A FACE
TO DIE FOR

A FACE
TO DIE FOR

IRIS
JOHANSEN

GRAND CENTRAL
PUBLISHING

New York Boston

Grand Central Publishing
Hachette Book Group
1290 Avenue of the Americas, New York, NY 10104
grandcentralpublishing.com
twitter.com/grandcentralpub

First Edition: June 2022

Grand Central Publishing is a division of Hachette Book Group, Inc. The Grand Central Publishing name and logo is a trademark of Hachette Book Group, Inc.

The publisher is not responsible for websites (or their content) that are not owned by the publisher.

The Hachette Speakers Bureau provides a wide range of authors for speaking events. To find out more, go to www.hachettespeakersbureau.com or call (866) 376-6591.

Library of Congress Cataloging-in-Publication Data
Names: Johansen, Iris, author.
Title: A face to die for / Iris Johansen.
Description: First edition. | New York : Grand Central Publishing, 2022. | Series: Eve Duncan
Identifiers: LCCN 2021059701 | ISBN 9781538713211 (hardcover) | ISBN 9781538724385 (large print) | ISBN 9781538713242 (ebook)
Subjects: LCGFT: Novels.
Classification: LCC PS3560.O275 F35 2022 | DDC 813/.54--dc23/eng/
20211209
LC record available at https://lccn.loc.gov/2021059701

ISBNs: 978-1-5387-1321-1 (hardcover), 978-1-5387-2438-5 (large print), 978-1-5387-2668-6 (Canadian trade), 9781538713242 (ebook)

Printed in the United States of America

LSC-C

Printing 1, 2022

A FACE
TO DIE FOR

PROLOGUE

GHANA, WEST AFRICA
TWENTY-TWO YEARS AGO

The sun was going down!

And she was late again.

There was no way Riley was going to be able to get back to the camp before her mother and father returned from the trip to the village.

But she had to try.

She skidded down the bank that led from the creek. Then she was deep in the jungle and heading toward the hills in the distance. The night creatures had not come out yet, but the stillness told her they were there waiting in the shadows for their turn. She had caught sight of a panther earlier this morning... This time of day always excited her, and she instinctively slowed down to let the sensations flow over her, the fear, the eagerness, the curiosity. But then she reluctantly speeded up again. She had to be more careful after that last warning from her mother. She was running at top speed through the jungle now. She jumped over another creek and could see the camp a short distance ahead. She didn't hear any

1

sounds of cooking or conversation, but that didn't mean Riley would get away with disobedience. It was fully dark now, and her mother didn't like the night creatures the way Riley did. She always insisted that her father be back at camp before the end of the day.

Well, she could only hope that something had delayed the purchase of the artifact at the village. She ran around to her own tent that was in the rear of the encampment. She lifted up the back of the tent and rolled underneath the edge.

A beam of light speared her face in the darkness.

"You were told to stay in the tent, Riley," her mother said coldly.

Caught!

Her mother lit the lantern on the table beside the bed and then gazed at her disapprovingly. "Not only disobedient, but you look like a filthy ragamuffin. I saw children in that village today who looked much cleaner than you."

"I'm not filthy. I took a bath in a creek right before I came home." Riley was careful not to mention that the creek had run through an underground cave and ended in a ten-foot waterfall. Her mother would not have understood. "And I finished the lessons you gave me before I took a walk. I didn't think you'd mind. You always say I should get exercise."

"You crept past the guard again. You know you're not supposed to go anywhere alone. You're eight years old. What if you got lost? Your father would blame me."

"I never get lost." She sat up. "I'm like Eleni. Remember all the stories you told me about her? She never got lost and she never got tired. She was a true warrior."

"You're not like Eleni," her mother said between gritted teeth. "You're just a disobedient child who causes me endless problems. And I'm sorry I ever told you about her."

"I'm not." Riley knew she should just be quiet and not argue, but she couldn't accept those words. She lifted her chin. "I remember every one of those stories. Maybe I'm not like her, but I try to be."

"You're impossible." Her mother shook her head. "Now clean up and then go to bed. And if you've lied to me and didn't finish those lessons, you'll hear from your father. I've told him that we should send you to a private school in Egypt. I shouldn't have to handle you by myself."

"I didn't lie to you. I even did an extra lesson before I left for my walk. That should please him." She changed the subject. "Did you get the artifact?"

"We got it," she said curtly. "But it was hardly worth the trip. It was far too primitive and led us nowhere that we wanted to go." She turned to leave. "I suppose he'll want to know if you've had anything to eat."

"Berries," Riley said quickly. "Lots of berries. I'm not hungry."

"Good. Then go to bed. I don't want to hear anything else from you for the rest of the night. Your father and I have work to do." She left the tent.

Yes. Riley jumped to her feet and ran over to the table and hurriedly washed up and brushed her hair. Then she was in her pajamas, turning off the lamp, and crawling into her sleeping bag.

She closed her eyes. Sleep. Forget everything her mother had said. Remember the jungle, the strange sound of the chimps high in the trees, the way her heart had pounded as she'd run down the path this morning after she'd left the encampment. Let everything else go so the dreams could come.

Freedom. Power. Eleni.

———◆———

"You got in trouble again." Riley heard Eleni laughing even before she saw her sitting on the stool beside the arched windows of the palace. She was dressed in a white tunic; her blue eyes were lit with amusement and her golden hair was short and shimmering around that wonderful face. "Won't you ever learn, Riley?"

"That's what I'm trying to do." She didn't care if Eleni was laughing at her. There was only humor and mischief and no hint of scorn or bitterness when Eleni came to her. "You kept bragging how fast you were, how none of the young boys of the city could beat you. But I had no one to teach me. I just had to do it on my own. I was very fast today."

"Not as fast as me. Probably because they don't let you run naked as I do sometimes." Eleni tilted her head. "But you did well, and I was proud of you." She was suddenly chuckling again. "And I'll be more proud if you don't make mistakes and cause your mother to be angry with you. I've warned you about that. Running a race is one thing, but handling the people who can hurt you is more important." Her smile faded. "And your mother does hurt you."

Riley couldn't deny that. "Sometimes. She said she was sorry that she'd ever told me about you." Riley frowned. "I had to tell her that—"

"No, you didn't," Eleni interrupted. "Because she did tell you about me, and that means you win no matter what she thinks now. When you close your eyes, I'll always be with you."

"She thinks you're only a dream." Riley scowled. "She laughed at me."

"A dream?" Eleni nodded. "She could be right. But what does it matter? I'm here and you're here and together we're strong enough to shape the world to suit ourselves. Would you like that?"

"Yes." Her eyes narrowed on Eleni's face. "You're different tonight. Why?"

She shrugged. "I can't stay the same all the time. We all change, Riley. Sometimes life changes us. I just found out that I have to choose a husband and I'm not certain that pleases me."

"Then don't do it."

She chuckled. "But what if I miss something interesting if I don't? I've never been afraid of taking a chance. You mustn't be, either." She leaned back on her stool. "But we won't talk about it now. Perhaps I'll tell you how it worked out the next time we're together. Or perhaps not, maybe I'll have wonderful secrets that I won't want to share."

"You'll tell me," Riley said flatly. "How can we shape the world to suit ourselves if you keep secrets from me?"

"True." Eleni was grinning again. "But for now you have to tell me your secrets. Start at the beginning of your day and tell me everything. How fast did you run? Did you see any new, wonderful creatures? What about your endurance? I've told you that's just as important. Share with me, Riley." Her smile was luminous as she coaxed, "And I promise I'll always share with you . . ."

CHAPTER

1

AZERBAIJAN FOREST
PRESENT DAY

S o much blood...

And Riley couldn't stop it. It was too late. She knew it
was too late, but she kept her hand on the pressure point. Her
father was gasping for breath and staring up at her in despera-
tion. "Hurry. Get...out of...here, Riley. They were right...
behind me."

"Hold on. Don't give up. I'm not going to leave you."
Tears were pouring down her face and she impatiently wiped
them away. "I don't care about those bastards. I'll hear them
coming, and I'll pick them off one by one. You've just got
to hold on until I can stop this blood. Then I'll get you out
of here."

"Hold...on? I regret...I can't...help you there." A trickle
of blood was coming from the corner of his mouth. "You never
did...do anything I told you. But I can't allow it this...time."
He looked at Dan, who was standing behind her. "Your uncle
Dan is...always more...reasonable, thank God." He stared
him directly in the eye. "You'll never get...what you want if

they...get their hands on Riley. You know...that, don't you, brother dear?"

"I know it," Dan said roughly. "But she might be able to get you out of here alive. I've seen her do harder things."

"You were never good...at calculating odds. I always had...the brains in the...family. That's why I have...all those degrees."

"But I had all the fun. I've been thinking lately that wasn't quite fair. All the more reason for me to let her try to help you."

"Don't throw...that in my face now. You know...what has to be done." His gaze shifted back to Riley. "And so do you. Don't let them...take you. And don't...ever let them take *her*."

"I can't worry about that right now," she said shakily. "It's not too late. I think I might be able to cauterize this wound if Dan helps me."

"Oh, Dan is going...to help you." He looked back at his brother. "Aren't you? *Now*, Dan!"

A blinding pain in her temple!

Darkness!

———◆———

ROBAKU, MALDARA
CENTRAL AFRICA
THREE MONTHS LATER

Eve Duncan pushed back from her desk and gazed critically at the reconstruction she'd just completed. She was glad Gila was finally finished. Eve just hoped that her work would give back to the child's mother a little of the joy and humanity she'd known before those guerrillas had broken into her daughter's schoolroom and butchered her and her classmates. Only her mother had survived the attack on the village, and it was important that when Eve returned the reconstruction to her, she'd be able to see and remember all the love she'd known with her daughter. "What do you think, Gila?" she whispered. "Did I bring you home?"

"Sure you did," said a voice from the doorway behind her. "You bring them all home."

Eve whirled around in her chair to see Jill Cassidy leaning on the doorjamb and smiling at her. "Jill?" She jumped to her feet and ran across the space separating them. "I thought you were still in Egypt." She gave her a hug. "When did you get in? What are you doing here?"

"What I do, wherever I am." She grinned. "You know me. I'm a reporter and I always have a story to tell or one to investigate. When Novak called me in Cairo and told me you'd come back to do a few more reconstructions at the request of the local government, I decided that I should hop a plane and come and see you. The last I heard was that you'd gone back to your lake cottage in Atlanta and were refusing to budge."

"Situations change," Eve said. "And Joe and I decided to change with them. Michael was old enough to go to a wonderful school in Scotland that he's crazy about. Jane and Seth Caleb have a house there and are keeping an eye on him."

"And Joe?" Jill's eyes were narrowed on her face. "You've left out Joe. And he would never allow that to happen."

"Of course not," Eve said. "Joe took a leave from his job so that he could spend more time at Scotland Yard and visiting Michael's school, in between running over here to see me whenever he could." She tilted her head. "So you can see we're all accounted for and very content."

"Are you?" Jill slowly shook her head. "You forget I got to know you very well when we were here together trying to survive that post-civil-war madness. You wouldn't be content unless you and your family were together. What went wrong?"

"Nothing." Eve looked her straight in the eyes. "Everything is going exactly the way we want it to. Back off, Jill."

Jill studied her for a moment and then smiled. "Never mind. I'll find out on my own, and then I'll fix it for you. You forgot what a good reporter I am."

Eve definitely had not forgotten that, she thought ruefully. Jill wouldn't have won that Pulitzer before she was thirty if she hadn't been super sharp. "I don't want you to fix anything for me. All I want is to enjoy having you here, Jill."

"That's what I want, too." She shrugged. "You know me, I tend to screw things up for myself when I see something not quite . . . right. It's my journalistic instinct." Then she made a face. "But I definitely don't want you to be wary of me. That's not why I'm here. Let's start over." She strolled over to the reconstruction on the table for a closer look. "She's absolutely wonderful. What's her name?"

"Gila. She was six years old when she was murdered. I just finished her today."

"I thought you were finished with doing the reconstructions on the village children before you left here?"

"I did, but it was a terrible war. Those bloody mercenaries' favorite sport was attacking the villages and killing innocent children. It didn't end here in this village. But the government appreciated the job I did when I was here and asked if I'd come back and do several more reconstructions from a school in the northern province. I had the skulls brought to my studio here." She gently touched Gila's head. "She's the last one they brought to me. I'm glad. I know it's worthwhile, but it breaks my heart. I want it to be over."

"I can see how you would. But there's no way they're going to let you escape without a good reason. Everyone knows you're the best forensic sculptor in the world."

"I have a good reason," she said lightly. "As you've pointed out, I have a family that occasionally likes to have me around."

"And that you've mysteriously been avoiding." She suddenly chuckled as she saw Eve's pointed glance. "Okay, sorry. Let's grab a bottle of water and walk down to the creek. I'll tell you all about my research into the Egyptian tombs in the Valley of the Kings and Queens, and you can tell me about Joe and Michael." She was already at the fridge across the room and pulling out two bottles of water. "My research was fascinating. But I'll bet you had more fun than I did."

"No bet." Eve took the bottle from Jill and headed for the door. "A walk will do me good. I've been working on Gila since dawn. I wanted to finish her."

"And you did a great job." Jill was looking straight ahead. "But you're right, all those tragic kids might be too much for you. Maybe you need a change of pace."

"What?" Eve turned to look at her. "Just what are you saying? That sounds suspiciously like the snow job you gave me to get me to come here and do those reconstructions a few years ago."

"It does, doesn't it?" Jill asked cheerfully. "And I admit that was a snow job, but I only told you the sad story and let you choose for yourself. And in the end, I believe you found yourself agreeing that what we did was damn good for this entire country."

"After you brushed the snow job aside and let me see what I really had to do," she said dryly. "It took me a while to forgive you for that."

"But you did forgive me, and I promised I'd never do it again." Jill sat down on the bank of the creek and crossed her legs. "And I won't, Eve."

"But there's a reason why you suddenly hopped a plane to see me when Novak told you I was here?"

"I had a few days before I have to fly to Paris to cover a conference." She took another drink. "And I did want to see you. It's been too long."

"But?"

"It did seem to be a stroke of fate." She smiled. "You were here, almost where I needed you, when I'd thought you were still in Atlanta. How could I not accept that we'd been brought together again for a purpose?"

Eve made a rude noise. "You've been spending too much time in those musty tombs."

"Maybe." Jill laughed. "But it sounded pretty good, didn't it?"

"Of course it did. You were always a great storyteller."

"And you just told me that Gila was your last reconstruction on this job." She snapped her fingers. "Stroke of fate."

Eve chuckled. "You're impossible." Her smile faded as she searched Jill's expression. "But you're only half joking, aren't you? What are you up to, Jill?"

She didn't speak for a moment. "I have a friend who is in trouble, and it's a very complicated problem." She paused. "And I need you to do the job that you do best."

"Forensic sculpting?" She tensed. "Why? You know DNA always rules. Get someone else, Jill. I have enough complications in my life right now. The last time I agreed to help you, it almost started a revolution."

"But it didn't, and this isn't the same thing. I promise. All I want you to do is listen to me and then let me introduce you to my friend." She added coaxingly, "I'm not going to insist. But if you decided to do it, it will be something different for you, and you'll be doing good for so many people."

"That's what you said when I came here to reconstruct those twenty-seven schoolchildren."

"Did you regret it?"

"You know I didn't."

"Then listen to me." She finished her water and got to her feet. "But not now. I can see you bracing to turn me down. I'll give you until tomorrow to prepare yourself. Have dinner with me then. I'm going to dinner with Novak tonight. I'd have to talk to him about this anyway."

"You do?" Eve repeated warily. Besides being Jill's lover, Jed Novak was CIA, and he practically ran everything to do with the Company and law enforcement in Maldara. "Why?"

"I just want some advice." Jill made a face. "And I haven't seen him for over a month. He wasn't able to get to Cairo as we planned. Juggling two careers can really suck in a relationship."

"Tell me about it," Eve said. "Try juggling two continents."

"But you'll have dinner with me tomorrow evening? You can always say no when I start my pitch."

"And I probably will."

"We'll see." She reached down and pulled Eve to her feet. "I'm going to offer you something absolutely unique. The least it will do is intrigue you. Think about that until we're together again." She was walking down the path toward where she'd parked her car. "And remember the good we managed to do when you gave in to me the last time." She waved at Eve as she got into the driver's seat. "Tomorrow!"

Eve shook her head ruefully as she watched Jill drive down the village road toward the main highway. She probably wouldn't be able to stop herself from thinking about those weeks with Jill she'd experienced a few years ago. Everything she had said was true: She couldn't regret it. But Jill's profession as a reporter led her into situations that were both dangerous and sometimes bizarre, not to mention tragic. She didn't need that in her life right now. She and Joe were having enough trouble making their actions appear understated and totally normal so they wouldn't attract undue attention.

Which reminded her that it was almost time to call Joe now. She wasn't looking forward to it. He wasn't going to like the news that Jill was back in their lives again.

———◆———

Jill waited until she'd reached the road to Jokan before she called Novak. "I've left Eve and I'm on my way to the hotel. I dropped a few teasers, but I'm holding off until tomorrow to talk to her. It doesn't look promising."

"I wonder why," he said dryly. "She's always had excellent good sense, and you knew it was iffy."

"But I promised Riley I'd try to persuade Eve to at least listen to her proposition." She added, "It might help if you volunteered to go along."

"I told you that I couldn't leave Maldara right now." He

stopped a moment, then said impatiently, "Okay. Okay. I'll try to get someone else who might fit the bill. I'll make a few calls. There's one person who might be interested." He added, "But I have no intention of discussing this anymore tonight. It's been too damn long since I saw you."

"That's what I told Eve. I can't wait. Make reservations at my hotel for dinner and give me time to change. I'll meet you in the lobby."

He chuckled. "It's a deal. I'm on my way." He ended the call.

Jill smiled and instinctively pressed the accelerator. Time to forget everything but Novak and what she felt for him. She'd started the ball rolling today, but life was more than ancient artifacts and centuries-old tombs and she intended to explore every bit of it tonight.

———————◆———————

What the hell!

Novak frowned impatiently but then fifteen minutes later he pulled his SUV over to the side of the road and reached for his phone. Okay, he'd told Jill that he wasn't going to let her involve him with her attempt to help her friend at the moment, but he had an idea he was already involved. At any rate, he knew he wasn't going to be able to put it out of his mind until he found a way to strike a balance that would keep Riley and Eve as safe as possible if Jill did manage to talk Eve into listening to her.

So get it over with and make the call. Cade could sometimes be difficult, and who knew where the hell he was right now.

He quickly placed the call to Morgan Cade and waited for him to pick up.

"Novak?" Cade's voice was wary as he answered. "I haven't heard from you since Nigeria. That was three years ago. Are you still in Maldara?"

"Yes. Where are you now?"

"My place outside London. But I'm leaving for Morocco tomorrow."

"I don't think so. I believe you'd enjoy Azerbaijan more."

Silence. "I have a commitment in Morocco."

"They'll wait for you. Everyone always waits for you, Cade. You're the golden boy."

"Bullshit."

"Of course you are," he said mockingly. "One of the richest men on the planet. Congressional Medal of Honor recipient. Famous environmentalist and archaeologist. We're all in awe of you. Tell me, who did you have to bribe to get those elephants into the UK?"

"What do you want, Novak?" Cade asked bluntly.

"Just thought I'd touch base. Is Jon Kirby still with you? I have such fond memories of that son of a bitch."

"He was only obeying my orders." Cade repeated, "What do you want?"

"You owe me for Nigeria."

"I'll pay you when I get back from Morocco."

"That might not be in time. I'm not sure what's going down there."

"Then you have no business trying to pull me into this."

"But I thought of you immediately when I was told about the magnificent artifacts just waiting for you in Azerbaijan."

"What artifacts?"

"Curious? Of course you are. Jewels and vases and ancient treasures that you'd find interesting. You wouldn't even have to locate them yourself. Your partner has already done all the initial work."

"Partner?"

"I'll explain later. I'm sure that the project will intrigue you enough so that you'll agree it's worth your while."

"I'm not intrigued yet."

"Then I'll have to add the pièce de résistance." Novak waited a moment before saying softly, "Ralph Dakar is after the artifacts, too. He's in Azerbaijan now. You're bound to run into him at some point in the next few weeks."

"Dakar?" Cade repeated. He muttered a curse. "You're sure?"

"I'm sure. I've heard you've been searching for him. Now are you intrigued?"

"Talk to me," he said harshly. "I want to know every damn thing."

"I don't have time. I have an engagement. I just wanted to catch you before you took off again for parts unknown. I thought you'd need time to prepare. I'll call you tomorrow."

Cade was silent. Then he said, "You're enjoying this."

"A little. Those two nights in the jungle in Nigeria were hellish. You wouldn't give up."

"But I got what I wanted, and now you'll get what you want. But not if you leave me hanging like this. I'll walk away and head for Azerbaijan on my own." He continued brusquely, "At least you're going to tell me about this partner you're wishing on me. Name?"

"Riley Smith. She has excellent credentials, and I've been assured she'll be of value to you. Have Kirby check up on her. I'm hanging up now."

"Go ahead. That will be enough to get me started. Call me tomorrow." Cade cut the connection.

Mission accomplished, Novak thought grimly as he drove back onto the road. But bringing Cade into the picture might be a mistake even if he was lethal enough to handle Dakar. He'd learned just how intense he could be in Nigeria. Still, it was too late now to step back. He could imagine Cade exploding into action the minute after he'd hung up the phone...

CAMBRY HOUSE
WILDLIFE HARBOR SANCTUARY
OUTSIDE LONDON

"Cancel Morocco, Kirby," Cade Morgan said as he strode into the library. "We're heading for Azerbaijan tomorrow."

"Why the hell?" Kirby looked up from the tiger cub he was feeding. "I thought you wanted to zero in on that merchant in the bazaar. I was looking forward to it." He gave the tiger's throat a last affectionate rub and got to his feet. "What's in Azerbaijan that's worth canceling that scumbag Hamad?"

"Dakar."

Kirby whirled to face him. "Shit! How do you know?"

"Novak. He wants payment for Nigeria."

"I don't blame him. It was rough as hell. But he waited long enough."

"I knew it was only a matter of time. He wanted to make it worth his while." He added grimly, "And he wanted to make sure he'd have something to dangle that would bring me into line. I wonder how long he's known Dakar was in Azerbaijan."

"We can eliminate Novak. I can trace Dakar for you now that we have a general direction."

"No, I owe him. And he dangled not only Dakar but some exceptional artifacts that the bastard is going after." He was suddenly grinning recklessly. "There's nothing I'd like better than taking a prize like that away from Dakar before I cut his throat."

"So what do you want from me?" Kirby asked.

"I've changed my mind, don't cancel Morocco. I don't want Hamad to be able to operate one more day either. Just get Brandwick to bring in his team to go after those poachers. Then get Lewis and the crew ready and secure the sanctuary." He made a face. "And I want a report on a woman called Riley Smith whom Novak promises me will be just the partner I need. That's all I'll know about her until tomorrow morning. It would help if I knew if that artifact she's going after is worth my while. Try to get ahead of the game. See if I can buy her out or find a way to neutralize her until I can get rid of Dakar."

"You don't want much," Kirby said sourly.

"Stop complaining. Even Novak trusts you. He told me to have you check her out." He glanced back at the tiger at Kirby's feet. "And I told you not to make a house pet of that tiger. He's getting too old for that. He's happier outside."

"He's got a couple more months. He likes it in the house. He thinks this mansion just might be worthy of him," Kirby added slyly as he was reaching for his phone. "And at least he's not an elephant like that baby you brought back from Nairobi..."

———◆———

EVE'S WORKSHOP
ROBAKU

"Jill didn't give you even a hint what she was going to ask
you to do?" Joe asked Eve impatiently after she'd finished
telling him about the reporter's visit. "You should have pinned
her down."

"As you would have?" Eve asked. "She took me off guard.
And okay, I was glad to see her again. It took me back to
that time when we were fighting a common battle. I've always
liked and respected her."

"When you weren't having to make sure she didn't cause
you major trouble."

"I never worried about that. When she found out that I
might be in danger, she always looked out for me. You saw
that, Joe."

"Yeah," he said grudgingly. "And I liked her, too." He added
harshly, "But I don't like the fact she just dropped in on you at
the worst possible time."

"It might not be the absolute worst time," she said quietly.
"I finished Gila today. My job here is over. That means I'll
have to be looking for another logical reason why I need to
stay away from the U.S."

He muttered a low oath. "You could come here to Scotland,
dammit."

"We discussed that and decided an occasional visit would be
safe, but if I settled there with you for any length of time, it
would send up a red flag. It would look like I was trying to
avoid him."

"Well, what else are we doing? Son of a bitch!"

"Yeah, I know. It's killing me, too. I haven't seen you or Michael for two months." She leaned wearily back in her chair. "But you know as well as I do that Adam Madlock's men have extensive dossiers on both of us. They know our past and present, and probably have psychological mock-ups that tell them which way we'll jump. We do the wrong thing, and they'll zero in on us."

He was cursing again. "Screw Madlock."

"I agree. Or something much worse. But we can't do that, either. Adam Madlock has too much power. Now stop raving and let's talk through this."

"We can't talk through it. Jill didn't give you any information we could latch on to." Joe paused. "Sorry. I'm just afraid she's going to spring something on you that will scare the hell out of me, and I won't be able to do anything because I'll be stuck here." His voice roughened. "And I love you and miss you, and I've been wondering if all this is worth it."

"You know it is. If there's anything in the world worth it, it's what we're doing. We've just got to stick with it. It can't last much longer." She drew a deep breath. "Let's talk about something else. I haven't had a chance to talk to Michael since I congratulated him on his soccer game a couple nights ago. How is he?"

"Missing you, too. Doing well in his classes. Zooming on his computer with his friends back home in Atlanta. Caleb and Jane are taking him up to their house in the mountains this weekend."

"And how are you?"

"Grouchy as a bear. I've turned into a complete workaholic." He added thickly, "And I *need* you."

"Me, too." She was getting teary-eyed. She had to hang up. "I've got to package up Gila and arrange for her to be picked up. I'll call you tomorrow night after I talk to Jill."

"That's a plan. And don't let her talk you into anything."

"She promised it wouldn't be like last time. I believe her."

"That's what I'm afraid of. Good night, love."

Eve ended the call. She sat there a moment looking at her phone. She was tempted to call him back and tell him that she was going to be on the first flight tomorrow to Edinburgh. She could be careful. She *needed* her family. Surely if she stayed only a week or so, it wouldn't start any conjecture stirring in the White House.

She would think about it.

But right now she had to box Gila and send her to the northern province. Because the work she did was also a deeply ingrained need that was almost a passion. That was why she had chosen to come here when she and Joe had decided it would be wise to leave their lake home. It would be the natural thing for her to go back to the profession she loved so much.

None of Madlock's men would question that decision.

But would they question it if she abandoned her work now as if it had no value? Yet Joe and Michael had value, too, and she desperately wanted to be with them.

Tomorrow, she thought wearily. Think about it tomorrow. Nothing was really pushing her one way or the other.

Jill had just been joking when she'd called her visit to Eve a stroke of fate.

———◆———

CAMBRY HOUSE
WILDLIFE HARBOR SANCTUARY
OUTSIDE LONDON
NEXT DAY
10:40 A.M.

"You're not going to be able to buy Riley Smith," Kirby said as he came into the library the next morning. "I thought we might have a chance when I found out her connection with Dan Smith. He's her uncle, and he's been involved in everything from artifact smuggling to confidence games in both Africa and Europe for the last twenty years." He threw down the Riley Smith dossier on the desk in front of Cade and then dropped down in a chair across from him. "He's been picked up but never charged in half a dozen countries. Probably because he's smart as a whip, and he was never shy about mentioning his older brother, Professor Edmund Randolph Smith, as a character reference."

"Was the professor getting a cut of the loot?" Cade frowned. "No, I think I've heard of Edmund Smith. He's well respected as an archaeologist. Maybe he was just a dupe? Almost every family has a black sheep..."

"Or maybe Daniel Smith was useful to his brother," Kirby said. "I told you he was smart. At any rate, he spent a lot of time on treks with Edmund and his niece, Riley. No sign that either of them is anything but clean as the fallen snow. Though there's a mention of Riley being tutored at one point by a witch doctor." He made a face. "But it's hard to be anything else since they've spent most of their lives in jungles and archaeological sites."

Cade grinned. "Oh, I don't know. We've managed to raise an adequate amount of hell wherever we've landed."

"Entirely your fault," Kirby said. "You get bored and start looking for trouble. I merely trail behind in case you need someone to call a lawyer." He started laughing as he saw Cade's expression. "Admit it, Morocco was going to be too dull for you."

"Maybe." He picked up the photo of Riley Smith. "Exceptional. So she can't be bought? None of her uncle's weaknesses?"

"I'm not saying she's perfect. She's been known to go after her uncle Dan when he got into trouble, and she wasn't above using unusual means to get him out of it. But she's been her father's right-hand person since she was ten years old and she's as brilliant as he was. If you don't believe me, check the age she was invited to join Mensa. She has degrees from several online universities and has taken courses at others when they settled close enough for her to do it. Her father evidently didn't want any other assistant. Her mother died when she was nine, but before that they'd occasionally hire a nanny from one of the villages or just leave her with the guard on duty. Edmund decided that was enough of a concession to parenthood for him."

"Connection to Dakar?"

"The darkest. Edmund Smith was murdered in a forest in Azerbaijan three months ago. No one arrested in the killing."

"Ah, then I may not have problems getting her to agree to what should be done to the son of a bitch. That's the kind of partnership I appreciate."

"Why did I think that would be your reaction when I threw together this report?"

"It's a very good report." He was going down the columns. "No mention of the artifact?"

Kirby shook his head. "Both Smith and his daughter were very confidential regarding their work. Completely secretive. I couldn't dig up anything about it. I'll keep trying."

"You might try bribing her uncle Dan," Cade said. "He appears to be her only weakness."

"It may come to that. How much time do I have?"

"Not enough right now." He was reaching for his phone. "I'll call Novak and get the rest of the information I need. He'll realize I won't try to snatch the brass ring he's dangling until I know what's on the other end."

Kirby was looking down at the dossier. "You know, she sounds like a tough kid who's ready to take on the entire world. I think I'd like her. We'd get along just fine."

"You've already got one tiger cub. You don't need another."

"Just giving an opinion. Anything else you want me to do?"

"Not until I decide whether I'm going to be blackmailed into having a partner." He waved his hand. "Go feed your tiger his breakfast. He's going to miss you while you're gone. You're the only sucker he's able to play around here."

"Bastard," Kirby muttered.

CHAPTER

2

Eve had a dining table set up in her studio workroom when Jill came back the next evening.

"Very nice," Jill said as she glanced around the studio. "I brought the wine. What are you going to feed me?"

"Stew. It's very good. Leta sent it to me from the village. Do you remember her? She's the grandmother of Amira, the first little boy I did a reconstruction on when I came here. One of the reasons I wanted to work from this village in Robaku is that I know most of the people here. I can always count on them to not let me starve if I get too involved in my work."

"And that's an excellent reason." Jill sat down at the table. "Last night Novak took me to a glitzy restaurant at the hotel, but I would have rather had the privacy we have here."

"Come on." Eve grinned as she sat down opposite her. "I'm quite sure you made sure you had complete privacy later."

Jill nodded. "Naturally, I told you that it's been a long time." She started to eat her stew. "Which reminds me, you called Joe last night? Did he tell you to send me on my way?"

"He definitely had reservations. However, he did mention he liked you."

"How kind. Since he's always on guard about you, I guess I can't expect more."

"Not when you didn't tell me what you wanted me to do for you." She lifted her water goblet and took a sip. "You're lucky to get that much. I'm having the same problem."

"Okay. Okay." She made a face. "You're not eating. Can't we wait until we finish dinner?"

"No." Eve leaned back in her chair. "Now, Jill. Who do you want to introduce me to?"

"Riley. You'd like her. She's unique, and you met her father several years ago. Riley said you got along fine, and he had tremendous respect for you. He told her that when the time came, he was going to choose you."

"Choose me for what?" Eve asked impatiently. "And who the hell is he?"

"Professor Edmund Randolph Smith. He was on the board of the Natural History Museum in London for a while when he wasn't touring the world hunting for artifacts. He met you there when you were speaking at a seminar about a forensic sculpture you did of a woman from ancient Herculaneum for a museum there."

Eve thought for a moment. "I do remember him. We only spoke for an hour or so. But he was very enthusiastic about the possibilities of my work, and I recall that everyone at the seminar was treating him as if he walked on water. Marvelous credentials..."

"Yes, that's the man." Jill tilted her head. "Though I hoped you were more impressed."

"I *was* impressed. Smith struck me as a bit of a fanatic

about his work, but then so am I." She met Jill's eyes. "But that was years ago, and I haven't heard anything about him since."

"You're hearing about him now. And he evidently never forgot you. According to Riley, his daughter, you've been a household name since that seminar. He's been keeping track of all your projects through those years. He even sent Riley to check on your work here. She paid a visit during the time you were working here before."

"Riley Smith? I never heard of her, and she certainly never dropped in to see me." She smiled. "But you know how busy both you and I were back then. It was still dangerous country after the civil war and not safe for a casual visit. Maybe she changed her mind."

"She didn't change her mind. Her job wasn't to contact you and appraise your work. She knew her father wasn't yet ready for you. She just visited a few of the villagers who had children you'd done reconstructions on. She talked to them, saw what you'd created for them."

Eve frowned. "I'd have known about it. These villagers talk to one another."

Jill shook her head. "Riley is . . . unusual. She has the gift of fitting in almost anywhere. She'd choose carefully and make sure she wouldn't be noticed. I'm a reporter and I didn't know that she'd slipped into Maldara or what she was doing. I didn't even meet her until I later went to Cairo and started research-ing those tombs in the Valley of the Kings." She shrugged. "But then she deliberately faded into the background because she wanted her father to take center stage when he visited me at my hotel. I didn't have even a glimmer of what she really was until later. She just sat there and smiled and only spoke when she thought she could insert something that would add ammunition to accomplish her father's objective."

"And what is Professor Smith's objective?" Eve asked. "It's starting to sound very convoluted, and I'm beginning to be wary. Why are you here, Jill?"

"His objective at the time was to impress me with his credentials and talk to me about his work of some thirty years. He'd been everywhere, made some amazing discoveries that were in museums in Europe and London. He succeeded. I wanted to write a feature article about him before the evening was half over. I was even trying to get his input on my research about the lost queens of Egypt." She made a face. "He was polite, but said he hadn't been doing much exploration and research on Egypt lately. He was going in another direction now. Then he asked me very casually about your work here in Maldara. He should have been a journalist. He squeezed me dry on everything I knew about you. And he was so genuinely admiring and complimentary that I knew I wasn't betraying you. Then he dropped you as the subject and invited me to spend the week with him and his daughter at their house in Cairo. He was there to do some research himself at the Cairo Museum and would introduce me to people who might help me. You can bet I took him up on it, and I spent the next week wheeling and dealing with museum executives during the day and getting to know Edmund Smith and his daughter during the evening."

"That was his first objective?" Eve asked. "You still haven't told me what the hell he wants me to do."

"I'm getting there." She took a sip of her wine. "I just wanted you to get the background so you'd know I'm not the victim of a con game. It may sound like I've been played, but it wasn't like that. I knew what they were doing, and I took as much as I gave. And I enjoyed that week and getting to know them." She paused. "Particularly Riley Smith. I'd never met anyone like her. She's a true wild card. I guess it would have been a miracle if she hadn't turned out that way, considering how she grew up."

Eve's brows rose. "Being brought up as the daughter of a prestigious professor of archaeology? I'm afraid I don't see your point."

"Riley trailed after her father and mother all over the world, through deserts and jungles in some of the wildest places known to man. Then when her mother died when she was nine, her father decided she was independent and smart enough to still travel with him. He was sure she was getting a much better education with him than she would in a boarding school." She shrugged. "Maybe she did. She's certainly brilliant." She dialed up a photo on her phone and handed it to Eve. "This is Riley. And I got the impression that, though he might have neglected her at times, she picked up some incredible talents and esoteric knowledge from the tribes and villagers they ran across. And even more from her uncle Dan, who appeared in her life about that time." She made a face. "Daniel Smith is something of a loose cannon himself. Not at all like big brother Edmund. He was a black sheep whose talents weren't always legal. It's a wonder Riley managed to strike a sane balance between them."

Eve was looking down at the photo. Her first impression of Riley Smith was of vivid color and vitality. Shining, tousled copper curls, tan skin, wide hazel eyes, and a smile that lit her face with humor. "Well, I've never seen anyone who looks more alive. And from your description she sounds very unusual." Eve suddenly chuckled. "Shades of Tarzan, or maybe that comic-book character Sheena of the Jungle. You could write a story about her. I'm surprised you haven't yet. I can definitely see why you might find her worthy of interest." Her smile faded. "But it's Professor Edmund Smith who appears to be the one behind your trip here to see me. Let's get his offer out of the way so that we can finish dinner, because I'm not likely to accept." She looked her friend in the eye. "And I'd have had more respect for him if he'd come himself. Evidently he wasn't shy about trying to enlist you to do it."

"No, he wasn't," Jill admitted quietly. "But he'd probably be here to do it himself if it had been possible. He wouldn't stop at a little recruitment job when he'd been working on this project for most of his adult life." She was silent a moment. "He died in the Azerbaijan forests near the village of Lahar three months ago."

"I'm sorry to hear it," Eve said sincerely. "As I said, he was a scholar I respected. And I can see why his daughter might want to do everything she could to have his lifework completed. But you'll have to get someone else to do it, Jill."

"Hold on." She held up her hand. "I haven't even given you my pitch yet. Why do you think I'm so determined to get you to do this? I struck out on finding any of the tombs of the lost queens of Egypt. But Edmund Smith told me he hadn't failed in the project he devoted his life to." She leaned forward, her expression intent. "He'd also been hunting for a lost queen, and she was even more lost than anyone could imagine. That's why he'd been searching for decades for her tomb. This year he'd thought he'd zeroed in on the exact location, but there were difficulties that made it impossible for him to take the final steps to find her."

"A lost queen?" Eve repeated incredulously. "You're telling me that Smith wanted me to go with him to Egypt to rob a royal ancient tomb and work on the reconstruction of the face of a queen from that era? Are you nuts? Do you know how carefully the Egyptian government watches for any violation like that? And to actually violate a mummy without civil authority by doing a reconstruction? They'd throw me into jail and toss away the key."

"Easy," Jill said soothingly. "I'm not crazy. Though I admit I had the same reaction when Smith was telling me about it. But it actually isn't as bad as it sounds. There are a number of elements about the situation that would make it almost legal. It would depend on how you look at it."

"Almost legal," Eve repeated. "I can only think that our Professor Smith must have either drugged or hypnotized you. I don't do anything that's illegal. You know that, Jill."

"Of course I know that," she said soberly. "I realize what a lost cause this might seem. I wouldn't have even been persuaded to go this far if I could have thought of a way that would have been safer for you."

"Safer?" Eve frowned. "The safest thing I can do is to kick you out of here and forget this weird offer."

"Not exactly," Jill said. "Because Professor Smith used your name constantly in his research papers. Anyone going through them would be sure you were an integral partner in Smith's search. He's tied you into his project whether you like it or not."

"I *don't* like it. And I can't believe it." She threw up her hands in disgust. "And what difference would it make? I could just deny it and set about proving in court that I wasn't connected. That should take—"

"You might not have time," Jill interrupted. "And it's not a court of law you're going to have to worry about." She paused. "You mentioned that you thought that I was trying to get you to rob a tomb? Well, we had no intention of having you do that, but grave robbers are a problem that could raise their ugly heads. Not only for the treasure. Do you have any idea of the fortune that thieves could derive from either selling or exhibiting a tomb and mummy from the Bronze Age?"

"I've never explored it. I wasn't particularly interested."

"This particular queen could be worth millions. Even more after you do the reconstruction."

"Which I'm not going to do," Eve said sharply. "Do you realize what a picture you've painted for me? A chance of being arrested for violating a tomb. Grave robbers..."

"Not a great story for a decent journalist like me. Because I wanted to be honest with you." She made a face. "But I hurried through it and left out some of the details that might make it more palatable for you. I'll fill you in on a few of them now. One, you wouldn't have to deal with the Egyptians and their rough tactics with people who interfere with their handling of historical artifacts. Smith's queen was not Egyptian...though she might have visited there once. Any work you'd do would have to be in Azerbaijan. That's where the site of the tomb is, and I guarantee that nothing about their methods compares to Egypt's. They're amateurs in the game. Two, it will be difficult to determine the queen's actual ancestry, though you might find it fascinating to try. But there won't be any nation trying to claim her before you'd have a chance to finish your work."

"Anything else?" Eve asked caustically.

"Nothing that I want to tell you. I'll leave the rest to Riley. I only volunteered to come here and give you the broad strokes and let you know that you can trust Riley." She stopped. "One more thing. I promised her I'd let you know how Edmund Smith died. He was shot and killed in that forest in Azerbaijan. Almost certainly by a Ralph Dakar, who currently heads a gang of artifact thieves specializing in tomb raiding. There were signs he was also tortured. Riley said Dakar wanted to force him to tell them where the tomb was located."

Eve tried to smother the ripple of shock she felt. "All the more reason for me not to even consider this madness."

"In the end, that will be up to you. In a way, I almost hope you do turn Riley down. I don't want to be responsible for you getting near Dakar." She thought for a moment. "Smith wasn't the first person who has been killed by those gangsters. There have been other villagers tortured and butchered by them in the past year to get information. That's why Riley and her father asked her uncle to find a place in the hills to hide while they were searching for the tomb. But you might not be safe even if you do walk away. Dakar knows you're the only one who was considered to do the forensic sculpting work on the queen."

"Which was more than I did," Eve said bitterly. "Why should I be afraid if I just turn my back and walk away?"

"Because Smith had constructed a package he wanted to present to the world, and you're a special part of that very lucrative package. Though I'm sure Dakar wouldn't want to kill you right away."

"How comforting. Just how dangerous is this Dakar?"

"Very. Tomb raiding is rather a new and unique addition to his agenda. But he has contacts everywhere in North Africa and the Mediterranean. Riley thinks that's how he heard about what they were doing in Azerbaijan. He runs a criminal organization that generally deals in thievery, poaching, smuggling, and human trafficking as well as being often hired by local politicians and other racketeers to do their dirty work in North Africa."

"Nasty," Eve said grimly. "What did the local police say about Edmund Smith's murder?"

Jill shrugged. "Not a great deal. They went through the motions. Bribery is pretty common in most of the small towns and villages in Azerbaijan. Dakar evidently pays well. The police are content to let him do what he wants as long as he doesn't antagonize any local big shots." She met Eve's eyes. "Edmund Smith was a scientist and an educator, not a big shot. So Riley is on her own. I asked Novak if the CIA could help, but I knew the answer. It's a country close to both Turkey and Russia and there would have to be an important international reason why they should step in. Besides, Novak is swamped just handling Maldara right now. The most he said he could do was to recommend someone who might be able to help."

"Then give your friend Riley his name. I'm not interested."

"I will." She took another sip of her wine. "But she'll want to hear it from you. She's worried about you. Dakar stole her father's notes, and as I said, you're featured prominently in them. There's a good chance that he'll think you know more than you do." She hesitated. "Would you consider me staying overnight for a few days until you get resettled?"

"No, you said this was only a quick visit. I'm not having you babysit me," Eve said. "The villagers will take care of me. I'll be leaving in a couple days anyway. I've been thinking about going to Scotland."

"Joe and your son." Jill nodded. "I can understand. Though I might ask Novak to send a man to watch this place until you leave. Okay?"

"Whatever." She smiled. "Now will you stop trying to talk me into going to Azerbaijan and tell me what you were doing in Egypt before you became distracted by the Smith family?"

"I might, but the professor and Riley were much more interesting." She chuckled. "Okay, I'll drop it for now. And yes, sure, I'll fill you in on everything I've been doing for the last months. But I got pretty frustrated, coming up with zeros when I was searching for the lost queens. That's why I found myself looking for a story that was far more fascinating." Her eyes were twinkling. "Particularly when I found out that story was apparently looking for me, too!"

———◆———

JOKAN HYATT
FOUR HOURS LATER

Jill unlocked her hotel room and opened the door.

Then she froze.

Someone was there in the darkness!

She could *feel* it.

She swiftly moved to one side of the open door and reached for the gun in her handbag.

"Don't shoot," Riley called out from across the room. "It's me. Just close the damn door and I'll turn on the light."

Jill drew a relieved breath and slammed the door. "You weren't supposed to come. I told you to leave it up to me."

"You're too smart to believe I'd do that." Riley Smith turned on the lamp on the bedside table. "Did you talk to her?"

"Of course I did." Jill threw her handbag on the chair. "She turned you down, just as I told you she would. We'll have to go about it another way." She came over to where Riley was propped up on the bed. "How did you get in?"

"I climbed up to your balcony and picked the lock on the French doors." She swung her legs to the floor and got to her feet. "I was afraid to go through the lobby. I didn't want anyone to know I was in Maldara."

"Good move. I was afraid I might be watched. Which is why I didn't want you to come at all."

"Dakar already knows about Eve Duncan," Riley said harshly. "He has to have someone watching her. Do you think I'm going to let them take her? You know she'd fight, and then she might end up dead. Did you warn her against him?"

"Naturally. I even asked her to let me stay with her, but she turned me down. She said she'd be safe with the villagers. She was having trouble believing in the entire scenario. You have to admit it's a bit unusual."

"Not when you've lived with it as long as I have," Riley said wearily. "I grew up with it."

"Well, I checked out the grounds before I left her work-room, and everything appears to be safe enough. You should have trusted me and stayed away where *you* were safe. I would have called you and reported."

Riley shook her head. "I've been waiting for years to have a chance of convincing Eve Duncan to do that sculpting. I knew you wouldn't have a chance."

"And you believe you would?" She shook her head. "No way."

"Then I would have found a way to keep her alive and not let Dakar get his hands on her. I let you persuade me that you might be able to pull it off, but I should have relied on myself." She rubbed her neck tiredly. "It's okay, you did your best. I wasn't really expecting anything. Everything is different now than when my father thought we could use you as a bridge to Duncan."

"Obviously." Jill wryly shook her head. "And did you think I didn't know there might be a reason why you happened to run into me that day in Cairo? I've been used by experts, Riley. Usually because I'm a reporter, and media is everything these days. But I liked you and I was willing to see what you were up to." She shrugged. "And then I became fascinated and wanted to see how the story would resolve itself. I didn't mind being used." She paused. "Though I didn't expect your father to be killed. I was hoping for a much tamer story."

"So was I," Riley said hoarsely. "But that's not going to happen. It shouldn't be a surprise. Nothing connected with Eleni was ever tame or lacking in violence and drama." She suddenly turned and gave Jill a hug. "Thank you for trying." She was heading for the balcony doors. "I'll let you know if I find a way of using you again. I hope I don't. I don't have that many friends who are willing to step up and volunteer."

"Do that." Jill followed her out to the balcony and watched admiringly as she lithely climbed down the trellis. Riley was all grace and sleek compact movement. "I haven't stopped trying, you know. When I finish up in Paris, I'll come back and lend a hand. In the meantime, I've set her up for you, if you still want to make the attempt."

"Maybe." Riley reached the ground and then looked up at Jill with a reckless grin. In the moonlight her entire face was suddenly lit with the vitality and eagerness to which Jill had become accustomed. "Hell, why not?"

She disappeared into the darkness.

Jill shook her head as she turned to go back in the suite. There hadn't really been any doubt that Riley would choose to make contact with Eve now that she was here. She and her father had been heading in that direction all her life. Jill just hoped that she wouldn't be too disappointed when Eve turned her down. There was no telling what Riley would do if she grew too desperate.

A knock on the door. It had to be Novak.

She flew across the room and threw open the door.

"Hi! You've got great timing." Then she was in his arms and kissing him. Again. And then again. "I needed that. It's not been a very optimistic evening."

Novak kissed her again. "Glad to oblige. Can we go right to bed, or do you have to unwind?"

"Just hold me for a minute." She nestled closer. "This is good, too."

"Damn right." He put his hand on the back of her head and stroked her hair. "Eve turned you down? But you thought she would. You said you couldn't even give her the entire picture."

"Riley wouldn't let me. She was afraid it would just seem too weird and scare her away. She thought that she could explain it better. Maybe she was right. She has the passion. I'm only a good storyteller."

"Yes, you are." He pushed her back and kissed her forehead. "But I've never noticed a lack of passion. You do very well in that department." He added, "And you gave me all the details and it didn't scare me off. I'm glad you have that assignment in Paris and won't be involved, but I admit I still found it very interesting."

"Of course you did. It appealed to your Sherlock streak." She looked up at him intently. "Did you change your mind?"

He shook his head. "I'm swamped. But I found someone who might be able to help. I filled him in on all the details last night, and it didn't scare him off, either." He waited a moment before saying: "Morgan Cade. You've probably heard of him."

"Damn right I have," Jill said. "Who hasn't? The Elephant King? I didn't even know you knew him. How did you get him on board?"

"He owes me a favor."

"Doesn't everyone?"

"I've lost track. I admit I tend to encourage the process. It does help when you need to barter." He smiled. "Cade was reluctant to redeem that favor at this time—until I told him about Riley and Eleni. That caught his attention. One of his passions is for ancient artifacts."

"I've heard he has a passion for a hell of a lot of things. Most of them involve big-time trouble. You did tell him about Dakar?"

He nodded. "He was one of the lures I used to make Cade change his mind. I remembered that he'd had a run-in with Dakar once before. I guarantee Cade is going to relish going after him again. Though I told him he might need a crew. I caught him at his country house outside London, and he'll be on his way to Azerbaijan right away. He told me he'd research Riley, and he was in the process of finding out everything he could about Dakar's setup in Azerbaijan right now."

"Good. I don't know how much time there is to waste."

"I agree. I don't like wasted time, either." He kissed her again and lifted her so that her legs curved around his hips as he headed for the bed. "And I don't intend to waste one more minute..."

CHAPTER

3

The lights in Eve's workroom studio were still burning.

Riley parked a little distance from the building and got out of the rental car, then took a little time to look around. The village down the hill was dark and quiet. Jill had said she'd checked out the perimeter before she'd left, but there was no harm in taking another look around. Riley made a complete circuit of the studio building and the jungle in the rear of the structure. The moon was now behind the clouds, and once the jungle closed in around her it was pitch dark back here; she could barely make out a rear door.

She stopped to listen.

Only night sounds. Birds, small animals...No one moving in the bush.

But was it a little too quiet?

Maybe not.

She moved through the shadows back toward the front of the building.

"Stop right there. Or I'll blow you away."

Riley froze. It was a woman's voice behind her, but it was full of purpose. Riley drew a deep breath. "I assume that means you have a gun. I'm not moving. I also have a gun, but I'm not going to draw it. It's very dark back here, isn't it? I'll turn around and step out of the shadows, and you'll see that I won't have my gun in my hand." She was thinking quickly, drawing conclusions. "You have to be Eve Duncan? I'm Riley Smith. I know I'm trespassing, but I wanted to make sure that you were still safe." She slowly raised her hands and stepped out of the shadows. "I didn't like it when Jill told me that she wasn't sure you believed there was a threat." She added, "Evidently she was wrong, since you were waiting here with a drawn weapon for intruders."

"I know how to take care of myself." Eve came toward her. "I've been doing it for a number of years, and you're not the only threat I've faced. I don't like surprises, and I always check out the perimeter before I close up the studio for the night."

"So you weren't relying on the villagers for help. But I'm finding it curious that you'd be quite so wary if you didn't believe Jill." She smiled as Eve stopped before her. "May I take my hands down now? You can see I haven't drawn a weapon. All I wanted was to make sure you were safe and spend a little time talking to you."

Eve hesitated. "Jill didn't say you were coming here tonight."

"She didn't know I'd followed her to Maldara. She wanted to talk to you first herself."

"Yet she made it clear she knew that you wouldn't give up if she couldn't persuade me to listen." She lowered her gun. "Oh, for Pete's sake, put your hands down. I'm sorry you lost your father." She slipped the gun into her jacket pocket. "He was a very impressive man. I think I would have liked him if I'd known him better."

"Maybe. Sometimes he was hard to know, but he could be charming when he wanted to be. He would have taken the trouble with you. Are you going to let me come back to your studio and talk to you?"

Eve nodded jerkily. "Come on. We might as well get it over with." She turned on her heel and strode back toward the front of the building. "I'm probably going to leave here tomorrow anyway. I've decided to go to Scotland for a while."

"No!" Then Riley caught herself. "You're going to visit your husband and son? That wouldn't be a good idea. Not right now."

"That's hardly your affair," Eve said coolly as she paused at the front door to unlock it. "And I don't believe I like the idea of you knowing where my husband and Michael are. I had to tell Jill. It makes me wonder exactly how much you've confided to her if she didn't know that."

"I didn't deliberately keep anything from her. That bit didn't seem important. It's just that I had to know *everything* about you. My father gave me orders when we knew we were getting close. It wasn't necessary that Jill know every detail."

"*Every* detail?" Eve pushed open the door and gestured for her to enter. "Just what do you mean by that?"

"Probably more than you'd want me to know," she said soberly. "But my father knew it wasn't going to be easy to get you to help us. We needed all the help we could get. We know how much you love your family. Naturally, we had to focus attention on them. And then we discovered a few more things about your more recent life that we found very interesting." She entered the studio and quickly looked around. "There's a coffeemaker on that cabinet. Could I make you a cup of coffee?"

"No, you can't." She nodded to a chair beside her desk. "This is my territory and I make the rules. Sit down. I'll make the coffee, and while I'm doing it, I want you to start telling me what you think you know about me." She was at the cabinet and reaching for the coffee. "How do you like it?"

"Black." She frowned. "Look, I might have spoken out of turn. Before you start questioning me, why don't you let me tell you first why we were so desperate for you to help us."

"I don't care what you want." Eve looked over her shoulder. "You just said something that definitely put me on edge, and I've got to know how much your snooping might hurt me. Now I'm the one who wants all the details, Riley."

"I don't want to hurt you," Riley said quickly. "That's not what I meant. And it wasn't exactly snooping. It was just that we had to know."

"Do you know how ridiculous that sounds?" Eve turned around and leaned back against the cabinet. "Jill told me you were very intelligent, but *your* need to know does not give you the right to probe in *my* business. We both realize that's basic truth."

"Yes, we do," Riley said quietly. "It was a lousy defense, and I was trying to backpedal because I didn't want to deal with the situation yet. But that's clearly not going to happen. What do you want to know?"

"You said you've been keeping me under surveillance for years. How?"

"My father paid investigators to keep an eye on you and your family for the past five years. Before that he only checked on you every now and then to make sure you were doing well and progressing with your work. There was no problem with that as far as he was concerned. Your talent was growing by leaps and bounds, and so was your reputation. The only problem was that he noticed you occasionally appeared to take on high-risk assignments. That began to worry him more, but it wasn't as if you didn't have a husband who was a detective and able to protect you." She shrugged. "He would have felt even more confident if he'd seen you out there tonight holding me at gunpoint. But he was concerned only with your forensic skill and not your lethal talent. It was only when he thought we were getting close to finding the tomb that he felt we had to make sure you weren't doing anything that would be truly dangerous for us."

Eve vehemently shook her head. "I wasn't aware of being watched. And Joe would surely have noticed."

"The investigators my father chose were experts, and it's not as if they had to dig deep and report constantly. They were there to watch from a distance and report when something was definitely off kilter that couldn't be handled by you and your family. That's what they did." Her lips twisted in a sardonic smile. "My uncle Dan has a number of contacts on both sides of the law, and it was one of the only times my dad asked him to recommend someone. I can't be sure if they were crooks or reputable businessmen, but evidently, they were good at what they did. All I know is that they didn't fail us."

"What's that supposed to mean?"

"You're not dead, and they gave us some damn interesting reports," she explained. "Particularly in the last year or so. That's what you're really interested in hearing about, isn't it?"

Eve tensed. "Should I be interested?"

Riley nodded. "I would be, if I were you. It was a very busy period for you. There were times when our investigators couldn't keep up with you, when you disappeared from view. They could only patch it together in pieces later for us." She leaned back in her chair. "It started when your husband Joe's ex-wife Diane Connors showed up in your lives. She was a doctor who worked for a global health organization, and she appeared to stir up the pot. She was in and out of your lives often during the next months. Then, toward the end of that time, your husband ended up in the hospital with you by his side and Diane as his attending physician. But all of you disappeared on the day that the hospital received a surprise visit from Madlock, the president of the United States. He'd come to visit your husband, but you were there, too. Evidently neither of you wanted anything to do with him." She paused. "Because the next time our investigators had anything of interest to report about you was when you'd left your home in Atlanta and came here to Maldara, and your husband and son were in Scotland."

"We had perfectly good reasons for doing both," Eve said quickly. "Which are none of your business."

"Absolutely," Riley said. "If no one knew how close you were to your family. But if they did, it looked like you were hiding out. Not that I care."

"Really?" Eve asked skeptically. "And you're telling me that's all you know about why we left Atlanta?"

"I told you, it was distant surveillance. It appears you're in trouble, but it doesn't affect what I need from you. Maybe we can help each other."

"I doubt it." Eve got two cups down from the cabinet. "And I'm not sure how much you actually know about that period, or if you're ready to make trouble for us." She was pouring coffee into the cups. "Blackmail, perhaps?"

"It won't be blackmail," Riley said. "Though I'm sure my father would have considered it. He would have thought he'd paid his dues and should get a return. But I won't play that game."

"And what about your uncle Dan?" Eve asked as she carried the cups across the room toward her. "He sounded like a man who took advantage of opportunities whenever they presented themselves."

She nodded. "One has to be careful around Dan, but he is what he is. Most of the time I can trust him. I'm not saying you could." She took the cup. "Thank you. Does this mean you're going to listen to me?"

"It means I realize that if I don't listen to you, you'll never leave me alone. It doesn't mean that I appreciate being stalked, or that I'll believe what you tell me." She sat down in a chair opposite Riley. "And it means you know a little too much about me, and I have to determine how that's going to affect how I handle you." She lifted her cup to her lips. "So start talking, Riley Smith. You might begin with telling me who the hell you're trying to force me into doing a reconstruction on."

"Persuade you," Riley corrected. "Neither my father nor I wanted to force you. It might influence the quality of your work. That would be a disaster."

"I'm sure you wouldn't want that," Eve said sarcastically. "Who is this Bronze Age queen you want to *persuade* me to do the reconstruction on?"

"Her name is Eleni," Riley said quietly. "And that's the last thing I want. It would be a disservice to her, and I won't have that happen. She had enough problems in life; they shouldn't follow her in death. I won't allow it."

Eve's expression suddenly altered as her gaze searched Riley's face. "You do care about her as a person. She's not just a prize exhibit to show off in a museum, is she?"

Riley shook her head. "She's been a part of my family since before I learned to read as a small child. Other children were told bedtime stories. My mother told me about Eleni. She became my friend. I even dreamed about her." She smiled faintly. "And that's why I could understand why my father said that you had to be the one to do the work on her. He told me that every skull you worked on you treated as if they were still alive and you had to bring them home."

Eve nodded. "But you have to admit it's not quite the same thing. In what century did your Eleni live?"

"Thirteenth century B.C. or thereabouts. There's some dispute on it." Riley grinned. "It's all how you look at things. People are people."

"Really? Yet everyone seems to believe she's so unusual. Particularly your father."

"And she was," Riley said. "But don't the people left behind by those poor victims you deal with believe the same thing? Most people have someone to mourn them."

"If they're lucky," Eve said. "I always pray they do."

"So do I," Riley said. "But Eleni had no problem. Though there were others who didn't feel the same way about her."

"Jill said her tomb is in Azerbaijan. Did the stories your mother told you about her take place there?"

Riley shook her head. "Not exactly. She was kind of a world traveler, but she ended up in Azerbaijan. And she made enough of an impression that her descendants kept her story alive for all these centuries. Some of the tales became almost mythical as they were passed down through the family."

"Then why did Dakar think raiding her tomb would be so lucrative?"

Riley hesitated. Then she decided to go for it. "Besides rumors of the treasure buried with her, sometimes a myth can be worth more than the truth. Particularly this one."

Eve's gaze narrowed on her face. "Don't play games. Tell me what the hell you mean."

Riley shrugged. "She's always been Eleni to me because that was what my mother called her. It's Greek for 'the shining one,' and some people thought it must have been meant to refer to this queen." She added, "And because the mummy in that tomb was known for a good portion of her life as Helen of Troy."

Eve's jaw dropped. "What! Don't give me that shit. What are you trying to pull? Everyone knows that Helen of Troy never existed."

"Do they? Then why do stories about her persist in practically every library on the planet?" Riley asked. "And why did my father spend the last thirty years searching for her?"

"I have no idea, but my respect for him is dwindling by the moment." She frowned. "And I never heard any tall tales about him searching for Helen of Troy. Though he made several other discoveries that earned him credit over the years."

"Yes, he did. He valued his reputation, and he was always careful to not try to be compared to Schliemann, who spent years searching for the site of Troy. Schliemann earned a hell of a lot of disrespect from the scientific community until he found Hisarlik. But the search for Helen was the driving force of my father's career. Whenever he was off on any other projects, he was always on the alert for any other information that might pertain to her." She smiled wryly. "I believe he married my mother because he was able to convince her that someday they'd discover Helen's tomb. My mother was also a scholar, and I'm sure that idea excited her more than marriage to him. My father had only one real passion in his life, and it wasn't my mother. I think I was something of a surprise and inconvenience to both of them, but he was very relieved to have her along on the treks to help take care of me."

"And how did your mother feel about the situation?"

She shrugged. "I think she liked me better when I was a toddler and didn't cause as much trouble. I remember her smiling more then, and that was when she started to tell me the Eleni stories. Though she really didn't know what to do with me. I was a wild child, and she and my father became a little impatient when my lessons didn't go as well as they thought they should." She grimaced. "But you're not really interested in me. You want to know about Eleni."

"Actually, I don't," Eve said coolly. "I've told you that I have no intention of becoming involved with this fairy tale you're spinning me. The only reason I even wanted to hear about it was that you managed to get my friend Jill to come here and speak to me about it. Otherwise, I wouldn't be listening."

"I know that," Riley said. "I would much rather have approached you in a different manner, but there wasn't time. I had to reach you as soon as possible. That's why I asked Jill to help me." She held up her hand as Eve started to speak. "But since I'm here and you've heard the start of my spiel, would it hurt to learn the rest so that you can tell Jill you've totally heard me out?" She smiled coaxingly. "Aren't you the least bit curious?"

Eve hesitated. "I'd be lying if I said I wasn't. I've always been a sucker for a good story. And if Jill is intrigued, it's probably a very good story. But I don't want to encourage you, Riley."

"I've lived with a myth all my life. Don't you think I've grown callous to discouragement?" She added softly, "Give me a shot at convincing you. I wouldn't be here if it wasn't important to me."

Eve shrugged. "Go ahead. Entertain me. You've been warned." She took a sip of her coffee. "By all means, tell me how your mythical Greek queen ended up in a tomb in Azerbaijan."

"First, I'll have to go back to the basics. Have you read Homer's *Iliad*?"

Eve shook her head. "I'm afraid not. I wasn't heavy into literature when I was in college, since my sole purpose in going was to become a forensic sculptor and to learn the medical information I'd need to reach that goal." She smiled. "And later when I tried to get into it, I couldn't stomach reading a book about gods and goddesses and sea monsters who were the villains. Not when I dealt with the real thing whenever I started working on a skull."

"I can see that," Riley said quietly. "Particularly when the reason you became a forensic sculptor was that your little girl had been killed."

She stiffened. "Jill told you that?"

"No, my father had a complete dossier on you that he gave me to read. You were always part of his long-range plans. I can see how you were turned off by Homer. But I'll leave you a copy, if I may. Once you get through the bullshit, you'll recognize that Homer knew human nature very well. Though it's possible that it's the fairy tale you called it, Helen's story has been told and retold over the centuries until no one can tell what was true about her and what was total lies. Most people believe she's the myth you called her. But you have to start somewhere, and Homer is as good a place as any. I can give you dozens of other things to read, but everyone has their own twist on who she really was."

"Including you?" Eve asked. "No, thank you. I've seen the movies and the TV shows and that's enough for me. I'm afraid I was disappointed. All the Helens were pretty but not unusual or stunning enough to cause a war. And why were most of them blondes? I kept wanting something...different."

Riley chuckled. "Lord, you're tough. I can't answer for the casting, but I might be able to answer your blond question. The casting directors probably thought they were doing their research. In most literature, Helen is referred to as having fair hair. Homer's Helen certainly did, and Alcman, a poet from the seventh century B.C., praised the Spartan female athletes with their golden hair and violet eyes. There were both dark- and fair-skinned Greeks and Spartans, of course, but the poets of the day evidently were more inspired by light than dark. Even some Greek vases in museums portrayed women with fair or red hair and with blue eyes. So blame the poets and the artists."

"Interesting. But I'd rather skip the research and form my own opinions."

"Suit yourself. I'll leave the *Iliad* for you anyway. But you should know that almost everyone agrees that Helen wasn't Greek. She was a Spartan princess who later became a Spartan queen after she chose her husband from all the suitors who wanted her."

"*She* chose? In the Bronze Age?"

"She was a princess, and an heiress, and Spartan women were trained and treated much like their warrior brothers and cousins while growing up. Very strong, very tough. She could probably take any of them down if she chose. That kind of upbringing was different from that of the women of Greece, who were encouraged to love the arts, be meek, and speak only when permitted. Helen was a warrior. She would fight to get her own way." She shrugged. "According to Homer, she wanted Menelaus. Though she was probably too young to know what she wanted at that time in her life."

Eve's eyes narrowed on her face. "You seem very sure of that."

Riley chuckled. "I've studied everything about her background and the problems she must have faced. She's no myth to me. I've lived with her all my life."

"Imagination?"

"Perhaps. Call it what you like. Imagination. Obsession. These days she's like an old friend." She paused. "And I wouldn't like to have an old friend's grave robbed or her story used to feed the media. She deserves better than that."

"If she even existed. You still haven't convinced me that she did. Or that you've managed to find her. Azerbaijan?"

"Sorry. I became distracted. Eleni has a habit of doing that to me," Riley said. "Over the years my father and I traveled all over this part of the world, trying to find proof that she did live. We visited Greece, Crete, Egypt, and of course Turkey, where the supposed ruins of Troy lie. But during that period when Helen lived, the entire area was being torn apart by earthquakes. City-state after city-state was leveled, and new ones took their place. If the Trojan War did happen, there's no proof that Helen had a part in it outside the works of Homer and other storytellers.

"My father was getting very discouraged, but he decided to try one other path. He began to gather the ancient stories and tales of the bards in all the countries we visited. Some of them were fascinating, and a good many had references to Helen. Of course, they didn't all tell the same stories about her. Some said she was a demon temptress; others that she was a beautiful martyr. But a few were worth checking out the locations where they originated. None of those proved interesting." She smiled. "Until we discovered the works of a young poet, Charon, in northern Turkey near what later became the Azerbaijan border. He described a beautiful, rich woman who had fled the wars of the south and come to live in peace with her lover in the hills of his homeland. The time was exactly right. His description was of a golden-haired woman as fair as the moon. He was obviously besotted with her. He spent no time telling us about her lover, Demetrius. He didn't exist for him." She added ruefully, "We had to find out more about Demetrius later when we followed up on the young poet. But thankfully, Charon couldn't seem to stop writing about the woman. He made her his lifework. He referred to her as Eleni, the shining one. Only now and then would he call her by another name." She met Eve's eyes. "It was Helen. She ran away from the life that had almost destroyed her after one of those earthquakes I mentioned. But she took her lover, Demetrius, for company and several chests of treasure with her. She might have been in hiding but she had no intention of living the humble life. I'm sure she thought she deserved the best at that point."

"You actually found her?" Eve asked.

"We found the story of her last years. We only got hints about where her tomb was located. We spent three years in the small village of Lahar just searching for every scrap of information that poet had written. The story was passed down from generation to generation in his family. First by mouth, later by tablets that they hid in caves in the hills." Her face lit up with excitement. "After several years searching the property, my father found several references to the tomb on tablets from one of the caves. We actually discussed possible locations. I'll be able to find it."

"While you're being hunted by this tomb raider?" Eve asked sarcastically.

She nodded. "There has to be a way. I'll find it."

"Good luck to you," Eve said. "You tell an interesting story, but I'd advise you to get help before you take a chance like that."

"I will." She hesitated. "I realize how dangerous it might be to have you with me, so I want you to know that I won't try to persuade you if I can't do it safely. And I'll make sure that there won't be a threat to you if you agree to go with me."

Eve shook her head. "Even if I believed you'd actually found that tomb, it's too much of a risk. For one thing, the government would probably claim it."

"They'd have a difficult time doing that. My father bought the property from the descendants of the Charon family, including all rights to any tombs or treasure found on the grounds. He had the documents approved and certified by the head of the Azerbaijan government. He was very specific."

"That might not help if the local politicians are crooked enough."

Riley nodded. "Which is why we'd have to remove the tomb from Azerbaijan as soon as we find it and take it somewhere safe."

Eve gazed at her skeptically. "Where?"

"I'll find a place. It would have been easier if my father were still alive. He could have appealed to one of the museums he worked with to accept custody until he worked something out."

"That should have been one of the first things he considered after he thought he'd found it," Eve said.

"He didn't have time. It was a dream to him, and then suddenly it wasn't." She gestured impatiently. "Now it's up to me, and I'll do it. But first I have to find it and make sure it's the genuine article. That's why I need you."

Eve shook her head. "No way. I told you that before you began."

"Yes, you did." Riley was nibbling at her lower lip. "And I understand perfectly. But you really do need to come with me so that I can take care of you."

"Take care of me," Eve repeated incredulously. "What do you mean?"

"What Jill was trying to tell you. Dakar knows about you from my father's notebooks. He's going to try to get his hands on anyone who might be able to give him more information. That's why I didn't come with Jill. I've been worried that he might have already connected you to my father. I didn't want to make the situation any worse by showing up here."

"Yet here you are."

"I was careful, and I made sure no one was watching your studio."

"And might have gotten yourself shot."

"Not by you." She held up her hand. "I can tell I'm just upsetting you. Look, I'll leave right now, but think about what I said, and I'll call you in the morning." She was heading for the door. "Lock up after me. Okay?" The next moment she'd slammed the door behind her.

Riley drew a deep breath and stood there until she heard the key being turned in the door.

It hadn't gone well, she thought as she moved away from the door and into the shadows. She hadn't really expected it to, but she'd had to start the action rolling. It would have been so much better if it had been her father approaching Eve. That might have had a chance, at least.

What to do now? Maybe she'd go back to her car and try to take a nap.

You tell me, Eleni. I don't seem to be having much luck. It used to seem so simple. It would be nice to go back to those times when I could close my eyes and you'd be there. But that was a long time ago, and then one day you were gone. And I've lost too much lately. Even my father is gone. What am I supposed to do?

She was being foolish, she thought impatiently. Sniveling like a child when she should be thinking of ways to keep Dakar from winning. She would work it out. But there was no way she was going to leave Eve Duncan until she was certain she was safe.

———

"Helen of Troy?" Joe repeated. "It sounds totally bizarre. How did Jill get herself involved with Smith and his daughter?"

"The way she always gets involved," Eve said. "It's one hell of a story. Professor Smith must have dangled it in front of her and been convincing enough to make her believe he'd actually found that tomb." She paused. "It even intrigued me."

"I can see how it would," Joe said grimly. "With every

reconstruction you've ever done, you've wanted to bring home the lost ones. You can't find a subject more lost than Helen."

"If she even existed," Eve said. "And Riley almost convinced me that she did."

"Did she also convince you that it would be worth going up against this Dakar? Forget it. Get on the next plane, dammit."

She chuckled. "Calm down. Not the next plane. But I'm leaving here tomorrow. I've already told Riley I'm not interested. But I won't stay long," she added. "The last time I saw Novak, he told me that he kept getting inquiries about how I'm doing with my project in Maldara. They might have been casual comments, but I'm not taking a chance. Madlock may not be sure I had anything to do with Diane's discovery, but he's watching me. There's no way I'll draw attention to you and Michael. You know you're both safer without me."

Joe cursed low and vehemently. "Son of a bitch. This has to end."

"And it will, Madlock has a lot of enemies. We just have to be patient until one of them takes him down. You have to keep Michael safe until Madlock loses interest in me." She changed the subject. "Can't wait to see you. I'll let you know what flight I'll be on so you can meet me. Love you." She cut the connection.

She leaned back in her chair. There was no way that she'd persuaded Joe to be patient. It would be better when she could be with Michael and him tomorrow. Everything would be better then. She'd call for airline reservations in the morning, but she could do something productive tonight. She got to her feet and moved toward the closet to pack.

As she passed the desk, she saw the white paperback novel.

No, not a novel. The *Iliad*, an epic poem by Homer. She hadn't seen Riley take it out of her bag before she left. But of course Riley had said she'd leave it for Eve, and she'd done so. Eve was beginning to believe she was a woman who always did what she'd promised. She picked up the paperback and leafed through it. She might read a little before she went to bed. Now that there was no pressure, there was no reason why not. She tossed the book on her cot. First, she would finish packing...

CHAPTER

4

Riley was still sitting in her car, watching Eve's workshop, when her phone rang two hours later.

She glanced down at the ID.

Dan Smith.

She answered it. "I'm fine, Dan. Stop worrying."

"Why should I be worrying? Unless it's that you shouldn't even be down there when I told you that Dakar was hunting for you. Stupid. Very stupid, Riley."

"I couldn't just sit there while Jill was doing my job. I had to make a move."

"Well, you made it."

She didn't like the tone. "Are you telling me that Dakar followed me?"

"No, I'm telling you he followed Jill Cassidy," he answered. "Though it could end up the same way. Because if I'm not mistaken, you're both leading him right to Eve Duncan."

Riley swore beneath her breath. "You're sure? How much time do I have? How many men?"

"Dakar didn't go himself. Evidently, he didn't think Duncan was a real threat. He sent two of his men, Carl Zangar and Paul Jolbart, and they boarded a flight to Maldara this afternoon. They should be there by now." He was silent a moment. "And it might not have been your fault. We both know Duncan had to be on Dakar's list since he found your father's notes. Maybe when he learned that Jill had left for Maldara, it nudged him a little."

"Yeah, maybe." She opened the car door. "Maybe not. Thanks for the tip, Dan. I've got to go check the premises again."

"You're welcome. It's what I do. There's nobody better." He was silent. "What premises? Duncan's?"

"I've got to go."

"Remember everything I've taught you. And for God's sake, be careful." He hung up.

There wasn't the least doubt she'd be careful, she thought grimly. She'd had a good view of the road and the village from where she'd been parked. But that didn't mean Dakar's men might not have circled around and gotten in through the rear door. She moved silently around the building toward the rear.

She stopped before she entered the jungle and listened.

Darkness.

No sounds.

She glided toward the door at the rear of the building.

A sudden screech from a tree across the way and then the sound of wings.

She froze in place.

Her heart was beating hard.

Listen.

Watch.

Movement in the darkness!

Two shapes...moving toward the rear door. The taller one was Zangar, whom Dan had once pointed out to her at the market at Lahar. She didn't recognize the other, who must be Jolbart.

Zangar made a motion to Jolbart, gesturing to the lock. Then he was gone, moving around the side of the building.

Probably to attack from the front entrance, she thought. She didn't have much time. Because Jolbart was bending over the lock, absorbed in trying to pick it.

That absorption was her chance.

She started forward.

Move with the stealth that Dan had taught her all those years ago.

It had been a game to her then. It was no game to her now.

No sound. Even her breathing must be shallow and silent.

She was almost there. He was so intent on the lock that he was completely unaware of her.

Close enough!

She leaped forward and swung the edge of her hand down to the back of his neck in a karate chop.

He grunted and fell sideways. She gave him another blow to his throat!

He slumped forward, unconscious.

She took off running around the side of the building.

The front door had already been thrown open when she reached there.

She heard a cry from the rear of the workroom.

Eve!

Then she was inside and barreling across the workroom

toward the bed in the corner where Eve was struggling with Zangar who was kneeling on top of her. His hands were gripping her throat, choking her.

"Get off her, Zangar." Riley pulled out her gun and struck him on the side of the head.

"What the hell!" He jumped off the bed and punched Riley in the stomach. Then he grabbed at her gun, and it went off.

A hot pain in Riley's side . . .

Her hand tightened on her gun, and she fired at him blindly as he started toward her.

"Bitch!" Zangar screamed, and then he was clutching his arm and turning and running out the front door of the workroom.

Riley staggered after him to the door, but he was gone . . .

An instant later she heard the sound of a car engine at the rear of the building. She'd been sure her bullet had hit Zangar's arm, and it was possible he was no longer a threat, but Jolbart, the man she'd taken down before, might have recovered. She had to be sure they'd both left the property. She started to run toward the corner of the house.

"What the hell are you doing?" Eve was beside her, grabbing her by the arm, pulling her back toward the open doorway, and slamming the door. "Are you crazy enough to try to go after him?" She was locking the door and then pulling a table in front of it. "Now sit down and let me see how badly he hurt you."

Riley didn't move. "I'm okay. He wasn't alone. Can you turn on the outside light in the back? I have to make sure they're both gone."

Eve muttered something under her breath and switched

on the overhead lights. The exterior lights cast a harsh glow through the windows. "Satisfied?"

Riley went to the back windows and looked out at the stoep and the jungle stretching toward the back road. "He's gone." She turned away. "They must both be gone. I couldn't be sure..."

"Well, now you are." Eve pulled her away from the windows and pushed her down on a chair. "Be still while I take a look at this." She was examining the wound in Riley's side. "I don't think it's bad. It's only a flesh wound. Not much blood."

"I told you I was okay," Riley said quietly. "You're making a fuss over nothing."

"We'll see." Eve went to the sink and got a bowl of water and a cloth. She applied a damp cloth to the wound and put Riley's hand on it. "Keep pressure to make certain there's no more bleeding. I'm going to call a friend and have him come out and take a look around the property."

"Jed Novak," Riley identified. "Don't do it. It's not necessary. I don't think they'll be back tonight. But I should get you out of here before they get their nerve back. My uncle Dan said it was Zangar and Jolbart, two of Dakar's men. They're not going to be pleased. They didn't get what they wanted, and I did shoot Zangar. He'll be too embarrassed to go back to Dakar until he either completes Dakar's orders or thinks up a good excuse. Dakar doesn't like failures."

"I'll decide if it's necessary," Eve said curtly. She was already punching in the number. "I promised Joe I wouldn't take chances while I'm here. This definitely qualifies." Novak answered and she said, "Eve Duncan. I need you at my studio at Robaku, Novak. If Jill is with you, tell her that she might as well come along. Her friend Riley Smith has been shot. I don't think it's serious, but she's being stubborn, and I don't want to have to be the one to argue with her." She cut the connection and turned back to Riley. "How do you feel? Any dizziness?"

She shook her head. "I told you, this is just a scratch. I'm tough. I've gotten worse than this just going for a trek in the jungle."

"Well, I think I'll just clean that 'scratch' and bandage it." Eve opened the cabinet and pulled out a first-aid kit. "While you tell me what this Zangar wanted with me. I woke up and his hands were on my throat. Was he trying to kill me? How did he get in?"

"Skeleton keys. I told you Dakar was also a thief. His men are usually very competent. I don't think he was trying to kill you. My bet is that he was just ordered to scare you and take you back to Dakar for questioning." Her lips twisted bitterly. "Then if Dakar wasn't satisfied, you might have been killed. He knew why my father needed you. He probably also thought you knew more than you do." She added impatiently, "Where was that gun you pulled on me tonight? You should have kept it handy. I told you to be careful. I could have been wrong. Zangar might have been told to just eliminate you so that I'd have no chance of using you."

"I did have it handy. It was in the drawer of the table by my cot." Eve was pulling Riley's shirt away from the wound and cleaning it. "I was trying to fight him off and reach for it when you broke in." She put antiseptic on the wound. "I didn't have much time before you swooped down on us."

"That wasn't close enough." Riley was looking at Eve's throat. "You have bruises. You were probably hurt worse than I was."

"I doubt it. No one shot me." She began bandaging the

wound. "You should really go to an ER and make sure that there's no real damage."

Riley shook her head. "Zangar might be on the lookout for a move like that. Besides, I can't be stuck in a hospital. I have to get back to our camp at Azerbaijan. Dakar murdered my father. I won't let him steal Eleni." She paused. "You won't come with me? Is there any way I can persuade you?"

Eve gazed at her in frustration. "Don't do that to me. I won't be given a guilt trip because you rushed in here and took a bullet for me."

"I didn't take a bullet for you," Riley said quietly. "I told you, he might not have had orders to hurt you yet. He could have been trying to frighten you so that you wouldn't struggle. And don't you know that I realize that none of this was your fault? You were just caught up in my father's obsession." She shrugged. "My obsession, too. I had to attempt to get your help, but I'll find another way. I just had to make certain that we hadn't hurt you, too."

"Other than a bruised throat and a rather wild encounter, I appear to have survived fairly well," Eve said dryly.

"Then will you take my advice and *not* rejoin your family right now? They won't be safe. Dakar uses people. He won't be happy that he didn't get his hands on you tonight. He might decide to go after someone you care about. Can't you just disappear?"

Eve gazed at her incredulously. "Disappear? I know how to keep my family safe, Riley."

"I thought that about my father," Riley said quietly. "I watched him so closely, and my uncle Dan and I also watched Dakar and his mob, but they still got to him. I don't want any more deaths."

"Then you could forget about Eleni."

"Too late. Dakar knows too much to give up his chance at finding her." Her lips tightened. "Besides, I won't have my father cheated. Dakar took his life; I won't let him steal his dream."

"Then you'd better have a plan that—" She broke off as they heard a thunder of knocks at the door.

"Eve." It was Jill's voice. "Open the damn door."

"It seems our rescue has arrived," Eve said as she got to her feet. "They were very quick, weren't they?"

"I told you that you shouldn't have called them." Riley was already on her feet and heading for the door. "We're coming," she called as she started to tug at the table. "Help me with this, Eve."

"Go away." Eve pushed her aside, shoved the table away from the door, and unlocked it. She threw the door open to see Jill and Novak standing there. "Come in." She stepped aside. "Novak, this is Riley Smith, and she's been trying to convince me that I shouldn't have called you. I decided not to pay any attention to her."

Novak nodded at Riley. "I've sent four of my men to scour the property and see what they can tell me. We should know soon. You were shot? Can I take a look at it?"

"No, thank you. Eve took care of it." She turned to Jill. "Sorry to disturb your evening. Eve overreacted. It was two of Dakar's men, and I shot one. Then they both bolted."

"Eve doesn't overreact," Jill said as she looked at the blood on Riley's shirt. "You're sure you're okay?"

Riley nodded. "No problem. But someone should probably stay with Eve until we can find a safe place for her." She turned to Novak. "From what Jill tells me, you're probably the one to do that."

"Stop trying to run my life, Riley," Eve said impatiently. "I told you I was going to Scotland to be with my family. You haven't convinced me that I won't be safe there."

"Then perhaps you should think about it a little longer," Novak said quietly. "From what I've been hearing lately, it might not be a bad idea for you to disappear for a while. I was going to suggest it. I'll be glad to help."

"Hearing lately?" Jill repeated. "What are you talking about? It's not anything I mentioned to you since I've arrived here."

"Because it wasn't necessary. Why worry you? You kept telling me that there was little or no chance of her going along with Riley's request, and that was the principal threat. I was just going to keep an eye on her until I could sort out why she was attracting so much attention from Washington."

"Washington?" Jill took a step closer to him. "You mean Langley? Why *worry* me? Since when have you kept secrets from me, Novak?"

"Not Langley. The orders and information might have gone through them, but they came from much higher up than the CIA. I had to find out why. Then I got word of a weird connection I was supposed to ignore." He met her eyes. "Secrets? Secrets are my job, and you know it. I would have told you when I could. And you know I would have protected Eve."

"How very kind," Eve said caustically. She brushed Jill aside as she came to stand eye-to-eye with Novak. "The two of you can settle your personal problems later. I have to know what the hell he's talking about. Why did you say that it might be safer for me not to go to Scotland? And don't give me that CIA bullshit when I ask you what you heard that was weird enough to make you say it."

"I won't," Novak said. "Because it's something you and

Riley should know about." He pulled out his phone. "Just let me get a report from my agents and then you can interrogate me." He turned away from them as he made contact and started to ask questions.

"Washington, Eve?" Jill murmured. "What have you been up to?"

"Exactly what I should have been doing," Eve said curtly. "Minding my own business and trying to keep a low profile."

"Well, evidently you haven't been doing the latter," Riley said. "Or you wouldn't have attracted the interest of Jill's friend here."

Novak heard that as he hung up from his call and turned around to face them. "On the contrary, Eve's been very low-key ever since she came back to Maldara. Until tonight. And I imagine that might be laid at your door, Riley." He put away his phone. "The property seems to be secure. I'm having my agents search the huts in the village just in case."

"Tell them not to frighten the villagers," Eve said quickly. "Those people are my friends."

"I know that," Novak said. "They're good agents and will handle the situation appropriately. But it's not a bad idea that they be warned in case your visitors come back."

"There will be no reason for them to come back if I'm not here," Eve said. "I appear to be the main attraction." She returned to her initial question. "Which brings me back to asking you why you said that it might not be smart for me to go to visit my family right now. Why not? And why would the CIA be interested in what I do?"

"I told you that there had been a few inquiries about you after you returned here," Novak said. "I didn't think anything of it at the time. You gained quite a bit of publicity with your project the last time you were here. But day before yesterday I received a call from Herb James, my director, asking for a report about what you were doing in Maldara."

"Novak!" Jill said.

He held up his hand. "I had no intention of giving him one. He didn't give me a reason why he'd want to know. James is more politician than agent these days and, like I said, I could sense that someone in the background had an ax to grind." He grinned at Eve. "Besides, I know your husband's capabilities very well indeed, and I didn't want to go up against him. I decided to stall the director until I could find out what the hell was happening." He looked at her invitingly. "Unless you'd care to tell me?"

She ignored that. "You still haven't told me why I shouldn't leave here and go to Scotland. I'd think you'd want to get rid of me."

He shook his head. "I like and respect you. But I have a hunch you've gotten yourself involved in something pretty nasty. Even if Jill hadn't asked me to help, I'd still want the best for you." He made a face. "And I don't like politicians."

"Neither do I. But as you told Jill, it's your job."

"James isn't going to fire me. Maldara is too tough to keep afloat after that civil war. And besides, he pissed me off with something he said right before he hung up."

"What was that?"

"He said that sometimes it's necessary to bring in a third party to deal with a difficult subject." He added, "If that proved to be the case, I wasn't to get in the way."

"Holy shit," Riley said.

Novak nodded. "And then I get the call from Eve tonight about the attack on this workshop. It was entirely too convenient. Dakar's men would definitely qualify as a third party."

"Yes." Riley was nibbling at her lower lip. "And I'd heard Dakar is for hire to the highest bidder. I just didn't think that included the CIA."

"Not generally." Novak shrugged. "Or I wouldn't still be working for them. There are always exceptions. Particularly when pressure is applied. But I'm curious to learn who decided we should get in bed with filth like Dakar."

"I can guess," Eve said bitterly. "No problem. It shouldn't even surprise me that Dakar was tapped to join the party."

"Would you care to share?" Novak asked. "I've risked my job being honest with you, Eve."

"No, I've got to think about it." She frowned. "You were questioned only about me, not Joe or any other members of my family?"

He shook his head. "You were the only one James was concerned about. He obviously had your dossier in front of him. Will you let me send you somewhere you'll be safe until I can find out what the hell is happening?"

"Then I'm the target," she said absently. "If he didn't mention Joe or Michael to James, he believes I'm the only one who could be a threat to him."

"Who?" Jill asked. "You're not being fair, Eve. I was pretty pissed off with Novak, but he's obviously trying to save your neck. But he can't do it if you're not going to tell him what's going on."

"Stay out of this, Jill." Eve turned to Riley. "You were the one who told me it wasn't safe for me to join my family in Scotland. Why did you say that?"

"Because I've heard of cases where Dakar tortured and killed other family members to get information from people," Riley said quietly. "It's practically his trademark. I didn't want that to happen to you. It's not your fault that my father decided he had to have you for the queen. I can't let you suffer for it."

"How generous of you," Eve said sarcastically. "Much less Joe or my son?"

"No one," Riley said firmly. "Eleni wouldn't have wanted that to happen, either. She was tired of all the blood and pain long before Charon met her that day she showed up in his village."

"I almost believe you." Eve glanced at Novak. "Did you hear the same stories about Dakar?"

"I haven't researched him," Novak said. "But I don't see why she would lie about him, do you?"

"No," she said wearily. "I guess I just wanted to find a reason to go and see my family."

"You'll let me find a safe house?" Novak asked. "It might not be for long. I'll talk to Joe about it." He paused. "But it would help if you'd tell me what I'm up against."

"Perhaps later. I haven't given up yet. I'm going to call Joe myself." She turned back to Jill. "But I want you and Novak to take Riley to an ER in Jokan and have that wound checked. I think she's okay, but it won't hurt to make certain."

"I'm not leaving you alone here," Riley said flatly.

"Dammit, I don't want any of you here while I talk to Joe. This is our business, not yours." Eve turned to Novak. "She was shot trying to keep me from being hurt. Send for a couple of those agents to stand guard here while you take care of Riley. Then when you come back, we'll talk."

"Yes, we will," he said grimly. "Count on it." He reached for his phone and punched in a number. "I'll get Carlisle and

Peterson up here right away." He opened the door. "Lock the door behind us. I guarantee we'll be back in a couple hours, and if I don't get the right answer from you, I'll call Joe back myself."

"It's not your business," she repeated. "But I promised we'd talk."

She slammed the door and locked it. Then she leaned back against it and tried to catch her breath. Too much had happened tonight and all of it was bad. The idea that Madlock might have teamed up with criminals like Dakar's mob was terrifying but not unbelievable. He was probably growing greedy and wanting to move forward on the attack.

They couldn't let him do it. No way. But how to get around it?

They'd work it out. But she couldn't do it alone. She sat down at the desk and called Joe.

———◆———

"Son of a bitch!" Joe exclaimed. "Madlock and this Dakar are joining up?"

"That's my guess. It has to be Madlock who's pulling the strings with the director of the CIA," Eve said. "I don't know who else would furnish James with my dossier and have him give an order like that to Novak. I hadn't even heard of this Dakar before Riley Smith showed up in my life."

"Oh, I've heard of him," Joe said grimly. "When I was working with Scotland Yard and Interpol, they had a lot of dealings with him. He has a vicious reputation in the Mediterranean, Azerbaijan, and Russia. I don't like the idea that he got anywhere near you. Tell Novak to put you on the next flight here."

She was silent. "He offered to find a safe house for me somewhere in Maldara."

"Screw that. I want you here with me."

"And I want to be there."

"Then why the hell are you hesitating?"

"It might not be the best thing to do." She heard him start to speak and interrupted: "From what Novak said it's clear that I'm the one Madlock is after. We knew it might happen when he found out that I agreed to help Diane by identifying that body. He must believe that I'm the person who can tell him what he wants to know about her work. If I join you in Scotland, then I'd automatically put all of you in danger. I can't do that, Joe."

"You *will* do it. Do you think I'm going to leave you there and let Novak stash you in some safe house in the jungle? I'll be on the next plane to pick you up."

"And leave Michael over there by himself? I told you what Riley said about Dakar's trademark."

"Caleb and Jane are here. Michael would be safe with them."

"This is our fight, not theirs. I won't have any of you threatened. You stay there and take care of our family. I'll make sure I'm safe here."

"You *are* my family. I don't have anyone if I don't have you."

"Sure you do." She had to hang up, her voice was starting to break. "But you're not going to get rid of me. We're going to handle this, but it may take a little while. I have to figure it all out. I'll let you know when I do. I love you, Joe." She ended the call.

But she knew Joe wasn't going to give up anytime soon. Even if he didn't hop on the next flight as he threatened, he'd be planning, researching, finding any way he could to get them out of this mess efficiently. He knew Michael was his responsibility and it might take him a little while to find the safest solution for him. But he would find it and then be on his way to her as soon as possible. There was no one more protective than Joe, and the love they felt for each other wasn't going to fade.

So find a way to make him believe she was safe and keep him in Scotland where he and Michael were equally safe. It wasn't going to be easy.

Damn, she wished Zangar and Jolbart hadn't shown up tonight. By tomorrow she would have been with Joe and Michael, and it would have been an entirely different situation to worry about. Yes, and probably an even worse one, she thought. Best to accept what fate had given her and just work it out. She had a little time before she would be invaded by Novak, Jill, and Riley. It would help if she had some idea what she was going to tell them.

———◆———

"No one's following us," Jolbart said as he looked in the rearview mirror. "Do you think we should go back and try again? They might not be expecting us. Dakar isn't going to like it that that Riley Smith bitch took us down. He was mad as hell that he didn't get hold of her after we killed the old man."

"You're the one she took down," Zangar said coldly. "If I hadn't yanked you off the back doorstep and into the car, you'd still be there. If you'd done your job, she would never have been able to stop me before I'd grabbed Eve Duncan. She *shot* me, dammit." He looked down at his left hand, which he'd wrapped in a scarf when he'd gotten into the car. "It's still bleeding."

"Not much," Jolbart said sourly. "You didn't answer me. Are we going to go back and get Duncan? I don't want to run to Dakar with my tail tucked between my legs."

Neither did Zangar. He'd been so close to getting Duncan before Riley Smith had shown up. And Dakar could be a total son of a bitch. He looked down at his bleeding hand. "I'm thinking about it."

"Think hard," Jolbart said. "We can do it. We can still get Duncan and maybe show Riley that she's not such hot shit."

That sounded even better to Zangar. Revenge could be sweet. "It would have to be something special." But if he offered a punishment that pleased Dakar, it might make it easier for him. "Keep driving. No hurry. Like I said, I'll think about it..."

———◆———

Eve heard Novak's SUV pull up in front of her workshop two hours later.

After glancing out the window, she threw open the door as Riley got out of the passenger seat. "How are you? Any problems?"

"No, I told you that there wasn't. Just a minor wound. Waste of time." She wrinkled her nose. "And it annoyed Novak when he and Jill wanted to get back here to you."

"I wasn't annoyed," Novak said. "On the contrary, I figured I'd get more results if Eve had time to consult with her husband. But Jill was concerned, and I was already in her bad books."

"You should have been upfront with me from the beginning." Jill gave him a distinctly cool look. "I trusted you."

"And I'll never betray you. I didn't this time, either." He turned back to Eve. "Did I give you enough time with Joe to make your decision? Did he talk you into going to Scotland and telling me to go to hell?"

"He tried very hard." Eve gave a half shrug. "But there was a problem. I asked him if he thought you were capable of keeping me safe. He gave me a very reluctant yes. Jill might not trust you, but Joe does. Of course he believes he'd be better at it. He probably would be, but then I'd have to worry about both Michael and him, and that's not an option. I won't lead Dakar to my family."

"Then are you going to let me make you disappear until I decide it's safe for you to come out of hiding?" Novak asked. "Or maybe you don't trust me as much as Joe does?"

"I trust you, but you don't know what you're asking." She thought a moment. "Or what I'm asking of you. And I can't let either one of us go into this blind. It's more dangerous than you realize." She suddenly whirled on Riley. "Isn't that right?"

Riley stiffened. "What are you asking me?"

"Just the truth. I was going to question you about it later anyway. That story about the detectives your father hired to investigate Joe and me during the last couple years didn't really hold water. I remember your father being much sharper than that. He would have demanded a more complete report. You might not have known everything, but you probably knew more than you told me. Correct?"

Riley nodded. "I was surprised you accepted it so readily. It's true that we didn't have a complete report, though."

"But you found out something that interested you?"

Riley hesitated, then nodded again. "We knew about the president of the United States."

Novak's eyes widened. "What the hell?"

Eve's lips curved in a wry smile. "You said that you thought your director was taking orders from someone high up in the government."

"Not that high up."

"This might be the time for me to ask you what you think about your commander in chief before we go on," Eve said. "Because I had no doubt that was who gave the orders to involve Dakar."

"How do I feel about the president?" Novak repeated slowly. "I didn't vote for him. Too much dirty laundry and bullshit. But then I don't like politicians." He thought about it. "And it wouldn't surprise me that he'd make a deal with a mobster if he could get away with it." He paused again. "But he'd have to think it was worth it."

"It's worth it," Eve said flatly. "I think you'll agree with me once you hear the stakes." She tilted her head. "If you want to hear them. Madlock would consider it top secret and probably put you on a death list." She looked at Jill and Riley. "I think Riley might know more than she's telling, so she's already in too deep. But I'd rather not involve you, Jill."

"Neither would I," Novak said quickly.

"Be quiet, Novak," Jill said. "Eve's my friend, and she wouldn't cheat me of a story as juicy as this one is shaping up to be."

"Yes, I would," Eve said soberly. "If I thought I could get away with it. Because you may not be able to write it for a long time. But you'd definitely have the exclusive."

"Good enough," Jill said to Novak. "So you go and check out your agents. I'll give you ten minutes while I make coffee for us." She turned away. "A good story deserves all the bells and whistles . . ."

"You're late." Jill handed Novak his cup of coffee when he walked back into the workroom fifteen minutes later. "Is everything okay?"

"Yes. Sorry to mess up your planning. I had to make arrangements," he said caustically as he dropped down in a chair across from Eve. "You don't run my unit, Jill."

"You've made that clear." She settled down on the couch beside Riley. "Go ahead, Eve. It's over to you now."

"Then stop throwing sparks at Novak," Eve said. "He's probably been doing the best he can. It's not his fault he's been caught in the middle of my particular nightmare." She wrinkled her nose. "And I might need him to help me fight my way out of it."

"That's why I'm still here," Novak said. "But let's jump back a little to Adam Madlock. He can cause me a lot of trouble, and since he's one of the most powerful figures in the world, that probably goes double for you. What does he want with you? How did you manage to get on his bad side?"

"He wants information, and to use me to get to a prize that he's been after for a number of years. He's been playing it cool, but now he's ready to make a move." She shrugged. "Actually, he came fairly late onto the scene. Before Madlock ran for president, he was a friend of Joshua Nalam, the owner of one of the biggest pharmaceutical conglomerates in the world. Nalam was pouring money into Madlock's campaign for president when I first heard about him." She made a face. "And they were both scum of the earth. But my main problem was with Nalam until we managed to get rid of him. He was the one who was trying to kill

Diane Connors, Joe's ex-wife, because of the bullet she'd discovered."

"Joe's ex-wife," Jill repeated. "What the hell? I didn't know he was married before."

"It was a long time ago," Eve said. "And it didn't seem important until she showed up on our doorstep asking me for a favor a couple years ago. But then, of course, it was tremendously important because of the bullet."

"I don't give a damn about Joe's ex-wife," Novak said. "But I want to know what a bullet has to do with this."

"It wasn't a real bullet," Eve said. "That was only what Diane called it." She waited a moment, then just went for it. "Some people would call it the silver bullet. The medical cure for all human afflictions."

"What?" Novak shook his head. "No way. That doesn't exist."

"That's what I thought you'd say. That was my response when she first told me she'd created it. But now I believe she did it. She had proof," Eve said. "And later both Joe and I became certain enough that I agreed to go with her when she needed me to perform a reconstruction and DNA confirmation. However, Nalam also believed she'd succeeded and was trying to hunt her down and kill her because it would have caused him terrible financial losses if all those expensive miracle drugs he was selling were no longer necessary. We had to stop him. Because Diane's bullet was going to be a miracle for everyone on the globe."

"And did you stop it?" Novak asked.

"We stopped Nalam, but he'd told his buddy Madlock about Diane and her silver bullet. By that time Madlock had won the presidency, and that made him even more of a threat than

Nalam. Diane had to vanish until it was safe for her to release the bullet. Madlock was into power. If he'd gotten his hands on either Diane or the bullet, he would have been able to control more than the presidency. We're talking about global domination. He would have had the power to call the shots with any nation on the planet. But we were warned in time, and we sent her into hiding."

"And went into hiding yourselves," Jill said.

"It was safer for us. Madlock knew I'd done that reconstruction for Diane, but he didn't have information about Joe or Michael. He couldn't prove we knew anything about the bullet. We split up and we've just been waiting for an opportunity to help Diane . . . or get back together. But that seems to have been blown out of the water tonight. If he's been watching me, Madlock almost certainly believes Diane may get in touch with me, and he might get an opportunity to snatch her." She shook her head. "Not good."

"Evidently Madlock is getting impatient," Novak said. "But I'm curious why he chose Dakar as a partner."

"Eve," Riley said suddenly. "She's world-famous and he couldn't take her prisoner without getting flak, but when he was searching for a partner to do the dirty work, he probably had his men look for someone influential but willing to cooperate with his agenda. By now a good many of Dakar's men know what was in my father's notes, where Eve was mentioned prominently. She'd be a gift to Dakar."

Eve frowned. "Maybe."

"Makes sense." Novak met Eve's eyes. "Far more than the rest of your story."

"You think I'm lying?"

"Not intentionally. I know you're an honest individual and

a professional. But I'm also aware that anyone can be fooled. Perhaps you wanted to believe Diane Connors's story. You're an idealist, and you probably went through as much hell as the rest of us during these last years with the pandemic. It would be understandable if you were looking for a happy ending."

"I'm glad you understand," Eve said dryly. "Even if you came to the wrong conclusion. One thing you said is true. I do want a happy ending, and I'm going to fight to make it happen. Do you believe enough of my story to risk helping me?"

He was silent a moment. "That was never in question. Not from the minute the director started talking about making a deal with a group outside of the Company. Not from the minute I promised Jill I'd do what I could for both you and Riley."

"Hallelujah," Jill said. "You had me scared, Novak."

"Then it was a learning experience for both of us." He looked her in the eye. "Though a trial like this was bound to haunt us sometime. But you should have known better. You will next time."

"Bastard. You couldn't resist rubbing it in, could you?" Jill turned to Eve. "He's right about that 'bullet' tall tale. It's hard for me to believe, and I specialize in storytelling."

"No tall tale," Eve said quietly. "Diane proved it to me." She grinned. "But I'm not going to tell you how or when. You've got to trust me. I'll accept Novak's cynicism, but anyone who would come here and try to talk me into proving to the world that Helen of Troy was no myth hasn't got a leg to stand on." She shot a glance at Riley. "And you're very quiet. How much of that story did you know already?"

"Not much. We had a report about Diane Connors. Rumors about Madlock," Riley said. "Nothing about the bullet.

You must have kept everything about that top secret." She shrugged. "As it should have been. I understand about secrets. I've been trying to unravel one myself all my life."

"So did you believe mine?"

A smile lit Riley's face. "Why not? A cure that solves the world's ills isn't any stranger than a queen like my Eleni who created a world of her own that lasted thousands of years."

Eve chuckled. "I suppose not." She turned back to Novak and her smile faded. "It's generous of you to offer to help, but I'm still not sure that I should accept it. What are you planning?"

"I haven't decided. This is unexpected. I'm having to juggle a few possibilities. But I have friends all over Maldara, and I'd have no problem locating a safe house for you that even Joe Quinn would find acceptable."

"I doubt that," she said. "Not unless it was in Scotland."

"No, it won't be there." His smile vanished. "And we'd better get you out of this village ASAP. My agents verified that none of the villagers had seen Dakar's men, but that doesn't mean it's safe."

"But you said you don't have a place to take me yet." Eve had another thought. "And are you sure that your agents won't prove to be more loyal to your director than you are? I'd be better off not being seen with you." She paused. "Besides, I don't like the idea of being the one who destroys your brilliant career in the Company. You were always good to Joe and me when we were here before."

"She's right," Jill said. "I don't give a damn about sabotaging your career with James since he's trying to use you for his dirty tricks. But I won't have it go down the tubes without giving you a chance to salvage it. I got you into this. I'll take Riley back to the hotel with me, and we'll figure out her next move between us."

"Back off, Jill," Novak said. "I'll handle it. I just don't know how to do it yet. Having Madlock to contend with makes it a whole new ball game. It's not as if I can arrest him or shoot him. I'll have to arrange a way to do it that won't put me in prison for the rest of my life."

"Exactly," Eve said deadpan. "Welcome to my world. Joe has been following his movements. Madlock has been gradually forming his own special army since he took office. He's looking for Diane, and he's getting ready for a big push of some sort. It doesn't matter what a scumbag he is or what damage he's planning on doing. Joe and I have felt as if our hands were tied. Except I don't believe I can take it any longer. We have to find another way." She got to her feet. "You're not the only one who has some thinking to do tonight. You're both out of this. I'll finish packing, and then I'll go spend the night down at the village with Hajif and his wife, Leta." She turned to Riley. "But you should get out of here. Dakar as well as those two mobsters will be targeting you for interfering in their nasty game."

Riley shrugged. "Then I'm not any worse off than I was before, am I? I was always a target. I'll stay with you until I know you're safe." She saw Eve open her lips to protest and held up her hand. "I told you that I knew none of this was your fault, but I still had to make a final attempt at persuading you to help me with Eleni. And you saw where it ended."

"Yes, I did." Eve smiled crookedly. "But I also saw that Dakar managed to hook up with Madlock. So where does the blame really lie?" She waved her hand. "Whatever. I can take care of myself, Riley."

"I know you can." Riley turned to Novak. "She can be stubborn. Will you assign one of your men to guard her friend's hut tonight?"

Novak nodded. "I'll send Peterson and Carlisle to escort you down to the village. And I'll swing by here early tomorrow morning. I might have come up with an acceptable alternative to offer her by then." He turned. "Come on, Jill, I have calls to make."

"I thought you would. I'll help." Jill started to hurry after him but stopped at the door to look back at Eve. "Novak will take care of it. You can trust him." Then she was gone.

Eve glanced at Riley as she started across the room where she'd left her half-packed duffel. "You might just as well have gone with them. You're wounded and I might end up taking care of you."

"No, you won't. I'm very strong. I grew up trekking in the jungle." She got to her feet and followed Eve. "When I was a little girl, it used to drive my mother crazy when I'd run away from camp at dawn and not come back until evening."

"Because she was worried about you?"

"Maybe." She watched Eve pack the final items in the duffel. "Or maybe my mother just liked to be in control when she could. My father definitely dominated their relationship. Is there anything I can do for you?"

"No." Eve carried her duffel toward the door. "Because I like to be in control, too. Let's get out of here."

CHAPTER

5

The village was brightly lit, and Leta ran toward Eve as soon as she caught sight of her coming toward the hut. "I was frightened. Are you well?" She embraced her. "Those men that Novak sent said that you were not hurt but it was strange that they came. It reminded me of the time those monsters attacked us when our Amira died. They have not come back?"

"No, those monsters are gone forever. But we both know there are other monsters in the world." Eve hugged her. "The attack was on me, but Novak wanted to make certain that none of the villagers had been hurt. I'm sorry you were frightened. I'll be leaving Robaku in the morning; would it bother you if I stay the night with you? Novak didn't like the idea of me remaining in the workshop."

Leta shook her head. "I will be glad of the company. I will not have my Hajif tonight. He is at a gathering with the other men in the village. They are talking about how to guard our homes. They were frightened, too."

"Of course they were," Eve said. "But I'm glad to tell you that there shouldn't be a reason for any of you to be frightened from now on. We have two guards with us and, as I said, no one in the village is targeted. Tomorrow I'll be gone." Eve turned and gestured to Riley. "This is my friend Riley, Leta. She was wounded for me tonight." Then she had another thought. "But you might know each other. Jill said you spent a few days in the village on your father's orders checking me out."

Riley shook her head. "I would never choose your good friends. I had a brief visit with a young widow in the next hut section who was very kind to me. She showed me the work you did on her daughter." She politely bowed her head toward Leta and the next moment she was rattling off conversation to the woman in fluent Maldara-Swahili. Leta appeared surprised and then answered Riley in the same language.

"Jill said you were a linguist," Eve said.

"Languages are easy for me. It was one way I could help my father." She shrugged. "And Maldara is a simple language. It's a blend of Swahili, English, and Maldaran itself." She spoke to Leta again before she switched to English. "I just thanked her for her courtesy and asked her if there was anything I could do to make my stay less of a burden." She was smiling at Leta. "She said that your friends were her friends. Thank you, Leta."

Leta smiled back at her. "But if you are wounded you should be in bed," Leta said. "I will put mats down for you in the other room." She turned and hurried out of the room.

"Nice woman," Riley said.

Eve nodded. "But the death of her grandson nearly broke her heart. He had to be the first one I chose for a reconstruction."

"I can see that." Riley ruefully shook her head. "You have

a unique talent. I'm standing in line to have you do the same for my Eleni."

"But your heart won't be broken if I don't do it."

"My father's would have been." She gazed at Eve. "And I also have a very special feeling for her." She held up her hand. "No pressure. I think I'll go offer to help Leta. I didn't argue when you made her believe I'd been hurt saving you. Now I'm feeling guilty about imposing on her." She moved quickly toward the other room.

Eve wearily shook her head as Riley disappeared. Riley wasn't like anyone else she had ever met, and she didn't know how to handle her. There was no way she could agree to do what Riley wanted. It would be crazy to go to Azerbaijan and do the reconstruction. Okay, she might feel grateful that Riley had possibly saved her life. But to follow up and go searching for that Spartan queen would be a terrible mistake that would prove dangerous and...totally fascinating. The challenge would be greater than any she had ever taken. But of course she wasn't going to take it. She must be exhausted to even consider the possibility. Tomorrow she would be more clearheaded and make a far more sensible decision...

Something was wrong...

Why was it so hard to breathe? Eve wondered.

Her lungs felt as if they were on fire.

"Smoke." It was Riley's voice. It sounded like a croak, and she was shaking Eve's shoulder. "Wake up, Eve. We've got to get out of here. The hut must be on fire." She was coughing. "I'll be right back. I have to go wake up Leta..."

"Wait. I'll go with you." Eve's eyes were wide open now and stinging from the smoke. She couldn't see any fire, but the entire hut was filled with thick gray mist and Riley was no longer in the room. Eve rolled off the mat, got to her feet, and staggered into the other room.

"She's not here," Riley said as she headed for the front door.

"Maybe she went outside to see what was happening."

Then Eve heard the screaming.

"Leta!" She threw open the door.

And then she saw the fire!

At first glance it looked as if the entire village was ablaze. She saw several huts on fire; one large hut in the center of the village was completely engulfed in flames. Over a dozen men were streaming out of it.

And Leta was running straight toward it! "Hajif!"

"No!" Riley was running to intercept her.

Eve started to follow her but Peterson, one of Novak's guards who'd been sent to protect them, stepped in front of her. "No, ma'am. You can't go there. You're safe in this area as long as you stay with us. We've checked the area out and whoever torched this village must have taken off. I've called Novak and he'll send help."

"Get out of my way, Peterson. The whole damn village will burn down by the time anyone else gets here. If you want to be of use, help these people draw water from the pond and put out the fires." She pushed past him and ran toward the burning entrance where Riley had followed Leta into the hut.

It was even worse inside the hut than the burning exterior. Spot fires were igniting all over the interior and the smoke was too thick to see anything... "Riley!" she shouted.

"Here!" Riley called from across the tent. "We need help."

Eve could see why after she made her way across the room. Leta was kneeling beside a gray-haired man, rocking him back and forth, tears running down her face. "My Hajif is dying," she said brokenly as Eve knelt beside her. "How can I live without him?"

"You won't have to do that. Not if we can get him out of here." She looked at Riley. "We don't have much time."

Riley nodded. "We'll drag him toward the door." She said to Leta, "You go ahead and see if you can find someone to help us once we get him out."

"I don't want to leave him."

"Go," Eve snapped. "Now, Leta."

Leta jumped to her feet and ran toward the door.

"Good." They started to drag the man toward the door.

It did not go quickly. They could barely see where they were going. Eve had to stop once to bat out flames on Hajif's clothing.

Then the door was just ahead of them.

They lunged through it and saw Leta waiting anxiously on the other side. Peterson was there, too, and he grabbed Hajif away from them. He was muttering an oath beneath his breath as he started to examine Hajif. "Why the hell did you run in there? Novak is going to kill us for this."

"No, he won't. It's not as if you could have stopped us from going after Leta," Eve said. "How is Hajif?"

Peterson glanced at Leta, who was holding Hajif's hand. "Not good," he said in a low voice. "He's an old man and he's having trouble breathing. But I told Novak that an ambulance might be needed. I hope to hell they get here soon."

"Leta and I will take care of Hajif," Riley told Peterson. "You keep an eye on Eve and see if you can help the rest of those villagers. Just look at them. Half their village is gone. Those bastards didn't care who they hurt. All they wanted to do was cause as much damage as possible to punish me and show Dakar they hadn't totally failed him." She added fiercely to Peterson, "Don't you let them get away with it. Do you hear me?"

"They hear you," Eve said as she turned on her heel and headed for the villagers struggling desperately to fill their buckets with water to douse the flames. "Call me if you need me. Take care of Hajif. I'll come back and check on both of you soon."

"I don't need you." Then Riley's whole attention was focused on Hajif.

———◆———

Novak and Jill arrived forty minutes later followed immediately by an ambulance and several cars with more of Novak's agents.

Riley flagged down Jill as soon as she caught sight of them and pointed to Hajif. "He needs immediate care. Get an EMT over here." She turned to Novak. "There are probably more in bad shape, but Eve didn't believe anyone was critical. She's over there with the rest of the survivors, and you can get an update."

"I'll do that as soon as I get an update from you," Novak said. "Are you both okay?"

"As okay as we can be." She was watching the three EMTs pour out of the ambulance and run toward Hajif's body. She muttered a curse as she saw one of them try to pull Leta away from her husband. "I can't talk to you any longer. I've got to go stop them from doing that. I did the best I could, but I think Leta's the only thing that's kept Hajif alive since we brought him out of that hut." She ran back and stood over Hajif's body, confronting the EMT.

"Go talk to Eve," Jill said to Novak. "I'll see that Riley doesn't cause problems with the medical team. She may be right about Leta." She was running after Riley as she spoke.

Novak shook his head and turned on his heel, striding across the grounds toward where Eve was standing. "What can I do?" he asked her.

She handed him a bucket. "You can help us put out the rest of these fires while you tell me if you've managed to track down Jolbart and Zangar."

"No. Peterson said they set charges at several of the huts, and they were long gone by the time the fires ignited." He was already motioning to several of his men to grab buckets as he dipped his own bucket in the pond. "They'll be across the border by now. I've sent a unit after them, but I doubt if we'll catch them." He threw the water on the nearest hut and turned back to the pond. "Did Peterson tell you that they also torched your workshop?"

She nodded. "It didn't matter. That was only a place where I worked." She gazed at the villagers huddled together staring in numb horror at the fires devouring their huts. "They've lost their homes. After all they went through losing their children during the civil war, this is sickening. And there are several men and women who have bad burns. Hajif may die. I should never have asked Leta to take us in."

"I told you that the village was safe." He added bitterly, "Who knew that those bastards would come back?"

"Riley did," Eve said. "She seems to know them very well. That's why she came with me. Thank heavens she did, because it appears she has a medical license among all her other credentials." She wearily shook her head.

"He's the headman of the village, isn't he?"

She nodded. "And the first person I met when I came to Robaku." She wiped her hands on a towel. "He begged me to do a reconstruction on his grandson because his wife, Leta, wouldn't believe he was really gone and thought he was just lost in the jungle." She started toward the place where the EMTs were working with Riley. "I'm glad you're here, Novak. Though I never dreamed that I'd be disturbing you again in the middle of the night."

"No disturbance. I was still working on getting you a safe house when I got Peterson's call." He was tossing another bucket of water on the burning hut. "You'll be glad to know I'd just closed the deal."

"Glad? I'd forgotten all about it." Startled, she looked at him over her shoulder. "I've been a little busy."

"And your problem is fairly complex. Which is why I had to make certain it would be suitable for all parties. What happened here tonight could have made it even more desirable. I believe I'm detecting a change of attitude...We'll talk about it later."

Eve shook her head. "Maybe. Right now, just put out the fires."

"That's what I'm trying to do." He turned back to his men. "You heard her. Put out *all* those damn fires."

Jill turned when she saw Eve approaching. "Good to see you," she murmured. "I'm tired of running interference between Riley and those EMTs. She's mad as hell and ready to explode. They've told her that she may have saved Hajif's life, but they still want her to go by their rules. They're trying to load Hajif into the ambulance and take him to the hospital, but they want to leave Leta here. I offered to follow them with her in my car, but Riley says their rules suck and Leta should do what she wants. She's not fond of rules."

"I've noticed that." Eve was looking at Leta, who was clinging desperately to her husband's hand, and she had to blink back tears. She knelt beside her. "It's going to be all right, Leta," she said gently. "You can go with him. They're trying to help. They just didn't understand. I'll talk to them."

"Your friend tried to tell them." Leta looked at Riley. "They wouldn't listen to her. She's very wise, and they should have listened."

"Evidently Riley thinks the same thing. I don't blame her. Sometimes rules should be broken." She got to her feet. "Let's go do it. I'll run your interference with Riley. You get going, Jill. I know you don't like trading on your relationship with Novak, but this is an exception. You know Novak can move mountains with everyone in Maldara. Tell him to go and break the stalemate."

Jill was already heading for the pond. "Right."

"Come on," Eve told Leta as she pulled her to her feet. "Let them get Hajif into the ambulance. You'll be there to greet him." She turned and headed for the ambulance. "Break it up," she told Riley as she inserted herself between her and the EMT. "You're wasting time." She opened the door of the ambulance. "Get in the ambulance, Leta."

Leta scrambled into the vehicle.

The EMT frowned. "You can't do that. I was just telling this lady that I couldn't—"

"New rules." Eve looked over his shoulder at Novak striding toward them. "Novak will explain them to you. I'll tell your partner that it's time to put Hajif into the ambulance." She pulled Riley back over to where Hajif lay. "Stop arguing. I know you're pissed off. So am I. But you've done everything you could without wasting time. Let Novak handle the rest of the battle." She quickly gave the other EMTs the orders to put Hajif in the ambulance, and they stood and watched until the gurney was placed in the vehicle.

"I'm sorry. I wanted to finish it," Riley said jerkily. "They were your friends. I told you that I'd take care of him for you. This is all my fault." Riley's hands were knotted into fists at her sides as her gaze circled around the burnt-out village. "All of it."

"The hell it is," Eve said harshly. "You didn't set those charges. And I'm the one who decided to come down here and spend the night. But we both know exactly who's to blame for this horror story. And there's nothing we can do right now about making any of it right with these people. We'll have to worry about that later." She turned away and moved toward the ambulance. "It's my turn to take care of Hajif and Leta now. I'm going to hitch a ride with Jill and follow the ambulance to the hospital. If you want to help, take my place with Novak and his men, and try to make these villagers as comfortable as possible. Then meet me at the hospital. Will you do that?"

"Of course," Riley said quietly. "Anything you want."

"That might not be possible," Eve said grimly. "I have an idea it might be too big a task. But it could be a good start."

She didn't look back as she reached the ambulance. "We'll talk about it when you meet me at the hospital."

———◆———

ICU
JOKAN MEMORIAL HOSPITAL
SEVEN HOURS LATER

"How is he?" Jill asked as Eve came out of the ward. "Any better?"

"Maybe a little." She wearily rubbed the back of her neck. "The doctor said we wouldn't know for another few hours. I'm waiting for him to come back with some lab reports. But Leta said she thinks he'll make it. I'm hoping. I just got a call from Novak, and he's on his way back here after he talks to Riley. They've done all they could for the villagers for the time being. He's called the Maldaran Government Charitable Office for help, and they'll be there shortly. Did he call you?"

Jill paused and then nodded. "He asked me to make a call for him. He said he wanted everything in place before he talked to you."

"'In place'?" Eve repeated warily. "What's that supposed to mean? Nothing's been 'in place' since this evening began. It's been a total nightmare."

"That's not Novak's fault. He's done everything he could to give you what you needed." She wrinkled her nose. "Actually, before he got that call from Peterson, he thought he'd managed to do it. Then everything blew up in his face and he had to get it back on track."

"I don't know what you're talking about. How could I

blame Novak? It's always been my problem. I just have to figure out a way to solve it." She shook her head. "But not right now. I'm going to go to the waiting room and get a cup of coffee and then try to think what I'm going to say when I talk to Joe. Because if he thought the situation was bad before, it's nothing to what it is now." She rubbed her temple. "I keep seeing all those burnt huts and those good people who have lost their homes. I can't *stand* it, Jill."

"Yes, you can," Jill said. "But don't call Joe too soon. Let Novak see if he can make the situation a little more palatable."

"Not bloody likely." She waved her hand dismissively. "Go make your call. You wouldn't care to tell me who you're calling?"

She shook her head. "It's not my story, it's Novak's." She plopped down on a bench in the corridor and took out her phone. "Go get your coffee. I'll call you if I see a doctor heading for the ICU."

"Do that." Eve headed for the waiting room. She hoped that doctor would bring good news. She'd like to give Joe something optimistic to mix with the story of fire and pain and disaster that was all she was going to be able to tell him when she forced herself to call him.

❖

ROBAKU

"I'm heading for the hospital," Novak said as he entered the tent they'd set up for Riley to treat the villagers. She was bandaging the burn on a little girl's arm while her mother stood anxiously beside her. "Eve told me to tell you that Hajif is still holding his own. The doctors said to send you their compliments and wanted to know where you'd studied."

"Besides Cairo Medical?" Riley asked wryly. "I interned with any number of villages in half a dozen countries, plus getting an advanced degree from at least two witch doctors."

"Interesting," Novak said. "Evidently you paid attention when they were giving their lessons."

"It was necessary. It was the one skill that could keep us alive on those treks through the jungle. I was useful enough that my father didn't want to spare me to go to school, but I insisted. Most things I could learn from books or computers, but that was definitely hands-on." She finished bandaging the little girl, smiled at her mother, and sent them both on their way. Then she turned to Novak. "If you don't need me anymore here, I could go with you to the hospital. I promised Eve I'd join her there."

"I'd prefer you stay here for a while longer," he said quietly. "I've made arrangements for you to meet with an old acquaintance of mine. I thought that it would be beneficial for both of you. I was going to have him contact you when you returned to Azerbaijan." He shrugged. "But since conditions with you and Eve have deteriorated considerably since yesterday, I gave him a call and told him to detour to Robaku so that we could use him here."

"Use him?" Her eyes narrowed on his face. "Why? Who is it? Look, I realized that Jill would probably ask for your help, but I understood when she said you couldn't do it. That doesn't mean I'd let you pull in one of your old buddies to take over because you're feeling guilty. It's not as if I'm completely alone. I'd rather handle it myself." She had another thought.

"And if you're trying to kill two birds with one stone after what happened here, anything you can do for Eve would have nothing to do with me."

"Are you finished?" he asked. "One, I'm not feeling guilty, because I've done the best I could for you. As for killing two birds, that will be up to Cade. No one could ever call us buddies, but he's been known to pull off some clever stunts on occasion. You might be able to negotiate with him. But everyone is in agreement that you need help of some kind. I've told him he has to regard you as a partner. He owes me a debt, but you'll have to decide if you want to meet his terms."

"Partner?" Then she caught up with the rest of the dialogue. "Cade?"

He nodded. "Morgan Cade."

The name froze her in place. She tensed. "Shit," she murmured, "I didn't expect this."

"No one does," Novak said. "Cade tends to hit the landscape like a tornado. At least, that's how my encounter with him went. But once he decides he needs you for something, somehow you get pulled into the morass." He was gazing at her expression. "I don't have to ask if you've heard of him. You've spent most of your life here. You must have heard the stories."

"I wouldn't have had a chance not to. According to the media, he's half Robin Hood, half Indiana Jones. My uncle Dan is one of his fans. But that's not saying a lot. Dan admires anyone who isn't establishment and can write his own ticket."

"Well he certainly falls in that category. What else did your uncle Dan tell you?"

"What didn't he tell me about him? He couldn't shut up. That Cade was born in California but raised by his father on an estate in the Atlas Mountains. That he's one of the ten richest men in the world, was a special forces sniper in the marines, and was eventually awarded a Medal of Honor. He traveled the world after he got out of the service. He appears to be a man of many talents. He's an archaeologist, environmentalist, philanthropist, but he didn't like the corruption he found when he came back to his father's estate in the mountains." Her lips twisted. "Or maybe he just missed being a marine, because he did serious damage whenever he ran across any militants or human traffickers that showed up on his radar." She shrugged. "Dan thought that was far more likely, and he got much more kick out of those stories. Like I said, he's a fan."

"So are most of the members of Cade's audience," Novak said. "But for the most part, he believes in what he does. He just doesn't give a damn how he gets there when he uncovers something that pisses him off. Not many people have enough money and power to indulge themselves when they see some-thing going terribly wrong. For instance, he gets really upset when he watches helpless animals being tormented and he tends to hunt down poachers whenever he runs across them. I was involved in one of his raids in Nigeria when he tracked down a group of poachers and went after them. It wasn't pretty. He'll be difficult, but if anyone has a chance of getting you what you want, it could be him."

"Why would he bother? Just because he owes you?"

"He was intrigued by your Helen when I told him about the tomb." He added, "And he doesn't like Dakar. That was paramount. Put them all together and you should be able to hold your own."

"You're damn right I will." She moistened her lips. "If I

decide that would be the best way to handle it." She was scared, and confused, and her mind was dizzy with possibilities. Cade. That name was synonymous with opportunities according to Dan. But she and her uncle didn't always agree on either objectives or the price for achieving them. "You said he owed you and he's evidently keeping his promise. But will he keep his word to me if we make a deal?"

"I've never heard him of him betraying anyone," he agreed. "But I warn you that he usually gets what he wants in the end."

"So I've heard," she said. "It's one of the things that Dan likes most about him." She frowned thoughtfully. "What have you told him about me?"

"Everything that Jill told me. It was the smart thing to do to give him all the weapons so that he could use them to protect both of you," he explained. "But if you've kept anything from Jill, he'll probably know that, too. He never goes into a project without researching anything connected to it."

"I've never tried to hide anything from Jill, but we haven't known each other that long."

"But Jill is a journalist, and she asks questions. She'd know more than most people." He shrugged. "And she wants to help you, and that would encourage more questions."

"Yes, it would," she said quietly. "And you don't want her any more involved with me than she is now. I don't blame you. It's too risky. I feel the same way. I wouldn't have let her do as much as she has for me if she hadn't insisted. I had to make a last try at getting Eve to help with Helen, and it seemed safe enough." She smiled bitterly. "But it didn't turn out that way, did it?"

"No, it didn't," he said. "And I'd be lying if I said I want her having anything else to do with Dakar. But it's her job to search out the stories, and I have to stand back and watch."

"Unless you can furnish a substitute that even she would accept as suitable?" She met his eyes. "Is that Cade?"

"That's Cade." He added, "Heaven help you. Though after tonight I may still have problems keeping her on track covering that conference in Paris."

She shook her head. "I'll find a way to make sure of that. And when am I to expect Cade?"

"Anytime now. He called me from the airport. I told him what the situation was here, and he may be making additional preparations to remove you."

"Additional preparations?" she repeated warily. "I don't like the sound of that. And no one 'removes' me but me."

"Then tell him about it. From now on it's between the two of you. Unless you decide to jettison him because you can't stand the flak. Can't blame you. But then I don't have your motivation." He turned toward the door of the tent. "I've got to get to the hospital and give Jill a report on the village. Maybe I'll see you there?"

"You'll see me," she said. "Count on it."

She watched the tent door swing closed behind him and drew a deep breath. It wasn't as if she'd made a decision. It was just intelligent to let herself be open to the possibilities that Cade represented. Why not take advantage of Novak's knowledge of Cade? It was a chance, when she'd been searching wildly for which way to go next. But it was all coming too fast for her. She was trying to put together memories of Dan's stories and the outrageous newspaper and media accounts of Cade's adventures. They were all blending together into one and making her feel very uncertain.

"Hi, you must be Riley. I'm Cade. Sorry to catch you at such a bad time."

She whirled toward the door. The man standing there was definitely high-impact. Thirtyish, dark hair, blue eyes, hard features that were more interesting than good-looking. He was dressed in jeans and a black shirt and smiling at her. Definitely Morgan Cade. Just seeing him caused her sense of vulnerability to increase and it was suddenly making her angry. "That's probably the understatement of the century," she said jerkily. "Or maybe you didn't notice the huts burned to the ground as you drove in?"

"I noticed." His smile faded. "We'll get to how we're going to take care of them later. Right now Kirby is looking the situation over and will give me a report when he finishes. Sorry if I seemed flip, but I got the impression from Novak and my research that you'd respond better to not being treated as anyone but an adult with a purpose. Perhaps I was wrong? I'll go back to square one. No, I'll try one more time." He tilted his head, but his voice was as cutting and hard as a whip. "What do you want from me, Riley Smith? Can we talk and maybe make a deal that will suit us both?"

He was right. And behaving just as she would have if she hadn't been on edge. So she smothered the anger and nodded. "You took me by surprise. It won't happen again. Novak just told me that you were going to be a possible factor. Yes, we can talk. Give me ten minutes to wash up and I'll be with you."

He looked her up and down. "You need more time than that. You look pretty rough, and you must feel the same way. I want your full attention. I understand I'm supposed to eventually take you to the hospital to meet with Eve Duncan. We'll find a hotel next to it and let you clean up. Then we'll talk and you'll be able to concentrate on what I'm saying. Okay?"

"Do I have a choice?"

"Yes, but it's easier to give in to me on the simple stuff."

Why argue? She did need a shower. "I'll take your word for it this time." She grabbed her duffel. "Let's go."

They'd only just started to make their way toward a dark blue Range Rover parked down the way when a tall, sandy-haired man dressed in camouflage gear approached them. He nodded to her but spoke directly to Cade. "It's not as bad as some that we've seen. Novak brought in some charitable group to put a Band-Aid on the damage, but they obviously don't have the means to go very far with it. How far do you want me to take it?"

Cade glanced at Riley. "All the way. She's pretty involved in all this. She's not going to be able to concentrate otherwise. But don't use the main crew, bring in outside construction and medical."

"Right." Then the man turned and smiled at Riley. "Hi, sorry not to introduce myself, but I had to get that out of the way. I had to be certain I wasn't going to have to argue with him before I exposed myself to something more pleasant." He shook her hand. "I'm Jon Kirby. You must be Riley Smith. Cade didn't have to tell me how involved you are. In the short time I've been here, I've talked to four villagers who have been singing your praises."

"They wouldn't be difficult to find," she said. "They were hurting, and I could help heal them."

"I believe it went a little farther than that. They said you were kind, and one little girl said you smiled at her while you were bandaging her wounds." Kirby released her hand. "That counts a lot. I told him that I had a feeling we were going to get along, didn't I, Cade?"

"Yes, you did." He took Riley's arm and nudged her toward the Range Rover. "But I had to take it with a grain of salt. After all, you do have a taste for tigers."

Kirby was laughing behind them, and Riley glanced over her shoulder. "Tigers?"

"He'll probably tell you later about Cubby."

"Cubby? Odd name..." She was still looking over her shoulder. "I think I...like him."

"Of course you do. It's one of Kirby's main attributes. Together with how different he is from me." He opened the door of the vehicle for her. "I understand he's a great relief to be around after you get a little too much of me."

"I can see how that might be true. You're...unique, and no one would know how to take you." She settled in the seat as he started the car. She was silent for a moment. "But he must have another attribute. You talked about me with him. He just gave you a report. Does he do your research?"

He nodded. "Very good. Yes, he does most of it. He has contacts all over the world, and he's been with me long enough to know what I need."

"But he argues with you when he doesn't think you're right. You appreciate that, too."

"Yes, I do." He was silent. "Though I'm not sure I like the way that you've been collating all that information about us in such a short time. It makes me uneasy."

She made a rude sound. "No, it doesn't. If it did, you wouldn't let me get near to knowing anything about you. You probably think that letting me believe I might be able to pierce the armor you wear will bring me closer to doing what you want."

He was silent. "You're being very open."

"I have no choice. We both can see I'm scrambling to maintain a foothold with someone who has all the cards." She was looking straight out the windshield. "But I'm fairly smart and I don't give up. So it's not going to be easy for you. You'd be amazed at all the ways I can find to give you massive headaches if you don't cooperate with me."

He suddenly chuckled. "I wouldn't be amazed at all. I can hardly wait to watch you in action." He added, "But it's hardly fair to poke the tiger when she's already just had one battle to contend with. So if it's all right with you, I'll wait until we get to the hotel for you to give me your list of weapons you're ready to hurl at me."

"I don't mind." She was relieved. She was suddenly bone-weary and she needed a little time to gather herself together before she dealt with Cade. "I didn't mean to be aggressive. I only wanted you not to make a mistake about me. It would waste time."

"And we wouldn't want that," he said, straight-faced. "Thank you for your concern."

He was amused, she thought. And that hadn't been her intention. She had to be more careful. Cade had to take her seriously. She had to study him so that she could not only communicate effectively but play on his emotions effectively. It might be the only way she could control him. "You're welcome. I'm certain we'll come to an understanding soon."

"I'm certain, too. That's why we're going to have that talk." He shot her a glance. "Why don't you lean back and rest? If you doze off, I'll wake you."

"I don't need to rest." She sat up very straight. "I slept a little before I smelled the smoke."

"Oh, then that should do you." He nodded seriously. "No problem." He was exiting the village and was on the road to Jokan. "I'm glad you told me."

Humor? Sarcasm? She wasn't going to either challenge or define it. Accept it and just concentrate on continuing to sit very straight and not show him weakness...

Cade pulled up to the front entrance of the Maldara Hotel fifteen minutes later. "This will do," he said as he got out of the driver's seat. "It's the closest to the hospital." He ran around and opened her door, got out her duffel, and handed it to the doorman. "It's owned by Sam Gideon, a friend of mine, and he has very good taste. I think you'll like it."

"I'm sure I would," she said dryly. "But Jill tried to make reservations here and they were filled up for the next four weeks. She had to settle for the Hyatt. He'd better be a very good friend."

"He is," he said as he followed the bellhop into the lobby. "We've run into each other several times over the years. Sam used to be the acting president of Maldara before he got bored with politics and eventually found someone to take his place." He walked up to the front desk and presented his credit card to the clerk. "A suite, please. The lady won't register. She was never here."

The reception clerk took one look at the card and hurriedly checked his chart. "Certainly." He motioned to the bellhop. "The penthouse. Make certain all is in order."

"A very good friend," Riley murmured as she got on the elevator. "Why am I not surprised?"

"I have no idea. I tried to be honest with you." He smiled. He handed her the key but didn't get on the elevator. "I'll order breakfast and make a few calls. I'll see you in about fifty minutes?"

She nodded. "That's fine." She watched the elevator doors close and then leaned back against the wall. She was suddenly aware how dirty and disheveled she must look in this elegant lobby. Not that it mattered, she thought tiredly. After all, the lady was never here according to Cade...

———◆———

Forty minutes later Riley felt enormously better. It was amazing how just a shower and washing and drying her hair made her feel almost human. She hurriedly redid the bandage on her abdomen, put on clean khakis and shirt, and was ready for the room service knock on her door.

Only it wasn't room service. It was Cade who wheeled the table into the suite. "I ran into the waiter on the elevator." He rolled the table over to the French doors leading to the terrace and poured a glass of wine and handed it to her. "I didn't think you were up to having any strangers coming in and fussing over you right now. Much better to get all your questions over first and then eat. Sit down and have your wine." He glanced at her as he poured one for himself. "Actually, you look exceptionally good at the moment. How do you feel?"

"Fine." She sat down on the couch and tried not to reveal the tension she was experiencing. "But I felt fine before, it was you who thought that I was going to fade away just because I had a rough night. I'm not that fragile, Cade."

"No." He was gazing down into the wine in his goblet.

"Kirby told me that you weren't, but I wanted you to be in the best possible condition before I put any propositions to you. I don't want you whining later."

She stiffened. "Whine? I don't whine, Cade." Then he lifted his gaze from his glass, and she saw that his eyes were twinkling. "That was supposed to be a joke? Not funny, Cade."

"I couldn't resist." He took a sip of his wine. "You're so clearly expecting me to try to take advantage of the situation and desperately thinking of a way to foil my evil plans. The truth is that I always believe taking advantage of someone is a waste of time. Particularly when our aims might be similar. You impress me as being intelligent and might be better swayed by persuasion than coercion. I thought about bribery, but Kirby said that you couldn't be bought. He's usually right, and I abandoned that lure immediately. So the only other option is to form a partnership that might appeal to you." He said softly, "I can be a very generous partner if you return the favor. You have at least two things I want that I'll pay highly for."

"That still sounds like bribery."

He shook his head. "Mutual cooperation. Entirely different. Give me what I need, and I'll give you terms you can't refuse. Sound reasonable?"

"If I trusted you. You know everything about me. But I hardly know anything about you that can't be read in the tabloids." She met his eyes. "And you could find so many ways to fool or cheat me. You have ... weapons."

"I imagine you have a few yourself. But you're right, mine probably outnumber yours." He tilted his head. "And I doubt if Novak would let you go into this blind. I've found he's more honest than most. That means you probably know more than the tabloids would tell you." He smiled. "But if you want to know anything else, just ask me. I'm at your disposal."

"It would take a decade for me to get past all that armor. I don't have the time or the inclination." She paused, her gaze searching his face. "But if you tell me about those two things you need from me, I might be able to see past some of the bullshit to who you are. Novak told you about Helen? I'd heard archaeology was one of your obsessions. I can see you becoming intrigued by the idea of being first to bring her back to the world. You'd probably enjoy all the arguments and controversy it would bring."

"Perhaps. I'd certainly like the challenge. You have no concept of all the brouhaha it's going to cause when we spring her on the public. Cleopatra, Nefertiti...nothing compared with what we might expect from Helen."

She tilted her head. "You seem to be very certain. You've probably already got the great unveiling planned. You've actually been thinking about it."

He nodded. "From the moment I decided I was going to take the job. It's one of my idiosyncrasies that I have to see the beginning, the middle, and the ending. It might not turn out to be quite the way I plan, but sometimes I come close. Though I'll probably have trouble with Helen because I'll have to rely on you."

"What a pity," she said ironically.

"No, just an interesting diversion." He met her eyes. "But I'll never try to dominate the process. I promise I'll always remember it's a partnership. We find it, we retrieve it, we dispose of it."

She found herself believing him. "And what about Dakar."

He was silent. Then he said, "I don't promise not to try

to dominate where he's concerned. I've been hunting him for a long time. But I realize he killed your father and I'll try to remember that when I'm tempted to close you out."

"How very kind."

"It's as good as I can do."

And he'd been honest when he could have lied, she thought.

His brows rose. "Did I pass your test? Do you know me?"

"Probably not. But perhaps a little better."

"Okay, you've decided that you might be able to tolerate me. Now it's time to ask me what you'll get if you go into business with me." He shook his head. "You're not very good at this negotiating, Riley."

She was on edge, and she wanted to sock him. She lifted her chin. "And what will I get?"

"Everything you want. Money, and an experienced crew that's more than capable of taking on Dakar's men," he said. "I'll search until I find that tomb and then I'll find a safe haven for your Helen. I'll hunt Dakar down and protect you, and you won't have to worry about exterminating him yourself. Is there anything else that you need?"

She shook her head. "You seem to have covered everything."

But he was frowning. "No, there was something else." He snapped his fingers. "Eve Duncan. Novak said you needed Duncan."

"No," she said quickly. "It would be too dangerous for her. Besides, she would never come."

"You can never tell what people will do. I'll see what I can do to persuade her."

She said firmly, "No, I said it's too dangerous."

"That's really up to her. I'll talk to her when we get to the hospital."

"No, you won't."

He gestured dismissively. "We'll discuss it later. I just remembered I forgot to check that wound." He dropped to his knees beside her, took her wineglass, and set it on the coffee table. Then he began unbuttoning her shirt. "Be still for a minute."

She tensed. "What the hell are you doing."

"Exactly what I said." He spread the shirt and looked down at the bandage. "Novak told me you'd been wounded. I want to make sure that you didn't do any damage in the shower."

"I took care of it. And it's none of your business."

He was ignoring her as his fingers gently pulled back the bandage. "It seems okay." He began to button her shirt. "And until you tell me that you're not my partner, I'll assume that it's a done deal. Which means that everything about you is my business. I can't let anything happen to you. It's best to get used to the idea."

"The hell I will."

"You're probably hungry." He got to his feet, then pulled her up and led her over to the dining table. "It's making you bad-tempered. You'd better get a bite to eat so that we can get out of here." He was lifting the lids of her serving plates. "Still warm. It doesn't look bad."

It looked very good to her. She hadn't eaten all day. She forgot about being annoyed with him and reached for the salad. "You're not going to eat?"

He shook his head. "I ate on the plane coming in to Maldara. I'll have coffee." He dropped down in the chair opposite her and leaned back, watching her eat the salad. "How close did I come to convincing you?"

She didn't look at him. "I'll have to think about it. I can't be certain."

"That means fairly close. What else could you want?"

"Being sure that all you promised is the truth," she said bluntly.

"That might take a little longer," he said. "But maybe by the time we get to Azerbaijan you'll feel comfortable." He poured himself a cup of coffee. "Actually, I believe we're moving along quite well considering the circumstances. But judging by what happened at the village tonight, it might be wise to step up the pace a little..."

CHAPTER

6

Jill was no longer at the ICU when Riley and Cade reached the hospital. But Riley saw Eve coming out of the waiting room down the hall.

She hurried toward her. "Hajif?"

"Still unconscious," Eve said. "But he has a chance of surviving." She gazed at her. "You look better than when I last saw you. Novak stopped by and said that Robaku owes you big time. Thank you."

"Don't be ridiculous. I did what I had to do. So did you. Where's Jill?"

"She's down in the business office on a Zoom call with her editor in Paris. Then she's going to the cafeteria to join Novak and have a sandwich. I told her that we both didn't have to watch over Hajif and Leta."

"Have you called Joe?"

"Not yet. I'll have to do it soon." She looked beyond her to Cade, who had just caught up with Riley. "You must be one of Novak's men. He said that he'd asked someone to bring

117

Riley here. I'm very grateful, but you can leave now, we'll take care of her."

"That's okay, I'll stick around. I wouldn't want to irritate Novak." Cade smiled. "Always happy to oblige."

"This is Morgan Cade," Riley said quickly. "He's a friend who Novak thinks may be able to help me with Helen, if we can come to terms. He's also agreed to invest in the rebuilding of the Robaku village as part of the deal. I knew that would relieve you. All you have to worry about now is Hajif."

"Cade," Eve repeated. Her gaze flew to his face. "Novak told me all about you when he arrived here tonight. You have quite a history. But he has a good deal of respect for you."

"On occasion."

"More than that." Eve was gazing at Cade searchingly. "Or I don't believe Novak would have been quite so enthusiastic. He was quite explicit. It almost resembled an audition. You obviously must come with the highest recommendations, Cade. I'd like to hear more about them."

"Would you? That can be arranged." He glanced at Riley. "With my partner's permission. She doesn't seem to wish us to get together." He added softly, "No pressure, Riley. But perhaps there's something I can give her that she can't get anywhere else. I know you wouldn't want to cheat her."

"I also don't want her caught up in something I can prevent," she said coldly. "She could have died in that village tonight and it would have been my fault."

"It wouldn't have been your fault; it would have been Dakar's." Eve's expression hardened. "Or maybe his brand-new associate. They're both to blame for the suffering in that village. I've been thinking about that a lot while I've been sitting in that waiting room next to the ICU."

"Ah, revenge," Cade murmured. "I can understand how it could drive you. I'm definitely a fan of the concept." He tilted his head. "Audition...Do I detect a more personal reason for you to go after those bastards?"

"Perhaps. My family and I have a lot to lose. I'll have to consider whether the possibilities are worth the effort."

"Hmm." He was still studying her. "Then permit me to offer to find you a way to eliminate your problems with both men. I'm very good at doing that kind of manipulation. I'd regard it as a challenge."

She went still. "Are you suggesting taking them out?"

"Only in the most extreme circumstances. It would require examining all sides of the problem. I'd have to investigate the subjects very carefully before I went that far. But Dakar has already passed that test. And I've found that assholes usually gather together in the same foxholes." He shrugged. "At any rate, I'd find a way to see that they no longer bothered you."

"This isn't bullshit? You'd actually be able to do that for us?"

He nodded slowly. "I've done it before. You just have to find the key, set up the plan, and then execute it. I'd make it happen. In fact, considering the dirtbags I'd be dealing with, I believe I'd be inspired."

"And all I'd have to do is find the tomb, do the reconstruction, and turn it over to you?" she asked mockingly.

"To me and my partner," he said. "And we'll locate the tomb, you'll only have to do the reconstruction. I'd even swear I'll find a way to keep your professional reputation intact. Plus, I'd give you the option that you can back out at any time if you get nervous."

"And I would," Eve said. "Stop pushing. I'm not promising anything. I'm only thinking about what would be best." She turned and headed toward the ICU waiting area. "I'll let you know, Cade."

Cade was looking after her. "Interesting."

"You were a little too interested," Riley muttered.

"How could I help it? I was intrigued that I didn't have to persuade her. I admit I wasn't expecting her to have an agenda of her own. Novak only mentioned that you regarded her as necessary to the project." He glanced at her. "But I need more details. You wouldn't care to discuss it in depth?"

"No, I wouldn't," she said through set teeth.

"I didn't think so. I'll go find Novak and explore it with him." He was heading for the elevator. "I'll be back shortly. If you need me, give me a call." He added gently as he punched the button, "You can't save her, Riley. She's too strong, and she'll make up her own mind. She's the only one who can do it. We can only make it safer for her."

"It would be safer if I hadn't come to Maldara," Riley said bitterly. "I can't take that back. And it would be safer for her if I didn't let you come with me to Azerbaijan."

"No, it wouldn't." He stepped into the elevator and pressed the button. "Because I'm the one who's going to keep both of you safe. Consider me your lucky charm." He grinned as she started to swear. "Or not."

As the door shut, Riley whirled away and headed for the ICU. The only thing she could do now was be with Eve and try to help her. It wasn't the time to try to convince Eve that Cade could probably be more dangerous than the situation that Riley had originally confronted her with. But she might get a chance later.

She could only hope.

HOSPITAL CAFETERIA

"Son of a *bitch*." Cade gave a low whistle after Novak had finished filling him in. "You didn't get around to mentioning that the president of the United States might be involved. It didn't occur to you that this might change the odds?"

"I only recently knew there was anything more to tell you about her. Besides, I wasn't sure that Eve would be involved." He shrugged. "It seemed likely she'd opt out of going with Riley. She still might. Though I did get an idea that her attitude might have changed when we were back in the village. She was furious." He leaned back in his chair. "Hell, I wasn't sure you would give a damn one way or the other. The chances were that you'd be more interested in bringing Dakar down if you had to work a little harder. Isn't that right?" He smiled with amusement. "Or maybe you feel bound to save the president? But I don't recall you contributing to his campaigns."

"He's a crooked asshole who's driving the U.S. into being a third-world country," Cade said succinctly. "I just didn't realize he was also trying to take over the world health system while he was doing it."

"Neither did I," Novak said. "Nor trying to make my director one of his yes-men. That annoyed me." He frowned. "I can't abandon my duty here in Maldara, but I might be persuaded to offer a little help if you run into difficulty." He stared him in the eye. "You'd better be ready to show me proof, though."

He nodded. "Or not involve you at all. I remember in Nigeria you asked far too many questions." He finished his coffee. "I'll work it out." A smile lit his face. "But you're right, it's going to make the job much more entertaining. I only had to become accustomed to the idea." He got to his feet. "So I'd better get back to Riley before she gives in to the temptation to try to persuade Eve to let her go after Dakar alone. Believe me, she's on the verge . . ."

Kirby met Cade as he got off the elevator near the ICU. "Here's the report you wanted." He handed him the paper-work. "Donovan and his crew will be here first thing tomorrow. Don't blame me for the price. You wanted it done right away."

"I'm not blaming you." He scanned the contract. "He agreed to put the villagers up in temporary quarters until it was finished?"

"No problem." Kirby nodded. "But did you get Riley Smith to go along with the agreement?"

"No, but she will. Why wouldn't she? The Helen mystery is irresistible. She's wanted this to happen all her life. I'm giving her everything anyone could want. I've just got to handle her carefully." He made a face. "Very carefully."

Kirby threw back his head and laughed. "She's intimidating you. I told you that I liked her."

"She's not intimidating me," Cade growled. "I can just see trouble on the horizon."

Kirby looked at him. "And?"

"It's going to be one hell of a difficult project, and she's a target. I promised I was going to keep her alive. I won't have her die on me."

"And?"

"I like her. She kind of strikes . . . sparks." He started toward the ICU. "So you make sure she's protected once we're on the road."

"Anything else?"

"Yeah, stop grinning. And I've just found out that Eve Duncan may be higher than we thought on Dakar's kill list. She might not have survived that attack if Riley hadn't been around. So she has her own bodyguard at all times. Get on it right away."

"Right." Kirby pulled out his phone. "Though it might be awkward with all those bodyguards stumbling over one another."

"Then it's your job to keep that from happening." He paused. "Because you also have to find out everything you can about Dakar's connection to Adam Madlock."

"Madlock?" Kirby stopped dialing, eyes widening. "What the hell, Cade?"

"I wasn't keeping it from you. Novak thought it might not be pertinent." His lips twisted. "Or he might have just wanted to remind me of Nigeria. At any rate, Madlock's going to be a major player, so I have to be prepared. Pull out all the stops." He thought about it. "Particularly his contacts in Azerbaijan. He's going to want to protect his reputation from everyone in that world including Dakar and Eve Duncan. There's only one way to do that efficiently. He'll have to have help."

"I'll start there," Kirby said as he headed for the phone bank in the waiting room. "I'm on my way. Damn, Cade, you couldn't have been satisfied with Morocco?"

"Not a chance. Think of the possibilities." He opened the door and saw Riley, Leta, and Eve sitting across the room.

"Madlock put environmental issues back thirty years with that last—"

Alarms erupted from the bank of machines next to the door!

"Shit!" Riley jumped to her feet and then ran the few feet to the hospital bed where Hajif lay. "He's crashing! The nurses will be in here any second, Eve. Get Leta out of here. She shouldn't see them working on him. It will scare her."

"Right." Eve grabbed Leta's arm and half pulled her toward the door. Leta was screaming and fighting desperately to get back to her husband even as the corridor doors flew open, and the room was flooded by the medical team streaming toward Hajif's bed, almost knocking Eve and Leta aside.

"Come on." Cade ducked forward, picked up Leta, and ran back out of the ICU with Eve trailing closely behind. He set her down on the bench in the corridor and turned to Eve. "Should I get you help from the nurses' station?"

She shook her head. "She just didn't understand, and she was scared." Eve took Leta in her arms and held her close, murmuring to her. Leta was clutching at her, tears pouring down her cheeks. "It doesn't have to be the end for him, Leta. You know how strong he is. They just have to take special care of him right now."

"They are doing the very best for him now," Riley said as she came out of the ICU. She knelt beside Leta. "I watched them, and I saw how wonderful and skilled all those doctors and nurses are, and how careful they're being with Hajif. As soon as he is stabilized, they're just going to take him up for more X-rays and tests to see what they should do next."

"I want you to go with Hajif," Leta said.

"Of course she will," Cade said. He glanced at Eve. "And I'll call Kirby out of the waiting room to help you. Okay?"

She nodded absently, her eyes on the ICU door. "Anything you want."

Cade took Riley's elbow and nudged her down the hall. "We'll be in touch as soon as we hear something."

Riley pulled her arm away as they reached the elevator. "They're not going to let me do anything, you know," she said jerkily.

"But Hajif's wife will feel better thinking you're with him," Cade said. "Sometimes it's all in the perception. Besides, it will keep her from asking you questions. I got a glimpse of your face when you came out of that ICU, and I thought that wouldn't be such a bad idea. But maybe I was wrong. Was he still alive when you ran over to look at him when the alarms went off?"

"He was still alive. Unconscious. Barely breathing." Her lips tightened. "You notice that I didn't give you much argument about going with you." She shivered. "I don't know what those tests and X-rays are going to show. Hajif and Leta are both Eve's friends, and I didn't want her to go through any more hell." She shook her head. "But you don't have to stay with me. I'll get all the information I need."

"I said I'd stay," he said quietly. "We'll go down the list again. We're together until this is over." He paused. "And if you want me to break any bad news to Leta and Eve, say the word."

"No way," she said definitely. "Stop treating me as if I'm an imbecile. I can handle anything I have to. I just don't want to inflict it on Eve." She looked back over her shoulder and said pointedly, "That goes for everything. No matter what you found out from Novak, keep Eve out of it."

He shook his head. "It won't work that way. As I said, she's not going to allow it. But we'll discuss it later. Do what you have to do, and I'll stay out of your way."

"Yes, you will. I'm going to have enough problems just getting them to allow me to observe."

———◆———

NEXT DAY
6:15 A.M.

Riley knew she had to make the call.

She leaned back against the wall and braced herself.

She had to do it.

She'd give herself just a moment more.

Stop stalling.

Eve had to have warning.

She quickly dialed Eve's number.

Eve picked up the call immediately. "Riley? How is he?"

"Not good. The doctor is on his way down to talk to you now. Hajif is in a coma." She said the next words quickly. "The doctor believes there may be brain damage and he might not come out of it. I wanted you to try to prepare Leta before he got there."

"And how am I supposed to do that?" Eve asked hoarsely. "They've been together almost all their lives. Leta was only fifteen years old when they were married."

"I don't know. Just do your best. Look, I'll be down right away." She hung up the phone and walked to where Cade was standing down the corridor.

He straightened as he saw her face. "Not good? I saw the nurses whisking Hajif's bed out of there a few minutes ago. Is he still alive?"

She nodded. "He's in a coma. They don't think he'll come

out of it. They were taking him to ICU." She punched the button for the elevator. "I called Eve and told her the doctor needed to talk to them. I need to be with them." She held up her hand as he opened his lips. "You can't do anything. Don't even offer it."

"I wasn't," he said quietly. "I'll go with you and give his wife my regrets, and then I'll go see if there's anything I can do for Hajif. There's such a thing as second opinions. We'll see what we can find." He got on the elevator and pressed the button. "If that's okay with you."

"Of course it's okay. I didn't want interference, but I want him to live. I'm not looking forward to facing Leta and Eve when I get off this elevator."

But it was even worse than Riley thought when she saw Leta and Eve with the doctor only a few minutes later. "Damn," she murmured as she hurried toward them. She could tell Leta was almost falling apart, and Eve's face was pale and agonized.

"I'll speak to Leta later," Cade said as he stopped short in the hall. "No interference as promised." He called to Eve. "Phone if you need me, Eve."

"We won't need you." Riley braced herself as she drew closer to Leta. "I'll take care of them."

Cade muttered a soft oath. "I'm sure you will." He turned and moved away from them. "I'll let Jill and Novak know the news."

Riley was no longer listening to him. She was standing with her arm around Eve's waist and her eyes were desperately fixed on the doctor's sympathetic face.

HAJIF'S HOSPITAL ROOM
2:37 P.M.

"Is she sleeping at last?" Riley asked Eve softly as she came into Hajif's room. She walked over to the cot where Leta was curled up in exhausted slumber. "I thought she might, if we got permission for her to sleep in Hajif's room."

"Good call." Eve leaned wearily back in her chair. "Though the sedative helped. She was out in ten minutes."

"You need a nap yourself," Riley said. "I could stay and watch her."

Eve shook her head. "I wouldn't be able to sleep. I'm too angry and sad and every time I look at Hajif I want to reach out and *crush* something." She paused. "And I've been avoiding phoning Joe since last night. I didn't even answer when he called me an hour ago. I have to talk to him."

"Do you?" She tensed. "What are you going to say?"

"The truth. I always tell him the truth. But he's not going to like where that truth is taking me right now." She shook her head as she looked at Riley. "And I've got to clear my head so that I can persuade him that my way might work, when I'm not sure it will."

"Then maybe this isn't the time to talk to Joe."

"You think I'm too emotional? You're right. But that doesn't change anything. I just have to work through it." She added gently, "Go get yourself a cup of coffee and then find Jill and spend some time with her. She's going to have to leave for Paris tomorrow and she's been a good friend to you."

"Sometimes too good a friend," she said wryly. "I'm used to doing things on my own, and I shouldn't have relied on her when I needed to contact you."

"Jill always does things in her own way. I bet she not only stepped up to the plate, she probably offered."

"You'd win," Riley said as she turned back toward the door. "And I definitely have to spend more time with her to convince her that I don't want her to lend me another helping hand when that conference is over." She looked back over her shoulder. "I'll be back soon. If you need me to bring you anything, let me know." She paused. "Did Cade drop by while I was down at the business office arranging for your Wi-Fi?"

"No," she said. "I thought perhaps he was staying out of the way and avoiding all the commotion. Neither one of us was in any shape to be sociable."

"He wouldn't have avoided us," Riley said. "He'd be more likely to attack than do that. He'd move forward to take over the action."

"You appear to know him very well," Eve said. "Odd, since you only met him last night."

"Cade doesn't waste time." She added ironically, "And he certainly doesn't hide his light under a bushel."

"But you're still considering taking him up on his offer."

She nodded. "I've heard he's not a cheat, and he does get results. I have to consider it. I haven't been doing so well on my own." She glanced at Hajif. "At least I wouldn't be endangering innocents." She smiled crookedly. "No one could say that Cade can't take care of himself."

Eve watched the door close behind her and then her gaze went to Hajif and Leta. So many of Riley's words had struck a familiar chord in her own situation.

I haven't been doing so well on my own.

At least I wouldn't be endangering innocents.

No one could say that Cade can't take care of himself.

Joe would probably think she was crazy. He might be right, but she was sick and tired of hiding out from the monsters of the world. And now the monsters were stirring and hurting people all around her. How long would it be before they went after her family?

No! She instinctively reached out for her phone.

Don't think, just rely on Joe to understand and work with her. She quickly dialed his number.

He picked up on the first ring. "Why the hell didn't you answer my call?" he said harshly. "I was going to try once more and then head for the airport. What's happening there?"

"Nothing good. I didn't know what to say. I had to figure it out. I've been second-guessing myself ever since the fire." The words were suddenly tumbling out. "But I finally decided we couldn't go on hiding like this. I'm not going to be tucked away in a safe house somewhere and worry about you. Madlock is on the move, and we've just got to be smarter than he is."

"What fire?" Joe asked impatiently. "Slow down, Eve."

"You're right. I'm not being fair. I'll start at the beginning and tell you what happened. Then I'll tell you what I want to do, and I'll have some questions to ask you. You can let me know if you think I'm nuts, which you probably will. And then you can tell me if you'll find a way to help me pull it off."

Joe was silent. "You're scaring the hell out of me, Eve. But I knew you were desperate the last time I spoke to you, so I've gotten used to the idea while I've been trying to get in touch with you." He waited a moment. "So talk to me."

She drew a deep breath and then started out. "The fire was in the village. Riley and I decided to spend the night in the village because it would be safer than my workroom. I asked Leta and Hajif to take us in and..."

Joe was still silent after she'd finished speaking. Then he said, "Stop blaming yourself. You didn't know those bastards would come back. You said Novak's told you the village had been checked out."

"I should have found a way not to involve them at all. Hajif may never wake up from this coma. Of course I feel guilty. There's nothing I can do that will stop that except do what I can medically for him." Her lips tightened. "But maybe we can guarantee that this won't happen to anyone else. I told you that Madlock had hired Dakar to do his dirty work in Azerbaijan and evidently here in Maldara. That means if we strike at Dakar, we might be able to find a way to bring Madlock down."

"Wishful thinking?"

"You're damn right. With all my heart. But maybe through all this ugliness we might see an opportunity. We can't touch Madlock in the U.S., but this is a different place with different rules." She was thinking hard. "He's reached out to Dakar, and he wanted to grab me that night. That probably means that he's so impatient that he regards me as fair game. That could work for us . . . if we let it."

"Don't go there, Eve," Joe said sharply.

"I can't go anywhere else," she said gently. "But I don't want to go alone. Madlock has tied us up in knots for the last few months. We have to break free."

"And use you to cut the chain? Not a great idea."

"It's the only one I could put together." She tried to smile. "I've been a little distracted. I'm open to other suggestions, but I believe this can work. Riley has offered me an excuse to go after the tomb, which can keep Dakar occupied, and maybe even intrigue Madlock enough so that we can set a trap of our own. We'd have to play it by ear. But right now we have nothing." She frowned. "And she's throwing Morgan Cade into the mix, which could be a plus. What do you think about him?"

"I don't know what to think about him," he said flatly. "No one can predict what he's going to do next. And I've heard he likes to run his own show. That's dangerous."

"But then so do you."

"But I know I'm not going to risk your neck."

"Then why don't you give him a call and discuss it?" she asked. "If you've decided that we're going to do this together."

"Don't be an idiot. Of course we are. I know I can't change your mind. I just have to decide how we can do this as safely as possible. I've got to get more info on Dakar from Scotland Yard and MI6. And promise me you won't take off tomb hunting until I make arrangements with Jane and Caleb to keep Michael safe."

"You know he comes first with me." She could almost feel the energy Joe was emitting. His mind was working, going over possible scenarios and then discarding them, even though she'd just given him the primary objective. It was a relief to know that though Joe might not approve, he was always with her. "We'll talk later. I think this has a chance of working, Joe."

"Of course it does. We'll see that it does," he said gruffly. "Get some sleep. I love you." He cut the connection.

She leaned back in her chair. She was exhausted, but she couldn't sleep yet. She had another call to make.

She quickly dialed Morgan Cade. "You said to call you

if I needed you. I need you. I'm with Hajif now. Can you come?"

"I'll be there in fifteen minutes."

He was there in ten. "What can I do?" he asked quietly. He was looking at Hajif. "I've arranged to have a specialist flown here from Rome to take a look at him tomorrow. He's not stable enough to be moved. Maybe I should have told you before, but I just got the confirmation. Salano is supposed to be the best in his field. If anyone can do anything for your friend, it will be him."

"Thank you. I'm very grateful." She shook her head. "Did you think I brought you here to nag you?" She shrugged. "I suppose you get a lot of that. No, I promised you I'd let you know when I made up my mind about whether I was going to take up Riley's offer. I've decided I'm going to do it. Which will mean that you'll have to make adjustments in your planning to accommodate the fact I'll be doing the work Riley wanted on her queen." She paused. "And Novak told you that I might also be a handicap because of Madlock. Are you going to have to rethink your proposal to Riley?"

He shook his head. "I'll still get what I want from the deal. It will only mean that I might have a more interesting path to get there."

"More interesting than you think," she said dryly. "My husband, Joe Quinn, isn't going to stay on the sidelines. You'll be hearing from him."

"As long as he doesn't get in my way."

"That's exactly his attitude. I'm sure that you'll come to an agreement." She waved her hand. "That's all I wanted to say. Now I need a nap before Leta wakes up. She'll be glad to hear about your specialist from Rome. She's not had much hope."

She curled up in her chair. "Why don't you go find Riley and firm up that partnership? I want to get moving. You can tell her I'll be glad to have you along." She yawned. "And you'd better not make a liar of me."

"I won't." He took off his jacket and gently tucked it over her. "Even your Joe Quinn will swear that I'm an asset beyond compare before this over." He turned and headed for the door. "I'll see you later, Eve. Sleep well."

———◆———

Cade ran into Riley as she was leaving Novak and Jill in the cafeteria. "I have a mission," he said as he took her arm and led her toward the sliding glass doors down the hall. "Come out in the garden and I'll tell you about it."

She hesitated. "I was going back upstairs to be with Eve."

"She won't need you, and the message is from her. I was supposed to tell you that she approved of me coming along to Azerbaijan with the two of you. The second was to get you to commit to working with me." He slid open the doors. "She said it was important. I believe she's becoming impatient." He added, "So am I. How about it?"

"You talked her into going with us?" She smiled without mirth. "It was bound to happen when you made up your mind. I was only waiting for it to happen."

"I told you that it would be Eve who made up her own mind," he said quietly. "She had a talk with Joe Quinn, and that made the difference. But I have to confirm the agreement with you. Am I doing that now?"

She frowned. "I want to keep her safe. I don't like it."

"Am I doing it? Is it a deal?" he repeated. "Answer me."

She didn't speak for a moment. "It's a deal," she finally said reluctantly. "But it's not going to be all your own way, Cade. I'll have something to say about the way we go after Eleni. She's been in my life for too long. I've waited too many years to just turn her over to you."

"Do you think I don't know that?" Cade made a face. "I'm aware I'll have to contend with both you and Eve whatever I do. But that will be okay. I can handle it. I'll just make adjustments and get this show on the road." He was suddenly vibrantly alive, his eyes glittering in his taut face. "It's about time. I'll talk to Kirby to arrange a plane to get us out of here by tomorrow. That means anything we do about the village and Hajif will have to take place today. Can you be ready?"

She nodded. "It's not as if I have an entire camp of men waiting for me to come back and take over. That's something you'd do. I don't have your clout or your force of arms. I'll call my uncle Dan and that will be the end of it." She added sarcastically, "But he'll be happy I'm bringing a superhero into the match. I'm certain he'll be impressed."

"That's good. I'll probably need everyone you can furnish to give me support. Neither you nor Eve is impressed by me."

"Why should we be? You have the entire world at your feet." She saw a bench nearby and sat down. She waved her hand. "Go on and make your plans. I'll sit here in the sun and make a few of my own."

He hesitated, gazing down at her. "This is going to be a good move, Riley. I'll make it work out for you."

"No, I'll make it work for me," she said. "And maybe if we're lucky, we'll make it work for each other." She closed her eyes, letting her skin drink in the sunshine. "Go away, Cade. I'll be ready to go back to Azerbaijan tomorrow. And I'm not whining because I'm going to have to worry about Eve. That would be hypocritical. I deliberately came here because I wanted her to play her part in Helen's story just as my father did. It was all part of the big dream. And it all came together, didn't it? You want her to come, she wants to come. Who am I to change my mind because I'm feeling guilty?" She opened her eyes and stared up at him. "But we *will* keep her safe, Cade. Do you hear me?"

He nodded. "Without question." He turned and headed back toward the sliding doors. "But the deal is set in stone now. I'm not going to let you back out."

"I'll do what I please, you arrogant bastard."

He laughed. "Just thought I'd stir a little fire into the mix. You were being a little too reasonable and philosophical. I didn't trust it." He winked at her over his shoulder. "Now I feel much more comfortable."

And she didn't know how she felt, she thought in frustration. But she knew it wasn't comfortable. Cade was a combination of sheer mischief and devilment with the sharpness of a machete. She was never sure what side he would show her. But she'd better learn very soon since she was clearly going to have to put up with him for the next few weeks.

And she wasn't going to sit here in the sun and worry about the blasted man. He was moving and stirring and trying to shift the world to suit himself. It was time for her to do a little stirring herself. She pulled out her phone and called Dan. "Hello, Dan. I'll be coming back to Azerbaijan tomorrow and I'll be bringing one of your favorite people with me."

CHAPTER

7

The next morning Novak drove Eve, Riley, and Cade to a private military airport north of Jokan. Riley could see a Gulfstream landing as they entered the wire enclosure. A few minutes later she saw a truck with several men in the rear dressed in camouflage pull up beside a small utilitarian building near the runways and jump out.

"There's Kirby," Cade said. "The rest of the crew is on their way by the north road, but I thought we should have a small force with us."

"Small? Twelve men? There's nothing small about either that crew or the plane," Riley said as she got out of Novak's SUV. "Very nice..."

"I'm sure the commercial plane I'll be taking later to Paris won't be that nice," Jill said. She glanced teasingly at Cade. "Care to drop me off on your way?"

"Paris isn't exactly around the corner," Cade said. "And Riley doesn't want you anywhere near Azerbaijan."

"We'll talk about that later," Jill said airily. "I wouldn't want to miss the story of the century."

"Yes, we'll talk about it later," Novak said noncommittally as he drew up beside the truck. "In depth. In the meantime they'll keep you informed. Right, Cade?"

"Of course." Cade jumped out of the SUV and then helped Riley out. "Neither of us would forget our friends." He smiled. "And you can never tell when you might need media coverage."

"You don't appear to have any trouble in that department," Jill said dryly. "You're all over the tabloids, Cade."

"And the press has been very helpful. Their coverage has saved thousands of animal lives and shone a light on some very nasty human traffickers." He shrugged. "Hell, I don't mind my mug being a draw if it accomplishes something worthwhile."

"Except sometimes you don't wait for that to happen," Novak said sourly. "Nigeria?"

"There wasn't time, and I notice we didn't have to spend valuable minutes coaxing you to take the bad guys down." He turned to Kirby. "Get our guys on the plane and give the pilot the flight plan. Did you get the info I needed?"

"Most of it. I'll get a follow-up when we're on the road." Kirby was motioning to the guys to board the plane. "I had to be really careful about the contacts." He was heading across the runway toward the Gulfstream. "But the airport is still run by Vaskinski. That was a break. We can trust—"

He broke off as Riley stepped in front of him. He took one look at her face and said warily, "Yes?"

"You won't set a flight plan for Vaskinski's airport," she said curtly. "Dan said there was word out that he began to take bribes from Dakar two months ago. I'll go on board with you and give the pilot a flight plan of an airport run by one of

Dan's buddies that's safe." She made a face. "It's not as close to Lahar but we're not going to need it to be. We'll be going into the mountains."

"Vaskinski has always been safe when we were in this area," Kirby said slowly. He glanced at Cade.

Cade's gaze was on Riley's face. "I don't know your uncle Dan, but his reputation precedes him. I'm risking my men. Should I trust him?"

"You have a right to doubt him," she said coolly. "But you have no right to doubt me. I'm your partner and I would never betray you. If I say something, you can count on it being true." She tilted her head. "And if you'd taken me into Vaskinski's airport, you would have betrayed me, Eve, and your men."

He was still looking at her searchingly. "Why didn't you tell me you were planning to step up to the plate?"

"You didn't ask me. You just took charge and assumed I'd do whatever you said." She looked him in the eye. "But this is my life and that's my territory we're going into. So I had to make advance plans in case you screwed up. I called Dan last night and got the rundown on who we can trust *this* week."

Eve chuckled. "Checkmate, Cade."

"No such thing," Riley said. "It's no game to me, Eve."

"I can see that." Cade was suddenly grinning as he inclined his head. "I have to apologize. I'm not accustomed to having a partner and I don't have a handle on the protocol yet. But I'm a fast learner and it won't happen again." He turned back to Kirby. "Tear up our flight plan and take Riley and Eve to the plane so that Riley can give the pilot the new one." He glanced at Riley. "Satisfactory?"

"Almost." She turned and walked back to Jill and hugged her. "Thank you," she whispered. "Be safe."

"You take care." Jill gave her another hug then turned to Eve and embraced her. "Remember, I get the exclusive."

"I believe you've mentioned that a time or two. Enjoy Paris!" Then Eve was taking Riley's arm and walking with her toward the plane. She waved at Cade as they fell into step behind Kirby. "You handled Cade well, "she told Riley quietly. "Not that I would expect anything else. I watched you at the village. But I was surprised he didn't realize that you might respond in that way."

"He probably did. He's brilliant and he wouldn't have been taken off guard," Riley said. "But I think he tests everyone around him until he's sure what to expect of them. He was a sharpshooter in the marines, and I understand most of the time that's their modus operandi."

"And that was your test?"

"Only the first one. He'll probably watch me for a while, and he may decide I need another one." She smiled. "That's okay, I'll be watching him, too. It's time to take each other's measure. I was never a sharpshooter, but I've always studied people until I find out how they tick. From Dan's smuggler friends to a witch doctor who *almost* convinced me that he knew black magic. It's actually a survival app in the jungle." She glanced back at Cade. "And he might prove more fascinating than that witch doctor..."

————◆————

The plane took off almost immediately, but Riley didn't have any other interaction with Cade until after they'd been in the air for over an hour. That was fine with her. One confrontation at a time. She watched him warily as he sat with Kirby at the front of the plane going over Kirby's notes. Then he spent some time in the rear where his men were sitting, and she heard laughter and conversation. That told her something, too. He was clearly popular with them, and they accepted him without question. His military background could have led him either way depending on his temperament; it was encouraging that they wouldn't have to face resentment from the ranks.

He stopped beside her seat as he was going toward the cockpit. "Comfortable? We didn't stop for breakfast. I could have Kirby fix you something. It will be another couple hours before we reach Azerbaijan."

She shook her head. "I'm not hungry." She glanced at Eve who had settled across the aisle with her computer as soon as they'd gotten on the plane. "You can ask Eve, but she's been texting Joe and her son feverishly since the flight took off. I doubt she'll want to stop."

"I'll ask her before I go up to the cockpit." He sat down in the seat next to Riley. "But the texting is probably about me, and I wouldn't want to stop the flow. Quinn gave me a call last night and told me how I was to treat Eve until he could arrange to enforce his will in person. He was quite explicit, and I meekly agreed to everything he suggested."

"Meekly?"

"There was no use arguing. He's obviously very protective and I would have done as he asked anyway. We can sort out any differences when we're face-to-face." He glanced at Eve. "She's probably been trying to smooth the waters and plan how she's going to get what she wants from the arrangement and still keep her family safe."

"Of course she is," Riley said. "It's probably tops on her agenda."

He nodded. "Though she's obviously got a more complicated one hovering in the background. I'll have to see if I can do something to keep her mind off Quinn and the kid. I want her concentrating on Helen."

"And she will be," Riley said. "My father studied her for years. She's the best forensic sculptor in the world, and totally dedicated. She wouldn't know how to be anything else. That's why I wanted so desperately for her to do Eleni. If anyone could make her come alive for the world, it would be Eve Duncan."

He was studying her expression with narrowed eyes. "That's important to you. It's not just the sheer cash value of being able to present a legendary queen to the public who was more beautiful than Nefertiti. Why?"

Riley hesitated. Then she said stiltedly, "I guess because Helen's taken such a rap over the centuries. There's never been a woman who has been more vilified or revered, and yet the experts still won't even admit that she actually existed. I want everyone to know that she was a force to contend with in her world. Beauty does that, but even if she wasn't more beautiful than Nefertiti, it might cause the historians to take a deeper look and get her story straight."

"A search for truth," Cade said mockingly. "But you did say you've been dreaming about her since you were a child. Did she whisper it in your ear?"

"Maybe." She shrugged. "I shouldn't have mentioned it to you. I knew you'd make fun of me. Call them dreams, or just part of my obsession. I'll accept either explanation. I always have. But I'm not ashamed of wanting everyone to know she was more than that bizarre story about Troy." She looked away from him. "I think if I'd lived back then she might have been my friend."

His smile ebbed. "Perhaps I was making fun, but it wasn't about your search for truth. I'm an archaeologist, and I know that can be the only way to find that truth. I was intrigued that Novak mentioned Helen when he was trying to lure me into throwing my hat in the ring. I always wondered about the stories concerning her."

"Why?"

"I lived in England for a number of years. I even had a few digs in Wales. But you can't live in England without being aware how deeply the Trojan story literature is entrenched in its history. I was particularly interested in how fascinated Eleanor of Aquitaine was by Benoît's version of the story. Though you can see how she'd prefer it. His Helen was polite, ladylike, and yet very strong and able to create her own world, the way she wanted it to be. Rather like how Eleanor saw herself. Not as the ruthless prostitute depicted by other writers of the time." He tilted his head. "What was your opinion of it? Weren't you tempted to stay around London and see if any of those writers could tell you more?"

"We stayed there for two years. But my father always believed her story took place in Greece or Turkey." She smiled. "I liked Eleanor's Helen, too."

"I thought you would. She's your kind of Helen."

"Not entirely. Helen was impatient, sometimes not polite when she became angry, but she was always smart...and she always listened."

His brows rose. "You rattled those qualities off as if you did know her."

"Perhaps I do. I've read so many books and poems in dozens of languages about her that I've woven a personality together."

"Really?"

She grinned. "The only other explanation would be if I actually believed in those dreams, and I'm much too practical for that."

"Maybe not as practical as you'd have me think," he said soberly. "After all, you're going after Dakar."

"But I've signed on a partner to absorb some of the flak," she said lightly. "He assures me he can do miracles." She added, "If I do my part. I'll do my part, Cade. Just don't underestimate me."

"I've made that mistake. It won't happen again." He paused. "You said that we'd be going into the mountains. Where?"

"South. Dan set up a camp in the middle of the rain forest after my father was killed. It's about half a day's hike from the airport. Or we could rent a truck and be there in an hour or so."

"We'll get the truck. We have ammo, and we may need a truck to pick up the other men Kirby is bringing into the area."

She shrugged. "Whatever. But trucks leave tracks, and we could lose ourselves in that forest if we're on foot."

"Point taken." He got to his feet. "But we'll take the chance. We both know how to get rid of tracks, and I want to get this show on the road. Now let me see if Eve needs that sandwich and then I'll go up to the cockpit and see if I can arrange for the truck..."

———

Riley watched Cade as he moved to Eve's seat across the aisle and began to talk to her. He was obviously talking to her about more than a bite to eat. He was smiling, but there had been a brief moment when Eve had tensed and then relaxed. Probably when he'd told her about Joe's call last night. But he'd evidently made her feel at ease with it because she was smiling back at him. Cade appeared to be an expert at more than the collection of talents he'd been displaying since he'd erupted into her life.

She suddenly stiffened.

Eleanor of Aquitaine. He'd faultlessly chosen one of her favorite historical figures involved in the history surrounding that Trojan myth and made her feel a warmth and sense of togetherness. Had it been a deliberate attempt to influence her? She instantly rejected it. She was not a fool, and she could tell truth from lies. He'd been absolutely genuine in that moment. As far as she could tell, he'd been frank and honest about everything he'd said to her since their meeting at the village. Even when there had been a danger of upsetting or making her angry. So there would be no harm in trusting him unless he showed her a side of his character she hadn't seen so far. If they had to work together, it would be ridiculous and time consuming to keep all the barriers up 24/7.

Cade was leaving Eve and heading toward the cockpit when he stopped to talk to Kirby again. Probably telling him about the truck . . .

"Riley."

Her gaze flew to Eve, who was smiling with amusement and flicked a glance at Cade. Then she deliberately winked.

Caught.

There was no doubt that Riley had been a little too absorbed and obvious in her study of Morgan Cade.

She shrugged and moved to the seat directly across from Eve. "I told you I'd be watching him."

"And was he as good as your witch doctor?"

"Maybe, but he might be trying to impress me as a regular guy. I'll have to see." She paused. "He said that Joe Quinn had called him."

"Oh, yes, Joe mentioned that to me, too. He wasn't at all satisfied with their conversation. He said Cade was entirely too accommodating. It didn't jibe with what he'd heard about the man." She frowned. "But when he stopped by to speak to me just now, he said he'd been thinking and wanted me to approach Joe with the idea of asking Seth and Jane to take Michael to Wild Harbor, his place outside London. It's exceptionally well guarded and it would be a ten-year-old's dream vacation."

"Wild Harbor," Riley repeated slowly. "It sounds like a port for ships. Does Michael like boats?"

Eve nodded. "But the harbor doesn't refer to water. It's a wildlife sanctuary. Cade said he owns several private sanctuaries around the world. But the Brits have been very cooperative about accepting any rescue animals he chose to bring in, from elephants and tigers to anacondas. Since the property is so well guarded and it's closed to the public except in rare cases."

"Elephants and tigers? Cade did mention a tiger named Cubby," Riley said. "I think Michael would definitely be intrigued. I'm not sure about the anacondas. I think he'd pass on the reptile, but I don't know your Michael."

"You will. But Cade might be right about it being a safe haven that my son might enjoy."

Riley nodded. "If Joe can talk Seth and Jane into taking him there. It would seem ideal. Particularly the heavy guards to protect him." She looked at Eve. "Is that what you told Cade?"

"Words to that effect. I'll confirm it with Joe when I call him back."

"He said that he'd try to offer Joe something that would keep you from being distracted by your family."

"That would be impossible." She smiled faintly. "But he might have come close." She went back to her computer. "I'll fill in Joe, then tell him about the truck."

Riley leaned back, her gaze returning to Cade and Kirby. She could sense intensity and barely restrained eagerness in both of them. She could almost feel the vibrations, and she suddenly wanted to be up there listening, talking, joining in the conversation.

Not yet. Soon.

It was going to come together. The excitement was building. She could feel it . . .

———◆———

LAHAR VILLAGE, AZERBAIJAN
1:15 P.M.

"Washington," Zangar said as he saw the ID on the phone on Dakar's desk. He tried to keep the anxiety from his voice. "Madlock. You'll tell him we did everything possible? I wasn't to blame. You told me you wanted her to learn a lesson. We took the risk and went back to give it to her."

"Stop whining," Dakar said. "You screwed up and you know it. You're lucky I didn't turn you over to him when she actually managed to shoot your ass." He picked up his phone and answered it. "I told you I'd phone you if I had news, Madlock. I'm tapping all my sources and I haven't heard anything yet."

"Then it's good that my people aren't such bumblers," Madlock said sarcastically. "Because I paid big time for one of Novak's agents to tell me that he'd put Eve Duncan and Riley Smith on a plane leaving Maldara for Azerbaijan this morning. They're flying right into your hands. Do you think you might have the intelligence to not let them slip through your fingers?"

"I don't have to take that from you, Madlock," Dakar said coldly. "You're nothing to me, and you're lucky that I agreed to help you out. I'm the one who has the power here."

"You'll take anything I hand out to you," Madlock said. "I told you that I wanted Riley Smith and Eve Duncan. I've already paid you for them and gotten nothing in return. I'll give you two days, and then I'll send a team after you to retrieve them."

Dakar instantly backed away. "There's no sense you being argumentative." Better not to irritate Madlock if he could help it. Though it was hard to hold his tongue. "It's not as if I didn't intend to fulfill our deal. You should just treat me with more respect."

"When you show me you deserve it. I'm an important man and you should treat me with respect." His voice lowered to lethal softness. "I didn't have to deal with you. The only reason I did was because I was told that you had information about Riley Smith that might make it easier for me to access Eve Duncan. Now you're not showing me even scant efficiency. I want to be assured that whatever I decide to do with Smith and Duncan will take place. Any other little plans you might have for them won't matter. Understand?"

He gritted his teeth. At the moment he couldn't remember why the hell he'd been so flattered when he'd been approached to work with Madlock. "I understand." *Just go along with the asshole, then find a way to screw him later.* "Of course we can do that. I'll be in touch with you as soon as we locate their plane. CIA plane and crew?"

"No, private plane. It belongs to Morgan Cade."

Dakar inhaled sharply. "Shit!"

"A problem?"

"No, just an inconvenience. I'll handle it."

"Yes, you will," Madlock said. "Time's running out for me. You'll have to move fast." He cut the connection.

"Madlock being an asshole?" Zangar's gaze was on Dakar's face. "I'll take care of it for you."

"Just like you took care of bringing me Eve Duncan and Smith's daughter?" Dakar asked sarcastically. "I wouldn't have to be making excuses if I could tell Madlock I'd be able to turn them over to him." He paused. "Morgan Cade flew them out of Maldara today. You know what that means."

Zangar gave a low whistle. "He found out you're here?" He shrugged. "That just means we get another chance at taking him down. I told you before that I could do it. You shouldn't have gone on the run after Nairobi. I could have fixed everything for you."

Dakar gazed at him in outraged disbelief. "I didn't go on the run; I just did what any intelligent man would do. The Nairobi government was after us and so was Cade's team. I had to disappear and start operations somewhere else until the situation cooled down."

"Of course you did," Zangar said. "But now we have our chance if the Smith bitch has hired him to go after that treasure."

"He's not for hire, you idiot," Dakar said. "If he's after the treasure, then he wants it for himself." He shrugged. "But it doesn't matter what he wants. He's not taking it away from me. I have Madlock in my pocket, and I'll use him to squeeze everyone I need to squeeze. Now go out and find that plane. Have you located any of Daniel Smith's contacts who are willing to talk?"

Zangar shook his head. "Even if I did, everyone says he's very closemouthed where his family is concerned. But I ran across one of his buddies at a bar in Lahar. I might be able to persuade him to give me a hint or two."

"I don't want hints, I want facts," Dakar said harshly. "Go get them for me."

DANIEL SMITH'S ENCAMPMENT

"It's just ahead." Riley leaned forward and pointed to a turn in the road. "A left and then a right."

"Got it." Cade made the turns and almost ran over a tall man in his forties with gray streaked hair, dressed in jeans and a white shirt, who was leaning lazily against a banyan tree as he made the last turn. He screeched on the brakes. "I believe I'm about to meet your uncle Dan."

"Yes, you are." Riley jumped out of the cab of the truck as Dan Smith started strolling toward them. "Morgan Cade, Dan Smith."

"Delighted." Dan grinned as he shook Cade's hand. "Sorry if I startled you. I thought I'd come to meet you."

"I'm glad I didn't pin you to that tree," Cade said, deadpan. "Since it was such a courteous thought."

"No danger. I'm very fast. And it was worth the risk. It's not often Riley shows up with anyone interesting. My brother raised her wrong. Though I've tried to remedy it."

"Knock it off, Dan," Riley said as she opened the rear door for Eve. "I've made up for all my faults today. Not only Cade, but you got the bonanza we've all been looking for. This is Eve Duncan."

"I've never been called a bonanza before," Eve said as she got out of the truck. "I'm pleased to meet you, Mr. Smith."

"I'm glad she talked you into coming." He never took his eyes from Cade. "We'll try to make you comfortable here. Riley and I have arranged to set up a workshop for you in the hills once we locate the tomb. Does that sound good?"

"It sounds good to me." Eve glanced at Cade. "What about you, Cade?"

"Great." He added wryly, "Though I'm not the bonanza."

"Could have fooled me," she murmured.

Dan was immediately aware of the misstep. He turned a warm, charming smile on Eve. "I bet not much can fool you. Just tell me what you need, and I'll get it for you." He turned back to Cade. "You have men and equipment? Who's in charge? I'll show them the encampment."

"Kirby." He nodded toward the back of the truck. "He'll appreciate the help. You'll need to show him the layout of the forest in this area so he can assign sentries. The road from the airport was as twisted as a jigsaw puzzle."

"My pleasure. I have four men of my own back at camp." Dan was already heading for the back of the truck. "Riley said the location had to be safe. I think it will meet your standards."

"As long as it meets Riley's," Cade said. "She got us here."

He grabbed Riley's and Eve's duffel bags from the cab and turned back to Riley. "I imagine you can get us the rest of the way to the camp?"

"No problem." She led them into the bush ahead. The camp was only five minutes from the main road, but they were challenged twice before they saw the tents.

"Good response," Cade murmured.

"Surprised?" Riley asked. "Dan is always careful of the things that matter. He only indulges himself occasionally these days."

"So you allow him to do it."

"If I had to allow him to do something, I'd walk away from him. He just knows how far he can go these days."

"How long have the two of you been together?"

"Since I was nine. He came to my mother's funeral and from then on every now and then he'd show up wherever we were camped and stay with us for six or eight months." She made a face. "He told my father that he was only doing it because he knew that I'd turn out to be totally boring if he wasn't around to keep it from happening. I don't think he was right, but his influence made sure it wouldn't. My father never knew all the illegal junkets he took me on and the crooks and bar girls he introduced me to. He didn't want to know. He just wanted someone to take care of me when he wasn't around. As long as I kept up my schoolwork, he was happy."

"And were you happy?"

"Of course. I had the jungle and the villages and every now and then my father would find out something new and wonderful about Helen. Besides, Dan is great company and he never let anything really bad happen to me. He was always around to run interference."

"But not to protect you or tell you right from wrong," Eve said suddenly.

"I had mountains of books to tell me what was right and wrong. My father and I even had discussions about them when they had something to do with ancient history. And Dan did object to things that weren't fair, and I was soundly punished for them." She made a balancing motion with her hands. "All in all, I think I came out okay."

Cade chuckled. "I do, too. I would have liked to have known you then." Then his laughter ebbed. "But I admit I'm feeling a bit raw at the thought of what it took you to get there. I don't believe I approve of your uncle Dan."

She shrugged. "He is what he is. Dan was part of my childhood. I don't care whether you approve of him or not."

Eve nodded. "I can see that. But it would have been much easier for you if you'd had moderate attention and reliable guidance."

"As you've given your son?" Riley asked. "That sounds so maternal. He's very lucky, but that doesn't happen in every family."

"Joe and I are the lucky ones," Eve said softly. "Michael is very unusual, and sometimes it seems as if he's the one teaching us."

"Then he must be unusual," Riley said ruefully. "I never taught anyone anything. I was just a sponge that absorbed everything around me. That appeared to be enough for my father because it increased my value to our research." They had arrived at the encampment, which comprised six tents with a campfire in the center. She gestured at a tent on the edge of the circle. "I thought we'd share a tent, Eve." She glanced at Cade. "Though by the look of all the equipment you had loaded in that truck, you might have provided her with her own."

He shrugged. "I always believe in providing for all contingencies."

"I'll share." Eve was already heading toward the tent. "If you don't mind me using my phone and computer constantly. I'll want to do some research on your Helen besides talking to Joe and Michael." She reached into her duffel, pulled out her paperback copy of the *Iliad*, and held it up to show Riley. "And I have some reading to do. I decided I could stomach the sea monsters and gods and goddesses to get an idea about her character."

"I have to warn you that there are descriptions of Helen. Though most of them are just flowery and vague," Riley said. "I know that you never look at photos of a subject before you start to work. I wasn't sure that you'd want to read about what Homer thought of her."

"But you told me that the *Iliad* is thought to be only a poetic myth. It shouldn't influence me any more than reading a fairy tale about Cinderella would. Plus you said that almost every nation has its own version of Helen of Troy. I'm sure some of those descriptions of her differ."

Riley nodded. "Physically and also in her character."

"Then I'll get an idea about who she is as a person and let her tell me the rest." She tilted her head. "If you think that's a good idea."

"I think that's a very good idea," Riley said gently. "And I think Helen would like it, too."

"Then it's settled." Eve pulled open the tent door and disappeared inside.

Cade gave a low whistle. "I can see why you and your father were so determined to get her on board. You think alike."

"Even if we didn't, she's magic. She's worth listening to and she knows exactly what to do with those sculptures. They come alive for her."

"That *is* magic." His gaze was on her face. "And your Eleni would have approved?"

She nodded. "I told you, she always listened. I have to do the same." She saw Kirby and his crew coming down the trail carrying weapons, tents, and other equipment. Along with two vehicles that caused her jaw to drop. "Motorcycles? What on earth are you doing with motorcycles in the jungle?"

"They're built for off-roading. You'd be surprised how useful they can be."

She shrugged. "I'll take your word for it." She turned away. "But I'll let Eve get settled so we don't trip over each other. I need to talk to Dan and get his report before I turn him over to you."

"Turn him over to me?" Cade asked. "What am I supposed to do with him? He's your uncle."

"But you already disapprove of him. You'll want to question him and make certain that you can influence him if it becomes necessary. You'd probably prefer to do it subtly over a period of time since you wouldn't want to offend me." She shook her head. "That's not necessary. Dan will want to be approved by you and will want to be in your company. You can get it over with quickly."

"You have it all planned. Did it occur to you that I might trust your judgment about him?"

"Yes, but you'll trust your own judgment more until you're sure of mine."

She headed toward Dan. "I won't keep him long. I just want

155

to question him about any movement lately in the hills. Then I'll send him to you..."

Kirby finished giving orders to the crew about the tent placement and sentry schedule before he strolled over to Cade. "Everything all right?" His gaze was on Riley and Dan Smith, who were having a cup of coffee at the fire. "That conversation looks fairly intense. Is she raking him over the coals? Smith seemed an okay enough guy when I was talking to him at the truck."

"I doubt if she's raking him over coals, but I wouldn't rule it out. They have a rather unique relationship." His lips indented. "I think I'm going to take her at her word and assume that she's wringing the information she needs out of him so that she can toss him to me for interrogation. She apparently believes that I won't be content until I'm in total control of our arrangement."

"Smart woman," Kirby said. "Maybe not total control but something close to it. This deal is important to her. She doesn't want to blow it. She's made a judgment and she's trying to accommodate you."

He frowned. "I'm not unreasonable. I told her that I'd keep to our partnership agreement. I might have wanted to discuss what Dan Smith is doing, but I wouldn't have been intrusive." He made a face. "Which is what she said I'd do and not to bother."

Kirby laughed. "Like I said, smart woman." He turned away. "And you don't have any problem with smart women. Where's all that sleek worldliness? What the hell is wrong with you?"

"Nothing. Maybe I don't like the idea of having to be so damn careful around her—no one else ever bothered. Her dear uncle Dan sure didn't." He shrugged. "I don't know. I'll get over it. I just have to figure out how to do it."

"Don't try too hard," Kirby said. "It's very amusing. Perhaps if you treated her as if she were a tiger cub or maybe a baby elephant."

"I just may murder you," Cade said softly.

"That would be much more in your area of expertise. I might actually be intimidated." He turned away. "And on that note, I believe I'll supervise setting up those tents. It's safer than baiting you."

—◆—

"There's been no action on the cliffs," Dan said flatly. "Do you think I'm an idiot? I would have called you and told you if there had been. I knew you were having trouble in Maldara, but the cliffs are important."

"You're damn right they are," Riley said. "But it's not as if I don't trust you. It's just that everything has been going bad since I left here for Maldara. I was afraid you'd missed something."

"I didn't miss anything. You should know that I'm never careless when there's cash on the line. I was the one who taught you the importance of that when you were just a little kid." He thought a moment. "You've figured out where the treasure is, didn't you? That's why you're so edgy." His eyes were narrowed on her face. "Or maybe you've known where it was since before they killed my dear brother, but you just didn't trust me."

She hadn't expected him to guess, but no one could call Dan dense. It had only been a matter of time. "I didn't know. He'd only given me hints about where he thought the cave was located. We didn't agree. As I said, I had to figure it out. And there was no way I would have gone for the tomb right after they'd butchered my father. You remember I was having enough trouble just hiding and keeping out of Dakar's hands."

"Yes, I know that." His smile was crooked. "Though I wouldn't blame you if you decided you didn't trust me enough to share the treasure. Brother dearest made it clear that Helen's treasure was yours and yours alone after he passed on to the great beyond. I accepted that through all the years he let me hang around and keep you company. I had a great time with you, Riley. Though you were better for me than I was for you."

He had never said anything like that to her before and she felt...awkward. "When I was a self-centered brat? I don't think so. Maybe we were a matched set." She paused. "And if you help us get the treasure, I will share my portion. I never intended anything else."

He laughed. "No, you won't. I've gotten used to the idea of being noble about Helen's treasure. I won't have you spoil it for me." He glanced over at Cade talking to his men. "And at least you brought him here to make it more interesting. He's an intriguing mixture, half Equalizer ready to tear up the bad guys, half savior out to save the planet. I wonder which one is more fun for him? What do you think?"

"I have no idea. I just know he's complicated, he detests Dakar, and I've heard he might be honest with me. That could be enough to get us through this." She smiled faintly. "Why don't you go ask him?"

"I intend to." He shot her a mischievous glance. "I was only waiting for you to finish with me before I wandered over there and let him get to know how valuable I can be to him. It's not often a man of my dubious talents gets to throw in his lot with a one-of-a-kind operator like Cade. I need to expand my circle." He added, "Besides, he's probably going to pump me about his new partner. You realize that I'm perfectly willing to be pumped?"

"When it's someone like Cade." For some reason she didn't like the idea that Cade might be cool to him when he was on Dan's semi-hero list. "You're amazingly discreet with anyone else. Though you may be disappointed. He'd already had me researched before he decided I might be a worthy partner for him."

"But does he know your innermost secrets? I still have an edge." He started to stroll toward Cade. "Everyone always wants to solve an enigma."

"For God's sake, I've never been an enigma," she called after him in exasperation.

"Sure you have. I never knew what you were thinking. Even when you were a kid. How would I have been able to tolerate you if you were just ordinary?"

He was gone.

A moment later Cade was turning as Dan approached. His face was totally without expression.

Riley shook her head in frustration. If anyone was an enigma, it was Cade.

CHAPTER

8

At supper around the campfire that night Dan appeared to be in great spirits. He was joking and laughing with Riley, Eve, Cade, and his men and seemed to be getting a response from everyone. Riley had thought there might be a stiffness in Cade's demeanor, but he was casual and easy, and Dan appeared to be amusing him. He'd evidently changed his attitude about Dan. Or not. How would she know? She'd bet Cade rarely changed his mind about anything, but she was glad that there didn't seem to be a conflict with Dan.

But Cade stopped her when she was heading back to her tent with Eve. "Walk with me. I need to talk to you."

Eve nodded. "I've got to call Joe, anyway. I'll see you later."

Riley fell into step with Cade as they moved deeper into the rain forest. "What is it? I thought everything was going well. Is something wrong?"

"Not wrong. Just not right, yet. I got a call from the specialist attending Hajif, and after examining him he said that he's not a lost cause, but it could go either way." He shrugged. "But he did say he'd seen worse and pulled them through."

"Not exactly encouraging," Riley said. There was bright moonlight, and she was staring searchingly up at him, trying to read his expression. "Is it, Cade?"

"I didn't ask him for encouragement. I asked him for the truth. Actually, I appreciated the bluntness. I thought you would, too. But I thought I'd leave it up to you whether you wanted to tell Eve or wait until the news was better."

"I'll tell her. I won't hide anything from Eve." She made a face. "And at least he said he's cured patients in worse shape. We can look on the bright side." She glanced at his face. "Did you tell him his reports were to go to you and not Leta? She's holding on by a thread and she needs hope, not bluntness."

"Everything will go through me or you first. That's the way we'll handle all our mutual business." After a moment he said, "Dan mentioned that he was almost sure you intended to go up in the foothills tomorrow. You didn't discuss that with me."

"I would have." She stiffened. "I was going to talk to you tomorrow morning. I wasn't trying to hide anything from you. I would have delayed the trip if I hadn't gotten the right answers from Dan."

"He also said that he thought you already had a good idea where the tomb was located. Were you going to talk to me tomorrow about that, too?"

"Perhaps." Her lips twisted mockingly. "You did have a good chat, didn't you? And here I was afraid that you and Dan weren't going to get along."

"I had my doubts. But I knew you were concerned so I made the effort. I found him a little verbose but entertaining. He didn't try to bullshit me, and it's clear he respects you very much." He added thoughtfully, "I think there's affection there, too. But it didn't stop him from telling me anything I wanted to know about you."

"I knew it wouldn't." She met his eyes. "Dan would have tried to be discreet if he'd thought you were a threat. But the chance to tell you something you didn't already know was so tempting for him." She gestured impatiently. "So maybe we won't wait until tomorrow to talk about the treasure. What do you want to know?"

"Everything, anything. Do you know where it is?"

"We were getting very close the week my father was killed. We were both very excited about it. We'd worked it down to three possibilities. There's a network of caves in the hills, but we could wander them for months unless we chose the right access. He was sure it was the ridge path through the cliffs. It branched off inside the cave in two directions. He said it obviously was meant to confuse."

His gaze was on her face. "But you didn't agree?"

"It was too simple. I told him Helen would never have chosen anything that easy. She would have made it harder for any thieves who wanted to steal from her. I wanted to try the lower access near the river."

"So we go for the river?"

She shook her head. "Not right away. I want to try the cliff road and see if Helen might have deliberately staged a little misdirection. And if Dan was wrong about not sighting anyone in those hills, I don't want to lead anyone directly to the tomb."

"Because you're that sure you were right?" Cade asked quietly.

"Sure? I'm not sure. How could I be? But I have a *feeling*."

Her hands clenched into fists at her sides. "She was so smart, Cade. She wouldn't let anyone take anything away from her. If she chose this place, she'd want to make certain that anyone would have to go through hell before they stole one bit of that treasure."

"But you couldn't convince your father?"

"I should have been able to. He'd studied her even longer than I had, why didn't he know her like I did? He said anyone would be insane to go the river way." She drew in a harsh breath. "But she's there, waiting for us."

"Then we'll go get her," Cade said. "After checking for misdirection, of course."

Her gaze was searching his face. "You believe me?"

"How could I help it?" He smiled. "I've never seen anyone who believed in anything with such intensity. I can't wait to explore it with you."

She tilted her head. "And you're not joking?"

"I never joke about business." His smile faded. "And you know more about this particular business than I do. I'll follow your lead. But there will come a time when I'll expect you to do the same."

She frowned. "I'm not sure that I can—"

"Then be sure," he interrupted. "Work on it. You may have a little time to become used to the idea, but I can't promise."

"I realize you may have a more extensive background than I do about certain subjects. Naturally, I'd take that into consideration. I'm not unreasonable."

"Great. Then I'll deliver you back to Eve so that you can get some sleep. What time do we start out tomorrow?"

"Six." It was going to happen. After all these years of searching, she was going to take those important first steps, and he was going to be a big part of it. She was suddenly brimming with excitement and enthusiasm, and she could feel her cheeks flush as she grinned at him. "Don't be late or I'll leave without you."

"I'd catch up with you. You wouldn't stand a chance." He turned and nudged her toward the encampment. "I assume you have a map of the caves. Will you lend it to me tonight so that I can study it?"

She nodded. "I'll run in and get it when we reach my tent."

"Are we taking the truck or are we hiking?"

"The truck. There's a place near the canyon we can leave it where it won't be noticed. I don't want to be stranded on foot in case we have to get out quickly."

"You're being very cautious. You double-checked with Dan, and now you're preparing for a fast exit in case we're noticed."

"Your experience with Dakar must be different than mine." She turned to face him as they reached her tent. "Wait here, I'll be right back." It took her only a few seconds to grab the map out of her bag and run back out. She handed it to Cade. "By all means memorize it if you want to. I know Dakar as a murdering son of a bitch, but he's not stupid. He has my father's notebooks, and there may be notes about our trips to the hills there. Yes, I'm cautious."

"Excellent." He tipped his hand to his head. "Then I'll be confident that you'll take good care of me. Good night, Riley." He turned and strolled away.

She couldn't keep from smiling as she stared after him. He was everything that was smart and savvy, and every moment with him was high-adrenaline and charged with electricity. What would tomorrow be like?

Though she supposed she should stop wondering and get some rest. She turned and entered the tent again. Eve was still on the phone, but she turned as Riley came into the tent. "I won't be long. I just finished talking to Michael. I'll cut the call with Joe short."

Riley shook her head. "Don't do that. I'm not tired. I'll go outside and sit and do some planning. I always like to hear the night sounds before I go to sleep. I have a few things to tell you later, but they'll keep." Eve opened her lips to protest but Riley was already outside again, sitting down beside the tent opening and crossing her legs. She'd been telling the truth; she wasn't ready to close herself away from this. She took a deep breath and stared up at the moon. Jungle sounds were all around her and the breeze softly touched her cheeks. It reminded her of all the other times she'd spent like this over the years. Always on the hunt, listening, the scents all around her. But this was a special night, and tomorrow would be a grand adventure. Morgan Cade was also an adventure, and he would make the experience even more special.

She lifted her head, closed her eyes, and let all the night magic wash over her.

I'm here, Eleni. Am I close to you? Tomorrow is just a dry run, but I still feel as if I might feel you there. Am I right about that? I'm excited, but you'd probably make fun of me. So many exciting things have happened to you. Thank you for sharing them with me . . .

———◆———

"I should hang up, Joe," Eve said. "I talked too long with Michael. Riley is being polite, but it's been a long day for us."

"She should be grateful you're there with her," Joe said. "I don't like the idea of you out there in the back of beyond with Dakar hovering nearby like a panther. There's been no sign of him yet?"

"Not one. Riley's being very careful. And Cade has his men surrounding the camp and has had Kirby checking with the sentries all evening." She paused. "He's not going to let anything happen to us, Joe. He knows exactly what he's doing. I think you'd approve of the way he's handling things."

"Maybe." His tone was surly. "But he's there and I'm not, and it pisses me off. I can't wait to get to you. I'll be on my way tomorrow and he'd better not let anything happen to you until I get there."

"I told you, he's doing everything right. You told me yourself that both Scotland Yard and Interpol gave him high marks for the way he handled those human trafficking cases in Ethiopia last year. He not only rescued the captives but also convinced that army to prosecute the politicians. And I don't know why he wants to bring Dakar down, but he's definitely motivated." Her voice turned crisp. "And we agreed that we might need to find a way to bring him down so that we could get to Madlock. If Cade can help, then we're going to let him. It's not as if I'm helpless, Joe. If you want to find someone to worry about, let it be Michael. What do you think about letting Seth and Jane take him to that wildlife place Cade owns? Cade said it's very safe, and Michael would probably love it."

"I'll check out its security before I leave tomorrow." He was silent a moment. "I think you can trust Morgan Cade if you have to. I just don't want you to have to. Riley only asked you to do the Helen reconstruction. Stick to that. Don't go running around anywhere near Dakar. Let me do that when I get there." He added, "I'll even let Cade tag along with me."

She chuckled. "I'm sure Cade will be grateful."

"I'll be grateful," he said quietly. "I hate the idea that you've set yourself up as bait. It sucks. I should never have let you talk me into it."

"But you did, and now we're going to make it worthwhile. So you'd better find a way to set a trap for Madlock that will save us all." She added lightly, "In return, I promise that I'll be alive and kicking when you show up here tomorrow."

"You'd better," he said gruffly. "Good night, love."

"Good night. Kiss Michael for me. Take care." She hung up and sat there for a moment. She'd known this was going to probably be harder on Joe than it would be for her. She could only hope that as time passed and circumstances changed, it would all even out. The good thing was that tomorrow she would see him, and they would be facing the problems together.

———◆———

"Tomorrow?" Eve repeated. "I wasn't expecting you to move so fast. I didn't know that you even had a concrete idea about where the tomb was located."

"Well, now you do." Riley was grinning. "There wasn't any reason to discuss it until I was in a position to make certain that it was safe for me to follow through. But Dan said it was looking good, and I want to take that first step. Cade didn't see why not."

"Oh, really?" Eve tilted her head. "Did that make the difference?"

"No, I was going to do it anyway. But it never hurts to have a backup. You can't say he's not qualified. He even understood why I wanted to wait before I tried the river entry."

"How nice he's turning out to be so understanding. So what time do we leave?"

"Early." She hesitated. "But I was going to talk to you about that. I can't tell you how grateful I am that you're going to do this reconstruction. But that doesn't mean you have to come with us to find the tomb. You can stay here and sleep late or read the *Iliad*. I don't believe that we'll run into any danger, but I'd rather keep you safe."

"You sound like Joe," Eve said. "If we do stand a chance of finding the tomb, of course I'd want to go with you." She thought about it. "But I did make Joe a promise that I wasn't going to take any chances until he arrived here, so it's good that you said that you're not expecting any problems. That's good enough for me."

She frowned. "I didn't say it was guaranteed."

"Nothing in life is guaranteed." Eve smiled. "And we'd miss so much if we demanded it. You didn't demand it tonight. When you came back into the tent tonight, you were glowing. Your eyes were shining, and I could *feel* your excitement. You were thinking about tomorrow and your Eleni and the chance to find her. You're still glowing, aren't you?"

Riley laughed. "Yes." She tossed back her hair. "But I should tell you to do as I say, not as I do."

"No way. Go to bed. You're not going to talk me out of it. See you in the morning."

Riley only hesitated for an instant longer and then she started to undress. "Okay. Maybe I'll try you when we wake up." A few minutes later she was in the camp bed, closing her eyes. Eve was right. *Glowing* was the correct word for what she was feeling. She would hold on to that anticipation for a little while longer before she allowed slumber to take her. She'd remember the darkness, Cade laughing, the moonlight, the night sounds, and that wonderful glowing over what was to come.

Or perhaps what might have been before...

———◆———

TROY

"The earth is trembling again!" Riley said as she ran into Helen's suite. "I saw some rocks tumbling from the terrace down to the sea. You're being foolish. You should be leaving here."

"The earth is always trembling here, and you are always saying that I'm being foolish." Helen chuckled as she sat down before her bronze mirror mounted on the wall, the skirts of her royal-purple tunic spreading gracefully around her. She always wore the purple these days, not only because she had become a queen after she'd married Menelaus, but because the material was grown in the fields of her home in Sparta and dyed especially for her. She brushed her long fair hair back from her face. "The earth shakes almost every day. And I'm not foolish. It's only that I refuse to let myself be frightened away until I'm sure that it's necessary. Demetrius is like all soldiers and has this idea that you never run from either the gods or man. He refuses to budge from this place. Now, that is truly foolish. But I'm patient and forgive him because he's such a splendid lover and swears that my soul is as magnificent as this face that has caused me such bother. Don't you think that warrants a little tolerance?"

Riley sat down on the stool next to her. "Not if it means that you risk your life. He doesn't deserve you. You should find someone else."

"Who does deserve me?" Helen turned to look at her. "Do you know how many men have possessed me since Menelaus? Yet I've never found one who gave me understanding as well as passion.

They don't seem to realize I might need it. I'm only a face and a body to them." She reached out and teasingly touched Riley's cheek. "But why should I care when I have friends like you? You're always here for me."

"But you haven't always been here for me," Riley said. "I've . . . missed you, Helen."

"Perhaps I'm too selfish to give all of myself. It could be that all of those great, wise men are right about me." Her eyes were sparkling mischievously. "Or perhaps I'm waiting for the man to prove me wrong. Do you think someday I'll find him? Do you believe someday you'll run in here to warn me, and I won't be here?"

Riley nodded. "I believe it. I hope it."

Helen smiled. "So do I. We shall see, won't we?" She leaned back. "But now I'm being selfish as usual and talking about myself. Tell me what you've been doing." Her gaze was raking Riley's face. "There's something different in your life that wasn't there before. A man? Yes, I can see it . . ."

"You don't see anything," Riley said impatiently. "There have been men before in my life. You just think there's a difference in this one because you're comparing him with Demetrius. And maybe there is a difference, but it's that men treat women with more respect now."

"I approve," Helen said. "But I always saw that men treated me with respect. They just sometimes didn't understand why they were doing it and had to be taught."

The bronze mirror was suddenly vibrating once more! Riley's heart pounded as she watched it sway on the wall.

"The ground is shaking again." Riley reached out and grabbed Helen's arm. "Listen, don't be patient with Demetrius. Make him do what you want. I think you're supposed to leave Troy, but I can't be sure. I don't want you caught here in an earthquake because you made a mistake."

"You're upset. You're the one who should leave." She gently removed Riley's hand on her arm. "Though I admit I never want you to go. You've been my friend for too long."

"Then will you convince Demetrius to either get you out of this castle or find yourself another lover? Will you do that for me?"

"I might. But you're very demanding, Riley."

"Please." Her voice was quivering with intensity. "It's important, Helen."

"Oh, very well. But next time I want to hear more about your lover. Don't I always tell you about mine?" She got to her feet. "And now I'm letting you tell me that I have to discard a perfectly good lover because you're worried about me?"

"Yes, and because you trust me as you've never trusted Demetrius or any of the others."

"That is true." She laughed. "So I'll just have to find a lover I do trust. I'll set about it right away." She blew her a kiss as she headed for the door. "Right now I have to go to the dining hall and listen to a wonderful new bard who is going to sing my praises. I've always thought poets are so much more pleasing than soldiers. They actually mean what they say." She held up her hand as Riley started to speak. "And I'll remember you're worried about the city crashing around me. I'll be prepared. Enough?"

"As long as you realize it could happen tonight or any night."

"Well, even I can't find a new lover in one night, but if I'm spared, I'll attend to it all tomorrow or the next day. Will that make you happy?"

"No, but you'll be worried about keeping your promise to me and you'll be on the alert. It could be sufficient."

"Never satisfied." But the look over her shoulder was warm and affectionate. "I promise you'll get what you want, Riley." Then the mischief was back. "And so will I!"

Then she was gone in a flurry of royal-purple tunic and beautiful golden hair.

But the memory was still there, though it was also beginning to fade.

As dreams always did, Riley thought sleepily. Yet this one had seemed more vivid than usual, the fear sharper, her concern for Eleni deeper. It must be because of what was going to happen in the morning...

———◆———

FOOTHILLS, LESSER CAUCASUS MOUNTAINS
NEXT DAY
10:05 A.M.

"The shrubbery in these foothills is dense as hell," Cade said as he got out of the truck and looked up at the brush-covered entrance to the cave. "I don't know how Dan's men were able to see if anyone was checking out the area." He motioned to two men to get out of the back of the truck. "Take a look around and make sure we don't get a surprise."

Dan jumped out of the truck. "I'll go with them. I know this area." He disappeared into the brush.

"See how eager he is to please you?" Riley grinned. "But he already sent out men day before yesterday and they didn't find anything." She looked up at the opening of the cave on the ridge above them. "I'm surprised you didn't send them to make sure we don't have company there."

"Not necessary." Cade took out his phone and dialed a number. "Secure?"

He hung up. "It's okay." He was taking flashlights out of the knapsack and handing them to Eve and Riley.

"How do you know it's okay?" Eve asked.

"I sent two men up there to the caves on cycles two hours before we started out from camp. I told you that those off-road cycles come in handy."

She chuckled. "You *are* cautious."

"I believe I said the same thing about you last night. But I have to be cautious. I promised you both that you'd be safe." He added grimly, "And I do realize I'll have to answer to Joe Quinn."

"That's why you wanted the map," Riley murmured.

"I like to be prepared." He gestured for them to precede him up the curving path to the ridge before following them. "Dan was new to me." He was putting on his backpack. "And so are the caves in these foothills. I wanted to get as familiar with them as I could." He glanced at Riley. "Even though this wasn't your first choice. Will we be able to see the river access to the other caves from that ridge up there?"

She shook her head. "It's nowhere near here. It's more toward the north side of the Caucasus Mountains. We'd go the opposite direction from camp."

"But it's still in the cave area?"

"Mostly. According to the maps we found. Some of it." She had reached the ridge. "But not enough to please my father. That's why he chose this site."

"It does sound a bit vague. But intriguing..." Cade jumped the last few feet to join Riley and Eve on the ridge. "So let's eliminate your papa's favorite cave first." He turned to two men in camo who were approaching from inside the cave. "Eve, Riley, this is Bill Spencel and Jack Ramey. They'll be guarding the entrance while we take a look around." His gaze went to Ramey. "Anything we should know?"

Ramey shook his head. "Just the two branches, like the map said. Pretty filthy inside and the second extension appears to be only about thirty feet deep and blocked by spiderwebs, branches, and debris. We didn't go any farther than the opening of the extension, but we could see that it was a mess. We didn't try to clear it for you, because we didn't know how far you'd want to go."

"As far as the ladies want to go," Cade said. "You didn't see anything of real interest or threat in the second extension?"

Ramey shook his head. "Like I said, it was a mess. Filth and debris. The only threat seemed to be if the cave might come crashing down on top of you. Do you want us to come with you?"

"No, stay here and keep watch." He turned back to Riley and Eve. "Ready?"

Riley didn't answer. She was already making her way through the darkness.

Eve nodded as she turned on her flashlight. "Let's go."

"You shouldn't come with us," Riley said over her shoulder to Eve after they'd traveled another ten minutes into the murky darkness. "Why don't you go back? It's not as if we're going to find anything but dirt and branches. And I don't think that Joe would appreciate me letting you get clobbered if the cave collapses on you."

"But what if there's a secret panel?" she said in a hushed tone.

"We'd call you to come and see it," Cade said.

"Not good enough. I'd want to discover it for myself." She sneezed. "But it is totally filthy in here. I can hardly breathe."

"Here's where the path branches off." Riley shone her light on a cluttered passageway to the left. "And it looks just as bad as Ramey said." She carefully entered the passage, flicking the beam of her flashlight from the ceiling on either side of the cavity down to the floor. "Branches and debris and I think I see—"

"*Freeze*, Riley! Don't move." Cade pushed Eve aside and entered the passage. "Eve, you get back to the front of the cave."

"Why should I—Oh, shit." Riley was looking down at her left boot. "Do what he says, Eve. Go tell the guys we may need help."

"Right!" Eve gasped as she forced herself to look away from Riley's boot and whirled and took off running.

Riley was still frozen as she gazed down at the long black-and-white-banded snake wound around her boot. Was it her imagination or was the snake tightening around her ankle? "I've never seen a snake like this. Is it poisonous?"

"Very. Don't make a move. I thought it was a local steppe viper. But it's a many-banded steppe krait. I've only seen a couple, and they were in Vietnam."

"Then what the hell are they doing here?"

"I'm not about to check passports at the moment. He's very long and that means he's a male. They're lightning-fast and could lunge up and strike your knee in the next couple seconds."

She moistened her lips. "Then I'd appreciate it if you'd do something so that won't happen. I know you're into preservation of wildlife, but I don't really like snakes."

"I'm thinking about it," Cade said. "I'm not sure I'm faster than that krait. They're part of the cobra family. In 'Nam, they call them two-step vipers because on the second step you're dead. That might be an exaggeration. You could have a chance with some of the kraits if you could get antivenin. But some are deadlier than others, and I think this variety is a true two-step. It wouldn't give you more than five or six minutes tops." His gaze was darting around the cave. "And it's a delicate situation because he's evidently got a family. There's another viper that just crawled out from underneath that board to your left. And one more against the far wall."

"Three? Tell me you're joking." Then she carefully turned her head and saw the snake sliding near the edge of the board. She swallowed, hard. "It's crazy," she whispered.

"I agree." He was reaching into his backpack and pulling out a pair of leather gloves. "But he's not going to stay that still for much longer. When I make the move, run like hell."

She gazed in horror at the gloves. "You can't just grab him. That would be totally—"

"Crazy," he finished as he put on the gloves. "But using a weapon might not keep him from striking at you. Get ready."

How? she wondered desperately. She was almost as terrified at what Cade was going to do as she was of that viper. "I'm ready whenever you are." Her voice was shaking. "Is there anything I can do that will make it easier for you?"

"Just don't hesitate, and stay out of my way. When I move forward, you're out of here." She could see he was bracing himself as he glided slowly forward.

Then his voice came like a whip. "Now!"

The next few seconds came lightning-fast.

Black gloves plunging toward her boot.

The gleam of the black-and-white snake as it was torn from her boot and thrown across the cave!

"*Go!*"

She was out of the passage and running down the dark corridor toward the cave entrance.

She stopped almost immediately to look back for Cade.

But Cade was beside her, grabbing her arm and pushing her forward. "Keep going. I've decided I don't like this place."

"Neither do I. Did he bite you?"

"No, but his fangs managed to get a bit of my left glove. It was close."

"Close? It was—"

"That must be Eve and the guys," he said, interrupting her as he pointed to the beams of the flashlights coming toward them. "She made good time."

"Good time? It seemed to take them forever."

"It was only a few minutes, Riley," he said quietly. "Though it did seem longer. I haven't felt that uptight about a situation in a long time."

"You almost died, dammit," she said harshly. "And I couldn't do anything about it."

"It was only a question of timing. And it turned out I was a little quicker after all." He turned to Ramey, who was coming toward them. "Emergency over. You didn't see any snakes when you were examining that passage?"

"God, no." Ramey shook his head. "Though we paid more attention when we were going through this primary passage. But we only saw a few spiders here, and we weren't even sure you'd even decide to go through that second passage. We thought you might skip it." He added ruefully, "I wish you had. Was the snake poisonous?"

"Yes."

"Shit."

"Exactly." He started toward the front entrance. "And he

wasn't alone. Which is why we're getting out of this cave because I don't know when or where another one might pop out of these rocks. We'll talk once we reach the main entrance."

Eve fell into step with Riley. "More than one?" she asked.

"Cade saw three. I only saw two." She shuddered. "Just that first one was enough for me."

"Me, too," Eve said. "I was hoping it was harmless, but I saw Cade's expression and decided maybe I'd better get help fast. How did you get rid of it?"

Riley silently looked at Cade.

Eve gave a low whistle. "I can see you don't want to talk about it. Maybe later." She took Riley's arm and nudged her faster. "Let's get you out of here."

"I'm fine, Eve."

"I know. But I'll be seeing snakes hanging from the rocks and trees until I'm back at camp." She smiled. "Humor me."

A few minutes later they'd reached the entrance of the cave and Riley saw that Cade was already on his phone. "No, get them all back to the truck, Dan. We'll join you there. Watch out." He cut the connection. "No sign of any of Dakar's men in the area. But that doesn't mean they're not there." He turned to Spencel and Ramey. "Get on your cycles and get back to camp. Go west and circumvent the area until you're sure you're not followed."

Ramey blinked. "You think those snakes were planted here?"

"I don't believe in coincidences. Get going."

"Right." Ramey gestured to Spencel, and they jumped on their cycles and roared out of the cave and down the path.

Riley's gaze shifted from them to Cade's face. "I take it that snake species isn't natural to this country?"

"It could be. I told you that there's a variety of steppe viper that's found here. But the particular variety that's also found in Vietnam isn't common to Azerbaijan." He was already leading Riley and Eve out of the cave and down the path. "Though this country is famous for its snake venom storage facility, and there would probably be several of that variety in captivity. However, there might be several less there than originally brought to the facility. I wouldn't bet there were only three snakes in that cave."

She shivered. "Dakar wanted to stage a surprise for anyone who showed up in that cave after he read my father's notes."

"He knew you wouldn't go near the place if you saw anyone nearby. But a poisonous bite would show up immediately and you'd have to get serum."

"Or die."

"Or die," Cade said. "Or it could have been Eve."

"Yes." Her eyes flew to Eve. "I should never have let you come."

"Joe will agree with you," Eve said. "So you'd better let me handle it. That was very ugly."

"No past tense. It won't be over until we get back to camp," Cade said. "And it will take a while to do that." He glanced at Riley. "I hope you know more than one way to get there, because the orders I gave to Ramey are in force for us, too."

She nodded. "I know these hills." She jumped into the driver's seat. "I'll drive."

Cade hesitated. "It might be better if—"

"If you're going to argue, shut up." She was checking to see if Eve was in the backseat and Dan and the guys were getting into the truck. "I can still see that damn snake flying across the cave. So this is my job. Get in the front seat so I can get out of here."

"Yes, ma'am. I'll be right there." He was bent over, doing something on the floor of the backseat. "Don't leave without me." Then he opened the passenger door and slid into the seat. "We can go now." He opened a gun case and took out an M24 automatic rifle. "Since you decided I have to ride shotgun, I thought I should be prepared."

Riley was already backing out. "That's no shotgun."

"Same application." He was gently caressing the butt of the rifle. "But an old and familiar friend."

"I can tell," Riley said. "I didn't even know you'd brought it." She was turning sharply to get back on the road. "I'm sure Dan would like to get a look at your old friend."

"He would if I'd needed to bring it out when they were searching the brush for snipers. You always appreciate a talented friend when you're in a tight corner." He glanced at Eve in the rear seat. "Are you okay?"

"Yes, other than I had no idea I was babysitting your rifle back here," she said dryly. "Is that the one you used when you were a sharpshooter in the special forces?"

He nodded. "I'm boringly faithful when I find a good fit. I've never found a better one." He turned to Riley. "Which way are we going?"

She looked at him with narrowed eyes. "Which way do you want me to go?"

His brows rose.

"You wanted to drive," she said. "You had a reason?"

He nodded. "I want to go south. And then west." He nodded mockingly. "If you please."

"The way you sent Spencel and Ramey."

"I figured if anyone was targeted by snipers it would probably be the first ones leaving the cave. Since they were on motorcycles, they'd also be the most vulnerable. That's why I wanted them to be sure to avoid anyone following them. Though that might not be enough, and they could need help. But if they were followed, the pursuer would be far ahead of us by now, so they wouldn't know we're trailing them. I'd like you to stay far to the rear, so we maintain the status quo. I'll be in communication with Ramey, and he'll tell me if there's a problem. Do you understand?"

"Of course I understand."

"And you'll keep a low profile?"

"Do you think I'm an idiot? I won't risk Eve again. I'm not going to get near those motorcycles while she's in the truck." She turned south. "Just give me directions where Ramey is leading Dakar's man."

"Maybe nowhere. It's all supposition, Riley."

"So was the damn snake. And it's instinct and supposition that you've lived and breathed for years. I don't know where I'm going in this scenario, so I've got to trust that you do. So get on the phone with Ramey and tell him to keep in touch and his head down."

Cade gazed at her for a long moment and then reached for his phone.

CHAPTER

9

I think I've spotted your targets," Paul Wilson said as soon as he got Dakar on the phone. "I was staked out on the far ridge, and I saw two women of their description coming up the path toward the snake cave."

"Saw? I told you I wanted them brought to me. It was a priority."

"You'll get them. The place was crawling with guys searching the brush and I had to keep my distance. But I'm zeroing in on two guys on motorcycles. As soon as I take them down, they'll tell me exactly where to find Duncan and Riley Smith. I guarantee it."

"I don't want your guarantees," Dakar said coldly. "When Madlock sent you to me, he said that you'd prove valuable to our arrangement. I haven't heard anything but promises since you got here."

"I'll get them. This is the first time I've had a chance to even get a look at them. All I had was a photo and description." His voice turned nasty. "And you don't give me orders, Dakar.

183

Madlock sent me, and I take my orders from him. He's not too pleased about the way you're handling his affairs. I'll help you out when I can, but he's my boss. Don't you forget it."

"I won't forget it, you asshole," Dakar said. "But you'd better report to me first."

"I'll even send you a photo of the man they were with at the cave," Wilson said mockingly. "How much more cooperative can I be?"

Seconds later a photo appeared on Dakar's phone.

Son of a *bitch*! Cade!

"Interested?" Wilson asked. "He's not one of the guys on the motorcycles, but I can go back and try to get him after I take down the current targets."

Dakar was tempted to tell him to do it. It would serve Wilson right to try to face down Cade. But Madlock was being a complete bastard about Riley Smith and Eve Duncan. "Maybe later. Concentrate on the two women." He cut the connection. It took him a minute to get over the frustration and fury coursing through him.

He'd never liked Wilson, not from the minute he'd shown up on his doorstep; he'd wanted to find a way to rid himself of him ever since. Cade would have been perfect. Dakar knew Madlock had given Wilson other assignments to make contacts in this area, but he should have been told to make Dakar a priority. Fat chance. No one got priority but Madlock himself.

So he'd have to give Eve Duncan to Madlock. But at least he'd get an opportunity to squeeze the information he needed out of Riley Smith if Wilson did a decent job.

"We've been on the road for almost an hour," Riley said. "Are we going around in circles?"

"Maybe." Cade lifted his binoculars to his eyes again. "Maybe not. Ramey hasn't seen anything, either. But if a sniper is any good, he'll be patient. He'll wait all day for his chance of a good shot."

"Well, Dakar isn't patient," Riley said. "And he won't want any of his men to be wasting time if he has a chance of getting his hands on someone who can tell him where either Eve or I can be found. I'll bet it won't be long."

"No bet. I remember that about Dakar. It's no good having skilled soldiers if the commanders are crap. He's probably pushing him right now..." He sat up straighter. "But that cliff up ahead would be ideal for a trap as the cycles go underneath it." He lifted his binoculars again and focused on the cliff. "And I believe I see a shadow behind that boulder that could be a vehicle..." He reached for his phone again. "Ramey, watch it! To your left and about a mile from your present location. It might be—"

A shot blasted through the canyon!

"Shit!" Riley could hear Ramey's exclamation. "Spencel's down! And the bastard is still shooting at him. I've got to get him under cover." He must have cut the connection because Cade was also hanging up.

"Pull over to the side. I've got to go and help him."

Riley pulled over into the shrubs. "By yourself? We've got men in the back. They could—"

"I don't know how many men are on that cliff," Cade said as he grabbed his rifle and jumped out of the truck. "And you swore you wouldn't risk Eve. I'll call you when I have more information." Then he was gone.

And Riley was sitting there, her hands clenching the steering wheel.

Another shot echoed in the canyon.

"A man down?" Eve asked. "What the hell. What do we do?"

"According to Cade, nothing until he gets more information," Riley said. "But I can't take that." She opened the driver's door. "I won't be stupid, but I have to get ready to move if needed." She was heading toward the back of the truck when she saw Kirby coming toward her. "I was just coming to talk to you."

"And Cade just called and told me to come up front and keep you company."

"That's all he said?"

"Judging by those shots, there might not have been time for anything else. What's happening?"

Riley briefly filled him in. "And if I'm going to sit here and twiddle my thumbs, I want someone to tell me I'm not being an idiot. Kirby, you know Cade. I wanted him to take a few of you with him. Does he usually close everyone out and go off to save the day by himself?"

"Sometimes," he said cautiously. "But it's usually when it's the smart thing to do. Or when he wants to keep the focus off a victim while he does his thing."

"His thing?"

"The skill he's best at. The one he got medals for." He changed the subject. "At any rate, we'll know soon if he needs help. Because we'll—"

More shots!

Then return fire!

Then another pepper spray of bullets!

"That's Cade's M24," Kirby murmured. "He's on the job."

More shots, farther away this time.

Kirby's head was tilted as he listened. "He's moving the shooter away from our guys," he said.

Riley's phone was ringing. Cade!

She jumped on the call. "What the hell is happening?"

"It's safe. Only one shooter. Don't worry about him. But Spencel's wounded and you need to get both of them out of here. Move, Riley!" He cut the connection.

She was already moving, running toward the cab of the truck. "Get back in the truck, Kirby. We have to get Spencel out of there."

Five minutes later she pulled up the truck in the brush where she saw Spencel and Ramey lying in a ditch. Ramey was working to stop the bleeding of a wound in Spencel's midsection.

No Cade.

Riley grabbed a first-aid kit from the truck and ran over to Spencel. "How is he?" she asked Ramey.

"Not good. The bastard shot him in the belly and the hip." He turned to Kirby, who had run up with Dan and four of the men. "Cade said he thinks he might have phoned in our location to Dakar, and we have to get Spencel out of here."

"We will." Riley turned to Dan. "You know this territory. You drive the truck. Kirby, I'll get in the back with you and the guys to administer first aid to Spencel." She said to the other men, "Move him carefully." She watched them start to move Spencel and then turned back to Ramey. "Where's Cade?"

He shrugged. "He came sliding down from that cliff like gangbusters and started shooting. He moved deeper into the brush and more shooting. Then he jumped on my motorcycle and took off back up the cliff. You showed up a few minutes later. Should we wait?"

She looked in frustration at Kirby. He shook his head. "Don't ask me. You're the one he called and gave orders to."

"But what the hell is he doing?"

"My guess? I'd say he's doing his thing."

And they'd already discussed what that constituted. She whirled away and started toward the truck. "Then we're not waiting around for him. Both of you get in the truck and we're out of here."

Ramey frowned. "I don't know if—"

"I do," Riley said curtly. "Cade can look out for himself. He told me so, and I have to accept it. I have Eve and Spencel to take care of." She was heading for the back of the truck. She caught a glimpse of Kirby's expression as she started to climb into it. "Objections?"

He shook his head. "Just a bit surprised. I didn't think that would be your decision."

"Well, you were wrong, weren't you?"

He grinned. "Yeah." He helped her into the truck. "I was wrong."

———◆———

ENCAMPMENT
9:05 P.M.

The truck drove into the encampment at shortly before five that evening and Joe arrived about an hour later. Definitely not enough time for the atmosphere of the camp to settle into calm or normal in any sense of the word. Which was why Eve whisked him into their tent the minute he appeared.

Good call, Riley thought. She was too busy stitching Spencel's wounds to want to worry about Joe's reaction to anything Eve was telling him. And she was making a concerted effort not to think about her decision to leave Morgan Cade out there by himself and come back to the camp. It had been the right decision. She was *certain* it had been the right decision. God, she hoped it had been the right decision.

Kirby stopped by the tent where she was working on Spencel shortly after Joe arrived. "How is Spencel doing?"

"Good enough. He'll be fine in a few weeks. Though he should be moved to a hospital." She got up from her camp chair beside Spencel's cot. "I was going to talk to you. You take care of all of Cade's arrangements. Where should I arrange to send Spencel? Or rather, where should *you* send him?"

"From this area, I'd usually send him to a hospital in Athens. Then after a couple days I'd have him transferred to London."

"That sounds very efficient. I told the driver who brought Joe that I'd need him to take someone back to the airport tonight. Will you call the pilot of the Gulfstream and tell him to be ready to take Spencel out of here to Athens?"

"I could do that. Just what Cade would want. I'll get on it right away." He was still standing there, gazing at her. "Everything you did was just as Cade would have wanted."

"Wonderful," she said flatly. "My fondest wish."

He was still looking at her. "Anything else I can do for you?"

"I'll let you know." Then she had to ask it. "You haven't heard from Cade?"

He shook his head. "But that's not unusual. He got used to working alone when he was in the service and going after a target. He'll be back when the job's finished."

"Or when the job finishes him."

"Not likely, Riley," he said quietly.

"I don't have quite as much faith as you or Dan do in the great man. I'm afraid I appreciate normal consideration and communication. Particularly in a partner."

"You'll have to discuss that with him. But I think you both acted as partners should today. You fulfilled each other's needs, just in different ways."

"Whatever." She gestured impatiently. "But I've thought of something you can do for me. I need to move out of that tent I was sharing with Eve. I don't believe Joe will want to have Eve out of his sight after what happened today. Will you have another tent put up for me?"

"It's already in the works." He turned to leave. "Just pack your bags and you're out of there." He grinned. "Think Eve can protect you until then?"

She nodded. "Eve is one tough cookie, and she and Joe seem to have a good marriage. But he's not going to be pleased with me." She gestured to Spencel. "I'll have him ready to go to the airport. Will you send a couple men to load him in the van?"

"They'll be here." He left the tent.

Riley drew a deep breath and then moved back over to the cot. She'd given Spencel a sedative when they'd gotten back to camp and he was still out, but she should probably give him something a little more heavy-duty to get him through the trip to the airport and plane trip to Athens. Then her responsibility would be over as far as Spencel was concerned and she could relax. But she didn't want to relax; it would only mean she'd probably be thinking about Cade.

Not worrying. Why worry when Kirby was being so casual about him? Just thinking and being frustrated and wanting to *shake* Cade.

And wondering if he'd managed to get himself killed when he'd ridden off on that motorcycle.

Or maybe she'd just pick up her bags and move into her new tent. It had been an exhausting day and she'd probably go right to sleep once she settled down.

———◆———

She was still wide awake after eleven that night when Cade stuck his head his head through the door of her tent. "Kirby tells me I'm in trouble." He came in and lit the lantern on her table. "If I am, let's get it over with now. I don't want it hanging over me."

She sat up in bed. "I don't know what you mean. Why should you be in trouble? Kirby said that you do everything right, and we have a perfect basis for a partnership."

"He's right, I am in trouble." He was studying her. "Kirby is really sharp, but we've been together for a long time and things that seem natural to us don't necessarily strike other people the same way. I believe that might have been it?"

"Really?"

"Brrr." He sat down on the ground beside her and crossed his legs. "Okay, let's go over it. I had a job to do, and I did it. You had a job to do, and you did it. Kirby said you did a great job. And I did everything I was supposed to do. We both had a good day, considering."

She just looked at him.

"Talk to me," he coaxed.

Why not? She said curtly, "We had a good day, considering..." She suddenly spat out in fury, "That there wasn't one moment that you couldn't have called me, and I would have told you what I was doing and if there was a problem. Or even if there was something that we could have handled together, you'd have known about it."

"Ah, the crux of the matter."

"*Yes!*" She could barely control the anger. "You shut me out. After what you did for me with that damn snake in the cave, there's nothing that I didn't want to do for you. I couldn't help you with that snake, but I was ready for anything. Then you gave me the minimum to do that you possibly could and then disappeared. Not even a text to say whether you were alive or not. You *cheated* me."

"I can see that," he said gravely. "By not taking enough."

"Or giving enough. Anyone should have understood that."

"Except me. I have a tendency to concentrate on getting business done in the most efficient way possible. And since I don't generally have a partner, I thought that philosophy would please you."

"It might have," she said. "If I hadn't already been in debt to you."

He suddenly chuckled. "So it's the snake's fault?"

She found her lips twitching. "It could be." She frowned. "But it's also your fault."

"By a gross lack of sharing? I can accept that, and it shouldn't be too difficult to fix. I gather you want more of a joint operation? Kirby's already told me about your day, and you were awesome."

"He didn't tell me about *your* day. He said that he never knew when you were going to be going after a target. You said that you'd taken care of it."

He tilted his head. "You want the details?"

"Not particularly. I'm sure you were amazing. I want to know if you had to contend with Dakar, too."

"No, I caught up with the sniper before he met with Dakar. Though it was close."

"How do you know?"

"I took him out when he was still in his van. I got near enough for a head shot, and he smashed into a tree. He had touch ID, and I managed to check out his ID and his phone info by using his thumbprint when I examined the body. His name was Paul Wilson and he's an American citizen. His phone had a few local phone numbers, and a number of calls to Washington, DC, as well as a few interesting contacts in Istanbul and Moscow. I need to check them all out. But one of the local numbers was Dakar, and Wilson was heading straight for an address that was maybe nine or ten miles from his collision with that tree."

"And bringing you with him."

He nodded. "I would have been a prize for Dakar. But I'd bet Wilson would have taken any of us who were in that cave today. Particularly you or Eve." He tilted his head. "Do you want to know anything else?"

She shook her head. "But I don't want to be shut out, either."

"I've got that straight now." He made a face. "I can't always promise to take you along. You don't have the training. But while we're partners, I won't shut you out. Is that good enough?"

"Not really. But I couldn't expect anything else." She slowly nodded. "That's good enough."

"Then can we scratch this day off as a miss and go after your river entry tomorrow?"

"It might not have been a miss if any of those phone numbers work out," she said thoughtfully. "You might talk to Joe Quinn. One of the reasons Eve agreed to take the re-construction was that it offered them the chance to go after an agenda of their own."

"Anything to get out of his bad books is a good move. You mentioned you'd arranged to set up a workshop in the moun-tains where Eve could work after we transfer the sarcophagus. How extensively did you do the preparation work for preser-vation of the mummification process?"

"Very extensively. My father did the research, but I did the legwork. I guarantee we didn't screw up."

"Do you mind if I do a little investigation on anything else new in the marketplace that might be beneficial?"

She shrugged. "Have at it. I realize you're an expert. But I think you'll find that we're up to date."

"I believe I will, too. And the principal thing right now is the discovery and removal of the sarcophagus. Should I arrange with Kirby to take the same number of men tomorrow as we did to the cave today?"

"We can head for the river entry tomorrow." She moistened her lips before adding hesitantly, "But I've never taken addi-tional men when I go to the river. It will take us nearly half a day to reach it and I didn't see the need. My father never mentioned it in his notes, so Dakar doesn't know about it. The area is practically deserted and it's nowhere near Dakar's stronghold."

He frowned. "I don't like running any risk with you or Eve."

"You brought a small army today and there was still a risk," she said dryly. "It's just a waste of manpower." She paused. "And I doubt if we'll actually be going into the river cave tomorrow. But once we get there, we'll want to discuss ways to get to the upper cave." She added, "And you might have problems with agreeing that Helen's coffin is there. My father did."

"And what would you do if I did?"

"Go by myself. But I'd demand that you at least have my back if you want any share of the treasure."

He shook his head. "Nope, I want my full share. You can leave everyone else here at camp, but you'll have to take me with you." He got to his feet and turned off her lamp. "I'll see you in the morning. Sleep well, Riley."

Riley lay back down and stared into the darkness. She hadn't been able to sleep before, but she thought she might now. She was not going to have to worry about that blasted Cade now. Not that she should have worried before. Yet she had to admit the disturbance had been there. But now he was here and alive and had cared enough about how she felt to come and make things right between them.

No reason not to sleep when tomorrow might be the day she'd been waiting for all her life . . .

———◆———

Joe checked the text he was receiving and then looked up at Eve from where he was lying on the cot. "It's from Cade. Evidently, he's back in camp and wants to get together with me first thing in the morning. He said he had information for me I might find interesting."

"I'm glad he's back," Eve said. "Kirby didn't seem worried, but I could tell Riley was on edge."

"Imagine that," Joe said with a grin. "And she had absolutely nothing to worry about but trying to keep alive one of Cade's men who had been wounded by some nut taking potshots at all of you."

"Not all of us," Eve corrected quietly. "I told you, only Spencel and Ramey. Riley kept the rest of us out of harm's way."

"But it could have been you."

"And it would have been my fault. Neither Riley nor Cade wanted me to come along. But it was supposed to be safe, and I was interested." She folded her arms across her chest. "And I explained all of this when you first walked in here this evening. I thought we were done with it."

"Do you think I was thinking all that clearly when I hadn't seen you in weeks? All I could think about was getting you into bed."

"And you did," she said softly. "Several times. Thank you very much."

"You're welcome. But it was very distracting, and I should have been paying more attention to what was happening here. I was just so damn glad to see you."

"Well, you're obviously paying attention now. Do you suppose you could forget about it for a while and just hold me?"

"It might be possible." He pulled her down into his arms. "Though I should really text Cade and tell him I'll meet him tonight instead. It could be important."

"*This* is important." She cuddled closer. "*We're* important. I know I was the one who talked you into this. And yes, we have a chance of beating Madlock at his own game, but our family and what we have together is just as essential. So we're going to lie here and you're going to tell me everything that Michael has been doing and what friends he's made." She brushed her lips across his throat. "And how much you've missed me. Okay?"

"Very much okay," he said huskily. "Where shall I start?"

"With Michael. The magic started before that, but we created him out of the love we shared. Let's start with Michael..."

———◆———

CAMP DAVID
CATOCTIN MOUNTAIN PARK

"I've got Dakar on the line, Mr. President." Charles Dunwoody, his assistant, held out the library phone to Madlock. "He says he doesn't know where Mr. Wilson is at the moment."

"It's his business to know." Madlock took the phone and said sharply, "What the hell is happening there, Dakar? I got a call from Wilson a couple hours ago, but I was in a meeting and couldn't take the call. Now I can't get him back."

"It's not my fault," Dakar said sourly. "The bastard always told me that he takes orders from you. There was some kind of uproar about Morgan Cade and the Riley Smith woman. I offered to send some of my men to assist, but he said it wasn't necessary."

"Morgan Cade? What was he doing with her? Dammit, he's a media magnet. I don't want him anywhere near any of my business. There would be leaks. Why couldn't you keep him away?"

"I will. It's not my fault that Cade and I had a previous encounter. I just have to convince Wilson that you wouldn't like him to be around. If he's as good an exterminator as you claim, that shouldn't be a problem. You might help, Madlock."

"Don't speak to me like that," Madlock said coldly. "You're playing with fire. I've put up with enough from you. Time's running out. I *want* Eve Duncan. It sounds as if Wilson may be doing your job for you, and you're just spinning your wheels. If you hear from him, tell him I'm trying to reach him." He cut the connection and almost threw the phone at Dunwoody. "What an idiot. I thought you told me that I'd be able to control Dakar."

"That was my report," Dunwoody said warily. "Dakar is a nasty operator who likes his own way, but he's supposed to be easy to intimidate. Since you're in the big leagues, he should have been scared to cross you."

"You didn't check thoroughly enough. I sent a good man like Wilson to him, and he didn't know what to do with him. Not only that but Dakar has brought Morgan Cade into the mix."

Dunwoody gave a low whistle. "That could be awkward."

"Awkward? Are you an idiot, too? Cade is a do-gooder and people listen to him. He's the worst possible contact I'd want for Eve Duncan. It gives her additional strength."

"Do you want me to send someone to clean up the mess Dakar's making?"

"I'm tempted." Madlock thought about it. "How is the search going for Diane Connors's lab? If I can get hold of her directly, I might not need Duncan right away."

"We think we might have traced her location to somewhere in Switzerland. But we haven't pinned down an area yet.

But I'll tell them it's a priority," he added quickly as he saw Madlock frown. "You'll have it very soon."

"Soon isn't what I need," Madlock said. "Unless you come through for me, it means I'll still have to deal with Dakar for a little longer."

"Then you do want me to send someone?"

He shook his head. "Just concentrate on finding that lab. I'll wait until I hear from Wilson and see how bad it is. But I don't think so. I may have to find an excuse to pay a goodwill visit to Russia or Turkey so that I'll be on the spot to handle it myself."

———◆———

DAN'S ENCAMPMENT
NEXT DAY
10:20 A.M.

"More than interesting." Joe gazed down at the names and addresses on the phone before he looked back up at Cade. "They might be exceptional. Are you going to check them out or should I?"

"I'll let you do it. At present, my only aim is to take down Dakar and complete my arrangement with Riley. I could get the information, but it would take longer and might not be pinpointed in the direction I want." He met Joe's eyes. "You have contacts all over the world. According to what Eve told me, your ambitions are much more all-inclusive, and you might not want to involve Washington, DC, in the inquiry. All I ask is that you give me whatever you find out about Dakar that might help me."

"Done." Joe suddenly grinned. "And, who knows, you might find your own ambitions becoming more extensive as time passes. Eve and I had no idea we'd be going down that path a couple years ago. It just seemed the right thing to do."

"And it still does?"

Joe nodded. "It still does."

"Incredible," Cade said. "I believe I'd have to think long and hard about it. I've saved a lot of wild animals in my career so far, but I've never gone after the big game you have."

"Life. The ultimate big game," Joe said. "And the most satisfying."

"Tempting," Cade murmured. "Maybe I'll catch you later. But right now I have a very demanding partner who insists I give her my full attention. Are you going with us to check out the river cave entrance?"

Joe shrugged. "I thought that was the plan, but Eve said that Riley gave her a map leading to that house in the mountains where she's going to be doing the reconstruction. She wants to go and look it over." He made a face. "And I'd just as soon do that rather than have her go coffin hunting again. It didn't go too well yesterday, did it?"

"Actually, it didn't go too badly. One wounded. No one died but Wilson."

"And that was the cave that had Riley's father's approval. Eve said he turned thumbs down on the river cave you're going to look at today." He grinned as he turned away. "Good luck, Cade."

CAUCASUS MOUNTAINS
SUNSET

"That's not a river," Cade said flatly as he got out of the truck. "If anything, it's a trickle." He was climbing down the bank. "A muddy trickle at that." He looked back up at her. "What are you up to, Riley?"

"I didn't say it was a big river." She was half sliding down the bank. "It gets a little deeper once you're in the cave. It was probably even deeper at the time when Helen's sarcophagus was taken to her resting place. It would have had to be taken by boat. Otherwise it would have been difficult for anyone to get it up to the lower mountain caves."

"Mountain caves," Cade repeated, gazing up at the snow-capped Caucasus Mountains towering over the cliffs and the sluggish river pouring into the dark cavity. "Not in the cliffs, but the mountains themselves."

She nodded. "But you have to get through these lower caves first. That's why my father said no one would have chosen this place." She looked at the sun. "It's almost sunset. We'd better get to the far side of the opening right away."

"Why?" he asked curiously.

"Trust me. Move!"

He moved.

And suddenly the sky turned black as a screeching blanket of dark flesh poured out of the opening in the cliff!

He instinctively ducked. "What the hell?"

Then he started to swear. "Bats. It's a bat cave!"

"Don't swear at them. They have seniority. Their ancestors have probably been here since before Troy." Riley sat down on

201

a rock at the side of the river. "But most people don't care for them. My father didn't."

"I can take them or leave them," Cade said. "I admit they make me a bit nervous. But I can see how he'd think they wouldn't be fitting guardians for his Spartan queen." He tilted his head as he gazed at her appraisingly. "However, you don't appear to feel the same way. Though I don't know many women who are fond of bats. They seem to equate them with vampires or rabid attacks."

"Then they're stupid people who haven't bothered to do their research. Bats are by nature gentle animals, and they don't attack humans. There are only three species of vampire bats, and they only take the blood that they need and never remove enough to do harm. Only a small percentage of bats go rabid, and you can almost always identify them because they appear sick and lethargic. Your real danger is their immune system and the zoonotic viruses they carry. You just protect yourself from that threat by wearing a mask and gloves."

"I'll be sure and remember all that. You've evidently done your research, and I doubt if it was all compiled here."

She shook her head. "I was a wild child. There was almost always a bat cave in the jungles and forests where I grew up. I found them fascinating. It drove my parents crazy when I was a little girl."

"I can see how it would. Perhaps that was why your father was prejudiced against accepting your view on Helen's burial place."

She shook her head. "My father always thought he was right. Most of the time he was." She smiled. "I always admired him even when we disagreed." Her lips tightened bitterly. "And he didn't deserve having Dakar steal his dreams."

"But then Dakar was expert at that particular kind of thievery," Cade said. "I experienced his talent myself a few years ago." He glanced at the cave opening. "Well, you brought me here. What are you going to show me?"

"It will wait." She started up the bank toward where they had parked the truck. "Let's get coffee and then have something to eat. I threw some bacon and bread into the portable fridge. I know I haven't convinced you that I'm right about this. I'll have to explain. We'll go into the cave later. The majority of the bats will be gone from the cave from dusk to dawn. I'll have time to take you deeper into the cave before they return."

"Did you stash a boat somewhere down here?"

"No need. You were right, it's barely a trickle by the time we get past the first twenty feet. We're both wearing boots and I brought elbow-length gloves and masks for both of us. We shouldn't have a problem." She looked back at him. "Unless you've changed your mind about going with me." Her smile was distinctly catlike. "It could be that bats bother you. You said take them or leave them? Maybe you'd much rather leave them."

He shook his head. "You're just trying to get out of paying me top dollar." He started after her. "Actually, I look forward to having you teach me more about your furry little friends."

"They're not entirely furry. Not their wings." She laughed. "And you'll do fine as long as you don't try to pick up any of them lying on the rocks. They object to that more than anything."

"I'll remember." He passed her and headed for the truck. "You build the fire; I'll do the cooking. You can tell me more about your mountain cave while I'm frying the bacon."

He looked up at the mountain in the distance. "It's already cooler since the sun went down. How much cooler will it get tonight?"

"Not much. The mountains are farther away than they look. This river basin creates a sort of cup effect and keeps it warmer close to the ground. The denseness of the surrounding forests helps, too. It's a good thing because the bats couldn't survive at temperatures colder than thirty-five, forty degrees." She met his eyes. "All of those natural elements seem to have been meant to make this place perfect for Helen to choose for her sarcophagus. I can see her ticking all of the items off..."

"I'm afraid I can't." He smiled. "But you know her better than I do." He turned back to the truck. "Which is why you're going to spend a long time explaining it all to me. I'm going to sit you down in front of the fire and you're going to answer questions. Agreed?"

She nodded. "Of course." She snapped her fingers. "As soon as I call Eve and see what she thinks of the workshop I had built for her."

He made a face. "I'd almost forgotten that was what Joe Quinn said they were going to do today. I'm sure she'll ask you how you're getting along here."

She frowned, puzzled. "So?"

"The last thing he said to me was to wish me good luck. Perhaps you'd better not explain in detail about this place until you explain it to me?"

CHAPTER

10

W ill it work for you?"

That was the first thing Riley asked Eve when she reached her forty-five minutes later. "I have you on speaker-phone so that Cade can hear if I did a decent job. I don't want him stepping in and bringing in outside help if you're having problems. Is there any way that I can improve it?"

"Not that I can see. I was expecting a small cabin, but this place is enormous." Eve paused. "And you did a terrific job, Riley. I have everything I need. The climate control room is great. I've seen workshops at Egyptian museums that didn't have the equipment you've set up here."

"It had to be as perfect as I could make it. We're taking Helen away from a place she chose for herself thousands of years ago. It has to be exactly right. That's why we chose you."

"Nothing like applying a little pressure," Eve said dryly.

"You can take it."

"I think I can, too. With a little help from my friends."

"What about the location? That spruce forest covers almost half the mountain. I tried to put the cabin and workshop deep in the woods so it wouldn't be noticeable. As far as I've observed, there aren't many people who live anywhere near that area."

"We've just left there and are on our way back to camp. We didn't see anyone on the road or when we got there. Joe was more interested in the location than I was. He spent his time outside planning how to protect the area while I was inside examining the equipment. He said there shouldn't be any problem."

"Good. I'll let you go now so that you can get back to the camp. If you've just left the workroom, it will take you at least another hour."

"Will I see you back at the camp when we get there?"

"We may be there a little later." She met Cade's gaze across the fire. "We're still in exploring mode."

"Really?" Eve was instantly alert. "Joe is looking very interested. Would you care to elaborate?"

"When we get back. I'm glad you're happy with the workroom. Bye." She cut the connection. "As requested, I didn't satisfy Joe's curiosity." She took the bacon, lettuce, and tomato sandwich Cade handed her. "But you heard that I got the prep right for the reconstruction."

"Yes, I did. Now convince me that she's going to have something to reconstruct." He poured himself a cup of coffee. "Why this place?"

"Because the young bard, Charon, who became Helen's friend when she and her lover ran away from Troy and came to live in these hills, wrote about many places that he visited with her. He became her personal poet." She added, "But one of the last poems he wrote in his life was about himself and his final adventure with Aphrodite."

"Aphrodite?"

"Even in death Charon was protecting his Helen. His name meant 'fierce brightness.' He was named after the fierce and brave ferryman of Hades from Greek mythology. His poem was quite touching; it described how he managed to save beautiful Aphrodite from the darkness surrounding her and gave his life to do it."

"Ferryman," Cade repeated. "The boatman. You're saying he was telling the world about his last glorious trip with Helen." He looked back at the darkness of the cave opening. "It's a stretch, Riley."

"But he wouldn't be able to resist doing it. He was a poet. She was everything to him from the moment she'd come into his life." She shook her head. "Particularly if that was a true poem and he ended up giving his life for Helen."

"I don't suppose you know if that actually happened."

"All we've been able to find out is that he disappeared about the same time. We can only track him by his poems." She paused. "But we do know that during that period it would have taken a boat to reach the back of those lower caves that lead to the mountain caves."

"And a brave ferryman to carry his Helen and her treasure to her last resting place." Cade smiled gently. "A fairy tale, Riley?"

"Not if you look at it the right way. She wasn't a princess from a fairy tale. She was very human and both bad and good. But I believe Charon thought she was worth his time and his effort... and perhaps even his life." She bent across the fire toward him. "And I thought it was worth my time to go down to that bat cave and take the trek all the way to the mountain caves."

"How far?"

"I went past the first cave, but I had to stop when I came up against several boulders on the upper level. I'd need help to move them, and my father wasn't going to volunteer. After he was murdered, I didn't want to ask anyone else for help. Things became . . . complicated."

"But then you got a partner."

"Who was almost as cynical as my father."

He shook his head. "Not at all. I told you that I want to believe you. How could I resist? All that passion." His gaze narrowed on her face. "Besides the ferryman, what made you think that your Helen could be in one of those mountain caves?"

"When I was standing in front of those boulders, I felt the cold."

"What?"

"I felt the waves of cold coming from beyond the boulders. It reminded me of Otzi, the iceman."

"Otzi, the Alps mummy?"

She nodded. "Before I'd been thinking of Egyptian mummies. Because there are so many of them in Egypt. But Otzi was preserved because of the ice. It would be so natural for Helen to arrange to be preserved for eternity in the same way. And the bat cave would terrify thieves and keep them from stealing her treasure. She was very possessive about keeping what was her own."

"So a blast of cold air was the final determination?"

"It was all a combination of facts and feelings." She tilted her chin. "But isn't most of life?"

"But we're talking about death."

"Are we? I'm not sure."

He finished his coffee and set down his cup on the ground. "Then let's go and see if we can verify." He stood and pulled her to her feet. "Take me into your bat cave, Riley."

———◆———

The sloshing sound of their boots kicking the water against the stones was echoing off the hollow high ceiling and stalactites. But suddenly Riley couldn't hear Cade behind her.

"Come on," Riley glanced over her shoulder. "What are you looking at?"

"Your bats." Cade was standing still and shining the beam of his flashlight on the ceiling, pinpointing four bats huddled together in the darkness. "I've seen several since you brought me here, and most of them appear to be healthy enough. Though these four appear a little lacking in energy. But I'm keeping an eye out for any that look sickly. You said that was a sign of rabies, right?"

"The most prevalent sign. But just the fact that they didn't go hunting tonight wouldn't indicate they were ill. Sometimes with viruses like Ebola, they don't show it themselves; they just spread it. And there could be other reasons."

"Such as?"

"I don't know," she said impatiently. "Maybe pregnancy, a bellyache. I don't know everything about bats."

"You appear to come pretty close. But I prefer to err on the side of caution when I'm dealing with the unknown. So I'll just poke along behind you and keep an eye out for the bad stuff. How long do we have until we start climbing to get to the upper mountain chambers?"

"About another ten minutes." She flicked her flashlight beam to the left where the ground started to rise and curve, forming a rugged stone ramp. "But one of the reasons why those bats may be sedentary is that it's colder back here in this rear section than it was near the front opening. Can't you feel it?"

"Maybe." He held up his gloved hand. "Perhaps a little." He grinned as his pace increased. "I believe I'll skip the poking along and get down to business."

"Excellent." She laughed, her face alight with mischief. "And perhaps I should confess that I've been keeping an eye on all the bats we've come across since we entered the cave tonight. I didn't notice any that were suspect."

"Wicked," he said softly. "Very wicked, Riley."

"I couldn't resist." She moved quickly up the ramp. "Keep close to me. Keep your gloves on, and don't touch any of the bats. From now on the ramp is like a maze as it curves around higher and higher."

"Until it comes to the boulders. I won't let you lose me."

"I know you won't." She felt the adrenaline running through her with the excitement she was feeling. Close. They were getting closer with every moment. She'd never shown anyone the boulders, not even her father. Soon she'd be standing there and feel that anticipation she'd had before.

Are you here, Helen? I've brought someone to see you. I believe you'd find him interesting. He's not like the other men you've been with.

"Hey, slow down. I can't keep up with you." But he was laughing, and she could sense the same zinging eagerness she was experiencing. It was wonderful being able to share that whirlwind of feeling.

"Yes, you can," she said teasingly. "You wouldn't let me get ahead of you. You always have to be best."

"Not true. I just never want to fall behind. How far now?"

"Around the next turn up ahead. You'll see the boulders..."

Then they were standing before the four enormous boulders that were fully fourteen feet in height.

"Impressive." Cade was examining the rocks. "Similar in height. But how did they get here?" He gave her a sly glance. "What do you think? If it was Charon, he was even mightier than his reputation."

"He didn't have to be mighty; he was a poet and had brains, and that would be enough. I did wonder about it. But he could have arranged to build ramps. Or maybe placed them on sleds like the rocks for the pyramids. I don't believe he would have tried to roll them; it might have started an avalanche." She shrugged. "We'll figure it out later. First things first." She reached out and touched one of the boulders. "It's cold." She stripped off her glove and put her palm on the crease between two of them. "I can feel cold air streaming from behind them." She put her cheek against the boulder. "She's *there*, Cade."

"Is she?" He smiled gently. "I want to believe you." He put out his hand and brushed it almost caressingly over all four boulders. Then he took off his glove and put his palm on the same crease Riley had and let it remain there for a long time. He shrugged as he finally took it away. "What the hell? Why not? In for a penny, in for a pound. Of course I believe you." He turned away and started taking photos of the boulders and the cave itself. "I want to get as much done as possible before the other bats come home to roost. Let's get to work, Riley."

———◆———

2:40 A.M.

They were only an hour or so from arriving back at the encampment when Cade asked quietly, "We've taken photos and you've shown me the lay of the land. When do we go after the sarcophagus? I'm sure you have a plan."

"Later today. And we'll bring more people with us then. Perhaps ten or twelve. We've no idea what we'll find once we get past those boulders. We don't even know how far we'll have to go into the mountain. We'll need the truck for transport and Dan's SUV, maybe even the motorcycles." She smiled. "We'll need plenty of help to bring the sarcophagus and the treasure down from the caves. Then we'll have to deliver it immediately to the workshop on Spruce Mountain. It's going to be a busy day."

"We'll make it through," he said. "It's all in how we finesse it."

"Wonderful philosophy." She wrinkled her nose. "Particularly when we're both not sure if you believe it's going to happen. How do you intend to finesse that outcome?"

"I'm thinking positive. You're smart and you believe it, and I've always gone where the action is."

"And if you find out I'm full of shit?"

"Then we'll have a talk and decide where we went wrong and decide how to fix it. But that will only be a last resort, because as far as I'm concerned *you* are the last resort."

She blinked. "Thank you. I don't think I've ever been called a last resort before."

"You probably have. But your father had his Spartan

queen and was so self-absorbed that he didn't make a big thing of it."

"He did value me, Cade."

He nodded. "How could he help it? But he should have let you try the bat cave first. Personally, I think he was just a wimp. I didn't like the idea myself, but I got through it, didn't I?"

"Yes, you did." She chuckled. "Reluctantly. Are you sure you were awarded that Congressional Medal of Honor?"

"Now, that hurt. You have to admit I was good with the snake."

Her smile faded. "I do admit that, and I'll never forget it."

"Please do." He grimaced. "I didn't mean for you to get soppy about it."

"I'll work on it." She added solemnly, "I have some recent memories to keep me from getting too sentimental. Why don't you lean back and go to sleep? I don't need you to help drive."

"Or clearly anything else." He yawned and leaned back and closed his eyes. "Wake me when we get to camp..."

———◆———

RIVER CAVE
NEXT DAY
SUNSET

"You're excited." Eve dropped down beside Riley on the riverbank. "So am I. You think it's the real thing, don't you?"

"Would I have dragged you all here if I didn't?" Riley asked. She gestured at the dozen men wearing jackets, masks, and gloves who were standing around on the bank waiting, talking to Kirby, Cade, and Joe. "They're all waiting to see if I'm crazy enough to force them to really go into that cave. But it's logical that she'd choose this place. I'm hoping like hell that I'm right about it."

"So am I," Eve said. "It wasn't the main reason I came, but it's the reason that I should be here. It's who I am."

"Yes, it is," Cade said as he came toward them. "But I promised Joe that you'd go with him, Eve. Even when I told him we didn't see any snakes when we were here yesterday." He held out his hand to Riley and pulled her to her feet. "Come on. You've got a job to do. That sun is going down any minute. You think I'd trust any of these guys to lead me through that bat cave? You have to be front and center. Like it or not."

"I like it." She smiled at him. Then she pulled up her face mask and turned toward the cave opening. The screeching, black veil of bats was pouring out of the cave as the sun went down, enveloping the world in darkness. "I like it very much. Come on and get a move on it. I swear I'll take care of you, Cade."

———

Three boulders down. One still to go!

Riley's eagerness was growing with every passing moment as she watched the seven men undertake the task of removing the boulders barricading the mountain from the lower river cave. She'd wanted to throw herself into the job herself, but she'd known that she'd be more in the way than a help. Cade had given her the honor of being first leading the expedition, but she didn't have the muscles to compete with Dan, Kirby, and the other men Cade had chosen to remove those behemoth boulders. As soon as the first boulder was taken down and moved to a higher position on the ramp, she and Eve had climbed on the massive rock to watch Cade and Joe supervise.

"You're right," Eve murmured. "Every time one of those boulders is taken down there's another blast of cold air."

"Which could mean nothing." Riley added, "Or everything." She was trying to get a glimpse of the stone facade beyond the boulders. There appeared to be only darkness. Although the men all had flashlights and she could see a flickering of light now and then on what appeared to be a stone wall and a ramp similar to the one that had led up from the riverbed. "My father would say nothing."

"But that's not what you'd say, or you wouldn't be here."

"You're absolutely right." Her hands were clenched into fists as her eyes strained to get another glimpse. "I don't see Cade now. He was behind that third boulder when it was moved."

But then she saw him again as he emerged from behind the last boulder. There was dust on his mask, and he was as sweaty and disheveled as the other men. "Riley." He was striding toward her. "Come on. I might need you." He lifted her off the fallen boulder. "Eve, stay put. I'll send Joe for you later."

Eve's brows rose in surprise. "Whatever."

Then Riley no longer saw her as Cade pulled her behind the last boulder into the darkness. "Turn on your flashlight." Cade was grasping her hand as he led up a curving ramp she'd only briefly glimpsed from a distance. "This ramp is much wider than the one leading from the riverbed, but it has rocks and wide cracks all along the path."

Her flashlight beam was already searching every niche and cranny. "It looks...old. Do you know how far it goes?"

"I have an idea. But I was already feeling as if I was cheating you when I took the opportunity to do a little exploring when we got toward the end of the boulder tear-down. I figured I should let you have a shot at it on your own." He grinned at her over his shoulder. "We'd better hurry, though, or we won't be the only ones exploring. Besides, the farther we get, the colder it becomes. Do you suppose we've run across another ice man?"

"No, that's not what I think." Her excitement was growing with every step. "You know what I think. Are you going to tell me if I'm right?"

"Of course not. I wouldn't dream of it. Why do you suppose I brought you along to help me? Just be quiet and you might see for yourself. The answer should be about half a mile down the ramp..."

"Then keep up with me." She was half running as she traversed the dark ramp.

Are you here, Helen? I'm almost sure you are.

"To the left, Riley," Cade said. "The far wall. Shine your flashlight."

She skidded to a stop. She lifted the beam of her flashlight to illuminate the wall.

It was there, written in ancient Greek in ornate amethyst script engraved on a limestone wall:

MY QUEEN

ELENI

THE SHINING ONE

Then down below in smaller script:

HELEN, THE BELOVED, GLORIOUS QUEEN OF SPARTA

"Dear God," she whispered. She couldn't stop looking at it. "The Shining One..."

"I was correct in the translation?" Cade asked. "I caught a glimpse of it, and I knew I had to get the expert. It is ancient Greek. Eleni, the Shining One?"

"Yes, you were correct."

"I think there may be a door at the end of the hall," Cade said. "Presumably leading to the treasure room where Helen lies in state. I didn't look inside. I just came to get you."

"Thank you." She felt a little dazed. "I suppose I should have brought Eve with me. But I was too excited."

"We'll go get her now." He was gazing at her face. "No, on second thought, I'll go get her. I think you want to stay here for a while, don't you?"

She nodded. "If you don't mind."

"Why should I mind? My partner has just made a very smart move that will benefit both of us enormously. You deserve a bit of personal time." He smiled. "I'll even run interference until you gather yourself together." He lifted his hand. "Congratulations, Riley. I'm proud of you." Then he was gone.

And Riley was leaning back against the limestone wall and slowly sinking to the floor. Even though her back was to the wall, she could still see those words that had so shocked and thrilled her.

MY QUEEN

ELENI

THE SHINING ONE

———◆———

Eve, Joe, and Cade didn't return for another forty-five minutes, and by that time Riley was not only fully recovered but eager for the next step to come.

Because the next step would be Helen.

Eve was shining her flashlight on the wall as she came down the ramp toward Riley. "Very impressive. Amethysts? And that was written by your poet Charon, whom you said called Helen the shining one?"

"We know he was one of the poets who referred to her in those terms." She shrugged. "We don't know whether the world took the description from him or some other place."

"But you prefer the former because you've studied him for so long," Cade said. "Including his inclusion in this final chapter."

She nodded. "I can see him writing those words as a final tribute."

"Then suppose we get down to the important business at hand," Joe said. "If Eve is convinced she has to do this, I want it over ASAP. We're not going to get there by standing out here admiring your poet. I know you and everyone else thinks this area is safe from Dakar, but I'd hate like hell to be caught in this bat cave if he paid us a visit. I'll feel a lot better when we have both her and the sarcophagus out of here and up at Spruce Cabin so she can get to work."

"And you can get down to checking out those phone numbers Cade got from Wilson," Eve said wearily. "I know the priorities, Joe."

"They're all priorities." He gently stroked her hair back from her face. "And we'll get them all taken care of, just like we always do." He gestured down the dark hall. "Let's go find your queen first, Riley."

But Eve put her hand on his arm. "No, we'll wait here for her, Joe." She turned to Riley. "You and Cade go ahead. She's your queen, and you should meet her on your own. When you're ready to invite us to the throne room, give us a call on the satellite phone."

"I will." Riley smiled brilliantly. "Thank you. Come on, Cade." She was heading toward the darkness at the end of the corridor. She looked over her shoulder at Joe. "And you'll forgive me if I continue to admire my poet and whatever else I find at the end of this tunnel."

"Nice thought," Cade muttered from where he stood several steps ahead of her. "Except we've just hit a dead end."

Riley stopped and raised her flashlight. About thirty feet ahead, the cave ended in a sheer rock wall.

"Or is it?" Riley moved the flashlight beam across the wall. "Look how smooth that is. It's not like anything else in the cave. It was ground and polished."

Cade walked over and ran his hands over the surface. "I see what you mean. You think perhaps it's a door?"

"Maybe. Ancient tombs often had secret entrances so family members could continue to bring offerings to the departed." She pushed on the rocks lining both sides of the wall. "But if this is a door, I have no idea what opens it."

"A crate of dynamite might do the trick."

"And maybe bring down this entire cave system. No, thanks." Riley stepped back. Then she froze. She hopped experimentally in place for a moment.

Cade gave her a curious look. "What is it?"

"The floor . . . it *gives*."

Cade shone his flashlight toward her feet. He took off his jacket and used it to sweep centuries of dust from the floor around them. "There are carvings here!"

Riley took a deep excited breath and backed away. She pointed to another area. "Clear it! Clear it all."

Cade finished brushing away the dust, revealing three rows of squares. They numbered eight squares across, decorated with nature-themed drawings.

Riley hopped from one square to the next, each time bending her knees to feel the slight movement beneath her feet. She crouched and ran her fingers over one of the intricate drawings. "Each of these squares moves slightly when I jump on it. This may be the trigger that opens the door."

"An ancient combination lock," Cade said. "I saw something like this in Cyprus."

Riley looked at the various carvings. There was a tree, a quarter moon, a flower, a horse...

She suddenly gasped as it all came together. "That's it! There was an anonymous poem thought to be written about Helen by a family member as a requiem to her. My father and I found the tablet in one of the caves." Riley reached into her knapsack and pulled out a worn leather-covered notebook. She flipped through the pages until she found what she was looking for. "Here it is. It describes Helen as shining with the intensity of the sun and the soft beauty of the moon. Her spirit will always soar with the highest of winged birds, and her memory will loom large over all who knew her, like the pines of Athens." She pointed. "Look, there's a sun over there, a moon here, a bird, and then a pine tree."

Cade smiled. "The combination?"

"Only one way to find out. Give me some room."

Cade nodded and backed away.

Riley stood there with narrowed eyes, plotting her path.

Could this be it?

She leaped from one square to the next.

Sun! Moon! Bird! Pine!

She jumped completely across the room and then whirled back toward the wall. Waiting.

Nothing.

Dammit.

"Too bad," Cade said. "It was a nice—"

A low rumble shook the cave.

The wall slowly rose upward!

"Oh, my God," she whispered. "It's working."

Cade stared in amazement as the wall continued its rise. "Incredible. It must be counterweighted by hundreds of tons of rock."

As they watched, an ornate passageway was revealed in the cave beyond. Jewelry hung from craggy walls, and sheets of gold leaf glittered on the ceiling.

The door finally stopped.

Riley's breath left her. She was almost afraid to move. But what she was feeling was a mixture of exultation and inner peace. Because she knew what was waiting for her down that passageway. There could be no doubt now.

She had found her Helen of Troy.

But Cade was suddenly there beside her, taking her hand. "As an acting partner, I'll take a first look, if you don't mind. I don't know what you're going to find in there besides grime and chaos. I prefer that this goes as smoothly as it's started out."

"For Pete's sake, you don't have to protect me." Riley was frowning impatiently. "Do you know how many tombs I've visited with my father?"

"I really don't give a damn," Cade said. "I warned you there would be times like this. I won't cheat you out of that first glimpse, but I want to make sure you'll be safe. I promise it won't be long."

Ordinarily she might have fought him, but she was still feeling that almost euphoric peace. What was in that chamber would wait for her as it had all these years.

And then Cade was back almost immediately, taking her hand again and smiling down at her. "No booby traps. Okay if we face this together?"

Together.

And that also seemed absolutely right at this moment.

———◆———

Darkness.

Cold.

She'd expected the cobwebs but the tomb was amazingly clean, perhaps because the cold was not friendly to insects.

"There's the sarcophagus." Cade was gesturing across the chamber to a long cylindrical container. "I slid open the protective lid for you. The coffin itself is in the Egyptian fashion with highly painted decorations, jewels, and a large pair of wings. Also silver and gold were used and, as you know, that was only done with royalty. It's decorated principally with amethyst, gold, and garnet. Perhaps Charon thought those stones suited his Helen?"

"If it was even him who designed it for her. She did have a lover." She found herself crossing the chamber to look down at the sarcophagus. "It's beautifully done." She touched the smooth stones with a gentle index finger. "Whoever created it took time and care. He wanted to honor her."

"Like you," Cade said softly.

She nodded. "Like me."

She couldn't look away from the glittering purple stones and the white linen that must be beneath them.

We're so close now. I could reach out and touch you. You've been here alone for such a long time, and you've always hated that. But I'm going to find a place where you won't be alone again.

"You're very quiet." Cade was studying Riley's face. "Are you disappointed?"

She shook her head. "I'm just...adjusting." She looked around the chamber at the sheets of gold leaf decorations on the ceiling and the cobwebs that were more like mist and seemed to pervade everything with a soft glow. "Everything here is so grand and formal and not...her. They wanted to honor her as queen, but I don't think they got it right. Maybe Charon didn't have as much to do with this particular chamber." She shrugged. "Oh, well, we'll just have to fix it. We'll make it what it should be. It will be a challenge. Helen always liked challenges."

"Did she?" He smiled. "Then I'm sure she'll furnish you with one literally for the ages."

"Of course she will."

"Do you want to look at the treasure?" Cade nodded to three sizable carved golden chests across the chamber. "I took a glimpse inside the first box, and it was fairly magnificent. Helen had good taste."

"Everyone knows that." Then she shook her head. "I'm glad she managed to keep her treasure, but that's not what's important. What's important is what's ahead for us. I need to go and bring Eve in here and show her that Helen actually exists." She headed for the door. "And then you need to go and set up the guys to come and take her away from this place. It's too bare and stark. The only really vibrant color is the sarcophagus, and she loved color. Everyone always thinks of the Bronze Age décor as dark and dreary. But when they dug up those ruined city-states, they found walls of brilliant blue and yellow ocher and deep salmon pink. So bright and happy. That's what she liked. This place might have been safe, but she didn't care about being safe. She was always taking chances." She suddenly shivered. "And it's cold here, and she was never cold."

"Then we'd better take all that into consideration," Cade said gently as he led her toward the door and stepped aside. "You go talk to Eve and I'll get the exodus under way."

SPRUCE CABIN
AZERBAIJAN
3:40 A.M.

"Anything else I can do?" Kirby asked Cade as he got into his SUV. "I'm going to leave four sentries on duty here with Eve and Joe until the job is finished. I'll try to be back soon, but I think I should get back to the camp right away. I trust Dan Smith, but I don't know about his other men. They helped carry the treasure and the sarcophagus from the bat cave to put them in the truck and to bring it here. They might decide they have something to bargain with if Dakar comes knocking."

"Dan trusts them. He swears they're loyal." Cade shrugged. "But it might be a good idea to keep an eye on them. At least check them out. I'll be staying up here with Riley until we get close to completing the job. But I'll have other work for you to do before I come back. It's time I tightened the noose on Dakar."

"I'll vote for that," Kirby said. "I've dropped off food, tents, and sleeping bags for the sentries. Will you need any equipment?"

"No, Riley said that she'd made sure that she'd added a few extra bedrooms when she'd designed the work cabin. No question she would volunteer her services to help Eve with the reconstruction."

"And what are you going to do?" Kirby asked.

"What I always do. Make calls, search for Dakar, and maybe find ways to entertain myself by helping Joe with his project."

"What project?"

"I'll let you know if I decide it's a go. In the meantime, start checking out the people from Wilson's phone book. Get Dan Smith's help with the locals here in Azerbaijan."

"That should give me a wide choice," he said dryly. "From the stories he's been telling me that could be either the village priest or the local mafia." He was getting into the SUV. "Either way, I'm sure they'll be characters to remember." He started to back down the driveway and then stopped, looking back at the large cabin in the trees. "Something's been bothering me. I wasn't here when you were ordering the sarcophagus taken into that cabin. That entire area beyond those four boulders was ice-cold. How is Eve going to keep the body preserved well enough to work on it if conditions aren't the same?"

"Good call. But Eve isn't going to have to worry about things like that. Riley had special generators installed to keep the sarcophagus at the exact temperature needed for maintaining preservation after Eve determines what that is."

"Incredible," Kirby murmured. "Riley is sharp as hell, isn't she? She must have been planning this for a long time. I thought she was nuts when you told me about the bat cave. How did she put this together?"

"I have no idea. She grew up in the jungle, and you told me yourself that she worked with witch doctors on occasion." He kept his expression deadpan. "Personally, I wouldn't put anything past her."

"Bastard." Kirby shook his head and started backing up again. "I just have to remember that it was you who brought all of us there to do her bidding. Now I wonder how she managed to convince you to do that?"

"It's that damn witch doctor," Cade called after him. "I fought it, but I couldn't help myself."

He was still grinning as he turned away from Kirby to see Riley coming out of the cabin. "Everything okay with Eve?" he asked.

She nodded. "Other than that she's on edge because she's eager to start working." Her gaze searched his face. "You're in much better humor than she is. What was Kirby saying to you?"

"Nothing important. We were discussing your ability to get things done. I was being very complimentary."

"Maybe," she said skeptically. "But I'm in too good a mood to call you out about it. I have Eleni." Her face was suddenly lit with brilliance. "There were times when I doubted if it would ever happen, but it *did* happen, Cade."

"Yes, but I don't understand how you'd doubt yourself. Particularly when you had me to fight and triumph over the bats for you."

"Stop joking." She grinned. "Even though that thought

was amusing. I keep seeing your expression looking up at those four bats wondering if they were going to attack. But I'm trying to be sincere, so listen to me." She stopped smiling. "You probably don't even realize how much this meant to me, but you might someday. I'll pay you back, Cade."

"You already have, we're partners. I just haven't shown you the bill yet."

"Listen, I'll pay you back. I don't remember anyone in my life that has done anything like this for me. First, that damn snake, then you helped me with finding Helen. So I'll do anything I can. I believe in paying debts. Screw your bill." She smiled. "You want Dakar? So do I. I'll find a way to get him for both of us."

"No, you won't," he said sharply. "I don't want your help with Dakar, Riley. I never did. The Helen story intrigued me, but I was only using you so that I'd be in a position to get Dakar myself."

She flinched and then drew a deep breath. "Well, then you made a mistake. Like I said, I believe in debts. Because it doesn't matter what your intentions were, I still owe you. I know how people use each other to get what they want. I've watched it all my life. But it doesn't change how I feel. The only thing that matters is that I want to be free when I walk away from you."

"Oh, shit." He stared at her in frustration for a moment. "What the hell am I supposed to do with you?"

"Probably not lie to me." She was studying his face. "Because I think you just did. I don't really know why you would, it confused me. I'd heard stories about you from Dan and I took them with a grain of salt. But I'm a good judge of character and I've watched you do things that made me think that maybe the stories weren't total bullshit."

"I don't want to hear about that blasted snake again."

"You won't. I'll just observe and make up my own mind as usual. But in the meantime, I don't see why I shouldn't also do what I'd ordinarily do. So I'll take all the help from you that I can get to make sure that Helen is safely settled, and naturally I'll keep to the strictest terms of our partnership agreement."

"And let me run my own game with Dakar," he prompted.

"I'll consider it. But I think I liked my own plan better." She turned and headed back toward the cabin. "I originally came out here to tell you that I've assigned you the guest bedroom down the hall, left of the door." She glanced back at him. "And that Eve has done the initial examination of the sarcophagus and she says she'll be able to give me the exact optimal temperature to maintain maximum preservation within a few hours."

"That means you'll probably have to make the adjustment right away. Will you need any help?" He smiled crookedly. "Since you've already decided that you'll make use of me to get your Helen settled comfortably, there's no reason why I can't start now."

"You're right. I'll probably be able to do it by myself, but I'll let you know." She disappeared into the cabin.

Cade muttered a curse as he looked after her. The last thing he'd wanted was to have Riley get it into her head to help him go after Dakar. Dakar had already targeted her even before he'd realized that Cade had thrown in with her. Cade killing Wilson after she'd been seen going into that cave was bound to make the heat on her more intense.

But how to stop Riley from doing anything she decided to do? She was a force unto herself. And she'd evidently chosen to save him from Dakar.

No way! The bare idea scared the hell out of him. Just find a way to get the reconstruction on her precious Spartan queen done by Eve and then whisk them away somewhere safe until he could take Dakar out.

Which sounded simple enough, but it could mean a more complicated scenario since Eve and Joe might have to be involved.

Worry about that later. Handle one thing at a time. Go check the men on duty and then go get a couple hours of sleep in case Riley called on him later to help with the generators...

CHAPTER

11

E ve threw open the door to Riley's room. "Where's Cade? I need him!"

"Well, what would he be doing here? The last time I checked this was my room," Riley said. "I haven't seen him since we worked on those generators together a few hours ago." She frowned. "Is there any problem with them?"

"No, they're working fine. That chamber is cold as a freezer. I just can't find Cade." She frowned. "Or Joe. I wanted to get an early start and now I can't find either one. I tried Cade's room but he's not there."

"Is there anything I can do?"

"You can find Cade. I placed the damn Skype call, and now Michael wants to talk to him." She turned to leave. "I'll try to stall him. I didn't want Michael to think anything was wrong with Joe and me both here."

"I'll go look for him." Riley pulled on her jacket and headed for the door. "I know you don't like to be dishonest with your son, but can't you fib to Michael?"

231

"No, it wouldn't work. Find Cade."

Riley was already calling him as she ran out of the cabin. But she hung up as soon as he answered because she saw him coming out of the forest with Joe. She waved and shouted, "Eve needs you, Cade. Not an emergency. Something to do with Michael."

"Right." Cade broke into a run and passed Riley a moment later.

Joe was right behind him, but he slowed as he reached Riley. "You're sure it wasn't an emergency?"

"It didn't sound like it to me. Except maybe to a mother. But I didn't want Eve to be upset. I was surprised she didn't want to talk to you instead of Cade."

"I'm not." He was grinning. "She mentioned she was going to call Michael last night and evidently I didn't fill the bill when she got hold of him."

"She said she didn't want him worried, and she couldn't fib to him."

"No, we both have problems with not telling him the truth." He took her elbow. "But you might as well come in and be introduced to him. We're very proud of him, and he's probably in a great mood at the moment."

"I don't want to intrude."

"You're not. And he probably won't want to pay attention to anyone but Cade at the moment. Michael was supposed to arrive at Wild Harbor late last night with Jane and Seth Caleb, and he's getting his first taste of Cade's magic."

"Magic?"

"For Michael it'll be magic. For a good many other people also, I imagine. Cade has a lot of endangered species at Wild Harbor." He broke off as they entered Eve's work area. Cade was already sitting beside her in front of a large computer screen, and on Skype was a boy of ten or eleven with mahogany-colored hair like Joe and hazel eyes like his mother. His entire face was filled with excitement and eagerness as he stared at Cade. "Can I really ride him? I won't hurt him or anything?"

"You won't hurt him. He'll like it. Elephants are very gentle."

"You're sure?"

"Look at his tail. Is it swishing back and forth?"

"Yes. It's kind of like a dog does."

"That's what they do when they're happy and relaxed," Cade said. "He probably knows you're a kindred spirit. You should be complimented. Elephants are very special. They're full of joy, laughter, and intelligence, and they have great memories. They live to be sixty or seventy years old and will remember things that happened to them when they were only calves, particularly things that are connected to food supply or a traumatic event with a member of the herd. You might need a little help to get on his back, but once you're there, you'll get along fine." He winked. "Unless the two of you run into a mouse. Then you might be in trouble."

"You're kidding."

Cade shook his head. "Elephants are sometimes scared of mice or other tiny creatures. There are stories about mice nibbling at their feet or crawling up their trunk, but I think it's because elephants have poor eyesight and seeing mice startles them. What do you think?"

"You're probably right," Michael said seriously. "If they're as smart as you say."

"They are. Are you ready to take a ride?"

Michael nodded. "If you're sure I won't hurt them. I

saw a baby elephant with the others, and I'd really worry about him."

"Kimbro? You'd be okay with him, too, but it takes time to make him comfortable with anyone. We'll let you ride Bansel, the big boy." He motioned to someone out of camera range. "Pauley, show Michael the rest of the animals and then bring him back. We haven't finished our discussion yet. I'm sure he'll want to know how some of the other animals came here. Be sure you let him feed Cubby, the tiger. I think Kirby is missing him. If Michael is going to stay around for a while, they'll become old friends. Is that okay with you, Michael?"

"That's great, Mr. Cade." Michael was smiling eagerly. "Maybe I could help Mr. Pauley while I'm here?"

"Cade, Michael. And I'm sure Pauley would be glad of your help. I'll talk to you later. Enjoy yourself." He cut the connection and glanced at Eve. "Okay?"

She nodded. "What kid wouldn't want to ride around that place on his own elephant? He'll feel like he owns the world. Thanks for indulging him, Cade."

He shook his head. "No indulgence about it. I could tell he's a great kid. He was more worried about wearing out the elephant than he was about enjoying himself. Let me know when he comes back, and I'll fill him in on the history of the rest of the animals." He looked at his watch. "And I might have time to cook breakfast for all of us before Pauley brings him back."

"Unless the elephant runs into a mouse?" Riley asked, straight-faced.

"Hey, I wouldn't steer him wrong," Cade said. "That would have been the mouse running up the elephant's trunk. He's obviously a bright kid. Michael and I came to a mutually logical conclusion." He headed for the kitchen. "You want to come along and help me cook breakfast, Joe? Providing you think Eve and Riley can get along without you. Though I have a hunch that we'll both be twiddling our thumbs before this reconstruction is finished. Or are we finished talking for the time being?"

"We might have a few things to still iron out." Joe strolled after him. "It might be the only way I'll be able to talk to my son today. You appear to have supplanted me."

"You'll live through it." Cade tilted his head consideringly. "Though I suppose I could let you borrow one of the elephants for a month or two when you go back to your lake cottage..."

Riley frowned as she watched them disappear into the kitchen. "What the hell was that all about?"

"I'm not sure," Eve said thoughtfully. "But I think it might have been a negotiation. Were Joe and Cade together when you found them?"

She nodded. "Coming out of the forest. Negotiation?"

"Cade has a staggering amount of money and power. Joe might be trying to persuade him into spreading a little of both to help us fight Madlock. Heaven knows, we need it."

"In return for what? Madlock is a huge threat and Cade is already committed to bringing down Dakar. That should keep him busy enough."

Eve shrugged. "That's up to Joe to negotiate. He's very clever. He should be able to think of something to make it worth Cade's while. I'm going to be too busy with your Helen to bother with it." She met Riley's eyes. "And so are you. I have to know everything about her and exactly how she responds and reacts. I want to know *her*, Riley. I want you to sit in there with me while I'm doing the initial work and tell me a few of the stories your mother told you about her when you were a child. Can you do that?"

Riley nodded. "Of course I can. It's not as if I could forget any of them. When do you want to start?"

"After breakfast. I don't know when I'll get a chance to be with Michael for a while, so I don't want to waste a moment. That's why it was important that Cade be there to make today special for him." Eve smiled gently. "I don't believe there's any doubt that Michael is going to remember that visit with Cade."

"I don't either," Riley said. "But with parents like you and Joe, I can't see him lacking in that special factor. You appear to do okay, Eve." She glanced after Cade and Joe. "And so does Joe if he's able to talk Cade into anything. From what Dan tells me, Cade has the reputation of making up his mind and generally not changing it."

"Unless he has a reason," Eve said. "I felt the same way when Joe's ex-wife, Diane, was trying to talk me into throwing my hat into the ring after she told me how her silver bullet could change the world as we know it. No way was I going to go along with it at first."

"You changed your mind?"

"I changed my mind. Because she had a wonderful dream and I couldn't resist trying to change the world, too. Neither could Joe." She shrugged. "We'll just have to see how long Cade can resist the temptation. I'd judge that a man who spends a good portion of his life rescuing animals might be a pushover."

"We'll see."

Eve nodded. "That we will, and probably sooner rather than later." She turned away. "Now I believe I'll run into the preservation room and take a look at the temperature controls. Tell me when Cade calls us for breakfast."

9:05 P.M.

Riley didn't leave Eve's main workroom until it was almost dark, and that was only because Eve and Joe were on a Skype call saying good night to Michael before he went to bed.

She was just as glad to have the moment to herself and drew a deep breath of the cold night air as she went outside.

"You look like you're escaping. Come over and have a cup of coffee." Cade was sitting in front of the crackling fire and looked up as he heard the door slam behind her. "I haven't seen you all day. Has Eve been keeping you busy?"

"No more than I wanted her to." She walked over to the fire and took the cup he handed her. "No busier than Eve was all day." She poured coffee from the pot warming near the flames. "It was just . . . different." She took a sip of the coffee. Then she frowned and looked down at the liquid in her cup. "Like this coffee you just gave me. Different. I don't think I've ever tasted anything like it." She tasted it again. "A combination of black coffee and very exotic spices. I can't even identify them."

"Sorry. I assure you that they're harmless. I didn't expect company, so I made a pot of a favorite Berber café of my childhood. It was one of the recipes that my father's cook, Ayla, always made for me. I was a spoiled kid from San Francisco, and I didn't like it at first. But he served it to me every day anyway. He said I should never accept the ordinary even if I hated the extraordinary. It took me almost a year to learn to like that particular brand of extraordinary. But now I'm addicted to it." He smiled. "Though I could go inside and make you a coffee that would probably appeal to a more normal palate."

"No, this is fine." She sat down on the ground beside him. "I'm used to extraordinary, but I never had a cook to prepare it. And rarely would spices be included in the recipe. It would more likely be berries and bugs or spiders."

"Ah, now you're trying to show me up by bringing up your witch doctor background." He shook his head. "We can't all belong to elite classes like that. What kind of bugs and spiders?"

"I tried not to identify them." She took another sip of coffee. "But this is nothing like them."

"Well, when I was in the marines, I did my share of scavenging when I was on a mission. Does that count?"

She nodded. "That counts." She lifted her cup to him in a toast. "That does count big time, Cade."

"Good. I always strive to be worthy of you. What were you doing with Eve today?"

"I think I was supposed to be telling her Helen stories that my mother told me when I was a little girl. It didn't work out that way. She became involved with examining the mummy itself."

"Really? Interesting?"

"Not for me. She wouldn't let me touch Helen. She was being super careful and making notes galore. She did let me make several notes for her myself. But mostly I ended up going through the treasure coffers and making lists and notes and taking photos of all the objects. I only managed to finish two coffers today. I'll do the other one tomorrow." She added wryly, "Unless Eve actually lets me help her with Helen."

"Eve's such a professional, it must be difficult for her to relinquish the responsibility," he said quietly. "You must have known that when you decided that she had to be the one to do the work."

"Of course I did. I expected it." She hesitated and then said in a rush, "I just didn't think it would be this hard to let go. Eleni has always been *mine*."

"And she always will be."

"No, she won't. She belongs to you now, too. And she'll belong to an entire world of other people when they find out about her. She's Helen, after all." Riley was looking into the fire. "And that's what should happen. She should be some-where safe where everyone will know how special she is."

"And they will when Eve shows them," he said gently. "And she *will* show them, because you brought her here to do it."

"That's right." She lifted her chin and smiled at him. "And we'll take care of Helen, won't we, Cade?"

"I wouldn't dare do anything else." His eyes narrowed on her face. "But I've told you that before. What's wrong?"

"Nothing. It's just that everything is different tonight." She added, "And Eve mentioned that Joe wanted you to help them with taking down Madlock."

"And you didn't want me distracted?"

"That's always been your choice. And I can see that you'd be drawn to a cause that would change the world." Her lips twisted. "When you're trying to single-handedly save the world's wildlife."

"Yes, I am, though I do have other agendas going on in my life." He frowned. "And I might decide to go along with Joe Quinn. But it wouldn't affect our arrangement, nor what else I might do. I'm going to do exactly what I promised you. How will I get you to believe me?"

"I believe you. I just watched you with Michael and the elephants this morning and I could see how absorbed you were with him and the animals. You were wonderful with him." She gave a mock sigh. "You have so many interests that I have to stand in line."

"Bullshit."

She threw back her head and laughed. "Right. And I was trying so hard to be humble and grateful. And all because I was feeling so depressed about Helen. Thank goodness that's over." She lifted her cup to her lips. "It might be this spiked coffee. Are you sure these are spices and not drugs that your cook was feeding you?"

"My father would have tossed him off the mountain," he said flatly. "He and my mother shared custody of me for the first few years after the divorce, and since my grandfather left all the family loot in trust to me, they were both very careful to make sure that they appeared to be model parents. But my mother remarried after six months and left me with my father."

"With the cook who wanted you to be extraordinary?" Riley asked. "How did that work out?"

"Pretty well. It turned out the cook had a big brother named Ridha who was a badass soldier and con man whom I got along with just fine. He was good with weapons, and he taught me a lot of things I used later in life. Though I think at one time he had plans to kidnap me and hold me for ransom."

"Charming."

"But he waited too long, and I already knew too much by the time he got around to it. I was able to take care of the problem."

"What was your father doing all that time?"

"He hung out a lot in the local casinos in Casablanca. Then one night he ended up dead in an alley, and I ended up with a bunch of banks fighting over custody."

"I'm sorry."

He gazed at her face and shook his head. "You really *are* sorry. Don't be. It was all about the money, Riley. No one gave a damn about me. I didn't find anyone who did for a long time. But I joined the marines before the bank could get their hands on my grandfather's money and that saved me. By the time I got out of the service, I'd learned to take care of myself, and I was on my way to independence."

"You were on your way to a lot more than that."

"There isn't much more than that from where I started. No one owned me and I could go my own way."

"And one of those ways led you toward those elephants you were talking to Michael about this morning."

He shrugged. "I ran into a band of poachers when I first came back to settle some business I had with the Berber estate. It made me sick to my stomach. It reminded me too much of how I'd felt being torn apart between everyone around me. Only those animals didn't have the chance I had to survive against those beasts." He smiled crookedly. "So I gave them one. And it felt so good, I kept on doing it. I started with the tigers, but it wasn't long until I began to track the elephant poachers. Somebody had to or they'd all be butchered. The money is too good, and it was too easy. Particularly with the elephants. Sometimes the poachers will kill up to a hundred a day."

"No." Riley shuddered. "That's terrible."

He nodded. "Dakar was very happy with his profits in Nigeria before we put a stop to them. We spent four days hunting him and his men down and rescuing what elephants we could. I'd promised Novak that it would only be a two-day job so that he'd give me his time and additional men to go after Dakar. It took a little longer, and I owed him."

"That was why you were willing to help me?"

"It wasn't as if he hadn't offered me a couple other attractive incentives," he explained. "But yes, I had to pay my debt."

"I understand."

"I thought you would." He made a face. "Which was one of the reasons I couldn't decide whether to tell you."

"Of course you should have told me. It wasn't as if I didn't know I was right." She went on to what was more important. "Dakar. Did you manage to save the elephants?"

"Most of them. It wasn't safe for them there, so I transported them to the London Wildlife Harbor. But we lost Kimbro's mother."

"That was the baby elephant Michael was talking about?" She was trying to remember everything Cade had said. "You didn't want Michael to ride him. You said he was . . . edgy."

"He saw his mother butchered by Dakar's men. The other elephants have been trying to help him to adjust, but he's not there yet."

"Adjust? What do you mean?"

"That may be a bridge too far for you." He hesitated, then said, "What the hell. It's a form of PTSD. Elephants do suffer from stress-related emotional traumas. So do military dogs and other animals who are under fire. Elephants are particularly sensitive and more likely to suffer from anything that happens within the family." He studied her expression. "You're not laughing."

"Why would I laugh? I didn't know that could happen, but I think it's sad. And I think you're kind to try to help that poor baby. Is he getting better?"

He nodded. "We make sure he's not isolated, and being with other elephants does help." He added, "And you're very accepting of the eccentricities of our four-footed friends."

"I might not be quite so tolerant of lions and tigers. But I wouldn't try to stalk or kill them." She tilted her head. "And I'm glad you explained to me why you're so angry with Dakar. I've been feeling as if you know everything about me, but maybe I understand you better now. Though you're not an easy person to read, Cade." She took a sip of her coffee. "Now I know about the extraordinary cook, and his brother, the soldier, and the elephants. It's not everything, but it's quite a bit."

"But I don't know everything about you," he said quietly. "We're both just learning." He leaned over and touched her cheek. "I'm looking forward to it." He rubbed his finger on the arch of her cheekbone. "Are you, Riley?"

She suddenly couldn't breathe. He had removed his finger, but she could still feel the lingering warmth of that touch on her skin. "I don't know. You make me feel..." She shook her head. "I don't know if we're looking for the same thing."

He studied her for an instant. Then he added ruefully, "Right now, I believe you're only looking for one thing and that's connected to your Eleni. I, on the other hand, am discovering all kinds of new sensations I wasn't expecting. I'd better back away until you catch up with me." He got to his feet. "So I think I'll say good night." He was suddenly smiling. "But in the interest of furthering a budding relationship, I believe we should each tell each other one thing we didn't know about each other. I'll go first. I've decided that I *will* help out Joe with bringing down Madlock because I've decided the asshole must have the instincts of a poacher to hang out with Dakar." He nodded at her. "Your turn."

"It's about Helen."

"Of course it is."

"Right before I came out here Eve told me that there would be no problem with doing the reconstruction on Helen's face. The neck bones were disconnected during the move either to or from the burial cave. She'll be able to mount the head to work on it separately from the skeleton."

"I'm surprised you didn't tell me that right away." He snapped his fingers. "That's right, you were a little depressed about losing Helen."

"But I got over it." She got to her feet. "I can't ever really lose her." She tapped her forehead. "She's right there. Good night, Cade."

"Good night." He was already on his way toward the cabin. "I'll see you in the morning. I believe we've taken a few interesting steps forward. Do drop in for another cup of coffee anytime."

She watched as the door shut behind him. More than a few interesting steps, she thought. Fascinating revelations from a fascinating man. And she didn't know where they would take her, where she wanted them to take her. For a few moments that touch had been both sensual and mesmerizing, and she had thought that perhaps...

But there was Helen and a dream that had been there since she was a small girl. Cade was right, she couldn't let it go; it was still with her.

So stop thinking of Cade and that brief sensual moment. Concentrate on helping Eve and then taking Helen to her new home. They were moving forward now and with any luck she was leaving Dakar and his threats behind. Go to bed and rest so that she would be ready to do even better in the morning. Now was not the time to step out of the magic circle when everything was going so well...

———◆———

3:15 A.M.

Riley's phone was ringing...

She reached out drowsily in the darkness to check the ID.

Dan, of course. It wasn't the first time he'd called her in the middle of the night, when he was drunk or just wanted praise for a successful ending to a difficult project. And it could be either, since one almost invariably followed the other. She punched the access. "It couldn't wait until the morning?"

"It *is* morning," Dan said. "And no, it couldn't wait. Dakar is getting impatient. I got a call tonight from Jim Bosworth, a buddy in Lahar, who wanted to see me. He sounded scared and said he was on the run." He swallowed. "I met him at the edge of town, and he was in bad shape. He'd been beaten up by Dakar's men, but he'd escaped. He said Dakar had wanted to set a trap for me. Which really meant a trap for you, Riley." He added mockingly, "Important though I may be in some quarters, I'm nothing to Dakar. While you've managed to piss him off in grand fashion."

"How much does Dakar know?" She was sitting up straight in bed now. "Could Bosworth tell you anything?"

"No hint that Dakar knew anything about the sarcophagus. My guess is that he was upset that Cade offed his sniper who shot Spencel. Evidently he just wanted to get his hands on you and thought Bosworth could help." He paused. "But he was also frustrated as hell that he couldn't give him any information. Bosworth is only my drinking buddy, so a trap was his only option." He hesitated. "But Dakar wasn't shy about talking in front of Bosworth. He probably figured he wouldn't live to tell anyone. Bosworth said that he mentioned to one of his men that he was going to talk to Washington and see if he couldn't get the big man to send him a few experts right away to help track you down."

"That's not good." It had to be Adam Madlock he was talking about, and that also meant tracking Eve down. "Anything else?"

"Isn't that enough?" Dan asked sarcastically. "It is for me. Because it means that I've got to find a way to get Bosworth out of Azerbaijan right away before Dakar's men find him. He did his best to keep me alive, so I guess I owe him."

"I'd say you do." She was thinking quickly. "Call Kirby. That's his area of expertise. Tell him Cade wants him out of here."

"I certainly will. Nice to have friends in high places. I'll let you know if I run into trouble." He was silent a moment. "We did fantastic work the other day, didn't we? It's good to know that asshole didn't get his hands on your Helen."

"Yet. The ice is very thin right now."

"But you have Cade." He added slyly, "And me. What could be better?" He cut the call.

She put her phone back on the nightstand, but she didn't lie back down. She was trembling. She went to the bathroom and washed her face and drank a glass of water before she went back to bed.

He's going to call Washington to get the big man to send him experts right away to track me down.

What was that supposed to mean? What experts? And how much time would she have before they closed in on her? She felt like prey being hunted. But one thing was certain: They had to finish the reconstruction ASAP and get Helen away from here. Because no matter how much time they were being allowed, it wouldn't be enough. Dakar was impatient, and *right away* meant exactly that as far as he was concerned. He would be even more impatient now that he had lost Bosworth.

She could probably expect—

The phone was ringing.

Oh, shit! Blocked call. No way could this be Dan again. But she did have an idea who it was.

She drew a deep breath and then answered the call. "Riley Smith."

"You know who this is, don't you?" Dakar said harshly. "I'm sure that bastard Dan Smith must have contacted you and bragged how he managed to save both himself and you."

"I know who it is, Dakar." She pressed the RECORD button as she added recklessly, "And Dan shouldn't really have bragged about it. It's no real accomplishment. You've failed too many times."

"I killed your father, bitch," he hissed.

She flinched. "Yes, you did. You and your men hunted him

down and killed him. Proud of yourself? But he still kept you from getting hold of me. So you lost out there, too."

"It's the last time I'll lose, Riley. That's why I'm calling—to let you know that you didn't really win anything." His voice was grating with rage. "I *want* that treasure. Did you think that because you brought in that son of a bitch Morgan Cade, he'd be able to protect you? He doesn't care anything about you. He just wants the treasure, too."

"Does he? Why? He doesn't need it. I think he'd rather eliminate you any way he can. That's the only reason he asked to be my partner. He was very angry with the way you killed those elephants. You're a monster."

"He told you about that? Good. I'll make it my business to go after another herd once I get the money from that treasure you're going to give me."

"You're not going to get any treasure."

"Oh, but I am. Very soon. You're not the only one who brought in the big guns. I made a deal that will give me everything I need to grab not only the treasure but even that sarcophagus your father mentioned in his notes." He laughed. "And you gave it to me. Without Eve Duncan I wouldn't have been able to do it. I might not have been able to cinch the deal with the big man. But you persuaded her to come with you. She's a prize that will take me all the way." His voice became venomous. "And then I'll come after you and your dear uncle Dan and that Cade, son of a bitch. I'll get all of you."

"The hell you will," she said fiercely.

"And you might not even see it coming. When you least expect it, I'll be there." He laughed. "Because I've got that ace in the hole and you won't be able to stop me."

He cut the connection.

She was shaking. She had tried to ignore the sheer ugliness of his words, but she'd found it impossible. She could only hope that he hadn't realized how afraid she'd been of those threats. It hadn't only been her that he'd hurled them at. Everyone in contact with her had been targeted.

Forget it. And try to forget Dakar for the time being. But that wasn't going to happen anytime soon. She needed to get away from this room and get some air...She grabbed her jacket, slipped on her shoes, moved out of her room, and glided toward the front door.

Then she was outside and leaning against the wall, gazing up at the stars. The campfire was out, but she preferred the darkness right now. It was clean and silent. There was no ugly voice spitting venom at her. But she had to remember some of that venom: There had been an important message in his words. She slid down the wall, leaned back, and linked her arms around her knees, her gaze on the stars.

Screw you, Dakar. You don't know anything. We're going to be fine...

"Are you okay?"

She jumped, her gaze flying to Cade standing in the doorway a few yards away. "Of course I am. I just wanted to get some air. What are you doing up?"

"I got a call from Garcia, one of the guards, he caught a glimpse of you when he was doing his rounds. He thought I should know that you were either up to something or might be having trouble."

"No trouble. As I said, I needed air." She added, "But are all your guards that suspicious? They must know I work with you and aren't likely to 'be up to something.'"

"If they weren't sharp *and* suspicious, they wouldn't work

for me. I do the final interview myself, and I'm far more suspicious than they are." He strolled toward her. "Bribery and corruption are rife when you go after the scumbags I do. There's always a Dakar ready to pour money in the pockets of one of my men if they're willing to betray me." He sat down beside her. "And you have to admit this hour of a bitter-cold night isn't the usual time you'd want to go for a walk." He leaned back his head against the building, his gaze on the night sky. "Are you going to tell me why you're really out here?"

"I'd prefer not to." She made a wry face. "But heaven forbid you think that I'm going to double-cross you. You'll probably hear about it soon from Kirby anyway." She reached in her pocket, pulled out her phone, and handed it to him. "I recorded the last call." She got to her feet. "But I have no intention of sitting here and listening to it again. So since you've spoiled my quiet time out here, I think I'll go back into the kitchen and make myself a cup of decent black coffee that's not at all extraordinary and has nothing to do with you or Dakar. Drop my phone off when you decide to go to bed." She turned on her heel and went into the cabin.

———◆———

Riley had finished drinking a second cup of coffee by the time Cade came into kitchen. He handed her the phone. "Nasty. Did it upset you?"

"Hell, yes." She slipped the phone into her pocket. "But I didn't let him see it."

"How did he get your number? There's a chance he could trace you here."

"No, there isn't. Do you think I didn't think of that? I knew someone would eventually get my contacts. After my father was killed, I had Dan take my phone to one of his IT buddies and modify it. He did an excellent job. Dakar would have to bounce over half a dozen countries before he even got close to tracing any call."

"My apologies. I should have known."

"But it didn't stop me from being upset. I couldn't go back to sleep. It brought back that day when he killed my father." Her lips tightened. "And Hajif and what he ordered done to those villagers. I knew he just wanted to frighten me, but it didn't make any difference. I could see him reaching out and killing everyone I knew and cared about." She took another sip of coffee. "I won't let him do it. He's not going to get anything he wants."

"No, he won't," Cade said grimly as he sat down and poured himself a cup of coffee. "Not that he was before, but now he sure as hell isn't going to ever worry you again. I'll cut the bastard's throat before I let you go up against him."

"No, you won't." She looked him in the eye. "It's my fight, and it always has been. I tried to tell you that before. He killed my father, but now he wants to take Helen away from me, too. That's not going to happen. You probably have a very good reason to go after Dakar, and I might let you help. But don't try to take over."

He smiled and shook his head. "I totally disagree. We'll argue about details later." He paused and his smile faded. "Because that phone call made me very angry. You gave as good as you got, but it made me almost as enraged as I was when I saw Dakar going after those elephants. I'm not going to let him touch you."

She looked at him incredulously. "Listen to you. Did you just compare me to an elephant?"

"Only the concept. But I like elephants. You should be complimented." He took a swallow of coffee. "I phoned Kirby after I finished listening to the call and told him to give Dan anything he needed for his friend. I think we'd better bring Dan out here to the cabin. Dakar is obviously targeting him."

"I was thinking about that," Riley said slowly. "But Dan is a unique character in his own right, and you won't be able to control him like you do your men."

"I'll handle him." He leaned back, studying her. "What else were you thinking about out there?"

"How clear the stars seemed," she replied. "And that Dakar said that I'd given him the way to take everything he wanted by bringing Eve here. It was scaring me because I was afraid he might be right, and I knew I had to fix it."

He went still. "And how are you going to do that?"

"The same way that you intend to do it. You decided to help Joe Quinn stop Adam Madlock. I didn't want to do that. I thought it would get in the way of what I needed to do with Helen. But if Dakar thinks he can call the shots with Madlock and get him to go after whoever he chooses, then I don't have a choice. I have to take Madlock down or risk Dakar destroying everyone and everything that I want to keep alive and well." She looked him in the eye. "I can't let that happen. Because Madlock is going to be the key, isn't he?"

Cade muttered a curse. "That's just the conclusion I didn't want you to reach."

"Isn't he?" Riley repeated. "You were really casual when you said you were going to help out Joe. But you'd already taken the situation apart and come up with the target you needed to destroy if you were going to accomplish your mission. You just didn't want me to realize what you were doing."

He was silent.

She shrugged. "You don't have to answer. I would have figured it out anyway if I hadn't so desperately wanted everything to be fast and simple where Helen was concerned. I tried not to even think about Eve's problem with Madlock. Dakar just made it all come together."

"Son of a bitch!" He added roughly, "Of course Madlock was the target. You always pick the most powerful figure to take out and then you hope the rest of the resistance falls apart."

"Just what you would have done in the military," she explained. "And you're probably making plans how you'll take down Dakar and not rely on hope to carry the day."

"I hadn't gotten that far yet. We've been a little occupied."

"Then you'd better get busy. Because it's clear Dakar is going to do everything he can to bring Madlock into the mix to help him get what he wants. Maybe it's already in the works. You heard how frustrated he sounded."

"That might not be all bad," Cade said. "I might be able to work with it."

Riley's hand tightened on her cup. "It doesn't sound good to me. But it's what I might expect of you. I won't ask what you intend to do. I'll be very busy helping Eve for the time being." She added slowly, precisely, "And I only have one thing to insist you promise me. I told you once that you couldn't leave me out of anything. You said it wouldn't happen. Was that bullshit?"

"No." He hesitated. "I admit I hoped to work around it. But you can't say that you haven't been involved in everything from playing with poisonous snakes to chasing down snipers. And you were the one who dragged me into that bat cave."

She made an impatient gesture. "That's all in the past. This is a new page," she said grimly. "And it's a page that has me front and center and that's how it has to remain. Dakar has seen to that. I won't be shoved aside when I have a responsibility to keep the people I care about alive. I don't have all your skills, but I'm intelligent and I have experience in forests and jungles, and I have contacts you might not have. You consult with me and give me the chance to do my part. All the way, Cade. Otherwise I'll close you out."

He didn't speak for a moment. "If you agree to listen to me. No one-way streets."

She nodded. "I'm not a fool." She tilted her head. "But I want to know what your first move will be."

"Talking to Joe and Eve and getting an idea exactly what they know about Madlock and that miracle formula he's trying to steal. Then I'll spread the net a little wider and gather more information. I might have to be patient. I can't promise anything. Whatever it takes, I'll do it." He finished his coffee and then got to his feet. "Don't worry, you'll have time to do your duty with Eve while I'm hunting and gathering. If I run across anything interesting, I'll stop and bring you into the picture."

"You'd better."

"I promised, didn't I?" He turned to leave and then stopped and said over his shoulder, "But it's not going to be easy for me. I'm feeling incredibly protective of you after I listened to that asshole Dakar. It's not that I don't believe you can take care of yourself. I know you can. And it's not because you're my partner and it's part of the deal." He smiled crookedly.

"Because of the way I was raised, in the end I've always thought everyone should be responsible for their own self-preservation. I don't know what it is. It's just *there*, dammit." He strode out of the kitchen.

She didn't really know what Cade was talking about and she was too weary to think about it now. He was too complicated and maybe he didn't know himself as well as he thought. Time to go to bed and get a few hours' sleep before it was time to get up. All she should care about now was that Cade had agreed to do what she wanted...

CHAPTER

12

No trace," Zangar said as he entered Dakar's library. "Sorry. We did everything we could. We would have needed a Pentagon cyber wizard to track it."

Dakar muttered a curse. "And now the bitch will think I've failed again." He scowled. "I should have been able to reel her in. I was hoping I wouldn't have to tell Madlock that I still have no idea where in hell he can find Eve Duncan." He reached for his phone. "Well, you want a cyber wizard? He can just get me one. What good is all that fucking power he's supposed to have if he can't get me what I need?" He dialed Madlock's private number. He started to speak as soon as Madlock picked up. "I thought I'd have Riley Smith wrapped up so that you could use her as a bargaining card to get Duncan, but there's been a small problem. I might need one of your tech people to fly over and help with—"

"You screwed up? First, you lose me Wilson, and now you've made another mistake."

"I didn't say that. I just didn't want to keep you waiting

until I worked out the problem. We agreed that we should do everything possible to get the job done fast."

Madlock was silent. Then he said, "Yes, we did. I've been thinking about it. I haven't been fair." His voice was suddenly smooth and even persuasive. "Naturally you deserve my full support. You'll get it. Not only will I send you whatever manpower you need, but I'll be on hand to supervise them."

Dakar stiffened. "What?"

"I've been making arrangements to fly over there so that you can deliver Duncan to me personally."

"You're joking? You're the fucking president of the United States. You can't do that without causing a media stir."

"I can do anything I want. I'll just take a rest week at Camp David and have my staff cover for me. I've already arranged for a yacht to pick me up at Istanbul. No one will know I'm on board, and I'll be available to get my business taken care of when you finally do manage to give me Duncan." He added caustically, "Whenever that may be."

"All I need is that tech help I asked you for. I don't really want you here."

"But you're going to have me. We're going to be close as brothers. I'll contact you when I reach Istanbul." He cut the connection.

Dakar was frowning as he put his phone away. "I don't like this. But this time he was agreeing with me and telling me that he'd get me anything I needed. It made me nervous." He paused. "And he's coming here so that he can get on-site reports."

Zangar gave a low whistle. "I wouldn't like that, either. What are you going to do?"

"It's what you're going to do. I'll take all the help that he'll give me. Then you're going to find Riley Smith and Cade and grab that treasure while I stall Madlock by dangling Duncan in front of him." He met Zangar's eyes. "Any problems?"

"Not as long as you're the one dealing with Madlock. You know I won't say no to you. Though I might want a bonus to keep me happy."

"You'll get it." He was beginning to feel better by the second. All that power Madlock wielded had made him think twice, but he'd find a way to get around it. "Now get out of here and start making lists. I'm not going to be caught being made a fool of again. I need to know all the contacts, equipment, and cyber teams we're going to need to locate Riley Smith and Morgan Cade."

SPRUCE CABIN
8:05 A.M.

Riley was just finishing her breakfast cereal when Eve came into the kitchen the next morning. "Do you need me?" she asked. "Can I make you breakfast?"

Eve shook her head. "Joe and I have been up for hours. I just came to have a cup of coffee with you before we get to work." She sat down opposite Riley, cradling her cup in her two hands. "There were a couple of things I wanted to discuss. I would have woken you when Cade came pounding on our door a few hours ago, but he persuaded us that you needed your sleep." She wrinkled her nose. "And after he told us about Dakar's call, I thought maybe he was right."

"Cade shouldn't have woken you," Riley said. "It wasn't as

if there was any urgency. There wasn't anything you could do about it. It was just threats."

"Cade thought it was also Dakar trying to locate you. He was probably right. Dakar was being especially vicious and obnoxious. He must have been trying to keep you on the phone until he could trace the call."

"It didn't do him any good. We were prepared."

"But what about next time? Technology advances whenever you blink your eyes."

She grinned. "Then I'd better get Dan to find a way to keep me from blinking."

"I think Cade is already working on it," Eve said. "I just wanted to warn you. I know you're going to be tempted to talk to Dakar if he calls you again."

"Yes, I will. I won't be able to help it. So you'd better work very fast to finish Helen and save me from myself." She added, "But I don't believe that Cade only told you about Dakar's call. He said he was going to ask you and Joe questions about Madlock."

"And he did. By the time he finished questioning us, he knew practically everything we did about Madlock." She hesitated. "And a few things that you should also know. I told you that the reason he might want to get his hands on me was that I worked with Diane Connors, the creator of the formula, when she asked me to do a reconstruction on the face of a murdered man to determine identity."

"That wasn't the truth?"

"It was the truth . . . as far as Madlock knew. But I was always afraid he might discover that there was another reason why I mustn't ever be taken prisoner by him."

"And what was that?"

"Diane had done some additional work on both Joe and me when Joe was wounded. It was the only way to save Joe's life." She shrugged. "But we don't want the results known, and I decided that I'd probably be the target if Madlock got suspicious since I was the one who was working with Diane. Needless to say, I don't want to be put on an operating table and examined if Madlock says the word."

"My God," Riley murmured. "Why did you even agree to come and do the reconstruction?"

"Because I wasn't going to hide in a hole and not be with my family. Besides, we can't let Madlock get away with cheating the world. We have to find a way to get rid of him." She smiled crookedly. "Cade said that you'd both be willing to help us do that, and we thank you. But I'd appreciate you keeping me away from Madlock if at all possible."

"I promise he'll never get his hands on you," Riley said fiercely. "I realize this is my responsibility. I'll do anything I can to stop him from finding you."

"That's all I ask. And you can't take full responsibility. Our problems with Madlock started long before I even set eyes on you." Eve finished her coffee. "And now I have a few questions about Helen that I've been waiting to ask you since I did a little more examination on her this morning." She pushed back her chair. "Let's go back to the preservation room and take a look at her."

Riley jumped to her feet and followed her. "You didn't ask me very much before. You seemed to want to find out everything for yourself."

"That's how I usually have to work. But a mummy is a bit unusual." She looked over her shoulder. "Particularly this particular mummy. I'm not sure what to expect and, since you're familiar with Helen and you've studied her past with her lover and Charon after she arrived in these hills, I was wondering if you could explain a few oddities I'd noticed. It might help me do the facial reconstruction." They were in the preservation room now and Eve was accessing the top of the sarcophagus to reach the linen-wrapped face. "I carefully examined the nose area this morning and I realized she might be ... different."

"Different?"

"And where are the canopic jars?" Eve asked. "There weren't any canopic jars in that burial chamber to store the body's organs as there usually are with Egyptian burials. Just the treasure chests and that magnificent sarcophagus."

"But she wasn't Egyptian," Riley pointed out. "On Charon's tablets he mentioned that he had accompanied her to many foreign countries and Egypt was one of them in the later years. But he also mentioned that she didn't approve of the way the Egyptians treated their dead. She thought it was disrespectful. It doesn't surprise me that she borrowed some of their customs and ignored others." She smiled. "Helen was very vain. She'd been a raving beauty all her life. She probably told Charon exactly how she wanted to be seen, even in death. And he was so much in love with her, I can see him agreeing with everything she said and to hell with burial custom or even the gods themselves."

Eve nodded slowly. "Then that might explain the nose." She spread the linen with ultimate care to reveal the skeletal facial structure. "Because there should be a cut here on the side of the nose where they put a hook. See? It was there on the other reconstructions I did at the museum in Herculaneum."

Riley reluctantly leaned forward to look down at Helen's skeletal face. *Sorry. You know you're always beautiful to me.*

She quickly looked away. "You're right. No cut and it's always done to draw the brain through the nose to get rid of it. Egyptians didn't think much of the human brain. The only organ they left in the body was the heart, because they thought all things good about a person came from the heart."

"Sometimes they were right," Eve said absently. "But if Helen wanted her brain left in her body, she would have had to make some kind of dehydration arrangement. Probably filling it with dry sand and salt. I'll have to be super careful when I start working with it. I wonder if she was that picky about her other organs?"

"My guess is yes," Riley said. "I think you'll find natron salt packets inside every orifice."

"Well, I won't have to deal with them immediately," Eve said. "I'll wait until Cade arranges to move the sarcophagus out of this area to a more permanent home before I deal with anything more than the facial reconstruction."

"That will be quite enough," Riley said dryly. "I've been waiting a good portion of my life for you to do that."

"Pressure. Pressure," Eve said. "But I admit I'm getting excited about working on her. I've never run across a subject who was quite this...colorful. She appeared to live life to suit herself."

"She had no real choice. And she could be kind." She tilted her head. "You'll see that when you start sculpting her."

"Will I?" Eve was studying her. "I usually let the subject dictate my work, and maybe you're right. But I haven't forgotten that I asked you to repeat those stories your mother used to tell you. I believe it's time you began."

"I'm at your disposal. Now?"

Eve nodded. "As soon as I get the skull set to put on the mount."

"Do you need help?"

Eve laughed. "No, I'll do it myself. I saw how you were flinching when you were examining your Helen. It bothered you. Unusual when you've obviously seen so much mummification. I won't even make you look while I'm doing the initial repairs on the skull."

She made a face. "Caught. But I'm not usually squeamish."

"I know. But everything about this particular mummy is different for you." She made a shooing motion with her hand. "Go away. I'll call you when I'm ready for you."

Riley was still smiling as she left the room and headed for the porch.

"I'm supposed to report to you," Dan said as he came toward her. "I tried to tell Cade that's not how our relationship works, but he wasn't having it."

"I wasn't expecting you up here so soon. How's Bosworth?"

"Okay. I turned him over to Kirby and they shipped him out to London. I like London. I wouldn't have minded hitching a ride. But evidently, I'm too important here to waste my time anywhere but on this mountaintop. Cade said that I was to stay here and keep an eye on you."

"And where is Cade?"

"Probably in Turkey by now. He said he was going hunting. He didn't like that call Dakar made to you. He's going down the list on the contacts he took from the phone of that sniper, Wilson. He's trying to see if he can use one of them to help blow Dakar out of the water. He said to tell you he'd be in touch."

"How nice of him." At least he'd left a message. And she

was going to be so busy she had no time to worry about what he was doing at present. "If I'm not too swamped, I might answer him."

"Do I detect a bit of edginess?"

"Not in the least. We understand each other." She added, "And I don't need you to keep an eye on me. I'll probably have to be watching you."

"That's what I told Cade. He'll get the picture once he gets to know us better. How is Eve's sculpting coming along?"

"I'll find out if I can get back to her and get to work." She smiled. "Take care of yourself, Dan, and don't get involved in any card games with the guards that I'll have to bribe your way out of."

"I'm turning over a new leaf," he said solemnly. "I'm considering going into hunting poachers with Cade. I figure it might be good for my résumé. I might broach it to him when he comes back."

"Heaven help us."

"It never has yet." He turned to go. "We'll see how it works out."

❖

KOLYA ESTATE
LOZAR, TURKEY
10 P.M.

"It's a damn armed camp," Kirby said as he slid down into the gully where Cade was located. "The main building is a bloody palace and there are women's quarters in the adjacent house that resemble a bordello. Evidently Szyman likes to live large on all levels. There's even a very sizable marijuana field for his convenience. Also a poppy field, though I don't believe it's large enough for him to use it for dealing with clients."

"But you verified he does deal? Mafia?"

Kirby nodded. "From what I found out while we were driving down here, he's a big player. Turkey is heavy into drug trafficking of all kinds. With an estate like this, he must pay a fortune to the government in bribes to keep them from investigating what's going on too closely."

"Which we might use. Anything else?"

"Two yachts in the boathouse."

"Names?"

"Does it matter?"

"It might if I wanted to identify a specific boat."

"The more impressive one is called the *Last Word*. The smaller one is *Liberty*. Satisfied? Can we leave now?"

"No, I want to take a look for myself. I'll see you back at the car."

"That's not your job. I'll go with you."

"No, you won't. I don't know what I'm looking for. I'll see you later." He smiled when he heard Kirby swear as he took off through the brush. Kirby always had his back, but he'd been on his own too long not to want to block everyone out when he needed to concentrate on making the kill.

And it would be a kill, he thought wearily. He'd try to avoid it, but when there was a man like Madlock who wanted to own the world, there was only one way to stop him. Maybe not tonight, but it would come. Kill or be killed. He'd had a hunch when he'd first taken that phone from Wilson's body and scanned some of the addresses. But it wouldn't be an easy kill and he had to be prepared. Kirby had given him everything he could, but the rest would be all instinct and it could only come from him. Go over the grounds, check the guards, even the women, then go down to the boathouse...

———————◆———————

"You were gone long enough," Kirby said when Cade got into the passenger seat. "Did you see anything that I didn't?"

"Maybe. I might not know until later. But I'll remember everything I saw. I'll draw a diagram when we get back to the cabin. Let's get going."

Kirby started the car. "Why did we even come? I would have thought you'd want to go to Dakar's stronghold in Lahar instead. What do you care about Dakar's mafia buddy?"

"Not a damn. But Dan Smith is already familiar with Dakar's location, and we can always tap him for information. I wanted to check out this one first. If this is a Dakar–Madlock operation, it will shape up to be a two-headed monster. I have to know which one has the most power. You'll recall when we were tracking Dakar down in Nairobi, your research indicated that Dakar never liked to share the spoils of his jobs with anyone. Why would he have changed when he moved to Azerbaijan? Particularly with a big mafia player like Szyman?"

"You tell me."

"Because he didn't change. All the personal contacts in the phone were Wilson's." He smiled crookedly. "Including one for a condo in a nice area of Washington, DC, that was quite close and convenient to the White House." He added, "And several other numbers in Virginia and New York. Not exactly Dakar's stomping grounds. If I had to guess, it would be that Wilson was paid by Madlock and on loan to Dakar. Which brings up the question of why he had Szyman's contact. What were his instructions regarding our mafia king? Don't you find it interesting?"

"You could be wrong."

He nodded. "That's why I asked Joe Quinn to verify Wilson's background and anything else he could dig up on him. As well as what he could find out about Szyman. I thought if we could find a common thread, it might clear up any confusion. But I couldn't wait, so I started to access a few of our own contacts myself about Szyman." He handed Kirby a photo on his phone of a fiftyish, dark-haired man with an aquiline nose, dressed in elegant sports attire. "That's him. You're right, he's into drugs and gambling on the Riviera as well as Turkey and occasionally Vegas, but he's reputed to be very smart and discreet when dealing with his more influential clients." He paused. "For instance, though he and Madlock have traveled in similar circles for years, there's never been even a hint of any association between them unless you go looking for it."

Kirby gave a low whistle. "And you told them to go look for it."

"When you consider what a dirtbag Madlock is, I thought he'd probably have wanted to use someone like Szyman at some point. And it seemed a little too convenient that Szyman had a place in Turkey within shouting distance of the Azerbaijan border. It took us no time to get down here. Wilson was probably setting up his own private outpost to keep an eye on Dakar in case Madlock decided to discard him and wanted to use his old friend Szyman instead."

"You could have asked me to check it out. You didn't have to do it yourself."

"I've been keeping you busy since we got here. I had more time than you did."

"That's never stopped you before. Don't do it again. I don't want you messing with my contacts."

Cade grinned. "Yes, Mr. Kirby, sir. I'll keep that in mind. So if you're that eager, you could get Dan Smith to tap any of his local buddies for any other info that might help."

"He'd take it better from you."

"And you evidently want to pick and choose. I'll think about it. But then I'd owe him, and that would be a mistake for me. He might use Riley for payback. That could be difficult. I'd either get angry, or I'd end up paying way too much for the information."

"Aren't you overthinking this?"

"Probably. So don't you do it. Just put several men on this property to tell us everything that's happening. I want to particularly know about any movement on those yachts." He leaned back in the seat. "Because I believe that the results might be very profitable."

SPRUCE CABIN

"What's wrong, Riley?" Eve's voice was abstracted, and she didn't look away from the reconstruction she was repairing. "You've been sitting there quiet as a mouse for the past half hour. Don't tell me you've run out of Helen stories?"

"No, I just didn't want to bore you. I wasn't sure you were listening."

"I was listening. It helped distract me from the measuring

I had to do. It's the most boring part of doing the re-constructions. Possibly also the most important because the measurements have to be absolutely accurate, but I've done so many of them that it's almost automatic." She glanced over her shoulder at Riley. "And it let me wonder about your mother who told her little girl all those stories of a queen who lived so long ago. It was almost like telling you fairy tales, but it wasn't really like that, was it?"

"No, because my mother made sure I knew that Helen was no fairy tale. My mother was a brilliant woman, but she wouldn't have wasted her time on telling a kid a fairy tale. She thought that it was perfectly acceptable to tell me about a part of her life that she lived every day. Helen was *real* to her, and she made sure she was real to me, too. She took stories about her from some of the great-est poets and writers of their day. Some of them were bullshit, but that was okay to her because they were true literature."

"So you ended up picking and choosing?"

She nodded. "And since I was also sometimes dreaming about her, the stories might have become a bit mixed up."

"But you don't think so?"

"No, I believe I kept them pretty much in order. She was important to me, the center of my life, just as she was to my mother and father."

"Well, they're all wonderful stories," Eve said gently. "You're making me see her as you see her."

"I'm glad. In spite of being such a star in her particular firmament, she was lonely sometimes. She liked to have people around her. Though she was never quite sure who she could trust." She smiled. "But she can trust you, Eve."

"Yes, she can." Eve turned back to the reconstruction. "But only if I stop asking questions and get back to work."

"But it's going well?" Riley asked. "You're making progress?"

"I'm making progress," Eve repeated. "I've finished the repairs and the measurements. It's almost time to begin the actual sculpting."

Riley sat up straight in her chair. "Exciting."

"Yes, it is. But you've got to remember to do your part. You've got to weave her story around me until I know her every bit as well as you do. No more sitting silent again, afraid to offend me. Before this is over, I want Helen to belong to both of us."

Riley shook her head. "She'll only belong to herself."

"Unless she chooses to let us come in and visit her occasionally. Sometimes that happens. Why don't you tell me that story about Helen when she was only a young girl and yet could beat all the boys in her city-state at sports. I like that one."

"So do I. She was happy then; life was simpler for her." She leaned back in her chair. "She was beautiful then, too. Though she wore her hair shorter, like all the other young girls of her age. She didn't mind. She said it made her feel more like one of the young men when she was running and competing against them..."

———◆———

It was after midnight and Riley had already gone to her room for the night and had just taken her shower when Cade knocked. "Open up," he called. "I've got good news."

She threw open the door. "From that town in Turkey? That was where Dan said you'd gone."

He shook his head. "No, that was just prep work. More later about that. But on the way here I got a call from Hajif's doctor, and he said that he'd regained consciousness. He's on his way back."

"He is? That's wonderful." She hugged him. "Isn't that great?" She stepped back. "I can't wait to tell Eve. This seems to be the day for good news."

"Does it? It must be. Because you're glowing." He reached out and gently touched her lower lip. "You look like warm satin. What other good news did you get today?"

Heat. Electricity. Her heart was pounding...Such a small touch to cause this sensation.

"What news?" he repeated.

She shook her head to clear it. "Nothing world shaking like the news about Hajif. It was just a good workday for Eve and me. She's almost ready to start the sculpting." She added, "And she made me feel as if I really helped."

"Of course you did. Just having you there must have made everything more clear. She must know you're rooting for her." His hand moved from her lip to the hollow of her cheekbone. "And she probably saw the glow, too."

She should step back. That touch was causing her entire body to tense, open to him, her breasts to swell. But she didn't move. "No glow." She moistened her lips. "I just got out of the shower."

"I can tell. Your skin feels clean and warm, and you smell of soap and shampoo." His hand moved down to the hollow of her throat. "And your pulse is beating harder and harder with every breath. Do you know how much I want to make it beat even harder?" He bent down and his tongue licked delicately. "Ah, there, I can feel it pounding.

It's very welcoming. I want to be inside you, Riley. Will you take me?"

She *wanted* him inside her. She could feel the muscles of her stomach clench. If she wanted him this much now, how would she feel if they went to bed together? "It would be a mistake. I'm sorry, I'm not that sophisticated. I can't balance casual sex with business. We're nothing alike. We don't want the same things. That's not why I opened the door tonight, Cade."

He went still. "No, you opened the door because it had been a good day and I promised to make it better." He took a step back. "However, it wouldn't be a mistake. I promise you. And how the hell do you know whether or not we want the same things? That's a question of discovery. But I won't take advantage of the moment." He turned to leave. "I'm not a fool. You want it as much as I do. You just don't want to get involved in a relationship when all you can think about is getting Helen finished and out of here. That's the second time; the next time I won't back off. We'll have a discussion. No pressure, but there will be persuasion." His smiled was reckless. "But if you change your mind, I'm right down the hall. You'll have to come to me, but I'll make it worth your while."

He was striding down the hall. "Until then you should remember that I'll take advantage of any weak moment to get what we both want. Be prepared." His door slammed behind him.

Riley stared at that door for an instant and then whirled back into her room and shut the door. She'd been tempted to follow him down the hall but that would have been as foolish as all her other actions tonight. She'd been clumsy and no doubt he thought her as unsophisticated as she'd told him. It would have been far more difficult to let him see that she might become too involved than she was now if she became closer to him. That would have been worse than having him believe she was immature.

But dear heaven her body was aching with pure sexual need, and she knew she wasn't going to be able to sleep for a long time tonight.

———◆———

She stayed in her room until she heard Cade's door open the next morning. Then she was hurrying after him. She caught up with him by the time he reached his car. "Could I speak to you?"

He turned to face her. "By all means," he said ironically. "I can hardly wait."

"I just wanted to tell you that if you don't want to continue with our arrangement, it's all right with me. You've done your best to help, and I'll still share the treasure. It's not your fault that you misunderstood the terms."

He stared at her incredulously. "I didn't misunderstand. They just changed as we went along, and they're still changing." He added, "And there's no way I'll walk away from you until this is over. Maybe not then. The situation is too promising on several levels. I meant every word I said last night." His gaze was fixed on her face. "And I'm betting that you didn't. You look tired, didn't sleep well? Neither did I. We should really take care of that problem." He got into the car. "But we both have work to do today. You're dealing with Eve, and I'm going on a road trip with your uncle Dan. We'll talk about it later."

"No, we won't. I've said what I came to say," Riley said. "If you change your mind, let me know. I can get along by myself. Eve is getting closer and closer to finishing the reconstruction."

"And you don't need me?" He was backing out of the driveway. "I guess I'll just have to change your mind. People say it's one of my talents." He stopped the car as Dan ran out of the forest, waved at Riley, and jumped into the passenger seat. Then Cade called back to her, "I'll check later and see what progress you've made today."

She watched him drive away. The conversation had been a total failure on her part, and she should probably feel frustrated. The reason she didn't had to be mixed up in the way she felt about Cade and the fact that he was just as persuasive as he claimed. She'd wanted to give him an out because she'd thought it was bound to be awkward between them. Yet there was a stream of relief running through the realization that he would still be here until the job was done.

And that might even be today or tomorrow. She felt a sudden ripple of excitement and enthusiasm as she turned back to the cabin. Stop thinking about Cade.

Eve was waiting for her.

And Helen is waiting for me . . .

———◆———

Riley knew that Eve was feeling that same excitement when she walked into the studio a few minutes later. She was sitting in front of the reconstruction, staring at it quietly, not touching it. But Riley could see the tension and eagerness electrifying the line of Eve's spine and the way she held her head.

"Is something wrong?" Riley asked as she moved toward Eve. "Is there anything I can do?"

"No, I'm better off handling it on my own. That's why I told Joe to go away and keep busy today so that he wouldn't hover. I'm just bracing myself."

Riley went still. "Because you're ready to begin the final? I hoped you would be."

"Well, then you're going to get your wish. Though you could give me a hint about how I'm supposed to start the sculpting." Eve made a face. "I know I told you that I wanted to know everything about Helen, but maybe I know too much now. It might be complicating my view of her. I think she's intimidating me."

Riley chuckled. "Not you, Eve. I won't believe that. But it's funny that you mentioned a complication. One of the things they called Helen was 'the beautiful problem.'"

"Now you tell me." Eve ruefully shook her head. "Were you afraid I'd get discouraged?"

"No, I knew that would only be a challenge for you once the two of you came together."

"What faith you have. Do you think it's going to be easy to create a sculpture of the most beautiful woman in the world? Perhaps the most beautiful woman who ever lived?"

"I do have faith," Riley said quietly. "I always have had faith in you. No, I don't think it's going to be easy. The beauty has always been there, and people see what they want to see. But you're the only one I'd trust to ignore the beauty and give us all the truth about her. She deserves that, Eve."

Eve gazed at her for a long moment. "Yes, she does," she said huskily. "Or she wouldn't have been able to make you feel this way. I'll do the best I can. Do me a favor, don't look over my shoulder while I'm working until you see that I've finished. It has to be between the two of us." She turned back to face the reconstruction. "But I can't do it alone, Helen. You forget about being a queen and help me, dammit."

"Call me if you need me." Riley backed away and sat down across the room as Eve began to slowly start the sculpting process.

You heard her, Eleni. You've always liked the best, and now you've got it. If you help her, she'll give you what we all want. So show her who you are.

———◆———

Eve had thought that the work on Helen would go faster but that hadn't happened yet. She had been very careful of the repairs and the packets of natron that occupied the skull, but she found that she was instinctively slowing down so that she wouldn't make a mistake. She knew that there was almost no chance of her damaging the skull, but the hesitance was still there.

"For Pete's sake, you're a damn icon," she muttered. "What do you expect from me?"

Then suddenly the tension was gone. She drew a deep breath of relief. "That's more like it," she murmured. "I don't know if it was me or you, but I think we can work together now. Let's start with the forehead. It's beautifully formed and simpler than the other features."

She started to work.

She carefully molded the clay.

As usual, it was cool to the touch. It would get warmer, the faster she worked. But she was in no hurry yet. Make the strokes slow and precise.

See? I'm not going to do anything you wouldn't like. We're in this together. I know you've been waiting a long time. But I might get impatient because I'm so eager. If you're as opinionated as Riley says, you'll probably let me know. And that's okay.

Because her hands were moving faster now anyway. She couldn't help it.

Mold.

Smooth.

Smooth was important because of the adjustment she'd had to make so that the skull would accept the clay and the repairs she'd had to make on the bone structure. She'd agonized over those repairs until she was sure that they were perfect and wouldn't change the integrity of the face. She wasn't about to ruin that work by being in too much of a hurry.

But no matter what she intended, her hands were even warmer now as they flew over the skull. *It's going well, isn't it? That's because you're helping me. But now we're going to have to do the hard part. I'm not going to think, I'm just going to feel. Are you ready for me? There are so many things I don't know about you. You'll have to help me with that. First, we'll do the ears. I'm sure they were very nice, but I can't let that influence me. Ears are difficult and I have no idea how they were shaped. So, it will be guesswork unless you tell me.* Her fingers were moving rapidly, her mind a blur of clay and shape...and something else...

The nose. That was generic, too. Make it ordinary length and width as befit a beautiful Helen. "You were right not to let them cut into your nose. Much better this way."

It seemed right. *Don't think about it. Just let it come to you.*

Go on to the mouth. Mouths were both a mystery and one of the most expressive features of the face. A smile or no smile? It was too important to make a judgment call.

She drew a deep breath. *A face to launch a thousand ships? If it was true, would there have been a smile on that face knowing what that war would bring? Only you would know. So I'll come back later when I do the final and maybe you'll tell me.*

Go back to the cheeks.

Mold.

Fill.

Smooth.

She was getting too excited. She was so close. It was almost time to do the final and that was always a dizzying, exhausting process that uplifted and yet drained her.

Exercise control. There were still the measurements to check. This time they were almost sure to be wrong. Helen was a queen in the Bronze Age and, therefore, smaller than a modern woman.

Nose width, 32mm. Cut it down to 31mm.

Nose projection, 19mm. Take 2mm off it.

Lip height, 13mm. Bring it down to 11mm.

Okay. Now do the final adjustment and she'll be ready for the final steps.

Steady. Her heart was beating crazily. She could feel the heat flush her cheeks. Her hands were trembling.

That was only the beginning, Helen. Now it's time for you to come through for me. I'll be good to you, if you'll be good to me. And maybe we'll end up with something that will make both of us happy. Riley says you deserve it and I believe her.

She straightened on her chair. *Here we go. You like adventure; consider this a great one.* She leaned forward, her fingers caressing the sculpture. *Just for the two of us.*

The fever was beginning to grip her. She couldn't wait. *Now let me see you!*

CHAPTER
13

4:35 A.M.

Eve..." Riley was walking toward her from across the room. "Are you all right?"

Eve looked dazedly over her shoulder at Riley and then shook her head to clear it. "Just tired. It was a long night." She stood up and arched her back to ease it.

"I hear it gets that way when you work your ass off and don't get any sleep," Riley said dryly. "You're exhausted." She was carefully avoiding looking at the reconstruction. "Are you satisfied with it?"

"I don't know. I think so. She seemed right while I was working on her. And now I feel a sense of peace." Eve gazed at Riley. "Why don't you tell me?" She smiled. "Of course, you'll have to actually look at her before you can do that. You're trying so hard not to."

"Am I allowed to do that now? I've been going crazy because you asked me not to watch you work. But since it was the only thing I could do that you said might help you, I did my duty."

281

"Then come along and see it with me." Eve took her by the arm and led her back several paces, then turned her back around to face the reconstruction. "I can't think of anyone that I'd want to share it with more than you. Who else can I trust to tell me the truth?" She waved her hand at the sculpture across the room. "Is it your Helen, Riley?"

Riley was standing frozen in place, staring in shock at the sculpture. "My God, she takes my breath away."

"That's not what I asked you."

"I don't know how you did it. She's . . . magnificent."

"According to you, she always was. But did I give you truth?"

"Yes," Riley whispered. "She seems to give out a kind of radiance. Eleni . . ." Suddenly tears were running down her cheeks. She turned and went into Eve's arms. "Thank you. Look at her, she's . . . perfect."

"I had no intention of making her perfect. It just happened. It must have been the bone structure." She was gazing at the sculpture critically. "But I can see how she might have caused all that stir. Those features are flawless. You'd never get tired of looking at her."

"She was more than a beautiful face. You must have seen it, because it's there in the reconstruction. The expression . . ." She was walking closer. "The mouth . . . a hint of mischief in the curve and yet so much more. A little weariness, wisdom, a knowledge of the world, but still a thirst for the next adventure." She reached out and touched the orbital cavity. "The shape of her eyes. A little slanted so that they'd crinkle when she smiled, and you'd want to see her smile again. But it also makes those eyes you chose for her a darker blue and shimmering under the light."

"Those eyes were difficult. They had to be that dark a blue.

Some color tones were different shades back in her day," Eve said. "Are you finished?"

Riley chuckled. "I could go on. But not right now. You're too tired. I just wanted you to realize that I appreciate your brilliant work." She paused. "And to thank you again. I wish my father were here to see her."

"You're welcome." She yawned. "I'm glad you think that I didn't fail her...or you. But now I'm going to bed. I suggest you do the same."

She shook her head. "I think I'll sit here for a little longer. Good night, Eve."

"Good morning," Eve said as she headed for the door. "I'll see you in a few hours." The door closed behind her.

And Riley sat down in front of the sculpture and gazed at it. "She did it," she whispered. "I knew she could. You would have liked the fact that it was a woman who did this. You'd like *her*." She leaned back in the chair. "Now, if you don't mind, I'll stay here and be quiet for a while and just be glad to have you with me..."

———◆———

"Finished?" Joe asked as Eve crawled into bed beside him. "How did it go?"

"Riley said I did good." She snuggled closer. "What about you? Did you have a good day?"

"It was productive." He kissed her cheek. "I'll tell you later. Now your mind is filled with Helen and all the joy of bringing her home."

"And Riley...she was so happy..."

"You've given her a great gift."

"But I haven't actually brought Helen home yet. I have to do all the computer work and the photos. I'll have to see about that when I get up. And remind me to talk to Cade . . ."

———◆———

"I hear Eve finished," Cade said to Riley when he came into the kitchen several hours later. "What do you think about it?"

She pushed her cereal bowl away. "I think I'll let you make your own judgment," she said. "I really wanted you to see it with Eve, but she's not up yet." She got to her feet. "So I'll take you."

His gaze was searching her face. "You don't want to tell me?"

He was still looking at her. "But you're not disappointed. There's a kind of serenity about you." He grabbed her hand and pulled her out of the kitchen and down the hall. "Show me!"

She had to almost run to keep up with him. "You don't have to drag me. You're my partner and naturally I would want you to see it." She opened the door to Eve's workroom, pulled free of his grip, and gestured. "Helen."

"My God." He stood in the doorway, his gaze on the reconstruction. "It's incredible." He went slowly toward it. "No wonder you look as if you're . . . bemused. It's wonderful."

She nodded. "I couldn't tell you. You had to see her." She smiled. "What do *you* think? Is she everything we wanted? Will she stun the world?"

"No doubt," Cade said. "She'll give you everything you wanted all these years. People will travel from every country on the globe to see her."

"And she won't be alone anymore."

"No, she won't," he said gently. "That's the last thing she'll be from now on."

She sat down in the chair in front of the reconstruction and looked up at it. "I stayed here with her for a few hours after Eve left. I was thinking of this minute that I could show you."

"Were you?" He smiled. "I'm honored that you let me share those moments with you. You were a bit upset with me when I left."

"None of that matters. Can't you see everything has changed?"

"No, tell me about it."

"I had to share it with you. I would have had a hard time even bringing her to Eve without you. I can't tell you how glad I am that I let you talk me into the partnership. This is so important I wanted to thank you."

"You're very welcome." He chuckled. "Thank you. It's enough that I can sit here and look at the expression on your face. You're almost as luminous as your Helen."

"You're crazy." She made a face. "I'm sitting here looking at her. She's perfect. Though Eve said that she'd had no intention of deliberately giving Helen additional glamour."

"Then she failed," Cade said. "We'll have to remember that when we ask her to do the rest of Helen's body. But we won't have to worry about that until we get her settled."

"I wanted to talk to you about that. We've got to decide where we'll take her."

"That's up to you." He paused. "Though I'd suggest that we take her to Wild Harbor outside London where I have security already set up at Cambry House. It would be a wonderful setting. It's what I had in mind for her if I could get you to go along with it. I believe you'd think it worthy of her. Eve could finish the remaining work, and you could make arrangements for the grand presentation. We'll give her the biggest hoopla she could ever want." He added, "Unless you have a different idea?"

"No." She was frowning. "But wherever we go, we should leave very soon. It was different when we hadn't finished the reconstruction yet. Now we have too much to lose. I'm feeling insecure."

"Agreed," he said promptly. "Should I make arrangements?"

"I'll have to talk to Eve."

"Then do it. Why don't you go get her? I'll stay here and wait for you. I want to congratulate her on this masterpiece anyway."

She nodded as she got to her feet. "And so you should." She headed for the door and said lightly, "Do keep Helen company. She's gone through a traumatic night, too. I'll be back right away."

"I'll watch out for her."

"I know you will." Her smile was radiant. "I trust you."

———◆———

I trust you.

Cade sat there, gazing at the reconstruction. Three words that meant such a hell of a lot. Why? It wasn't as if he hadn't gotten over the cynicism and distrust of the brat he'd been growing up. He'd had friends and lovers and made his way to the life he wanted.

"What do you think, Helen?" He looked at the sculpture. "You've had your share of entertainment over the centuries. What's different about this one? Sex?"

Of course it was. That had been self-evident. But it had been more than that as he had sat there looking at Riley. Not three words, only one.

Tenderness.

———◆———

"So, you think I've done a decent job?" Eve asked as she came into the workroom with Riley.

"You know you have. Modesty doesn't become you," Cade said. "Fantastic."

"It's not modesty," Eve said quietly. "I never know. Particularly when the subject is as special as Helen." She gestured to Riley. "But she said you already have plans to help me finish her. I meant to talk to you about that, Cade."

"If you're both in agreement. It seemed the most practical solution."

"Yes, it does. We have to get both Helen and the treasure out of here immediately," she urged. "But I can't go with you right now. I've done my part with the skull for the time being. I don't intend to leave you in the lurch, but Joe and I have something else that has to be done." She turned to Riley. "You know I do. I've told you from the beginning that we had another agenda." She added, "It's important to my family and to quite a few other families around the globe."

"The bullet," Riley said. "Of course. I was so involved with Helen that it slipped away from me."

"I wish it could slip away from me," Eve said wryly. "But it never will. Joe and I will stay here, and you can go to London and take care of details. I'll join you later."

"No, you won't," Riley said. "You gave everything to that

reconstruction. Do you think I'd leave you here when I might be able to help?"

"I was hoping you would," Eve said. "But I suppose that wasn't to be."

"Damn straight. Cade can take care of transporting the sarcophagus. It's his mansion and wildlife retreat, and he can give all the orders. They'd listen to him." She waved a vague hand. "And I'm sure he can give her all the hoopla he promised."

"Not necessarily," Cade said. "The first thing I learned to do when I took over my grandfather's trust was delegate. It saves me a good deal of trouble. I'm very lazy, I'm always looking for a way to avoid additional work." He turned to Eve. "I believe that Joe might have told you that I'm already involved in your project. You can't shut me out now." He smiled at Riley. "Stop trying to welch on me. I told you that you couldn't leave me until the partnership was officially over. There are a lot of details we haven't gotten to yet. You said you trusted me."

"I do," she said quietly. "I just didn't want you to have to follow me down a path like this. Dakar was very clear what he wanted to do to me."

"Then he'll be disappointed, won't he?" He turned back to Eve. "But the first thing is for you to get Helen set for travel. That might take a while. I want her to be ready to go by at least day after tomorrow. Possible?"

She frowned. "You're right, it will take a while. The difficulty of transferring both the sarcophagus and the skull safely from here to London is enormous. But possible."

"More than possible," Riley said. "I'll help you. You've finished with all the delicate stuff. I'm good at taking orders."

"I've noticed," Eve said. "Except where Helen is concerned."

"That's different. That was definitely a delicate moment. It's not as if I haven't examined other sarcophagi when I was with my father." She whirled on Cade. "What kind of transport? Who's going to handle it?"

"The Gulfstream. I figure you'd trust Kirby."

She nodded. "He wouldn't let anything happen to her."

"He'd be complimented." He added mockingly, "And I'll be sure to tell him not to let that tiger cub take liberties with your queen. All those bones might be tempting..."

"He'd have to face me if he did," Eve said grimly. "I'm a bit sensitive about my work."

"Heaven forbid. My apologies." He grinned. "Forget I mentioned it." He turned away. "I imagine we all have work to do in the next twenty-four hours, so I'll make my exit. Let me know if there's anything that you need."

Riley gazed after him. She wasn't sure that she was entirely happy about Cade's reaction. She'd felt warm and content that he'd jumped into the breach when she'd agreed to work with Eve. But that also meant that she was going to have to worry about him whenever she heard that Dakar was anywhere near. Just the thought sent a chill through her.

"Riley." Eve was looking at her inquiringly. "Are you ready to work?"

"Sure." She smiled. "It's the last stop in a long journey. I can hardly wait."

<hr>

Cade was calling Joe as he walked down the hall. "I've just heard that I may have a couple boring days sitting around and twiddling my thumbs. Want to go hunting?"

"Maybe," Joe said warily. "It depends on the prey. What did you have in mind?"

"Your favorite. I believe you called it the bullet."

"What the hell?"

"Ah, you're interested? I thought you would be. I've been doing a little reconnoitering and it seems the situation might be right up your alley."

"Reconnoitering? Where?"

"Turkey. I checked out one of the addresses in Wilson's phone and I found that Jan Szyman, the owner of the villa, had not only a criminal background, but an association with very influential people," he said. "I might have discovered a treasure trove there. Perhaps even one with a presidential seal."

"Shit!"

"And since I have an interest in ridding the world of Dakar, it occurred to me that we might be able to combine and conquer."

"You're not saying Madlock might be there? Would the arrogant bastard be that reckless?"

"No, I'm not saying that. You'd be able to read him better than I would. I'm saying that Kirby has had reports from his men watching the estate that there's been a hell of a lot of activity going on lately. Szyman's yacht the *Last Word* sailed out of the harbor before dawn this morning. Szyman got some kind of message that stirred him up, but we weren't able to intercept it. But I thought it wouldn't hurt to take a look at the situation. I'd like your input about how we should go about it. I might suggest you put a few of your police or government contacts in drug enforcement on alert there. I also have a few ideas about handling Madlock, but I wouldn't want to step on your toes."

Joe was silent a moment. "Madlock *might* be that reckless. He's definitely a narcissist..." Then he said bluntly, "Step on my toes. In Madlock's case, I can't afford to be sensitive."

"That's good news. I do like cooperation. I'm heading for my car, and I thought you might need something to do while we're waiting for Eve and Riley to prepare Helen for the grand exodus. The Turkey coast is quite lovely."

"I'm on my way. Don't leave without me." Joe cut the connection.

———◆———

ISTANBUL
NEXT DAY

"I know you'll be happy to see me," Madlock said sarcastically when Dakar answered his call. "I just boarded the yacht and I'm heading toward Szyman's villa. I should reach there in a few hours. I hope you're not going to disappoint me. My patience is at an end. I'm done with waiting for you to meet the terms of our bargain."

"You have to admit that it was really partly your fault," Dakar said. "If you'd given me more cooperation in the beginning, you'd have had Duncan long before this. You sit there in Washington and expect me to—"

"I sent you the tech people you requested," Madlock interrupted. "And I furnished you with enough equipment to run a small army. There's no reason why you can't hunt them to the ground and give me what I want. I want payback. Am I going to get it?"

"Soon. I'm still working on it."

291

"I thought that would be your answer," Madlock snarled. "It's good that I decided to take care of the entire problem myself. I'm already working on getting hold of that silver bullet, along with that damn bitch who created it. But I need to get Duncan so that I'll have leverage, and I'm not going to pay you for nothing. Produce or get out of my way. I'm taking too much risk as it is." He ended the call and sat there for a moment trying to smother the anger and frustration. Dakar had no idea how difficult this was for him, but he'd find a way to make him suffer if he didn't come through. Yet he still had to protect himself if Dakar was not going to help. He quickly dialed Szyman. "Your Captain Nomkar picked me up, but I won't come anywhere near your place. I'm going to have him anchor the yacht across the bay. Come and pick him up when you bring me a woman for the night."

"Certainly," Szyman said. "Anything for an old friend. I'll even bring you a bottle of your favorite brandy and we'll have a drink."

"No, we won't," he said flatly. "No one can know I'm there. Not Nomkar and not the woman. Once I'm done with them, they disappear before they can talk. You understand?"

Szyman was silent. "I don't mind about the woman, but Nomkar was useful."

"But you've also found me useful on occasion. Do you want our association to continue?"

"Of course. Naturally, I'll do anything you like."

"I thought you would. I look forward to both the brandy and the woman." As he cut the connection, he felt a savage burst of pleasure. That was what he'd needed after the frustration of dealing with Dakar. The knowledge that all the power of life and death was in his hands alone. That's how it should be, and once he managed to take that damn formula from Duncan, that's how it would remain.

But his phone was ringing. It was Dunwoody calling. He'd told Dunwoody that he wanted no calls after he left Washington unless there was an emergency or a major break-through. It had damn well be one or the other or he'd have his head.

He picked up the call.

———◆———

SPRUCE CABIN
2:40 A.M.

It was after two in the morning when Eve and Riley finally decided to break and go to bed. Eve had received a call from Joe after midnight to tell her that he'd arrived back at the cabin, but she hadn't wanted to stop.

"Okay." Eve held up her hands in surrender. "I'll stop being a damn taskmaster and let you go to bed. You've been very patient with me, Riley."

"Bullshit," Riley said with a grin. "I was enjoying it. We made good progress, didn't we?"

"Pretty good. I think we'll be able to finish up tomorrow to meet Cade's deadline." She made a face. "I thought we'd be farther along, but repacking that sarcophagus and securing it so that it was rock-solid took even longer than I imagined. There seemed to be problem after problem."

"But that was part of the challenge," Riley said. "We should have expected it. Helen was never easy."

"You're very cheerful about it," Eve said ruefully. "You even found a way to rig that portable generator to maintain the correct temperature en route."

"A challenge," Riley repeated. "I was glad I could meet it. Of course I'm cheerful. I could work another couple hours."

"Well, I couldn't. I'll hold off until morning." She yawned. "I'm going to bed. Good night, Riley."

"Good night." Riley followed Eve from the workroom but cast a final glance at the brightly painted winged sarcophagus across the room. *You're going to really fly tomorrow, Helen. How you would have loved it.*

She closed the door and headed down the hall. The light in the kitchen was on and she saw Cade at the table working on a drawing. She stopped, staring at him curiously. "What are you doing? I thought you'd be in bed."

"Just working on a few plans." He pushed the drawings aside and smiled at her. "I could say the same of you. Did it go well today?"

"Not according to Eve. But I think it went great." She sat down across from him. "Why not? It's a dream come true."

"And you're still walking on cloud nine." His gaze on her face was caressing. "And glowing. It's good to see."

"I'm glad you appreciate it." She chuckled. "Since you're partially responsible."

"I hate halfway measures. I'd far rather be entirely responsible."

"Would you?" Her smile faded as she met his eyes. Her breath caught and she couldn't look away. "Yes, that's like you. But you've always shared with me." She got to her feet. "At any rate, you've always made it right between us. That wasn't always easy to do. Our relationship was . . . fragile at times."

He laughed. "Really? I didn't notice."

"Liar." She turned to leave. "But it didn't make any difference. It all turned out wonderfully." She looked over her shoulder. "Did you make the arrangements for Kirby to take Helen tomorrow?"

"Yes. I told you I would."

She nodded. "You were right, Kirby will be fine with her. Good night."

She was almost running away from him, she realized. Ridiculous.

But as she closed her door, she realized she wasn't running away from Cade. She was running away from her bewilderment, because she'd wanted to run toward him.

Which was even more ridiculous since she was a woman who prided herself on thinking clearly and logically in every situation that presented itself.

Except perhaps the one that concerned Morgan Cade.

She dropped down on the edge of the bed, staring into the darkness.

If that was true, she'd better sit here and think long and hard about why he was the exception to prove the rule.

———◆———

TWO HOURS LATER

She knocked but didn't give Cade a chance to answer before she opened the door and came into his room. "It's me." She crossed to the bed and turned on the lamp on the nightstand. "It took you a long time to finish those plans you were working on. I've been waiting for you to come to your room. We'd probably better talk about it."

She plopped down in the chair beside the bed. "But not right now."

"No?" Cade raised himself in bed to look at her. "Why not?"

"Because we don't have much time before Eve will be getting up and I'll have to go back to work. I didn't want to waste it." Her gaze was moving down his body from the thatch of dark hair on his chest to the tightness of his abdomen muscles. "You're naked. That's good."

"I assume that you mean it will save time." He shook his head. "Don't count on it, Riley. The situation might have changed."

"Don't say that. You invited me here. I'm nervous enough without you trying to make me jump through hoops." She paused. "I've had practically no experience with seducing anyone, because it wasn't necessary. Why would I go to bed with someone if they didn't want it as much as I did? It wouldn't make sense. Sex should be joyous, not contrived."

"I see your point," he said solemnly. "I applaud it. But I wasn't trying to make you jump through hoops. Unless it was something you wanted to do. I just wanted to make certain you knew that the game had changed."

"I don't regard it as a game," she said soberly. "I was thinking about that after I went to my room. It's perfectly natural that you might, but I couldn't do it. I don't have that many people close to me. Like I said, sex gives joy. You have to be careful with anything that does that."

"Yes, you do."

"And I was confused about you before. You were right about everything you said. There wasn't any reason why I shouldn't have sex with you. I wanted it very much." She made a face. "Maybe too much. It kind of scared me. I've always had to be in control of my life. But I trust you, so that was foolish, too."

"But maybe you didn't trust me," Cade said quietly. "And maybe I wanted you so much I didn't care."

She shook her head. "No way." She was suddenly off the chair and kneeling beside his bed. "I told you, I thought about all this. You cared. You walked away."

"You seem determined to find excuses for me." He reached out and cupped her cheek in his hand. "And I've always been easily persuaded."

She made a rude sound. "Not true." She took his hand from her cheek and delicately licked his palm. "And all this conversation is wasting time." She put his hand down on the counterpane. "If you want to say anything else, it will have to be after I'm in bed with you."

She reached down and pulled her sleep shirt over her head and threw it on the floor. "Scoot over."

"In a minute." His gaze was on her breasts. "I'm enjoying the view. Beautiful . . ."

She laughed and tore the sheet off him. She nodded mischievously at his genitals. "I agree. Impressive."

"It's good to be appreciated." He grabbed her arm and jerked her into bed underneath him and pinned her arms above her head. "But you promised we'd talk once we were in bed. We have to do that before I lose track of what I was going to say." He glanced down at himself. "Which is happening even as we speak."

She was giggling. "We could talk later."

"No, we can't. Because I'm not at all sure that you came knocking on my door for the right reasons."

"I've tried to be very clear." She tilted her head. "Even volunteered to demonstrate. What else could you want?"

"I want to know that you're not getting the fact that I was able to help you with Helen confused with who I am. From the minute you showed me that reconstruction, you were so happy that everything I did was perfect." He smiled crookedly. "Now I admit I'm phenomenal, but perfect is a stretch."

She shook her head. "Not perfect. But I'm willing to audition you for phenomenal. If you'd let go of my wrists so that I could bring you down here and—"

"I'm serious, Riley."

Her smile faded. "I believe you are. Be for real. You're not taking advantage of me, Cade. As you said, the game has changed. Give me the chance and I'll show you. I trust you. I like you. I respect you. I'm not going to make you uncomfortable by asking too much. I know better than that. You can walk away anytime." She was smiling again. "But I've never had a partner before, and I find I like it. So if you don't screw up, we might be able to have a good time before you wander off into the sunset. Okay?"

He stared down at her, his expression enigmatic. "Why wouldn't it be okay? You're definitely not asking too much. You've been well trained by the way you've been brought up. All I have to do is keep you entertained?" He released her wrists and his thighs tightened on her hips. "I promise I'll do that, and you'll find that there are all kinds of intriguing benefits about partnership that you haven't discovered yet." He bent down and his teeth tugged at her nipple. He chuckled as he heard her inhale sharply. "You like that? There will be a lot more of it before I do any wandering into the sunset..." He was parting her legs. "This is the only place I want to wander at the moment. Ready for me?"

He plunged deep!

He laughed as she lunged up and grabbed him close, trying to take more. "Oh, yes, you're ready..." He grasped her buttocks and pulled her higher as he went still deeper. "Then talk to me." His voice was soft and intense. "Tell me what you want, and I'll give it all to you..."

———◆———

"I think it's time to get up," Riley said drowsily as she cuddled closer to him. "I told you that we didn't have much time. It was those damn drawings you wasted all our time on..."

"We made the most of it. I'm sorry I couldn't stop the clock for you. I'm but a humble man."

"Bullshit." She lifted her head to look down at him. He almost had stopped the proverbial clock, she thought ruefully. They had come together many times in the last hours and she could feel her body ready again as his hand began stroking her, probing, licking at her throat. Maybe it wasn't that late...

She forced herself to look at her phone. It *was* that late, and she was beginning to remember that there was something she'd intended to do...

She sat up in bed. "The drawings. I have to take a shower and get going. But I can spare a little time because you deliberately omitted telling me about those drawings you were working on."

"You didn't ask me." He pushed the sheet down to bare her breasts. "I would have gotten around to it. We were busy."

"Yes, but it would have been natural for you to work on

299

something that had a connection to Dakar while Eve and I were busy. What were you doing?"

He sighed. "I would have told you eventually. I made you a promise. I was just enjoying seeing you so happy."

"I would have been happier if you'd been more open."

He shook his head. "I doubt it. As I remember it, one thing led to another, and it took us to a very happy place. Admit it."

"I admit it," she said. "Now what were you doing?"

"I was making diagrams of Dakar's stronghold that I'd had Dan take me to. I'd already done the diagrams on the estate of Jan Szyman—who could be offering us a way to rid ourselves of two scumbags in one package." He shrugged. "I thought I should be prepared for any eventuality in either camp in case I can't combine them in one splendid disaster. It might get tricky where Madlock is concerned. I can't afford to leave any loose strings for Joe and Eve to have to tie up. I want them both to come out of this with reputations intact so that this silver bullet they're rooting for can save the world."

"Evidently you're doing some heavy rooting yourself," she said softly. "But then you were bound to head in that direction. It's your instinct."

"That's not the direction I want to head in at the moment." He laid his head on her lap and looked up at her soulfully. "I let you interrogate me; now do I get a reward?"

"No, I have to get in the shower." She reluctantly pushed him away. "And I'm going to be busy packing up those two treasure coffers to send with Helen while Eve finishes with the sarcophagus." She grabbed her sleep shirt from the floor and pulled it on. "And the reward would have been mine. We'll discuss it later."

"Wait." Cade's attitude was suddenly no longer lazy but laser-keen. "I just caught that number. You said you had to pack two treasure coffers to send. There are three."

She shook her head as she headed for the door. "I decided yesterday it might be smarter to keep one here. You're not the only one who was thinking about Dakar's next move. Dakar wants that treasure. I might need to lure him with a little preview of coming attractions."

"And when were you going to tell me?"

She grinned at him over her shoulder. "About the time you were going to tell me about those drawings."

The door closed behind her.

CHAPTER

14

*M*ore linen?" Riley's brows rose as she watched Eve carefully wind the thin white linen over and over around Helen's sculpture. "I don't want to critique, but don't you think that's a little overkill?"

"Maybe. But considering how much work I put in on making her the best she could be, I'm not taking a chance on anything happening on that plane trip to England. I'm surprised you'd complain."

"I'm not complaining. You're right of course." She shook her head. "You've just made her so wonderful that I hate to see her look like a mummy from a horror film. Maybe a classic Boris Karloff."

"Well, you'll have to put up with it until we're able to join her. I gave Cade orders no one is to touch her but me." She took a step back and gazed at it critically. "It's the best I can do. The damn plane would have to crash before she'd be damaged. Come help me put it in the case."

Riley held the case steady while Eve carefully inserted the

303

sculpture in place and then closed and fastened the lid. "Sorry, Helen," Eve said solemnly. "Blame me, not Riley. She's still your buddy."

Riley shook her head. "No, you'd be her hero. She always had a keen sense of self-preservation. She would probably have lectured me. So we're almost ready to leave for the airport?"

Eve nodded. "The reconstruction was the final piece to be packed. Joe has already had the sarcophagus put in the truck. He said that Cade was already at the airport taking care of some business with the airport manager."

Riley frowned. "What business?"

She shrugged. "Ask him yourself. Maybe something to do with the Gulfstream?" She took out her phone. "I'll call Joe and tell him we're ready to go. There's no use waiting for Cade to come back. We'll see him when we get—"

But her phone was already ringing before she made the call. "Joe." She spoke into the phone. "I was just going to tell you that we're ready to leave for the—"

"We're not going anywhere right now," Joe interrupted. "I just got a call from Cade, and he told me to check out the security and stay put until we're sure that everything is okay."

"Why?" Eve asked. "Is that all he said?" But Joe had already hung up.

Yet a few minutes later he walked through the workshop doorway. She suddenly tensed as she saw his expression. "Whatever it is, you don't look pleased." She gazed searchingly at Joe. "What's happening?"

"Nothing good. We may have to get out of here. Cade told me he'd received a message from one of the men he had watching Szyman's estate that he'd had company arriving late last night," he said grimly. "A very special guest who was picked up in Istanbul by the captain of Szyman's yacht and is still on board. The yacht is anchored a few miles offshore across from the estate, and no one has been allowed to go near it." His lips twisted. "Except one of Szyman's women sent to entertain him. He made two calls after he arrived. One of them was to Dakar. The other was to his personal assistant, Charles Dunwoody. Neither call was very long. I guess that teenager Szyman sent proved too distracting. Everyone knows he likes to play with little girls. Szyman probably keeps one on hand for Madlock."

"And it has to be Madlock," Eve murmured.

Joe nodded. "He didn't want any of Szyman's men to know he was there, so he wouldn't get off the ship. But Cade's man was able to get a photo—Madlock came on deck when Szyman dropped off a woman and picked up the captain who had brought Madlock from Istanbul."

"Slimeball," Riley said coldly.

"Without a doubt," Joe said. "Cade's on his way down there to Szyman's estate right now to check out the situation for himself. But Madlock's being even more careful than I thought he'd be when Cade and I discussed the possibility of him coming here. He's not going to chance anyone recognizing him." He looked at Eve. "You know he's probably here because he couldn't resist the temptation of maybe being able to scoop you up. He's not going to make it easy to stop him. And that's also why we're keeping you here at the cabin until we can find a way to determine if you'll be safer somewhere else. I'm thinking long and hard about sending you with Helen to London."

"Then keep on thinking," Eve said. "Because we agreed that we were in this together."

Joe muttered a curse. "We'll see."

"Yes, we will." She turned to Riley. "But it might not be a bad idea if you kept an eye on her. Right, Joe?"

Joe nodded wryly. "Cade mentioned both you and Riley when he asked me to make certain the cabin is secure and that you were safe."

"I agree with you, Joe. Keeping Eve safe is what we have to do."

Joe suddenly chuckled. "Well, maybe keeping you alive might be of some value, Riley."

"Thank you," Riley said solemnly. "But you did have your priorities straight in the beginning. I owe Eve big time. We're not going to let anything happen to her."

"I'm touched," Eve said. "Now be quiet and forget about me. Let's find a way to make Madlock go to hell in the most painful way possible."

"I'll keep it in mind," Joe said. "I'll leave Kirby here to keep watch. But right now, I've got to take a tour of the property, question the guys, and put them on alert. If you notice anything suspicious while I'm gone, give me a call." He gave Eve a quick, hard kiss. "Don't take any chances, do you hear me?"

Then he was gone.

"He's worried." Riley's gaze followed Joe. "Not that I blame him. But I wasn't sure that Madlock would actually risk coming after you."

"He's held out for the last few years," Eve said wearily. "He wants to own the world. Nothing is enough for him. But he's wanted that formula for a long time, and he's narcissist enough to believe that no one can really touch him. He hasn't been able to hunt Diane or the lab down, and he thinks that I'm the one standing in his way. He's ready to pounce."

"Not if Joe has anything to say about it," Riley said, dead-pan. "I'll be watching your back, too."

"Thanks. But you have enough problems with Dakar."

"What problems?" She suddenly grinned. "As soon as we get Helen to London, Dakar will be past history. All I've got is a lousy poacher to worry about. You've had a president chasing you down. I've been a little jealous."

Eve chuckled. "Yeah, what am I thinking? Glad you pointed that out."

Riley's lips were still indented in a small smile. "Anytime." She turned away. "Can I get you a cup of coffee or tea? I don't know how long we'll be here before we get to take off for the airport. I can't imagine that Cade will want to delay long."

Eve shook her head. "It depends if he thinks there's a threat. It didn't sound as if Cade was very optimistic."

"But then you're familiar with Madlock and Cade isn't. Do you believe the threat is imminent?"

"I believe that he's ready to pounce. He wouldn't have shown up here if he wasn't. But we've been very cautious, and neither Dakar nor Madlock knows our location. We should be safe as long as that remains the status quo."

"Then we do everything we can to make sure it does," Riley said. "That's what Joe is doing here now." She shook her head. "And I'm trying to soothe you when all I want to do is go jump in that truck outside and head for the airport." Her phone was ringing. She checked the ID. "It's Dan. I'd better tell him to get in touch with Joe."

But Dan didn't give her a chance to speak when she punched the ACCESS button. "Cade's going to kill me, but it's not my fault. He'd been with me for over three years, Riley."

"What on earth are you talking about, Dan?"

"I just went up to my camp to check on my guys, and I think we're in deep trouble, Riley. I'd bet Tim Farley has gone rogue. He might be in Dakar's pocket." The words were tumbling out now. "Hell, there's no *might* about it. I talked to Brian Evans, one of the other guys, and he said Farley disappeared from the camp early today and when he came back, he was bragging about going to Morocco and having a great time in the cribs. He was trying to talk Evans into going with him. He packed up and left the camp." He was swearing softly. "Though I'm surprised he's still alive. Dakar must have been pretty excited about what he was telling him to just let him take a bribe and leave."

"You think he went to Dakar?" Riley asked numbly.

"It's pretty clear. I thought Farley was a good guy. Like I said, he's been with me for three years. I told Cade when he asked me if he could trust my men. He's going to murder me."

"I might do it before he gets a chance," she said grimly.

"I wouldn't blame you," he said. "But you know that I wouldn't screw up like this ordinarily. I would have been able to read Farley and known what he was up to if I'd been here at camp instead of down at the cabin with you."

"That's not important." She was trying to understand just how bad this news was. She had a sinking feeling it was even worse than that jarring shock she had first experienced. "Was he one of the men who helped bring Helen and the treasure up here to the cabin?"

"Yes. Why do you think I called you? Get the hell out of there, Riley."

"Dammit!"

"I'm coming right back, but it will take me over an hour to get there. Are Cade and Joe there with you?"

"Joe is still here. Cade isn't. This isn't the first bad news we've had today. I've got to hang up and call Joe. He's out checking the perimeter." She pressed DISCONNECT and whirled on Eve. "Dakar knows we're here. We've got to get out of here. Call Joe and warn him."

Eve didn't even question. She started to dial the phone.

Shots!

Shouts from the woods!

Eve stopped dialing. "God, I think he already knows it!"

So did Riley. Too late for them to reach Joe and his team, she realized. "Dakar will be coming to the cabin." She was running toward the door. "Kirby!"

Kirby was already on the porch. "Come on. Jump in the car. I'll get you out of here."

But the gunfire was heavier now and appeared to be coming from all around them. "They'd block the road down the mountain first." Riley tried to think what to do. What did Dakar want? The treasure. Helen. Eve. All those things were high on his list. "The truck!" She ran around to the back of the cabin to where they'd parked the truck when they were packing it. "Eve!"

"Here." Eve was right next to her. She was tucking a 9mm gun into her jacket. "I thought we'd need a weapon. I can't get through to Joe. No surprise that he's not answering. We're going to try to leave in the truck?"

Riley shook her head. "Probably too late now. But Dakar doesn't know that Helen and the treasure are still here." She tossed the keys to Kirby. "Hurry. Take Eve and drive the truck deeper into the woods and stay there until Joe or Cade can get to you."

"Just Eve? No way," he said flatly. "Cade would break my neck. I'm not going anywhere."

"Yes you are." She took a step closer to him and punched her index finger into his chest. She said fiercely, "I like you, Kirby, but I'm not going to have you spoil things because you're afraid for your job." She turned and went to the chest of jewels she'd left out on the porch when she'd packed the other two chests into the truck. "I'm hoping for a distraction that will take his mind off Eve or anything else until Joe can get back here. All Dakar needs is to catch a glimpse of me and these jewels and maybe he'll forget everything else." She opened the chest, pulled a long gold chain out of the interior, and quickly draped it across the lid. "Eve, tell him to go. You know I can take care of myself in the woods. I've spent my entire life in jungles."

More shots. *Closer.*

"Go," Eve told Kirby. "Now. She's made up her mind. Neither of us will be pleased if Dakar shows up while this truck is still here. I put in too much work on that sarcophagus. I don't want him touching it."

He muttered a curse and jumped into the driver's seat. "Get in."

Eve shook her head. "No, I believe I'll stick around with her until Joe comes."

"No!" Riley said sharply.

"And now I have to contend with Joe Quinn?" Kirby asked sourly.

"No, I do," Eve said. "Get out of here."

He muttered another curse, pressed the accelerator, and took off.

Eve turned to Riley. "And you be quiet. Your ideas aren't bad, but I'm pissed off you didn't include me in them. And stop telling me what to do, Riley. I got used to being the one to give the orders when we were working together." She grabbed the shipping container that contained the skull that they'd readied for transport. She flipped the heavy latches and opened the lid. She took out the fabric-wrapped reconstruction, tightened the linen to make sure it would remain secure, and then dropped the box on the porch. "Now Dakar will see a chest full of jewels, *and* the empty box that held the skull. Two bits of evidence of a hasty departure. When there's no report of the truck on the road, maybe he'll think that we'd sent it on ahead before they got here and were coming back for the jewels. Let's get out of here before the bastard shows up."

More shots.

And Riley could hear shouts and the sound of footsteps in the brush in the forest.

Eve was right, Dakar could be in that forest coming toward them.

So accept it and get the hell out of here. "I'm sorry but you'll have to share the spotlight. You're on my turf now." She grabbed the reconstruction and started running in the opposite direction from the sound of those shots.

Eve followed Riley at top speed, though she was glancing uneasily over her shoulder for pursuit. "Do we have a destination? Or are we just trying to find a friendly foxhole to crawl into?"

"Probably the latter. I think there's no question Joe will be tracking us as soon as he realizes you're missing. We don't even know what we're hiding from," Riley said as she pushed through the brush. "We don't have faces or numbers yet.

We've got to assume that it's Dakar since Dan told me that one of his men had been bribed by Dakar, but it's odd that it all happened on the day after Madlock showed up."

"No, it isn't," Eve said. "Madlock has always been in the background waiting to pull the strings to get what he wants. It's been like that ever since I've known him. It's almost satanic." She was getting short of breath as she followed Riley up another hill. "But he might have met his match in Dakar. We'll have to see. He's not the devil I know."

Riley pointed toward a path on the right. "This way."

"What's there?"

"A stream. I saw it yesterday. I'm thinking we can follow it down the mountain."

"I'm right behind you."

They pushed through a clump of low-hanging branches, which splintered with snaps and cracks that almost seemed deafening in the still forest. They emerged at the edge of a steep embankment.

"Down there." Riley pointed to the bottom of the slope. "Slide!"

They dropped and slid down the ridge, with Riley hunched protectively over the fabric-wrapped skull. Eve looked back. Over the hill behind them, they heard men's voices, accompanied by the sounds of their machetes slicing through the brush.

"They're less than a minute behind," she said. "Faster!"

At the bottom of the ridge, they pushed through another clump of trees and suddenly found themselves up to their knees in ice-cold water.

Eve gasped. "Found the stream. What about Helen?"

"Do you think I wouldn't waterproof her?" Riley pointed

to the left. "That way. Follow the flow. It'll be harder to track us if we can stay in the water."

They navigated the stream, which increased in depth and power the farther they traveled. As they struggled to stay upright in the rushing water, they became aware of several distinct roaring sounds all around them.

"What's that?" Eve asked.

Riley tilted her head, listening. "Motorcycles and maybe some ATVs. Shit. We're being surrounded." She raised the skull to keep it above water. "And it's getting too deep in here for us to stay." She was looking frantically around for a way out. Then she thought she might have found it. She pointed to the far side of the stream, where the trees and vegetation were thicker. "Over there. It looks like there are more places to hide."

"I'll vote for that," Eve said grimly.

They waded toward the muddy bank and pulled themselves from the water. They ran for the tree line as a high-pitched sound roared just over their heads.

Eve looked up. "Is that what I think it is?"

Riley nodded. "It's a drone. Dakar has eyes on us."

"Dammit. What else can happen? I guess all we can do is—"

Eve pulled out her gun and emptied her clip into the sky. One of her bullets struck the drone, and the device spun out of control and crashed into the stream.

Riley half smiled. "That's one way of handling it."

Eve made a face. "Joe could have taken it out in one shot, so if he asks, tell him that's what I did."

"Deal."

They pushed ahead into the dense foliage at a dead run.

After a few minutes they emerged in a clearing below a

canopy of tall trees. Eve glanced around. "I haven't heard their motorcycles or ATVs in a little while."

Riley shook her head. "No way we could have lost them."

"I know. Dakar saw where we left the stream. It probably just means they're on foot. We'll just have to keep our eyes open." She motioned to the wrapped skull. "How's our girl?"

Our girl. Riley felt a rush of warmth. And Helen *did* belong to both of them in their own particular ways. "Good, I think. I've been cradling her like a baby."

"Want me to take a turn?"

"Thanks, but I'll hold on to her for a while longer."

A familiar male voice called out from the trees. "That won't be necessary any longer, Riley. It's my turn."

Dakar!

They whirled and saw Dakar and half a dozen men stepping from around the large pine trees. They were all wearing black military fatigues and holding automatic weapons pointed directly at Eve and Riley.

"Drop your weapon," he said to Eve as she reached in her pocket for her gun. "That's much too unwieldy a weapon for you to have to handle."

She hesitated and then threw the gun on the ground.

Dakar smiled. "Good. Riley, I assume that's the reconstruction your father was willing to die for? I was happy to oblige him, but since then you've caused me a good deal of trouble. Bring it here and let me see what I think of his fancy queen."

Riley clutched the reconstruction closer to her chest. "You son of a bitch. You already have her treasure, don't you? I had to leave it on the porch. Isn't that enough for you?"

"I want it all, Riley. The entire package. I've read your father's notebook and he thought that skull would be priceless."

He shrugged. "Though I can't see why. It's just a sculpture of a woman who's been dead for over a thousand years."

She stepped back. "Then why waste your time with it? As you say, my father has already died because of it. You don't want to be the second."

"But I do want to explore the money angle. And I killed your father, but I'm quite sure he wouldn't want you to give your life for a piece of clay, Riley. Especially if it means I'll have it anyway. If you make one more move, my men will have no choice but to shoot you where you stand. Give it to me."

"No."

"Do it," Eve whispered. "Let him have it."

Riley clutched the reconstruction tighter. "I can't. It means too much."

"Either way, he gets it. But if you hand it over, we live to fight another day."

Dakar nodded. "Listen to your friend. I'm not allowed to touch her for the moment, but you mean nothing to me. Bring me that skull."

Dakar's men raised their automatic rifles, and red dots from their laser targeting scopes suddenly played across Riley's chest and forehead.

Eve stepped closer to her. "Please, Riley. Do it."

Riley knew it was over. She looked at Dakar for a long moment. Then she moved toward him, still clutching the skull close to her, glancing down at the laser targeting dots on her upper chest. She slowly, gingerly, extended the wrapped skull in front of her.

"Wise choice," Dakar said. He took it from her and stepped back a few feet to a spot where a narrow shaft of sunlight penetrated the clearing. He started to unwrap the skull, but it took him several minutes to get through the linens. As the last of the fabric fell to the ground, he let out an audible gasp. He looked up at Eve and Riley in disbelief. "My God," he whispered.

He rested the reconstruction on the ground and stepped back, clearly mesmerized by what he was seeing. "I can almost believe all that crap I've read in your father's notebook. She's...stunning. It's hard to look away." He looked at Eve. "Your work? She didn't really look like that, right?"

"I believe she really did look like that," Eve said. "The stories, the poems, the legends...They might be true."

Dakar shook his head. "I wouldn't go that far, but I could put together a hell of a great con job around her."

Of course that would be Dakar's take, Riley thought. Shallow, lustful, self-serving. She glanced around and saw that Dakar's team was equally transfixed. Like thousands of men before them, they were entranced.

Riley took another step closer to Dakar. "It would be easy to do. Helen belongs to everyone," Riley coaxed. "Let me finish bringing her to the world."

"So sorry. She belongs to me now. I won't share." He laughed mockingly. "Serves you right, bitch. All the trouble that you caused me. I told you that I'd come out on top." His gaze shifted to Eve. "Including getting her as a special prize. Madlock is going to be very pleased. The son of a bitch has been nagging me about her. I can't wait to tell him." He laughed again. "In fact, I don't think I will." He was dialing his phone. "Hello, Madlock. I just thought that I'd make your day. I'm sending you a photo. I'll send you the real thing later tonight." He took the picture of Eve. "She looks a little worse for wear, but I didn't think you'd mind. I promised I'd get her for you."

"As long as I did half your work to make it happen," Madlock said sarcastically. "And, no, I don't care that you roughed her up a little. At this stage it may work to my advantage. I'm beyond being polite and pretending that I believe her lies. But I don't want her dead. You keep her in one piece and able to talk."

"You've told me that before," Dakar said. "I wouldn't think of damaging the merchandise as long as she cooperates. She appears to know which side her bread is buttered on."

"Does she? I've never found that to be true. Why don't you let me talk to her for a moment."

Dakar strode to Eve and handed her the phone. "I believe you know each other?"

"Hello, Madlock," Eve said. "What the hell are you doing? Do you think even a president can get away with crimes like this? I'm a reputable professional just doing her job. Tell your hired man to let us go."

"It's a little late for that, Eve," Madlock said. "I will get away with it. I've gone too far not to. But you made things easier for me by making yourself available where I could get at you. We would have been together much sooner if Dakar hadn't been such a fool. But now he appears to have redeemed himself, so I'll be forced to forgive him." His voice turned low and dripped with satisfaction. "Because things don't appear to be going too well for you. But they've been looking up for me since I stopped relying on Dakar. Do you think I didn't have my entire special service crew on the hunt for that Connors bitch? You were always just going to be a part of the puzzle anyway." He paused. "Yesterday I received word from James that my men had located the lab in Lugano, Switzerland, where your Dr. Diane Connors has been conducting experiments."

Eve froze. "Is that supposed to mean something to me? I have no idea where Diane is located or what she's doing."

"I think it does mean something to you," Madlock said. "Or it will soon. Unfortunately, she must have been warned—the lab was destroyed, but she got away. Still, I made sure that no one else escaped from that lab. I ordered that it be locked and then burned to the ground with everyone inside. I imagine she could hear the screams if she wasn't too far away. Since she's such a humanitarian, that would hurt her, wouldn't it?"

Eve felt sick as she visualized that terrible scene. "It would hurt anyone who wasn't a monster like you."

"I couldn't let her beat me. No one beats me, Eve. She had to be punished. But we'll catch up with her, and until we do, she'll have those screams to remember. It shouldn't be long. James said he already had information that would lead him to her within a few days." He added softly, "You've lost, Eve. Why don't you admit it? I have so much more power than you. If you hadn't had your uses, I could have destroyed you a long time ago. You might still survive as long as you'll agree to stop this pretense and give me the cooperation I need. I've waited too long to get my hands on that formula, and I'm out of patience. Turn it over, along with that bitch who created it, and you might live through this."

"I doubt it. I know too much."

He chuckled. "That's true, but perhaps we might come to an arrangement." His voice harshened. "Because, if we don't, I'll turn you over to a few of the operatives I have in my service who will make you talk. You'd do much better to give in without all that suffering, don't you think?"

"What a big, strong man you are. Do you enjoy threatening women?"

"Not unless I can follow through with it. And I promise I will. See you later, Eve. Now give me back to Dakar."

She handed the phone to Dakar. "Your master is tired of talking to me."

Dakar's face flushed. "Maybe I won't send you to him right away. Maybe I'll give you to my men first." He spoke into the phone. "I'm a little busy at the moment, Madlock. I'm sure you'll understand. As I said, I'll send her to you tonight after we get off this mountain."

"See that you do."

Dakar started to walk back to his men as Madlock hung up. "Though, Riley, I'd rather talk to you about that chest of jewels we saw on the porch. I was told that wasn't the only—"

Pfft! Pfft! Pfft! Pfft!

Muzzled rifle reports cut through the air, and four of Dakar's men fell dead to the forest floor.

"Son of a bitch!" Dakar scooped up the skull and the fabric wrappings and took cover behind a large tree.

Pfft! Pfft!

Another one of Dakar's men took a bullet as the remaining man took a position behind another tree.

"Get down!" Eve said to Riley. They dropped to the ground and scrambled for cover behind a boulder as a gunfight erupted between Dakar and his man and whoever was firing from the woods.

"Who do you think it is?" Riley asked Eve.

"I've no idea. I'm only glad they're obviously not firing at us. Maybe Cade and his men. Or it could be Joe. He can track my phone."

Pfft!

Dakar's one remaining gunman peeked around his tree just

319

in time to take a bullet to his forehead. He dropped to the ground, leaving a substantial part of his brain matter splattered on a low-hanging branch.

Then Joe and four of Cade's men emerged from the forest. They were dressed in full camouflage and moving low and fast toward them.

"Watch out, Joe," Eve shouted. "Dakar is still out there!"

"No he's not," Joe said as he came toward them. "He got away. I think he's wounded, but he took off just before we nailed that last man." He knelt down beside Eve. "Are you both all right?"

Eve nodded. "Fine. And very glad to see you."

"We got here just after Dakar, but I had to wait until I had clear shots." He glanced at Riley. "You insisted on making a target of yourself."

"Well, I didn't do it." Riley jumped to her feet. "He has the reconstruction. I have to find him."

"Hold on. We will," Joe assured her. "He won't get far. I just have to contact Cade and give him a report. He's been on my ass ever since he found out Dakar was stalking you." He punched in Cade's number and told him, "They're both fine. Dakar is wounded but still alive, though I have hopes of remedying that condition. Call you later." He pressed DISCONNECT and turned back to Riley and Eve. "Stay close to us." He gave instructions for one of his gunmen to cover their rear flank as they started to track Dakar through the woods.

They moved quickly through the trees, pausing occasionally for Joe to point out increasingly large pools of blood on the trail. He shook his head. "At this rate Dakar won't last long."

"I don't care. Why should I? He killed my father," Riley said. "As long as we get the reconstruction back."

After several minutes, they heard rushing water beyond the trees. They rounded a bend to see Dakar standing on the edge of a cliff.

Joe and his men aimed their weapons at him. Joe shouted, "Drop your gun, Dakar. Raise your hands!"

Dakar smiled shakily. His neck was covered in blood, and he struggled to form words. "I don't think that's really what you want." He showed them the linen-wrapped skull. "If I let go, Helen returns to history. Maybe . . . we can . . . make a deal." He gestured to the rushing water hundreds of feet below. "Go ahead and shoot me. Or let me go to that little patch of woods . . . over there and call some . . . of my men to pick me up. That way your precious Helen might survive."

Riley pushed past Joe and the others. "Give it to me. Please."

"Hell, no. You've heard my . . . terms."

"Then give us time to get someone to help you." She turned to Joe and said fiercely, "Let him go back into the woods and make that call. Don't let anyone touch him. I won't let anything happen to the reconstruction."

"Easy, Riley," Joe said quietly. "No one is arguing with you. Go on, Dakar. We're not going to stop you."

"I knew I'd . . . get what . . . I wanted . . ." Dakar coughed, and blood spurted from his mouth. He suddenly appeared woozy, and his body swayed toward the cliff's edge.

"Give it to me," Riley repeated in panic. "*Now.*"

Dakar shook his head. "So sorry. A deal is . . . a deal. Consider yourself . . . lucky."

"Luck has nothing to do with it. Just don't let anything happen to her. My father and I have put in a lifetime of work and sacrifice. Don't let it be for nothing."

"So much . . . emotion." Dakar's eyes fluttered, and he

clutched the skull closer to him. Blood dripped from his neck to the skull's cloth wrappings as he tried to stagger toward the woods.

Riley stepped closer to him, but he drew away, which put him still closer to the cliff's edge.

She looked helplessly back at Eve and Joe, then turned back to Dakar. "We can save you. Go make your call. We can save you *and* Helen."

"Helen…" Dakar's looked dazedly down at the reconstruction, his eyes fluttering again. His legs suddenly gave way as he lost consciousness. He tumbled over the cliff's edge with the skull still in his arms!

"No!" Riley screamed. "No! No! No!"

She ran to the edge of the cliff, followed by Eve and Joe, watching in horror as Dakar fell to the rapids hundreds of feet below, banging against tree limbs and protruding rocks all the way down. He finally landed in the rapids facedown. The rapids took him away in a shower of fine mist.

Riley felt sick. So close. She'd been so close.

Then she saw it!

"Look!" she yelled.

She was pointing to a clump of vegetation about thirty feet down. There the skull's fabric covering was snagged on a branch, suspending it in midair. Winds buffeted against it, and as they watched, the covering began to unravel.

Dear God, it couldn't last long.

She frantically gripped a clump of vines and tested them.

"What are you doing?" Eve asked.

"Don't try to stop me." Riley swung her legs over the cliff's edge. "I'm not going to lose her now. I think the vines are strong enough."

Joe leaned over and grabbed her arm. "Riley, stop. You can't be sure the vegetation will support you."

"It's a judgment call. *My* judgment. Let go of me, Joe. I need to do this."

He shook his head. "I can't let you go down there."

"It's not your choice. Get out of my way."

Eve leaned down toward her. "Riley, don't try it. I know what you're feeling. But look, I have photos, hundreds of them. And you know I did an entire computer program on her."

"It's not the same. You of all people know that." She met her eyes. "I need to do this, Eve."

Eve closed her eyes for an instant. "I know you do." Her eyes opened and she stared at Riley for a long moment. Then she finally put her hand on Joe's arm. "Let her go. She doesn't have much time."

Joe tightened his grip on Riley. "She could die."

"It's Riley's choice, not ours. Let her go."

Joe reluctantly loosened his grip from Riley's arm, then released her entirely.

"I'll be okay," Riley said. "I just need to work my way down."

"Be careful," he said gruffly. "I don't have to tell you how Eve would feel if you're wrong."

"I'll keep that in mind." She reached down and grabbed another clump of vines. She tugged, and they held in place. She kicked forward, scrambling for a foothold in the vegetation. She found one, and slowly lowered herself down.

A gust of wind blew the vines back and forth. Riley looked down and saw the skull rocking on its fragile perch. The cloth covering was becoming unfurled and flapping in the breeze.

"We may lose it," Joe said tensely.

The skull slid a few feet to an even more precarious position.

Riley increased her downward pace, occasionally slipping as the vegetation uprooted from its place on the cliffside.

Another gust of wind rocked the skull. Riley lowered herself another few feet. Almost there...

She reached for the skull, but winds moved it just out of reach.

She grabbed for it again. Another gust of wind kicked up and the skull tumbled from the branches!

As it fell, the linen covering waved in the air like a long tail. Riley swung herself over and at the last possible instant grabbed the fabric end. The skull continued its plummet downward, but after a few seconds, the cloth went taut.

"You have it!" Eve shouted. "The wrap is holding!"

Riley looked down. The skull was probably ten feet below her, still covered in layers of cloth. She slowly pulled it up, gently wrapping the covering around her wrist as she reeled it in. Finally she grabbed the skull and clutched it close to her.

Eve let out a long breath. "Can you make it back up?"

Riley nodded. She secured the skull to her chest by wrapping herself in the long fabric tail, securing it with a knot. She pulled herself up hand over hand, trying to grab vines she hadn't potentially weakened on the way down.

Eve leaned over the cliff's edge. "Just a few more feet!"

When Riley was within reach, Eve and Joe both reached down and pulled her up. Riley rolled over onto her back, still clutching the skull. She stared up at the sky and started laughing. She murmured something under her breath.

Eve leaned closer. "I didn't hear you. What did you say?"

Riley couldn't stop laughing, still staring at the sky. "I said, 'We did it, Helen.'"

CHAPTER

15

Cade called Riley when they were all hiking back to the cabin. "Joe told me what you did, you crazy woman," he said roughly. "You're an idiot. I told him he should never have let you do it."

"Be quiet, Cade. He couldn't stop me. I wasn't going to lose Helen after all we'd done to find her. I was being careful."

Cade was cursing beneath his breath. "Careful? One false step and it would have been over for you."

"But I didn't make a false step. As I said, I was careful. Since you weren't here, you couldn't see it, and you don't have anything to say about it. All that's important is that I'm carrying Helen back to the cabin when I could have lost her forever."

"No, I didn't see it, but Joe was very descriptive. I could imagine every step you took on that climb," he said thickly. "It scared the hell out of me. All I could think about was that it should have been me who was there with you."

"I told you, you wouldn't have been able to stop me."

"Probably not, you're too bullheaded. But I could have been

there to give you support, to share it with you. When you got back to the top, I should have been there to shake you and tell you to never do that again."

"We've already gone into that," she said. "And I'm a little tired right now, it's been a rough day. Is there anything else you want to say?"

"Only one thing," he said quietly. "I would have told you that there's no woman on earth like you, and how proud I am of you."

Riley hadn't expected those words and she could feel her eyes sting with tears. She didn't know what to answer. "You could have said that in the beginning."

"No, I couldn't. I had to get the rest out first. I didn't want to encourage you to ever do that again." He added, "And I wanted to spit out everything that had to be said because I'm sick to death of worrying about you. I want this over." His voice was suddenly harsh. "It's *got* to be over. I don't want any more surprises."

"Dakar is dead."

"But Madlock isn't, and now he seems to think he's going to get everything he wants. As long as he's still stirring up trouble, he'll be after Eve. Which means that you'll be trying to protect her and put yourself between Eve and him until he's removed. Right?"

"She gave me Helen. She risked her life to do it."

"That's a yes," Cade said. "And, as I told Dan, we might as well find a way to keep Madlock from getting what he wants while we have him here and conveniently away from his Secret Service guards."

"You told Dan?" Riley repeated. "When did you talk to Dan?"

"About five minutes before I phoned you. He called me right after he found out from Joe that Dakar hadn't killed you in spite of Dan's carelessness."

"Dan wasn't careless, he just misjudged an employee."

"That wasn't what you told him. He said you were pissed, and you should have been. He was groveling when he was talking to me."

"That's because you're his idol and he thought he'd let you down. The first thing out of his mouth was that you were going to kill him."

"It was close, but I'd just found out that you were still alive, and I didn't want to spoil a good mood by dire mayhem. I told him that he could make it up to me by helping me with a little job I was going to do tonight. He jumped at it."

"What job?" she asked warily.

"Madlock. I already had the beginnings of a plan in place, but then Joe told me about the phone conversation that he'd overheard between Eve and Madlock and it was too good for me not to use. It was too perfect."

"You're making me nervous," she said. "That bastard swore he was going to go after Diane Connors, and that means he might end up killing millions of people. There was nothing perfect about this day, except my getting Helen back."

"Yes, there was." He paused. "Two other things. One, Madlock doesn't know that Dakar is dead. And Joe can make sure that none of his men on that mountain will tell him. Two, he told Madlock that he was going to send Eve to him. That means if we send her to him tonight, I have an entry onto Madlock's yacht that Dakar made perfectly reasonable."

"Send Eve?" Riley vehemently shook her head. "No way, Cade. I won't let you use her as bait."

"You said you trusted me."

"I do trust you, but I don't have a right to let you use Eve."

"There's no permission required, Riley," he said quietly. "The whole problem was going to be getting close enough to Madlock to do what was necessary and get the information we needed when he was isolated out on that yacht in the middle of the sea. This is the way I can get to Madlock and remove him from Eve's and Joe's path. If I don't do it, he'll find another way to get his hands on Eve and there might not be a way to stop him from hurting her."

"I don't *want* this, Cade."

"I know you don't," he said. "Will it help if I tell you that I'll try to get what we all want without sending the son of a bitch to hell? Killing him would put everyone in danger. I know that, if I can avoid it, I might be able to stall until we can keep Joe and Eve safe, and maybe even keep their Dr. Connors alive to save the universe. So I'll do what I can. But Joe said Eve made him let you go off that cliff by telling him it was your call. Well, what do you think Eve is going to say when I phone her and ask if she'll do it? You know how much she wants it."

"Damn you." She knew exactly how Eve would answer. "It had better work, Cade. I want to be there to make sure it does."

"We'll arrange . . . something. Now I have to call Eve." His voice was soothing. "I promise I won't let anything happen to her, Riley."

"You'd better not," she said jerkily. "By all means talk to her. I know the answer she'll give you. But you may get an entirely different one from Joe."

"I know." Cade sighed. "Which is why I'd better have plenty of time to smooth the way with Eve before I talk to him."

KOLYA ESTATE
TURKEY
9:35 P.M.

"I left the raft about a mile down the shore," Dan whispered as he moved out of the darkness of the heavy brush toward where Cade was standing. "When do we move?"

"Soon. Kirby has stationed the unit where I designated all around the property. He knows exactly what to do when I give the signal. All we're waiting for is for Joe to show up with Eve," Cade said grimly. "He insisted on bringing her here himself. I think he's hoping to persuade her not to do this. I'm not his favorite person right now."

"Which means I must be in his bad books, too." Dan made a face. "It's like a chain reaction that's all my fault."

"True," Cade said. "And you're not going to be out of this chain reaction until you deliver Eve and then get off that yacht. You offered to do it and I'm trusting you to follow through. Are you sure you won't screw it up?"

"I'm sure." He shrugged. "I've had a varied career over the years, and I admit that it wasn't always on the right side of the law. I'm very experienced in the art of the con and bilking the suckers out there. I'll strike the note between deference and being just tough enough so that Madlock will accept me as Dakar's errand boy." He added wryly, "If Riley was here, she could give me a great recommendation. There's very few things she didn't learn about me while she was growing up. But I don't think you'd appreciate that."

"No, I wouldn't," Cade said. "It makes me want to break

your neck. But somehow, she managed to come out of it stronger, and she still cares about you. So I'll have to put up with you. That doesn't mean I won't keep an eye on you until you prove yourself to me."

"Thank God," Dan said fervently. "I thought that was where you were at. Now all I'll have to do is work on letting you see my good side. And I do have a good side, Cade. I can be loyal, and I love Riley. Even I have family feelings. You'll never see anything else when we're together."

"Tonight all I want to see is you doing your job in delivering Eve safely to that bastard and clearing the way for me." He added brusquely, "I've been watching the ship, and Madlock is still alone. He even sent the woman away, and he hasn't called in reinforcements from any of Szyman's men on shore. Once you have Eve, you call Madlock and tell him you're delivering her and ask permission to come on board. You can tell him that she's been properly handcuffed and won't give him any trouble. If we're lucky, he'll be so eager to see her he still won't request an escort from Szyman's men."

"And if we're not lucky?"

"Then we may need help from Joe's team that will be stationed here on the beach. But we'll work it out. The only thing you have to worry about is delivering Eve and making a show of leaving the yacht. By that time, I'll be on board, and you can leave the rest up to me."

"Pity." Dan was suddenly grinning. "That may be the most interesting part. You wouldn't like to tell me what you're going to do to Madlock?"

Cade shook his head. "It may go either way. I'll call you if I need you."

"What about me?" Joe asked bitterly as he stepped out of

the shrubbery. "Am I on call, too? You know I don't like this idea, Cade."

"But it might work?" Cade asked. "When we discussed the plan before, you thought it had a chance. That was always the question. You're just balking because I pulled Eve into it. And do you have any better ideas?"

"It might work," Eve said as she followed Joe out of the woods. "And we don't have any better ideas, Joe. You know that we have to make sure Diane and the lab crew are safe. Maybe there was a reason Dakar took a header off that cliff and gave Cade the opportunity to pull this stunt. We've each got our own tasks to do, so stop complaining. We both want it over and you've got this estate covered if anything goes wrong on that yacht. You'll swoop down like Superman if Cade doesn't keep his word to watch out for me."

"That won't happen," Cade said.

She smiled. "I know it won't. But I had to keep reassuring Joe and Riley." She turned in a circle. "Do I look dirty, disgusting, and totally beaten down? It was hard as hell not to wash up from that run on the mountain."

"You look pretty bad," Cade said. "Where is Riley? She was threatening to come with you."

"She'll be here later. I told her I didn't want to see her until this was over." She glanced at Joe. "It's going to be bad enough with him glowering at me."

"Tough," Joe said. "You had the solution."

"And I still do." She held out her wrists to Cade. "Handcuffs."

He reached into his pocket, pulled out a pair of metal handcuffs, and fastened them on her wrists. "They'll pass inspection if Madlock takes a good look at them, but if you try hard, you'll be able to pop them off if the going gets too rough."

"That's comforting. I may not need you at all, Cade." She turned to Joe and gave him a kiss. "I'm out of here, Superman."

"So I see." His hand gently stroked her hair back from her face. "Why didn't I ever think about using handcuffs on you?"

"Because you're a wise man." She whirled away from him and walked toward Dan. "Let's go."

———◆———

Eve turned her head from the sea spray as she and Daniel sped toward Madlock's small yacht. She was seated in the back of a Kodiak, her hands cuffed in front of her.

"Are you okay?" Daniel said as he gripped the steering stick. "The handcuffs aren't too tight, are they?"

"It's fine. They have to look good." She nodded toward Madlock's yacht. "Seems small for the president of the United States."

"That's the point. He doesn't want to attract attention from anyone, including the Secret Service. He's famous for giving them the slip." Daniel eased off the throttle as they neared the yacht. "It's bigger than it looks. There's two bedrooms, a galley, and a good-size interior common area, in addition to all the top deck space. But the boat is still small enough that he can man it by himself if necessary."

Eve looked around. The two boats were the only craft in sight on this lonely stretch of the Turkish coast near Kabak. They were miles from shore, and it was clear that Madlock couldn't have chosen a more remote spot for their meeting. "You called him when we reached this boat. That means he's probably watching for us now, doesn't it? Do you suppose he can see us?"

He nodded. "There's a light pouring out of that porthole beside the door. Good chance he'd at least see shadows."

"Well, it's time we gave him a show." She got to her feet and struck him in the head with her handcuffed hands. Then she tried to grab the steering wheel. "Hit me! The lips. They bleed more easily."

"What the hell!" He let go of the wheel and turned on her. His hands automatically warding her off. "Stop."

"Then hit me. You said he's watching, dammit!"

Dan backhanded her across her lower face. "Bitch, there's no way you're going to get away now." He hit her again so hard her head snapped back. "I've got my orders, or I'd drown you."

She collapsed back onto the seat, her fingers touching her lips. "Good. Blood. I was afraid you'd be too gentle."

"Not after you hit me on the head," he said sourly. "I could see where you were going. Did you have to have blood?"

"No, but I thought Madlock might have wanted me to show a little more pain than I did. It might save me a little punishment from him later. He's a bully and bullies like blood. Sorry I made you do it so close to the yacht. But I thought you might be nervous around Cade or Joe. Besides, it made it more effective."

"You shouldn't have been worried about Cade or your husband," he said gloomily. "I'm much more nervous about what Riley is going to do to me when she hears I slugged you." He added grimly, "But you've set the tone. I'll play by your rules."

"That's all I ask. Neither of us wants to get in Cade's way. We're just the window dressing at the   "

"Stop where you are." Madlock's distinctive voice blasted from the yacht's PA system. "Come no closer."

Daniel piloted the Kodiak into a tight circle about twenty yards from the yacht and glided to a stop.

Madlock appeared on the top deck. "Where's Dakar?" His voice was amplified by a small battery mic he held in his hand. "I know he told me he'd send one of his men with her, but I thought he might have changed his mind about bringing her in person. He knows how important she is to me."

"Otherwise occupied," Daniel shouted. "He's searching the whole damn mountain trying to find those treasure chests. It's all he can think about. He told me to deliver Duncan and then get back and help him persuade Riley Smith to tell him where she hid them." He gestured to Eve. "You can have her. The more I'm with her, the more I want to strangle her."

"So I saw. I may let you go after you secure her. I've already discovered Dakar doesn't know how to treat women like her. I'm in the process of bringing my own people to show him how to do it." Madlock smiled. "Hello, Eve."

Eve just glared at him.

"Too bad Quinn and Ms. Connors couldn't join you. But your presence here will ensure that they'll be along soon enough."

She shook her head. "Don't count on it."

"You underestimate your importance to them." He spoke to Dan. "Just so you know, if I so much as glimpse a gun, I will kill you both. I need you to drop any weapons into the water."

Dan nodded and pulled his handgun from a canvas bag. He showed it to Madlock and threw it overboard.

Madlock waved them in and pointed to the stern. "Permission to come aboard. Tie your boat here and climb the ladder."

They followed his instructions and climbed the chrome ladder to the small sundeck at the back of the boat. As Madlock walked toward them, Eve could see that he was now holding a Beretta. He looked extremely comfortable holding the gun, as befit a man who was elected partially due to TV ads showing him with an AR-15 laying waste to stacks of proposed gun owner background check laws.

Madlock chuckled. He appeared to be in excellent humor. "You've done a remarkable job staying out of sight and not letting me pounce, Eve. I have tremendous resources at my disposal, and even I haven't been able to find an excuse to zero in on you, Quinn, or your family. Then I thought I might be able to locate you through your son, but that went nowhere. I came close to finding one of Connors's labs in the South Pacific at one point, but we missed her by just a few days. I assumed you all must have split up and gone in different directions."

Eve stared at him, her face revealing nothing.

He shrugged. "It doesn't matter now. Wherever Quinn is, he'll come running for you. And once we have both of you, there's no way Diane Connors will let the two of you suffer on her behalf."

"Then you don't know her very well."

"Trust me. I have a thousand-page dossier on her, complete with an in-depth psychological workup. I literally know more about her than she knows about herself. Whatever problems she may have had with Quinn and you, she has a streak of loyalty that runs deep. You helped save both her and her precious bullet. She won't let you die."

"It doesn't matter. She's totally dedicated to her work. She knows what she's doing could save millions, possibly billions of lives in the long run. There's no way she'll throw all that away for the sake of her ex and his new wife."

"We'll see. All that's necessary is for her to poke her head up long enough for us to zero in on her. Believe me, it will happen."

Eve looked away. If Cade's plan didn't work, of course it could happen. They'd never been closer to the fragile edge of defeat than they were right now. *Don't think about it.* After what they'd all been through these past few months they couldn't let Madlock win now.

Cade. Where are you, Cade?

CHAPTER

16

Cade pulled himself from the water and climbed hand over hand up the nylon rope he'd slung over Madlock's bow railing. He'd ridden an underwater power sled from the coastline of the nearby Arhavi District, and he'd waited for Daniel and Eve's boat to pull up to the stern before timing his arrival to coincide with theirs. If there were proximity sensors in place on the yacht, he knew this would be his best bet to approach undetected.

So far, so good.

He knelt on the deck and peeled off his navy-blue wet suit, revealing the spandex shorts and T-shirt he wore underneath. He checked the watertight bag slung over his shoulder. The seal was secure. He pulled on the latch, and a rush of cool air hit him in the face.

Good. The air capsule he'd placed inside had been doing its job.

He reached inside and pulled out the mahogany box, six by eight inches, about the thickness of two decks of cards. He tapped its underside to activate the box's electronic component. He'd modified a small cigar humidor for this very special purpose, and although he didn't have access to every part he wanted, he was certain it would do the job.

Cade moved toward the row of windows leading to the main deck salon, or living room of the yacht. The windows were locked tight, but in his experience a hundred-million-dollar yacht was generally far less secure than an average suburban home. Cade wedged his fingers between a window and the black rubber weather stripping. He sharply pulled the window, and the lock broke with a loud pop.

He ducked below the window's lower edge.

After a moment, he raised his head again and listened. Madlock was still on the stern talking to Eve and Daniel.

He hadn't heard. Perfect.

Cade pulled the window, and it slid back on its track. When he had enough room, he jumped through the opening and slid the window closed behind him.

He looked around the salon. There was a wet bar on one side, and a long built-in leather sofa on the other. Leather swivel chairs were placed around the room, many facing a wall-mounted television over the bar. Cade looked at the beautifully carved mahogany box still in his left hand. He had to find the perfect place for it: not too conspicuous yet positioned well enough to do the job.

He put it down on a small round table next to the sofa. He stepped back to survey the scene. Yes, this should do nicely. He doubted Madlock would notice, particularly since the yacht was a rental and not his personal craft.

Cade looked up. Through the tinted rear windows, he could see that Madlock, Eve, and Daniel were moving toward the salon. He bolted for the stairs leading down to the galley.

He flew down the narrow passageway then stood very still. He heard the salon door open, followed by the sound of footsteps above him.

He'd laid the groundwork. The ball was in Eve's court now.

———◆———

Madlock swung the gun wide, motioning for Eve and Daniel to enter the salon. "Make yourself comfortable, Eve. You'll be here for a while." He aimed the gun at Daniel. "Your ID, please. You said on the phone your name was Carl Zangar. You work for Dakar?"

"I'm his main man." He shoved a wallet at Madlock. "That's why he wants me back tending to his business instead of baby-sitting this bitch." He saw Madlock frown, and he amended quickly, "Not that he doesn't consider what you want important. But I don't stand a chance of getting a share of that treasure if I'm not there to help."

Madlock glanced at the ID and then gave it back to him. "I'm all for claiming a share. I may even ask Dakar to keep me in mind."

"Dakar said you weren't interested in anything but making her talk." Dan's lips curled. "I wouldn't mind coming back here to help with that."

Madlock laughed. "I haven't dismissed you yet. Though I do like your enthusiasm." He looked over his shoulder at Eve. "He doesn't like you any better than I do. Do you have problems keeping friends?"

"Not if I want to keep them," she said coldly as she stepped around the swivel chairs placed through the salon. "What now, Madlock?"

He turned to face her. "You shouldn't be in such a hurry." He leaned down and touched her bloody lip. "You saw how frustrating it can be when you come up against someone better than you. And I'm much better than you, Eve."

"What now?" she repeated.

He shrugged. "I'll make sure your beloved Joe Quinn gets word of your precarious situation. When he's drawn out, I'll have a team standing by to capture him. As formidable as he may be, I don't expect he'll be that much trouble. We'll take him alive or dead. As long as Ms. Connors thinks that she can help save him, that's all that's necessary."

Eve could see Madlock searching her face for some reaction to his ugly threat.

Don't wince.

Don't look away.

Mustn't give that bastard the satisfaction.

Madlock leaned toward her. "You don't think Quinn would die for you?"

"Of course he would," she said simply. "And I would die for him. Not that you would understand that kind of love or devotion, Madlock. But you underestimate us if you mistake that for weakness. Our love for each other makes us stronger, not weaker."

"No, it makes you even more of a madwoman than I thought." Madlock chuckled, then turned and walked across the room.

Eve glanced around, trying desperately to find the mahogany box Cade should have left.

Had he not made it inside?

Dammit. If he hadn't managed to plant that box, then all their plans were shot to—

There it is.

It was in the middle of the small end table, a good ten feet away.

"I don't expect you to tell me where Dr. Connors is hiding out," Madlock said.

"Good, because I have no idea."

"I find that hard to believe."

"It's true. We never asked her. For her own safety, Joe and I didn't want to know."

Madlock paced back across the room.

Away from the box.

Dammit.

"No matter," Madlock said. "I have persuasive friends who will find out exactly what you and Quinn do and do not know."

She rolled her eyes and laughed. "Seriously, Madlock? 'We have ways of making you talk'?"

"After a session or two with my friends, I don't think you'll be laughing, Eve."

She cast a furtive glance at the starboard-side windows. Start him talking. Make him show his true colors. "I have friends, too. They'll be looking for me."

Madlock instantly whirled to Daniel. "Could you have been followed?"

"No, sir. No way. I was careful. She's just bluffing."

Eve was still staring out the windows.

Madlock walked across the salon. "What are you looking at?"

"Nothing. I was just thinking what a complete asshole you are. How you want to run the entire world but you're not even intelligent enough to conduct a simple conversation."

"You don't know what you're talking about," Madlock said roughly. "Everyone wants to talk to me. They know that all I have to do is pick up the phone, and I can get them anything they want." His face was flushing. "That's what power does. And soon I'll have even more. I have plans."

"What plans?"

"Russia. China. Everywhere l go, they'll bow down to me."

"Bullshit."

His hand shot out and slapped her. "You won't speak to me like that."

"Bullshit," she repeated.

He stopped just a foot or so from the mahogany box. "Your friends can't help you, Eve," he hissed. "It's about time you realized you're seriously overmatched."

Eve nodded and turned to face him. She raised her cuffed hands and lifted the green jade pendant on the large chain necklace hanging around her neck.

He raised his gun toward her head. "What the hell are you doing?"

She showed him the pendant. "It's a green cat. It's supposed to bring good health and wellness. You might call it a lucky charm. A friend gave it to me recently. I figure I need it now."

"You'll need more than that, Eve. Trust me."

"Maybe not." She affectionately squeezed the pendant and then let it fall to her chest. "I believe in luck."

Silently, just inches from Madlock's leg, the mahogany box's remote-activated lid slowly rose.

Eve and Daniel both quickly stepped backward.

"What are you doing? What's happening?" Madlock frowned in bewilderment.

A sharp hissing sound came from the box.

Madlock looked down. Before he could react, the black-and-white-banded viper leaped upward and sank its fangs into his neck!

Madlock screamed. He tried to pull the snake away, but it struck his lower arm. And his wrist. And then his cheek.

Cade leaped from the galley stairs with a steel mesh snake net at the end of a long telescoping handle. He snapped his net over the snake and pushed a button that closed the mesh around it. He grabbed Madlock's gun from the salon floor. "Hello, Madlock," he said with a smile as he gazed into his eyes. "I don't believe we've met. I'm Cade. If you'll stop all that wriggling and panting, you might last a little longer. That snake was very poisonous, and the venom is flowing through you very quickly."

"Cade!" Madlock was still scooting away, outraged. "I'll kill you. I'll kill all of you." He was falling to the floor. "You can't do this to me. Do you know who I am?"

"A mass murderer? Didn't you say that you'd ordered that lab blown up to kill all those technicians? I'm not impressed. Do you feel the pain? Are you getting short of breath?"

"Yes." He was panting. "But we can make a deal. Isn't there some kind of antivenin you can give me?"

"Yes, but why should I bother?"

"Money. I could cut you in to my profits."

Eve walked across the room and stood over him. She was shivering. "How much longer?"

"Several minutes," Cade replied as he took a step closer.

"Maybe even less." He turned to Dan. "Get her out of here. No one can see her. What are you waiting for?"

"He's waiting for me to finish what I started." Eve was still looking down at Madlock. "Death is a terrible thing, isn't it, Madlock? I keep thinking of what you said about wanting everyone to hear the screams of those medical technicians as they burned to death. You're not going to be allowed to hurt anyone ever again. Do you hear me?"

"No." Madlock's eyes widened in panic. "This isn't right. Save...me..."

Cade leaned closer to him. "Like you were going to save all those people around the world after you stole that formula? Yet now you want to be saved?"

"I'll give you...anything. Save...me." He reached out his hand, desperately clutching at Cade. "Can you save me?"

"Perhaps. Though it doesn't seem worthwhile. I did bring an antivenin in case Eve decided to be merciful." He looked at Eve. "Do you feel merciful?"

"No," she said. "But I'm not a murderess and I won't have him make me one."

"You might have gotten lucky," Cade told Madlock as he reached into the wire cage. "But I'm not going to let you get off without suffering a bit. You understand?"

"Save me."

"You do understand." He took out the hypodermic needle. "Is it still hurting you?"

"Yes. And my chest is tightening. Stop talking and give me the shot."

"I'm doing it. But since we're in a hurry, I won't waste time explaining the terms until I finish." He shot the serum into the president's arm. "Now breathe deeply and try to relax. Some of the pain should leave you soon."

Madlock's face flushed with anger. "It's fading a little, you bastard. Now get me to a hospital."

"Presently." Cade reached into the wire cage again and drew out a two-page document. "I took the precaution of having your confession drawn up. It's in great detail, including your latest ugliness in Switzerland that you told Eve about this afternoon." He handed him a pen. "If you'll sign at the bottom of each page, we'll have this nasty scene over with. Though copies will be distributed to the people who will do you the most damage if you don't stop trying to steal that silver bullet."

"I won't sign it," Madlock said defiantly.

"It's not really necessary," Eve said as she touched her jade pendant. "My lucky charm recorded and filmed everything you said anyway. I told you I believed in luck."

Madlock began to curse her.

"Don't be rude to the lady," Cade said. "I guess we'll have to forget about the hospital." He reached for his net, where the snake was writhing and hissing. "Your choice."

"Wait!" Madlock was scowling as he frantically picked up the pen and signed his name. "Get me to that hospital!" He tried to speak again, but his tongue and lips were too swollen. He only managed one word: "Hurry!"

"Sure." Cade got to his feet. "A deal is a deal. But you've got a little time now. And you should remember not to say a word about our arrangement when you get to that hospital or that confession will start appearing around the world immediately." He turned to Eve. "Get out of here, Eve. I'll send Joe a signal that you're on the way so that he can get ready for the fireworks. The two of you have to snatch Riley and be away from the estate and on your way to the plane before that happens."

———————◆———————

Riley saw Eve the minute her own Kodiak drew even with the yacht. Dan was helping Eve into his boat, and she looked across the water at Riley with a wry smile. "Why is this not a surprise? Couldn't you wait until I got back to shore before you tried to rescue me?"

"No, I only promised not to go with you. The minute you left I was making plans to follow you." She looked beyond her toward the salon. "Is it over? Are you okay? Your lip is bleeding. Is Cade safe?"

"Yes to all of those questions. And the lip wasn't Dan's fault. But you might still be going to cause us trouble. Cade told us to pick you up and take you with us to the airport. Well, he'll have to deal with you now. Unless you get in this boat right now, we don't have the time." She tapped Dan on the shoulder. "We have our orders. Let's get back to shore and take care of them."

"I'm not going anywhere," Riley said. "You're not leaving me out of this. I came here to help. No one even told me what the plan was before you took off after Madlock. What happened to Cade?"

"Nothing...I hope. He said he'd take care of everything. Another rescue, Riley?" Dan had started the boat and Eve said over her shoulder, "Why don't you go ask him? He's in the salon."

Riley jumped on deck and headed for the salon. A moment later she was standing in the doorway staring at Cade.

And then she saw the net and the multibanded snake. "Shit. Two-step?" she whispered.

Cade glanced over his shoulder and saw her expression. "Definitely. Ask Madlock." He got to his feet. "He'd testify."

Riley was staring at Madlock's pain-racked features. "I can see how he would." She moistened her lips. "Did the viper perform as you thought?"

He nodded. "Very fast. Four strikes before Madlock could even do more than gasp. And very potent, I believe he was carrying more than the usual poison, which made him a true two-step." He crossed to the door and took her arm. "But you can see Madlock is a little upset about it all. Let's go on deck and talk about it."

She didn't move. "A snake?" Riley shuddered as she gazed at the horror twisting Madlock's features. "You would have to choose a snake. No one told me how you were going to do it. Was that why Eve didn't want me along?"

"One of the reasons. She was in that cave with you and knew what it would do to you. She decided not to argue with you. It was easier to just let you stay behind."

"Not for me. And you let Eve go and face that krait."

"She hadn't had it curled around her leg, and I was there to watch her and Dan to make sure there would be no mistakes once it was released."

"I can almost guess how you did that." She swallowed hard. "And that viper looks very familiar. Was he the one that was curled around my boot in that cave?"

"I can't vouch whether he was the exact one or maybe one of his brothers," Cade said. "I didn't really care once I decided that it was the most practical way to get rid of Madlock if it became necessary to save Eve and Joe. It was bound to be a very difficult proposition. I can only guarantee the krait came from the same cozy alcove."

"Then how did he get here?" Riley asked. She glanced at the metal cage next to the net. "Complete with his own transport vehicle. A very ritzy delivery system."

"You're shivering," Cade said roughly. "You hate this. Why won't you go on deck?"

She shook her head. She couldn't seem to think of anything but that viper she knew was curled inside the steel mesh net. "How?" she repeated.

Cade took her arm, pushed her out on the deck, and slammed the door. "Before all this craziness started, the reason I went to the airport early this morning was that I wanted to rent a helicopter from the airport manager to fly back to that cave. I even had to scavenge to find a cage in one of the hangars that would work to carry him." He made a face. "I couldn't let the manager know what I was doing in case he was questioned later. Besides, I'm sure he wouldn't have liked the idea of hunting snakes any more than you do."

"You're the only one crazy enough to take a chance with that viper."

"It was worth the risk," he said quietly. "It was the only way his death might look accidental and maybe throw a curve into any investigation. Snakes aren't the usual weapons used when you want to take out a terrible dirtbag like Madlock. Also, this foreign location is ideal for confusion and corruption in any investigation that would involve a U.S. dignitary who wasn't supposed to even be in Turkey at all. This setup had to appear just right, with Dakar or Szyman as the possible bad guys and Joe and Eve nowhere near the place."

"So what's next?"

"Kirby will be arriving here in about another five minutes. We'll load Madlock on his boat and take him back to Kolya estate. On the way, I'll phone the local hospital in the area. When we reach shore, I'll deposit him near the poppy field...together with the two-step. We do want him to have company, don't we?"

She nodded slowly. "And a possible assassin." She paused. "And then what?"

"We wait until the hospital EMTs arrive. I did promise Madlock I'd get him to a hospital. In a few hours, the local police are going to raid Szyman's property. It seems they've been getting complaints for the last few days from several of his neighbors about the marijuana and the poppy fields. They've been remarkably silent about them before this but somehow, they must have been encouraged to risk Szyman's anger. There will have to be torches and flashlights burning bright so that the police can examine those fields. I want to make sure they find the two-step." He sighed. "But neither of us will be there to see it. You'll be on the way to the airport, and I have to start to lay a few other plans in place."

"Maybe." She straightened. "You said Kirby will be here in five minutes. We'd better get busy. What can I do first?"

"I suppose I can't talk you into getting back into your boat and going back to Joe and Eve to hitch a ride to the airport? Kirby's arranged to have the Gulfstream waiting for you. This is going to be my job tidying up here. You need to take care of Eve and Joe." He smiled. "And Helen."

She shook her head. "Not until we're finished. I told you that you couldn't shut me out. Not ever."

He shrugged. "Then you can help me finish with the cleanup. I was almost done. I don't want any traces of anyone but Madlock in that salon if the FBI comes calling. But let me go first and get the two-step into his cage."

"No. That wouldn't be fair." She braced herself and then turned and opened the door. "I'll even face that ugly viper. Just tell me what to do with him."

"Change your mind?"

She made a rude sound.

He laughed. "Okay, you can come with us to the poppy field. But then you go to the airport. You're the one who gave me your list of demands when I was begging you to be my partner. One of them was Eve, and I think you'd agree that Joe will always be with her. Now it's your duty to take care of them both while I tend to Madlock. It's going to be very tricky. This is one of those things I told you that you'd have to leave up to me."

She wasn't going to be able to win this one, and it was scaring her. "I don't want you to be alone."

"I'll take Dan with me." He reached out and gently touched her cheek. "He'll enjoy it."

She wanted to rub her cheek against his hand. She forced herself not to. "That's what I'm afraid of."

He smiled. "We don't have much time. Kirby will be here in a few minutes, and we have to get out of here. Remember, this is what Eve and Joe want. Maybe what a lot of people in the world would want."

"It's not what I want." She scowled. "When will you join me in London?"

"When it's safe. I'll wrap it up as quick as I can."

"That's not good enough. I want to see you no later than one month from today. And I want you to call me every day."

He grinned. "You've got it." He waved at Kirby, who was

drawing the motorboat next to the cruiser. He gave her a long kiss and then pushed her away. "We'll be just a couple more minutes, Kirby." He grinned mischievously at her. "Riley is going to catch a viper for me."

———◆———

KOLYA ESTATE POPPY FIELDS
FIFTY MINUTES LATER

"You've got to leave now," Cade said quietly after they'd watched the EMTs whisk Madlock off in the ambulance. He turned Riley around and nudged her toward Joe's car, parked near the woods. "Eve and Joe are waiting for you. They won't be safe until they get on that Gulfstream. You've done all you can here."

"I'm going." But she found herself leaning back against him. "But you're leaving, too? You're sure there's nothing else I can do for you?"

"I'm sure." His lips brushed her nape. "You're taking this partnership far too seriously. You don't have to hold my hand or save me from bats or snakes. If you want to help me, think about what you're going to do with turning that mansion and my sanctuary upside down in the next thirty days. Is it going to be expensive?"

"Very. You'd better come along and keep an eye on me."

"That would be my pleasure." He turned her around and kissed her. Then he stepped back and pushed her gently toward Eve, standing beside the car. "In thirty days. Keep her busy, Eve."

"I'll do my best." Eve was gazing back at him. "But you do

know that, once he's recovered a little, Madlock will still be causing us trouble?"

"I expect it," he said simply. "I only promised to save him from the two-step. I never told him there wouldn't be a third or fourth step to overcome. He's hurt too many people." He smiled. "Don't worry about it, Eve."

Eve smiled back at him. "I won't. If you need us, call."

"Only he won't do it," Riley said. "We'll probably need to go after him." She got into the backseat. "But this time, prove me wrong. You leave here right after we reach that road. Do you hear me?"

"Yes, ma'am." He saluted her. "I've already assigned one of the men to watch the fireworks from a safe distance from the estate. The rest of the unit, I'm taking with me. If you call me when you reach the plane, I won't be here."

"If I remember to do it." She smiled at him out the window as Joe started the car. "I haven't quite put a period to my stay in Azerbaijan yet."

He gave a mock groan as he stepped back. "Drive fast, Joe."

Don't drive fast, she thought as she blinked back the tears. She wanted one more look at him before she reached the road.

Eve was chuckling as she glanced back at Riley from the passenger seat. "Did I see terror in Cade's eyes? He's not sure if it's a bluff."

"It wasn't a bluff." Riley took out her phone. "I have to do one more thing before I'm finished here."

"What?"

"I have to keep a promise." She was dialing the phone. "I almost forgot about it." The phone was ringing and she unconsciously tensed. *Answer.*

Then Jill did answer. "Riley? Is everything all right?"

"I guess it's all how you view it. Right now it looks fine. Are you still in Paris? Have you finished with your conference?"

"Yes, I did the follow-up interviews this evening. I was going to call you and see if you needed me."

"Not right now." She paused. "I called to tell you just one thing. It's the last call I'm going to make to you for a long time. If you call me, I won't answer any questions, and neither will Eve or Joe or Cade. As far as we're concerned, nothing that happened here has anything to do with us. Do you understand?"

"I think I'm beginning to," Jill said slowly. "And I don't know whether to be excited or scared."

"I know which one you'll choose."

"And what was the one thing you called to tell me?"

Riley exchanged smiles with Eve.

"Why, I wanted to tell you it's time to come and get your exclusive, Jill."

———◆———

CAMBRY HOUSE
WILD HARBOR SANCTUARY
OUTSIDE LONDON
TWENTY-SIX DAYS LATER

"You're going to be early?" Riley's hand tightened on her phone. "Are you sure everything is okay, Cade?" she said quickly. "We're getting along just fine here. I know that I might have been a little demanding before, but it's not as if I can't wait."

"A little demanding?" Cade chuckled "You had me

thoroughly chastened by the time we got you to the airport that night. I wouldn't have dared disobey you."

"Bullshit. Stop it. I'm trying to explain."

"You don't have to explain anything to me," he said quietly. "Haven't you discovered that yet? We've gone way beyond that point. I'll obviously have to refresh your memory." He added softly, "Because it's me who can't wait. Tomorrow, Riley..." He broke the connection.

Hallelujah!

"He'll be here tomorrow!" Riley tore down the hallway of the mansion toward the new exhibition room where Eve was working. She threw open the door. "Cade's at Maldara today checking out the repairs on Hajif and Leta's village. The Gulfstream will pick him up tonight and bring him here."

"Just in time to rescue us." Eve grinned as she turned away from the sarcophagus. "Joe said that Michael is getting entirely too fond of the animals here at the sanctuary. We may not be able to get him to go back to the lake cottage if he stays too much longer."

Riley chuckled. "Cade did say he might lend him one of the elephants, remember? You've only got to hope that it won't be the baby. Your Michael would be constantly worried about his PTSD." Her smile ebbed. "It's absolutely safe for you to go home now?"

Eve nodded. "Joe checked it out with every one of his contacts from the director of the CIA to Homeland Security. Right after Madlock died of that massive heart attack two weeks after he was released from the hospital, everyone was looking for someone to blame. They couldn't believe it was a natural death even though that's what the autopsy showed. Then the CIA found a threat that linked Madlock, Dakar, and the Russian Mafia when they were searching Dakar's office. Joe doesn't know how Cade managed it, but now everyone is convinced that Dakar killed Madlock on Szyman's orders because the Russian Mafia wanted him dead." She shook her head. "And Madlock's political party is stumbling over themselves to find excuses why he'd be involved with Dakar or Szyman at all. They're trying to concoct a story on the Internet about Madlock being a martyr and hero of some sort."

"That was probably one of Cade's moves, too," Riley said. "He said it would have to be tricky."

"Well, it certainly turned out to be that," Eve said dryly. "But it also means Joe, Michael, and I can go home, and that the silver bullet can go safely into production. Joe has contacted Diane, and her team is already working on it. We're almost there, Riley. That's a pretty good trick on all counts." She turned away. "And now I believe I'll go hunt up Joe and Michael and tell them that they can start saying goodbye to all the animals. You know I've just been finishing up the last-minute details here for the past few days. It's over to you after today, Riley."

"No, it's not." Riley spun her around and hugged her. "Don't even think it," she said huskily. "You'll always be part of me, part of what Eleni is. Do you think I'd let you just walk away? I don't have that many friends that I could let a gem like you get away. I'll always be looking for a way for us to be together. Go home, live your life, enjoy your family. But don't be surprised if I drop in and maybe try to occupy a little corner of it now and then."

"I'd be disappointed if you didn't," Eve said gently. "Because I'd always wonder what you were doing. You're too much like Helen not to get bored if you don't have an adventure to keep you busy. It's not going to be long before you start searching again." She brushed her lips across Riley's forehead, her eyes suddenly twinkling. "I'll be interested to see what you come up with." Then she whirled away and left the exhibition hall.

Riley stared after her in bewilderment. It wasn't often that Eve was wrong about people, but this time it was clear she hadn't understood Riley's character or motivation. But she was right about her job being done here at Wild Harbor. Riley looked around the exhibition hall. Everything about the furnishings was elegant and glittering, from the crystal chandelier to the rich inlaid flooring. The colorful gold-and-amethyst sarcophagus lay in state on a raised platform cordoned off by maroon velvet ropes. Riley could imagine the throngs of people who would circle that platform once the house opened for visitors. She had promised Helen that she would not have to be alone again, and she'd had that in mind when she'd designed this room. It was everything that she'd wanted it to be.

But it was only the grand entry to the Helen chamber that lay beyond.

She opened the door and stood there gazing up at the arched stained-glass ceiling pouring light and brilliant color onto the granite panel in the center of the room. That ceiling had cost Cade a fortune because Riley had ordered special filters on the glass to let in the light but not harm the workmanship of the reconstruction. The sculpture of Helen also had its own raised platform, together with dark blue velvet cords to set off the glittering stand where the breathtaking beauty of the sculpture dominated everything in the chamber. But Riley had deliberately been careful that the purpose of this room was not to observe the magnificent reconstruction and then leave. There were several velvet couches around the room where people could sit and spend time with the sculpture, rather as if paying the queen homage...or perhaps merely visiting a dear friend.

Riley crossed to her favorite deep blue couch that was directly in front of the reconstruction of Helen. She sat down and gazed up at that wonderful face. *I think we did well, don't you? Are you pleased? Of course, it was mostly Eve, but I helped, too. And you do owe Cade a great deal of thanks. He not only helped enormously finding you, but I bet he spent more than a king's ransom letting me decorate this place for you. It was worth it, though, because it's exactly what we both wanted. You'd like Cade. He's not like anyone else. I hope you found someone that would compare to him. But that would be hard. I don't think it would be Demetrius. Maybe Charon? He seemed special...*

She leaned back, thinking about all the men who must have been in Helen's life. She truly hoped there might have been one who could have appreciated something about her beyond that beautiful face. It would have been difficult, but Helen must have learned to adjust. Adjustment was everything with a mystery like the Spartan queen. Riley was going to have quite a few adjustments herself now that she'd finally located and settled Helen. Her own life should be much more peaceful now.

Then she had an instant of uneasiness. Why did that sound boring?

Eve said I was like you and would probably be looking for the next adventure. But you were my adventure. Why would I need another? Besides, Cade would be an exciting enough adventure for anyone.

Yet that sounded somehow   wrong. She had never looked

to someone else to make life exciting. She'd refused to be that weak. Could Eve have possibly been right about her?

She was looking at the sculpture of Helen and she could almost see that little mocking smile that she'd never been quite sure Eve had given her.

So what difference does it make? she thought recklessly. Life would take Riley down whatever path it chose, and she would make the best of it.

No, that was entirely too tame and didn't suit her at all. She would be like Helen and change the world to suit herself.

She threw back her head and laughed as she gazed at the reconstruction. "What about it? Sound familiar?" she murmured. "There's no telling what's out there waiting. Back to square one? Yes, that would be much more exciting."

And Riley could swear that the smile on Helen's lips was not really mocking but full of mischief... and joy.

ABOUT THE AUTHOR

Iris Johansen is the #1 *New York Times* bestselling author of more than thirty consecutive bestsellers. Her series featuring forensic sculptor Eve Duncan has sold over twenty million copies and counting and was the subject of the acclaimed Lifetime movie *The Killing Game*. Along with her son, Roy, Iris has also co-authored the *New York Times* bestselling series featuring investigator Kendra Michaels. Johansen lives near Atlanta, Georgia. Learn more at:

  IrisJohansen.com
  Twitter @Iris_Johansen
  Facebook.com/OfficialIrisJohansen